W9-CLZ-111

FALSE DAWN

ALSO BY PAUL LEVINE

To Speak for the Dead

Night Vision

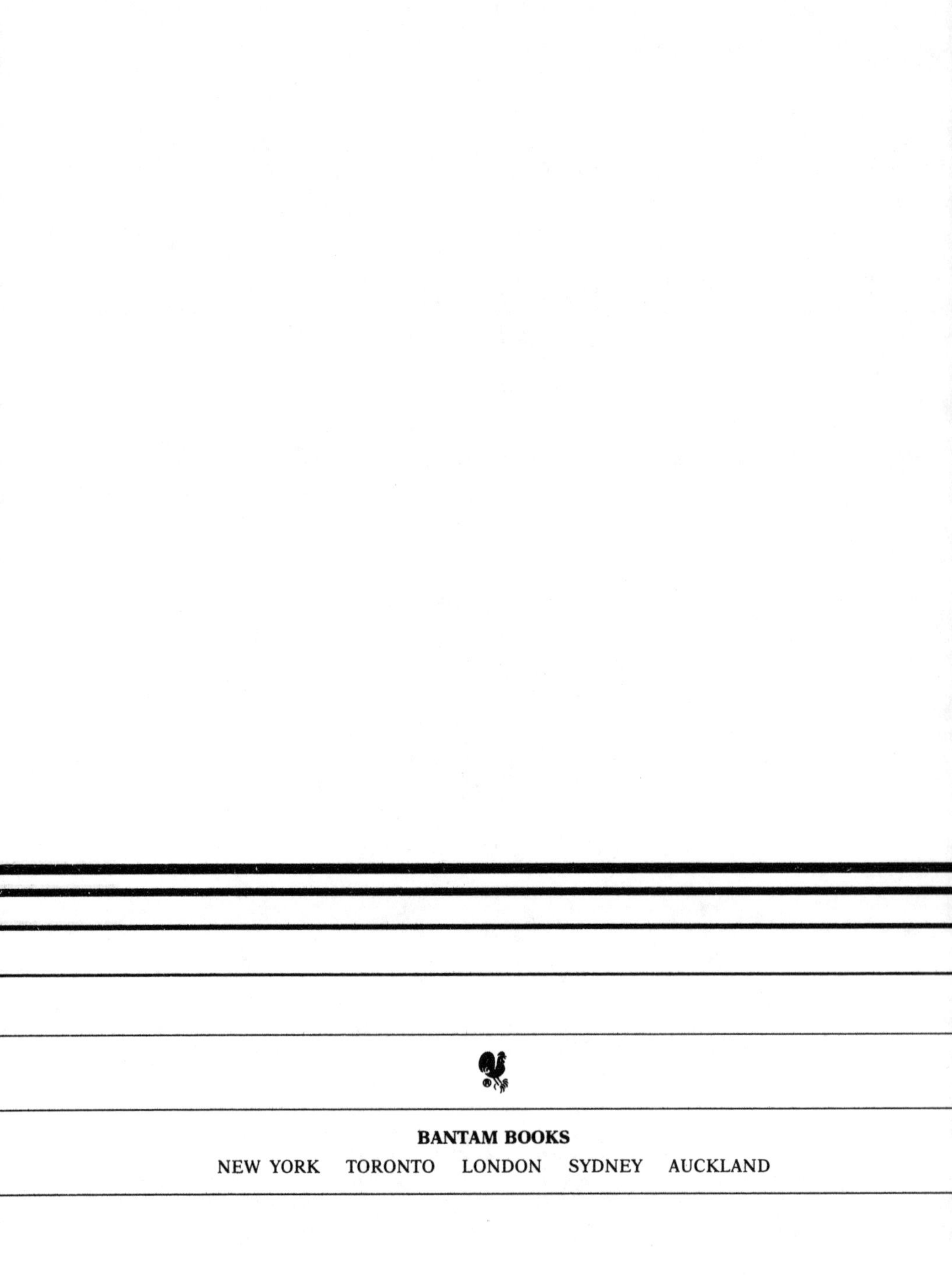

BANTAM BOOKS

NEW YORK TORONTO LONDON SYDNEY AUCKLAND

FALSE DAWN

PAUL LEVINE

This is a work of fiction. Names, characters, places, and incidents are either the product of the author's imagination or are used fictitiously. Any resemblance to actual persons, living or dead, events, entities, or locales is entirely coincidental.

FALSE DAWN
A Bantam Book / May 1993

Book design by Ann Gold

Library of Congress Cataloging-in-Publication Data
Levine, Paul (Paul J.)
False dawn / Paul Levine.
p. cm.
ISBN 0-553-08995-1
I. Title.
PS3563.E8995F3 1993
813'.54—dc20 *92-31456*
CIP

Published simultaneously in the United States and Canada

Bantam Books are published by Bantam Books, a division of Bantam Doubleday Dell Publishing Group, Inc. Its trademark, consisting of the words "Bantam Books" and the portrayal of a rooster, is Registered in U.S. Patent and Trademark Office and in other countries. Marca Registrada. Bantam Books, 1540 Broadway New York, New York 10036.

PRINTED IN THE UNITED STATES OF AMERICA

RRH 0 9 8 7 6 5 4 3 2 1

FOR MICHAEL AND WENDY

ACKNOWLEDGMENTS

I gratefully acknowledge the assistance of Stanford Blake, Gayle Bouffard, Angel Castillo, Dr. Joe Davis, Ginie Gorrin, Alan Greer, Stuart Grossman, Alice Holmstrom, Dr. Bruce Hyma, Abe Laeser, Lourdes Perez, Edward Shohat, Fred Tasker, Tom Templeton, and Gloria Villa.

I never like giving information to the police.
It saves them trouble.

—*The Quiet American,* Graham Greene

FALSE DAWN

1

HOOKED

Vladimir Smorodinsky ducked to the left, and the grappling hook, rather than piercing his skull, bit into the fleshy meat of his trapezius, just missing the collarbone. Okay, so maybe he wasn't Muhammad Ali in his prime, but still a pretty fancy move, since Smorodinsky was busy toting a hundred-fifty-pound crate of Mexican flatware at the time, expecting nothing worse than a hernia, and never seeing his assailant approach from behind.

Maybe the burly Russian felt something, air stirring or sneakers squeaking. Maybe he caught a whiff of the *café Cubano* on his attacker's breath, or possibly the last fragment of genetic matter derived from a hairy-knuckled Paleolithic hunter warned him of the danger. Whatever the reason, Smorodinsky ducked left, the grappling hook whizzed right and sliced through his blue chambray shirt, sinking into his shoulder.

He never cried out.

Not a sound.

Just the trace of a grimace, his jaw muscles tightening.

His assailant twisted the hook free, ripping out chunks of muscle and tendon and splattering himself with blood. Still, not a grunt from the big man, who dropped the wooden crate of knives and forks, turned, lowered his head, and like a wounded boar, attacked. The top of his skull caught the assailant squarely on the chin, knocking him backward and skittering the grappling hook across the floor and under a wooden pallet.

Both men stayed on their feet and, like cable TV wrestlers, clawed, gouged, and chewed on each other's vulnerable spots. They toppled into a tower of Scotch whiskey cartons and bounced off a stack of rectangular boxes of Taiwanese bicycles. They slugged and kicked and cursed—one in Russian, the other in Spanish—as they scuffed and bruised each other with a series of pokes and punches. An elbow caught Smorodinsky in the Adam's apple, but the Russian merely gagged before cuffing the smaller, darker man on the ear with a thunderous forearm that spun him sideways. Thirty pounds lighter than Smorodinsky, he threw a series of jabs, stinging the man's face but inflicting little damage. When the Russian moved closer, the man aimed a kick at his groin but connected with the hipbone.

Eventually, Smorodinsky got the better of it. He fractured two ribs with a decent right hook. He paralyzed the man's right arm with a two-fisted blow that did nerve damage to the shoulder. Then, moving inside, he bear-hugged the fellow, crushing his broken ribs and raising him off the floor. He dragged the man's face across the chicken-wire mesh of a freestanding refuse container, tearing off a goodly portion of mustache and some lower lip. With the man howling in pain, Smorodinsky did it again.

How do I know all this? I wasn't there, of course. I never am. In my profession, I hear tales of mayhem after the fact. Clients, witnesses, expert consultants all reconstruct what happened, seldom agreeing. They don't necessarily lie, but, the power of observation being what it is, they don't tell the literal truth either. Each of us sees reality through a lens of our own making. Our prejudices and self-interest shape the world into what we want it to be, or fear it is. So I was stunned that day when Francisco Crespo told a story guaranteed to get him twenty-five years to life.

Crespo sat in my office thirty-two floors above Biscayne Bay, watching me through eyes the color of burned toast, sipping a WASP law firm's watery imitation of espresso through torn lips. He wore baggy khaki pants and a Disney World T-shirt—Mickey,

Minnie, and Pluto—and was shivering in the air-conditioning. He had a grid of welts across his forehead and cheeks as if he'd been run over by a steel-belted radial tire. Good. That would help the self-defense claim, though it might be difficult to explain sneaking up on the Russian from behind.

I could think about that later, but the first task was to summon a photographer and tell him to beef up the contrast to emphasize the cuts and scrapes. The face should be shot in close-up to accentuate the damage. There's a personal injury lawyer in town who once hired a professional makeup artist to crank up the color of his clients' bruises. Using his experience with South Beach models who often tarnished their complexions with late-night drugfests before morning shoots, the artist found that reversing the process—*adding* eggplant-colored stains to perfectly fine skin—was easier and more profitable. But the lawyer got carried away, using a defrocked doctor to suture uninjured fender-bender clients, occasionally removing a healthy spleen or gall bladder. That seemed a tad excessive for the state bar, which suspended the fellow for sixty days or so.

For the full-body pictures, I told the photographer to stand on a ladder and angle down, making Crespo look even smaller. Up close, you could see my client was one of those sinewy guys who was plenty quick and twice as strong as he looked. All muscles and wires strung taut across a small bone structure. Work-hardened hands, wrists thickened from his latest job, hauling crates at a customs broker's warehouse for nonunion wages. The words "Cuba Libre" were crudely tattooed on his right tricep. His face was narrow, his complexion dusty, at least it had been before it had been bashed by the thick-necked Russian warehouseman. There was a gap where a front tooth should have been, but it didn't matter. Crespo seldom smiled.

When Smorodinsky finished shaving Crespo with the chicken-wire mesh, he just dropped him to the cement floor. While Crespo gagged and dry-heaved, the Russian gave him one good *thwack* to the temple with a reinforced work boot. The paramedics say the blow knocked Crespo unconscious, leaving him with a concussion. They found him that way, sprawled out alongside the refuse container. I would subpoena them as defense witnesses. Almost as good as alibi witnesses.

But no, Crespo insists, the lights never went out. Tucked into the fetal position, feeling the cold concrete floor against his bleeding face, Crespo watched Smorodinsky dab at the blood on his own shoulder and lumber down the aisle between thirty-foot-high rolls of Haitian cotton.

"You know it would help your case if you were unconscious just like the 911 boys said," I told him, as nonchalantly as possible. Okay, okay, I know all about the canons of ethics. *A lawyer shall not suborn perjury*. But there's a footnote. *It's okay to let the client know whether the truth will set him free or buy a one-way ticket to Raiford.*

I learned my ethics watching Jimmy Stewart coach Ben Gazzara into his temporary insanity defense in *Anatomy of a Murder*, and if that's too subtle for your tastes, how about James Mason teaching his client, a doctor accused of malpractice, a few courtroom tricks in *The Verdict*.

"If you were seeing stars," I continued, "somebody else must have—"

"Sí, yo sé, pero no paso así. The medics are wrong. I wasn't going to let the bastard get away so he could drink vodka with his *amigos* and laugh at me."

It got worse then, of course. It always does.

There was the Russian, heading for the exit, and here was my client, revving up his brain cells into the highest reaches of their two-digit IQ, seeking revenge on a guy who resented being mistaken for a side of beef.

Crespo said he watched the Russian turn left at the end of the aisle and head toward the loading dock. The Mitsubishi forklift was at the end of the second row. Crespo had used it that morning to move fertilizer crates, and now he wanted to cut Smorodinsky off before he reached the exit. Crespo ran to the forklift, started it up, and chased after the Russian, approaching him from behind. Why is it my clients are never inclined to face guys head-on?

"The big bastard heard me coming," Crespo said. He seemed to be staring at or through the photo of my college football team on my office wall. On the credenza is a no-frills white helmet with a single blue stripe and a crack that would do the Liberty Bell proud. I don't keep my diplomas here. My clients ask me to trust them; I figure they ought to have faith I studied some law, even if it was after the sun went down.

"He turned around," Crespo continued, "said something in Russki, and jumped onto a rack of Japanese transmissions. A tough *hombre,* big through the shoulders, like you, but shorter, and slow. Heavy legs." Crespo snorted, and his eyes focused somewhere else, probably remembering some barroom brawl where another big lug mistook him for an underfed *exilado,* then ended up with a busted nose or a shiv in the belly.

"You used the forklift merely to catch up with him," I suggested, helpfully. "You never intended to—"

"*Estas loco?* I intended to kill him."

Oh, brother. What would Jimmy Stewart have done? I decided to listen. Francisco Crespo stood and walked around my office. He picked up a deflated football from a position of honor on a bookshelf and ran his finger over the white paint that told the score of a long-forgotten Dolphins-Jets game. He stood near the floor-to-ceiling window without getting too close, and he avoided the draft from the air-conditioning vent. Then he finished the story in a matter-of-fact voice. I studied his body language and watched his eyes. No sign of deception. But how could he be lying? With every word, he incriminated himself.

Smorodinsky grabbed the rack's support strut like a rider pulling himself aboard a trolley car. Crespo zoomed past on the forklift and jerked it around, the back wheels whirling it into a steep turn. The Russian jumped down and was running the other way, grabbing wooden crates from the shelves, tossing them into the aisle behind him. The forklift smashed over them and caught up with Smorodinsky at an intersection of four aisles. He swerved right, wanting the forklift to rush past him. But the big Russian lost traction on the slippery concrete. I pictured his feet sliding out from under him, and I remembered trying to cut on artificial turf after a rain.

The fork was set about belly-high. It caught Vladimir Smorodinsky in midstep, slightly below the rib cage on the right side. The blade pierced the oblique muscles of the abdomen and just missed the liver, but, according to the medical examiner, plunged through the ascending colon, the right kidney, the duodenum, and worst of all, the inferior vena cava, which ordinarily carries blood to the heart from the lower extremities, but just then emptied itself all over cartons of beach towels from the Dominican Republic.

There is a lever to the right of the steering wheel, Crespo told me, happily demonstrating how he pulled it back, raising the fork, hoisting Smorodinsky off the floor. Crespo never hit the brakes. Instead, he accelerated, carrying the bleeding Russian with him.

"The bastard was stuck like, like . . ." He searched for an expression. "Like an olive on a toothpick," he said with malicious glee.

The forklift careened down the aisle, sideswiping metal racks with the *clang* of screeching metal and finally smashing into the corrugated metal door near the loading dock. The bloody steel fork reverberated against the wall like a pealing church bell. Vladimir Smorodinsky was impaled there, his feet four feet off the ground, his arms pinned to the wall in a macabre crucifixion, his insides oozing onto the concrete floor.

I peered out the window at Biscayne Bay three hundred feet below. A southeast wind rippled small whitecaps across the green water. At Virginia Key, three multicolored sails shimmered in the afternoon sun. Boardsailors. On cue, they jibed, and one of the masts dipped into the water, dunking the sailor who had flipped his boom too late.

I asked, "So why did the paramedics find you unconscious back at the refuse container?"

Crespo shrugged. "*No sé.* I must have walked back there and fainted."

Right. You could cut off both his legs at the knees, and he wouldn't faint.

"Francisco, listen to me. This isn't a simple A and B. If you tell that story, you'll take a fall for second-degree murder. Twenty-five years minimum. Now, I can't tell you to go up there and lie, but maybe you don't remember it all that well. You were under tremendous stress . . ."

He waved his hand as if to say it was no big thing, just a little fight to the finish in a warehouse hard by the docks of the Miami River. He wasn't going to help me, and that made it hard to help him. Outside my windows, one wet boardsailor water-started and pumped his sail to catch up with his two buddies. They were headed on a broad reach across the channel to Fisher Island, once a Vanderbilt retreat, now a condo sanctuary of vacationing millionaires who want the security of a saltwater moat to keep out the riffraff. If the boardsailors didn't have their papers in order, the security guards might pick them off for target practice.

"Here's how I see it. I can just keep you off the stand, and based on the state's case, all they've got is a fight between the two of you, and after you've passed out, somebody else came along and made shish kebab out of the Russian."

"*Pero,* no one else was there."

Sometimes, you just want to tell your clients to shut the hell up. "*Someone* had to be there. Someone in the office called the police, right?"

"*No sé,* you gotta ask them."

I already had. Somebody called 911 but wouldn't leave a name. Somebody saw what happened, but who?

"If we can show who drove the forklift, or if we just raise enough doubt that you did, you'd walk on the murder charge. I could probably plead you to aggravated assault right now if you'd tell the prosecutor who it was. Abe Socolow isn't stupid. An asshole maybe, but not stupid. It's a low-profile case. Nobody knew the victim. But if Socolow thinks you're covering for someone who ordered the hit, he'll go after the maximum."

Crespo shrugged again and touched a finger to the welts on his face. "You'll figure it out for me, *número cincuenta y ocho.* You always do."

I wasn't getting through to him. "You have no lawful excuse for attacking Smorodinsky. You're going—"

"He was a *comunista.*"

"I didn't know there were any left . . ."

Crespo shrugged.

"Or that you were political," I added.

Still, he didn't respond.

I rubbed my temples and stared out the window again. The boardsailors were hidden in the shadows of the Fisher Island condos. In a perfect world, I would be on the water, the wind crackling my sail. To the north, the cruise ships were lined up, single file, at the port along Government Cut, preparing for their Caribbean cruises, thousands of tourists clustered on the main decks, awaiting their prepackaged fun. For some reason, I thought of Pearl Harbor.

"So the two of you disagreed about politics," I said. Take what they give you, get a few anti-Castro Cuban-Americans on the jury, who knows?

"No, we *disagreed* because the cocksucker stole twelve dollars from my locker."

Oh, shit. I tried another theory. "You were defending your property. You caught him in the act, and in the heat of the moment—"

"No, he stole the money two months ago. *Pero,* I owed him thirty bucks at the time. He'd been bugging me about the eighteen I still owed him, and I just got tired of it. That's all there is to it. I killed the *hombre,*" my client said, "because he was a pain in the ass."

Atlantic Seaboard Warehouse was where it was supposed to be, on South River Drive, a pleasant thoroughfare if you like chain-link fences topped with barbed wire, vacant lots covered with broken beer bottles, and Doberman pinschers with psychopathic personalities. The warehouse opened to the rear, its loading docks fronting on the Miami River, home to rusty, overloaded freighters from the Caribbean and Latin America.

I had sent the photographer here the day after Crespo came to my office, but photos, diagrams, and police reports only take you so far. There's no substitute for being there. Photos and sketches often mislead. You can't pick up distances, lines of sight, the three-dimensional surroundings that make the setting real. That's why jurors are sometimes taken to the scene of the crime.

The warehouse was cavernous, piled high with goods from dozens of countries. Crates of foodstuffs—cereals, canned vegetables, bottled juices—filled several acres along the western wall. You could feed a starving country with the inventory. In another section, boxes of bicycles from Taiwan were piled to the ceiling, and nearby, thousands of concrete fence posts from Colombia were crisscrossed in stacks that resembled a house of Popsicle sticks. The open doors, the width of a tractor trailer, admitted the brackish stench of Biscayne Bay and the thick smell of diesel fuel from the river. I heard three toots of a horn, then the coughs and sputters of a tugboat nudging a barge under the Second Avenue drawbridge.

I retraced the steps, starting with the grappling hook attack, ending with the forklift. The layout was just the way Crespo described it. Once Crespo—or whoever—mounted his trusty steed of a forklift, Smorodinsky never had a chance to get to the exit. I heard an electric buzz behind me, and whirled just in time to see a forklift approach the intersection of two aisles. The machine carried a pallet of dog food cans, and the driver, a young Hispanic with a mustache, expertly steered the load around a corner.

The concrete floor was remarkably clean, but as I neared the cartons of beach towels, I saw the black spots. Concrete is just porous enough to soak up blood and ugly it. The drips continued down the aisle to the corrugated metal door, where a dark puddle of Vladimir Smorodinsky's innards left their spot for the ages. On the door itself, two indentations, at just the width of the forklift's prongs, just as Francisco Crespo said there would be.

There was a small office near the rear loading dock that led to the parking lot and a larger office overhead that could be reached by metal stairs and a catwalk. From above, you could see into every aisle. There were no witnesses to the fight, at least none I could find. None of the workmen in the warehouse or the office knew anything about it. No one admitted calling the police. No one knew much about the two workers, except Crespo was a hothead, always causing trouble. You want to know anything else, come back when Mr. Yagamata, the owner, is here.

Hothead was right on the money. I first met Francisco Crespo in his mother's house in Little Havana. He was a skinny *Marielito* just out of Castro's prisons who arrived in Miami barefoot and sopping wet. I remember thinking he must have been just off a raft, but it had been a rainy day, and he arrived at the little pink house off Calle Ocho in the back of a pickup truck.

I rented a room from Emilia Crespo in what had been the garage, having arrived in Miami—undrafted and unheralded—after a steady but unspectacular college football career. I wanted to live close to the Orange Bowl, not realizing the team practiced and virtually lived at the other end of town. It didn't matter. I never figured to make the Dolphins, and when I did, earning the league minimum, and hanging on a few years because of a willingness to sacrifice my body on kickoffs, I stayed put.

Emilia Crespo was a sturdy widow who always seemed to wear an apron. She cooked me *picadillo* and *plátanos* and taught me a smidgen of Spanish. She also asked me to look after Francisco, who refused to live with her, saying he wanted solitude. He rented a first-floor apartment on Fonseca, just east of Ponce de Leon Boulevard, and kept to himself.

To please her, I got him a job in the locker room, tossing jockstraps and towels into a washing machine with ample quantities of bleach and disinfectant. Just as often, he was brawling. I remember him flailing away at the assistant strength coach—a two-hundred-thirty-five-pound weightlifter—who smacked his lips at Crespo, suggesting he was one of the *maricónes* who recently washed up on the beaches courtesy of the Jimmy Carter flotilla across the straits. The coach slapped Crespo around, then tossed him into the whirlpool.

Crespo was reassigned to the groundskeeping crew. He got in less trouble outdoors and soon knew the vagaries of Kentucky bluegrass, fine fescue, and perennial ryegrass, as well as everything worth knowing about aeration, seeding, sodding, and mulching. Ignoring the automatic sprinkler system, Crespo hosed the field by hand, watering dry spots and patching the divots with patience and care. He seemed to like grass more than people, but then, most people he'd known the last ten years had worn boots and kicked him around.

I kept an eye on Crespo, slipping him some sweat socks when I saw his bare ankles sticking out of secondhand shoes. He returned the favor by giving me mangoes he filched from a South Dade farm. Then I gave him some old jerseys that could be turned into cash at swap meets. He sold Griese's, Csonka's, and Warfield's, but kept mine, hanging it in the front window of his apartment. It was not so valuable as to provoke a burglary or a call from the Smithsonian.

Once, in a close game against the Jets, I was in my usual position on the bench and Crespo was handing out Gatorade and towels.

"Ves al número setenta y nueve?" he asked me.

"I been watching him all day. Their weak-side tackle, a Pro Bowler."

"Why does he rock back on his heels when they're going to pass the ball?"

"What!"

"When he is crouching down in *cómo sé llame . . .*"

"The three-point stance."

"Sí, he leans forward when they are going to run, and rocks back when they are going to pass."

"Holy shit, Francisco, you oughta be a coach. We got thirty hours of game films plus Polaroids of every snap of the ball and nobody noticed that."

He shrugged and ambled down the sideline, carrying a tray of drinks to some guys who deserved them more than I did. "When you fight, must watch your *enemigo*'s every move," he called back at me.

Two plays later, we lost a starting outside linebacker to a hip-pointer, and I had a chance to get my uniform dirty. Two sacks and three tackles for losses in the fourth quarter. The only game ball of my career.

The year I retired—which is a nice way of saying I was placed on waivers where twenty-five other teams managed not to notice me—Crespo left, too. I spent the next year engulfed in booze and blondes, and by the time I started night law school, I had lost track of him. I figured he was either in jail or contending for the welterweight championship.

Then, a few years later, Emilia Crespo called me. I was in my last days as a public defender, copping pleas for guys too poor to buy a decent defense. Did I want to stop by for some *picadillo con frijoles negros y arroz blanco?* Did I ever! The years had added a few white streaks to the black hair pulled straight back, a little heavier maybe, but the apron was crisply starched and her greeting was the same. A hug that could knock the wind out of Dick Butkus. I ate heartily, and she watched in silence, nibbling at a plantain. I sipped a *mojito,* the rum and soda drink with fresh mint leaves from her garden. I asked Emilia Crespo about Francisco, and her dark eyes filled with pain.

"I don't know what that *asesino,* Castro, did to him in prison, but he has never been the same. Angry all the time. *Violento.* It is as if my son cares about nothing."

"He cares about you. And so do I. What can I do?"

Her answer was a tender plea. "Will you be his friend?"

"I tried in the old days. He isn't easy to get close to."

"Will you try again, Jake? For me?"

She knew I would. In my life, I have Granny Lassiter, who raised me, Charlie Riggs, who taught me, and Emilia Crespo, who put a roof over my head and meat on my bones. There was something else, too, a path of obligation that ran straight from Jake Lassiter, ex-football player, to Francisco Crespo, ex-*preso politico,* and it was something neither of us would ever tell his mother.

Two days later, I tracked Crespo down at the jai alai fronton where he sat in the back row, his feet draped over the seat in front of him, a program balled up in one hand. He was alone and seemed to like it that way. I sat to one side, watching him through the first three games, listening to the *plonk* of the pelota against the front wall. Nobody talked to him, and he reciprocated. Finally, I went up and said hello, how about a drink and a sandwich later. He said, fine, but if he was pleased to see me, it didn't show.

"What are you up to?" I asked him that evening, over a beer at a Calle Ocho *taberna.*

"This and that."

I took a sip of a Brooklyn Lager, a rare find in these parts. Burnt amber color, a taste of toasted malt, it goes well with spicy Spanish food. "Do you need work?"

"No."

"Money?"

"No."

"Anything?"

"No."

This wasn't going anywhere. Maybe I wasn't any good at reaching out. Maybe he thought I was there only because his mother asked me to be. Or maybe it was just hard for him to accept friendship, especially friendship sparked by obligation. My attempts at gratitude had always been awkward, his responses perfunctory.

"Francisco, you're making this difficult for me. I owe you. You haven't forgotten, have you?"

He dismissed the notion with a shrug. "It has been many years."

"Some things don't go away, even when you want them to. *Particularly* when you want them to. I still dream about it, nightmares really."

"Dreams are dreams," he said. "Life is life."

I wanted to reach out to him, give him a brotherly hug, but I didn't. He wouldn't have wanted me to. Or was that just my excuse? Maybe *I'd* been stiff-arming him because he reminded me of that night and my eternal obligation. "It's our secret, Francisco, something only the two of us share."

He finished his beer. His expression hadn't changed. *"Dos minutos*. That's all it was out of your life and mine."

"That's a lot," I said, "if it lets someone keep on living."

"You think about it too much."

"Don't you . . . don't you ever wake up, remembering?"

"My nightmares are different," Francisco Crespo said.

We finished our beer and polished off a couple of Cuban sandwiches with black bean soup on the side. I promised to stay in touch the same way Hollywood producers promise to call for lunch. He gave me his phone number, and I tucked it in my pocket, then taped it on the refrigerator door. When I finally tried to reach him, the phone had been disconnected. I could have called his mother. I could have tracked him down. I could have done a lot of things. But I didn't. Then came the call from the county jail; Crespo was booked on a second-degree murder charge.

I left my Olds 442 convertible, vintage 1968, in the parking lot, and walked along the river, a narrow, oil-slicked snake of a waterway that runs from just north of the airport to Biscayne Bay near the downtown commercial district. Half a mile away, the air horn on the Flagler Street drawbridge was tooting the alarm, the tender preparing to raise the span. I remembered a humid night on the MacArthur Causeway, the dark vision of death haunting me still. I shook off the cobwebs and stared at a Panamanian freighter loaded with bicycles and truck tires heading toward the bay. The bikes—nearly all stolen—would be headed for Haiti, where a battered old Schwinn can bring fifty bucks. Freighters routinely use the river to haul illicit cargo, but that's nothing new. During Prohibition, rumrunners from the Bahamas found their way up the Miami River with their contraband.

A few years ago, the city *padres* decided to clean up the polluted channel and decrepit surroundings where even the hookers can't be trusted: they're transvestites. The city planned a Riverfest extravaganza, which was going fine until a sewer line broke, spoiling the fun because it's tough to enjoy your lobster and *paella* when the afternoon breeze is ripe with the stench of raw sewage. Now, rustbuckets from a dozen Central American countries were tied up, their crews idling on the shore or heading to roughneck bars along Flagler Street. The ships are essential to Miami's commerce, hauling drugs and illegal aliens in, carting stolen cars and bicycles out.

I stopped at an outdoor fish market, bought a pint of cold conch salad, spicy with peppers and onions, and admired the fresh stone crab claws. The stoners were arranged in iced boxes, according to size—medium, large, and jumbo. In a triumph of marketing, even the smallest claw was labeled "medium." Apparently, "small" claws would have as much consumer appeal as "petite" condoms.

My canary yellow convertible was still there when I walked back to the warehouse, beating the odds in a county where a hundred cars are stolen every day. I haven't gone for any of the new devices so popular hereabouts: the LoJack transmitter to help the cops find your missing car; the Hook Crook Cane to lock the steering wheel; the electronic starter disabler and computer chip car key. If somebody really wants your car, they're going to get it, and love her as I do, the old 442 is still just a chunk of metal.

The radio was untouched, too, probably because it's older than most car thieves. It has no CD, no tape deck, not even an FM band. It does pick up Radio Havana, though, plus a big band station near the top of the AM dial. Some Filipino seamen were in the lot, but no one showed any interest in my antique, except a white ibis who was probably lost. The snowy bird was pecking at my tires with its long orange beak. Maybe I'd run over a juicy grasshopper.

I got in the car and drove five minutes to the Gaslight Lounge downtown. Once inside, I waited for my eyes to adjust to the darkness, then made my way to the bar. The conch salad had made me thirsty; the case of *State* v. *Crespo* required an expert consultation. I had come to the right place for both.

The Gaslight is fine for a beer and a bacon cheeseburger, onion rings on the side. The red imitation-leather banquettes and matching bar stools are right out of the Fifties, and so is the clientele. Usually I drink Grolsch. For my money, the Dutch brewmasters are the best. But everyone has his own tastes, and if the yuppies want to buy watery Mexican beer because the long-necked bottles are trendy, let them. If they impress each other with a pricey Swedish vodka that is indistinguishable from half a dozen other brands, that's fine, too. I stay out of the Misty Fern, and they stay out of the Gaslight, a place with no hanging plants, no pickled-wood latticework, and no nachos with salsa. Just a long, scarred teak bar with a brass foot rail, smoked mirrors, and barely enough light to read your check without striking a match.

For some reason, I didn't feel like a beer, so I pointed to a bottle on the mirrored shelf, and Mickey Cumello poured two and a half ounces of Plymouth gin into a mixing glass without using the jigger to measure. Why should he? Does Pavarotti need sheet music?

Usually, I only drink gin after being drop-kicked by a judge, a jury, or a lady friend. Come to think of it, I've had more than my share of martinis lately.

Mickey gently dropped in four ice cubes—the large square ones, so they won't melt the instant they hit the alcohol—and dribbled a splash or two of dry vermouth into the mixture. He stirred with a glass swizzle, but not out of fear of bruising the gin. Drinks don't bruise; only drinkers do, but shaking clouds a martini. Finally, he strained the drink into a chilled glass, sliced a sliver of lemon peel, and lit a match. He squeezed the rind above the burning match until oil dropped into the flame, shooting off little sparks, which settled into the martini, giving it a hint of burnt lemon.

Mickey Cumello is a bartender from the old school. No ponytail, earring, or track shoes. His gray hair was combed straight back, revealing a handsome widow's peak. He always wore a short-sleeve white shirt, charcoal gray pants, and polished black leather shoes, and he never spoke unless spoken to. In the dim light, he looked forty-five and had for twenty years.

I sipped at the cool poison and let it slide down the throat. "Mickey, you know every client I ever had is a liar."

He hunched his bushy eyebrows but didn't say a thing. Maybe he felt the same way about his customers. "They either lie to the jury or to me, or both," I continued.

Mickey allowed me a small smile while he polished an old-fashioned glass that was dry and spotless.

"But they always swear they weren't there, or the other guy started it, or the full moon made them do it."

A man in a dark suit sat down a polite three bar stools away and, without being asked, Mickey hit a long-handled tap and drew a glass of Canadian ale. Just as silently, he resumed his position in front of me.

"But until now, I never had a client claim he iced a guy when it's clear somebody else did it. Now why would he do that?"

Mickey wiped his hands on the towel and neatly folded it on a drying rack. "That's easy, Jake. To protect someone else."

"Right, but why?"

A swarthy man in a white guayabera slid onto the bar stool next to me. Mickey turned his body to shield our conversation. Is there such a thing as the bartender-client privilege?

"Because whatever he's involved in, Jake, is a lot bigger than he is."

My look told him to continue. He said, "And whatever a judge could do to him . . ."

"Twenty-five years to life."

". . . is nothing compared to what'll happen if he spills what he knows. So, not to tell you your business, but if I were you, I wouldn't be so anxious to hear this guy's story."

I drained the rest of the martini, tasting the sharpness of the gin against the smokiness of the burnt lemon. "Since when are you concerned about the health of my clients?"

Mickey Cumello shook his head. "Not his health, Jake. Yours."

2

THE CHICKEN AND THE EGG

The psychologist said I stood too close to the jury during opening statement. My client said I was too loud. The judge said I was argumentative. And Marvin the Maven wasn't talking to me.

Everyone's a critic.

"Be aware of horizontal space zones," Dr. Lester (Call Me Les) Weiner warned. "You're using social zones when the courtroom demands public zones."

I used to know a thing or two about end zones, but this was new to me.

Dr. Weiner toyed with the top button on his black Italian silk shirt. He wore no tie, and the sleeves were pushed up on his baggy sportcoat, a look favored by *Miami Vice* wannabes. The pleated pants were also black and had room for another Les inside. His dark hair was moussed and slicked straight back, and he studied me from behind dark-tinted aviator glasses. The general impression was Darth Vader with a Ph.D. "Jake, you're still a stranger to the jury, so keep a horizontal zone of at least eight feet. By closing argument, if you establish rapport, you may move up to the rail."

Marvin the Maven sat in the front row of the gallery pretending not to listen. Even at age seventy-six, there was nothing wrong with his hearing. He had said barely a word since learning I'd hired a psychologist to help with jury selection and trial tactics. For years, Marvin had the job, his only degree a lifetime of experience selling shoes, his expert's fee a cup of tea and a bagel with a *schmear.* Now, feeling abandoned, he threatened to spend the rest of the week watching the ticker at the Miami Beach Merrill Lynch office, tracking the path of his fifty shares of AT&T.

I was sitting at the defense table, half listening to the witness, half listening to Dr. Weiner, who kept reminding me of my many deficiencies. "Your directional gestures are also too strong. And your height power is menacing this early in the trial, especially when you encroach on the neutral zone."

Five-yard penalty, I figured.

"Did you notice the jurors crossing their arms and turning to the side as you violated their space bubble?" he asked.

"I thought it might have been the anchovies on the Caesar salad," I said.

The psychologist crossed *his* arms, and I wondered if it was something I said. Dr. Lester Weiner was deeply tanned, excessively self-confident, and for three hundred dollars an hour could tell you whether a woman will vote for the plaintiff by examining her makeup. A few blocks from the courthouse at Miami Marina, he kept a thirty-eight-foot Bertram—the *Pleasure Principle*—docked at what he called his Freudian slip.

"Perhaps a woman lawyer could approach the rail during opening statement," Dr. Weiner whispered, not letting it go. He was chewing on his lower lip, and his pencil had bite marks, but I refrained from asking whether he was bottle-fed as an infant. "It is easier for women to gain rapport, but a man of your size, well . . ."

He let it hang there, sort of telling me that I was a bull in the china shop. As if I didn't know.

"Now it is true the women on the jury will find you attractive in, shall we say, an animalistic fashion. The way your neck threatens to burst out of your shirt collar, it's quite provocative."

His *burst* had a faintly lascivious ring to it.

"But stay in the shadows at first. Approach too quickly, and you might intimidate them."

What am I, Phantom of the Courthouse?

"And the men will want to identify with you. The bald ones wish they had your shock of sandy hair . . ." He made a motion as if to run his hand across my head, and I leaned the other way.

". . . The small ones will envy your size." What did he mean by that, remembering that we had stood shoulder-to-shoulder in the men's room at the midmorning recess. Now, my legs instinctively crossed.

This was getting embarrassing. I wanted to use Marvin the Maven, but my client insisted I hire "Les Is More" Weiner, a guy who couldn't get into med school but had a booming business in hypnotic regression, sex therapy, and jury counseling.

I tried to pay attention. Percy Tucker, founder of Percy's Perfect Poultry ("The Cluck Stops Here") and my client, sat on one side of me, the psychologist on the other. Marvin the Maven sat directly behind us on the other side of the bar. Perched on the witness stand was icily smooth Christopher Middleton, president of Chicken Prince, Inc., the plaintiff and chief tormentor of my client.

"Your witness, counselor," H. T. Patterson, the plaintiff's lawyer, informed me with a confident smile that invited me to take my best shot.

"Mr. Middleton," I began, easing out of my chair and approaching the witness stand, "you never registered the name 'Chickee Tender,' correct?"

"Correct, but we spent millions advertising the name. It's nearly as well known as our Poultry Burger and our Milkshake Mucho."

"Yes, but really these so-called tenders are nothing more than breaded chicken breast with spices, correct?"

"Nothing more? They are the product of years of research, consumer testing—"

"So you've testified. But the name 'tender' is just an abbreviation of tenderloin, the meat covering the chicken's breastbone, correct?"

Christopher Middleton eyed me warily. His delay told the jury that he didn't want to answer the question, that he knew the question would lead to another and another, and somewhere down that road was a patch of quicksand. He touched a finger to the fringes of his blow-dried hair. "The meat does come from the breastbone," he answered, finally.

"And isn't it commonly called the tenderloin?"

Another pause. "I've heard it mentioned."

"I'm sure you have," I said quietly, causing the judge to stir, but no objection rose from the plaintiff's table. H. T. Patterson knew when not to call attention to his client's squirming. "Now, my client's frozen food product, Percy's Perfect Chickee Tender, also uses chicken from the tenderloin, does it not?"

"If you say so."

"Oh, come now, Mr. Middleton. You hired a testing lab at great expense to analyze my client's product."

"Objection!" Patterson was on his feet, realizing there's also a time to protect your witness. A former preacher at the Liberty City Baptist Church, my learned opponent was resplendent in a white linen three-piece suit. He stood ramrod straight, which took him to five-feet-five on his tippy-toes. "Mr. Lassiter is baiting, bedeviling, and badgering my client," Patterson railed in his seductive revival meeting singsong. "If counsel were a novice at the bar, we could forgive his transgressions, but given his experience, his erudition, his perspicacity, yea, his very wisdom, acumen, and sagacity, we must consider these malefactions to be intentional violations of the rules of evidence and trial procedure."

Was he talking about me, a guy who got straight C's in law school because they didn't offer phys ed?

"Sustained," intoned Judge Harold Bricklin, a man of imposing girth and sour demeanor. "Ask questions, Mr. Lassiter, and refrain from comments on the testimony." That was a mild rebuke from someone whose idea of judicial restraint is not plugging obstreperous lawyers with the seven-shot 380 Walther PPK he carried under his flowing black robes.

"*Did* you hire a testing lab—"

"Yes, yes. Your client uses the same meat." Middleton was growing edgy.

"So you don't contend Percy's Perfect Chickee Tender is misrepresenting its product?"

I knew the answer, of course. One of the trial lawyer's oldest tricks is to exclude allegations against his client that have never been made.

"No."

"And you don't claim trademark infringement?"

"No."

"And you can't possibly contend that consumers are confused, since my client's products are sold only in supermarkets while yours are sold only in your own fast-food convenience stores."

I tried to make "fast-food" sound like toxic scum.

"Well, maybe not," he allowed, "but Percy's trading off our name. We created consumer name identification with our advertising, and they're—"

"Thank you, Mr. Middleton. Nothing further."

I left him stammering while H. T. Patterson rose, bowed to the jury, buttoned his suit coat, and stroked the pink carnation in his lapel. Patterson knew he could still rehabilitate his client on re-direct.

Percy Tucker looked fat and happy as I sat down next to him. They always do when someone else is skewered on the witness stand. His turn would come.

"Now, Mr. Middleton," Patterson began in a tone of affection and deep respect, "how much money did your company expend on market research, consumer testing, and the like?"

I didn't hear the answer because Percy was whispering suggestions in my ear. Clients always second-guess their lawyers—and often sue them—so it's good to listen, or at least pretend. I doodled on a yellow pad so the jury thought I was taking notes. Percy was saying the jurors should taste both companies' products. I wasn't sure. The opposition's chicken was soaked in a slimy grease, while Percy's was dry, stringy, and coated with salt. I didn't want to make the jurors sick and risk a mistrial. Trying this case once was enough.

At the end of the day, Marvin the Maven stopped me in the corridor. "Even though you didn't ask, Jake, I think you're *meshuga*, leaving on that woman, number four."

Mrs. Kvajic. Late forties, a handsome woman with a big smile. "Dr. Weiner liked her earrings," I said. "Large hoops, a little flamboyant. Figured she'd go for the chicken farmer over the big company."

Marvin screwed his face into a septuagenarian's pout. "Earrings, schmearrings. Did you look at her shoes, *boychik*? Charles Jourdan, three hundred bucks at Mayfair. She's establishment all the way."

Then Marvin walked away muttering to himself, not telling me how much I needed him.

3

MASQUERADE

The waiter served hors d'oeuvres on a silver tray.

I turned down the phyllo triangles stuffed with curried chicken and headed for the table stocked with iced-down stone crabs. On a small stage, a woman plucked at the strings of a harp, lending a formal air to the festivities. I gathered my beer and a plate of crabs and parked myself in front of an ice sculpture that towered over a bowl of shrimp. At parties, you can always find me within a fourth-and-one of the food.

I heard his voice before I saw him.

"There are four manners of death—accident, suicide, natural, and homicide—and the coroner's first job is to ascertain one from the other."

Doc Charlie Riggs was surrounded by a gaggle of young women. Most were taller than the bandy-legged and bearded wizard. The women wore cocktail dresses and jewelry that sparkled in the flickering reflection of the patio torches. We were on the broad expanse of red Spanish tile behind a Mediterranean mansion on Palm Island, one of the luxury landfills between Miami and Miami Beach. Years ago, Al Capone was an island resident. The current neighbors—lawyers, investment bankers, bond traders—aren't as law-abiding.

"Right before I retired," Doc Riggs was saying, "we had a hanging death that baffled the detectives. They couldn't determine if it was suicide or homicide. A thirty-year-old married man was found in a hotel room. Bound, gagged, and dead. He was wearing a black brassiere and matching panties. His ankles were bound with a clothesline fastened to a dog collar around his neck. The body was positioned so that the man could see himself in the mirror, at least while he was alive. The panties were stained with seminal fluid."

"A ritualistic torture murder?" one of the women guessed. She was a platinum blonde who squirmed with delight inside a skintight red leather mini.

"Colombian cowboys?" another offered, licking her glossy lips. "A revenge killing in a drug war. Or maybe a Santería ritual?"

"A transvestite's suicide?" said a third, a willowy model in a bare-shouldered silk dress patterned with cheetahs.

While the women were cooing and fluttering, Doc Riggs scratched his bushy beard. He pulled off his old eyeglasses, still mended with a fishhook where they had tossed a screw. "No, no, no, just like the police, you've come to a *consensus audacium,* a rash agreement. You've all *assumed* it was a homicide or a suicide."

"But what else could it be?" asked the one in red leather, somewhat petulantly.

"Non semper ea sunt quae videntur. Things are not always what they appear to be. Or as Gilbert and Sullivan put it in song—"

" 'Things are seldom what they seem,' " I chimed in. " 'Skim milk masquerades as cream.' "

Charlie whirled toward me. "Eureka! Jacob Lassiter, my favorite downtown mouthpiece. Jake, do you know these young ladies?" Charlie gestured toward his admirers with his drink and wrinkled his forehead. "Gracious, I do believe I have forgotten your names, but they all end in *y*'s, *i*'s, and double *e*'s. Candy, Bambi, Sandee, et cetera, et cetera, et cetera, say hello to Jake Lassiter, shyster to the stars. So, Jake, what was the cause of death?"

"Got me, Charlie. And not for the first time."

"Accident!" Charlie thundered. "Sexual asphyxia. A botched attempt at a rather elaborate masturbation. The deceased intended to heighten sexual pleasure by increasing pressure on his neck. You probably know that Eskimos often choke each other during sex."

"Didn't know," I said. "My bedmates usually wait till afterwards."

"This poor soul got carried away, used too much pressure with his legs, and strangled himself. Just an accident, that's all."

While I was trying to figure the moral of the story, the young women started drifting away. I wondered if it was my body language again, but then I noticed that the music had stopped and so had most of the talking. Our host, Matsuo Yagamata, had taken the stage. He was short and stocky and wore his custom-made English suit a tad on the tight side. His eyes were dark and bright, and he had the air of unquestioned authority that successful men acquire if they are not born with it.

When I had arrived at the party earlier in the evening, Yagamata smiled pleasantly and shook my hand with a grip that could crack walnuts. "Still in shape, number fifty-eight?" he asked, flattering me with the recognition and drawing attention to himself with the show of strength. "And how are my legal eagles at Harman and Fox?"

"Fine and dandy, as long as Yagamata Imports has us on retainer," I replied.

He let my hand go and smiled. "Did you solve that duties problem on the European art, or do I have to bribe a customs inspector?"

You can never tell when some people are joking. "Better to pay your lawyers and let them sweet-talk the customs people," I responded.

"Right. Bribes aren't deductible."

Okay, so he wasn't joking. There had been a scandal in Japan, some government ministers on a secret payroll of his electronics exporting firm. With the investigation pending, Yagamata moved to Miami, a more forgiving place in both the private and public sectors. Businessmen here don't earn their bones until they've been subpoenaed by a grand jury. Local politicians courting publicity gain greater name recognition once they've beaten an indictment for bribery or tax evasion. County commissioners once named a street after a major campaign contributor who also happened to be one of the largest drug dealers in town. With his lobbyists and legislator pals, Yagamata could have a whole subdivision christened in his honor.

"And what of our hotheaded Latino friend?" he asked. "Will it cost me a fortune to tidy up that little mess?"

That little mess. The rich have quaint ways of dealing with other people's tragedies.

"I'm not doing Crespo much good right now," I told him. "He's covering for someone, and he's going to get hit with major-league time unless he opens up."

Yagamata stared at me with those dark, impenetrable eyes. "He told you this?"

A grand jury couldn't get that information out of me with a crowbar. But I was hesitant to brush off the guy paying Crespo's bills with a speech about the sanctity of the attorney-client privilege. On the other hand, Crespo had told me to keep his boss informed. *Señor Yagamata es mi amigo.* I felt Yagamata's eyes probing me. "I can tell he's holding back," I said, finally. "I've known Francisco Crespo a long time."

"So I am told. It is fortuitous, is it not?"

For whom, I wondered. Maybe for Yagamata. Get one of his expensive lawyers to clean up *that little mess,* some nasty blood on the floor of his warehouse. "I'm not sure," I said. "It makes it tougher for me. His mother is a saintly woman who's anguished by what's become of him."

"Ah, now I see. You are a sentimentalist."

"I just like to help out people who've helped me."

"An excellent quality. So what is stopping you?"

"Crespo told me a cock-and-bull story about how he killed the Russian all by his lonesome. It didn't hold up."

Yagamata shifted his weight ever so slightly. A look of discomfort crossed his face before he chased it away. "The authorities, they also will not believe it."

It was more of a question, and something struck me about it, but I couldn't pin it down. A faint tone of disappointment maybe. Around us, bartenders poured Cristal champagne into fresh-squeezed orange juice, and a fine ocean breeze stirred the palms.

Pleasant party noises were growing, the tinkling of glasses, animated chatter, and an occasional laugh. People just delighted with their own socially prominent selves.

"No, the prosecution will be so happy to close the case, Crespo will take the fall by himself. Keeping files open doesn't help the state attorney's statistics when it's appropriations time."

Yagamata smiled and let some light into his eyes. The foibles of government seemed to be something he understood. "Fine. If Mr. Crespo says he killed the man, who are we to say he did not?"

I'm not one of those self-righteous lawyers given to glorifying the lonely warriors of the courtroom, righting wrongs wherever we find them, blah, blah, blah. I'm just a lead-footed ex-linebacker trying to wade through the muck of the so-called justice system. I don't even mind getting dirty so long as the stains come out. But I've also got a big mouth, and sometimes a guy who sits on my shoulder puts words into it.

"My job is to do my best for Crespo whether he wants it or not." I sounded tight-assed, even to myself.

Yagamata's smile disappeared. He appraised me, probably wondering if I was a fool. That made two of us. I had never worked directly for him before, but the corporate and international lawyers in the firm had been glomming six-figure fees from Yagamata's business interests for several years. I was meandering on the fringes of an ethical thicket. No lawyer can serve masters with conflicting interests.

"I'm sure you will do your job splendidly, Mr. Lassiter," Yagamata said. "But perhaps you read too much into the situation. If Mr. Crespo is shielding someone else, it could be from a sense of honor, a commitment he has made. In my country, that would be praiseworthy."

"But it warps the system," I said. Jeez, where was I getting this apple-pie and flag-waving stuff?

Little lines formed creases at the corners of his eyes and he chuckled. He liked bantering with me. Maybe nobody ever argued with him, even politely. "The system," he told me pleasantly, "is made to be warped. If I had not retained you, Mr. Crespo would have employed the—"

"Public defender."

"Yes, and the representation would have been, shall we say, perfunctory?"

I nodded and grabbed a mimosa from a passing silver tray. The orange bubbles sparkled in the torchlight. "The state's case looks open-and-shut until you get into it, and the P.D.'s office is so overworked, they might not even talk to Crespo until just before the trial."

"Then I would say that Mr. Crespo is quite fortunate to have you as his attorney and me as his employer." Yagamata moved closer and used his broad back to shield us from the party guests. His voice was little more than a whisper. "They tell me you are a pleasant fellow and a decent if undistinguished lawyer, but that you have problems with authority."

Who was I to argue with the truth? I downed the sparkling drink and kept listening.

"In my country," he continued, "the failure to adhere to a rigid structure is considered a major personal failing." Yagamata paused and looked toward the channel just off the patio where a huge Bertram chugged along at no-wake speed, its running lights glowing in the darkness. He seemed to resent the intrusion on his personal space. "On the other hand, I have always believed life is more interesting if you have your own identity. My country cultivates faceless technicians. A man needs personality, singularity. That is why I love your country so much, Mr. Lassiter. Land of the cowboys. Rugged individuals. You understand this, I know."

Somehow I heard a "but" coming.

He gave me a wintry smile. "But it is one thing to be an individual and another to be disloyal to those who are willing to assist you. In our lives, Mr. Lassiter, we cross paths with many people. Most will be of little use. Loyalty to them is misplaced, a waste. Others will be in a position to further careers, to look after interests. Loyalty to these people will be rewarded. Disloyalty will bring shame and dishonor, pain and ruin."

"What happens," I asked, "if personal loyalty conflicts with moral principles?"

"Then it would be the truest test of loyalty, would you not agree?"

I could have objected to the leading question, but I didn't.

Before I could agree or disagree, Yagamata turned to greet two local politicians who attended every high-society bar mitzvah, communion, and bayside soiree on the public service gravy train. Yagamata didn't turn back. He just left me standing there, my paw wrapped around a slender champagne flute. I guess it hadn't been a question after all. It was a message. Dockworker Francisco Crespo was a damn lucky guy to have his millionaire boss paying a downtown mouthpiece to look the other way. And me, I was being paid handsomely to keep the boss's name out of the papers and deliver Crespo into the garbage disposal we call the criminal justice system. Do the job right, there'd be others to follow. Screw it up, there'd be pain and ruin.

You and me both, Francisco. Just a couple of lucky guys.

Now perched on the stage, Yagamata was introducing the local celebrities, a collection of county judges, city commissioners, TV anchorfolks, business executives, even a monsignor and two men who claimed to sit on the water and sewer board. Then Yagamata announced he was giving three million dollars to preserve some Art Deco properties on South Beach. In lieu of the mayor, who was on trial for bribery and extortion, the vice mayor of Miami Beach handed him a plaque, and all the politicos applauded politely and jockeyed for position as a local TV crew taped the event. Charlie and I moseyed over to a Henry Moore sculpture that looked like a gray marble camel. It made a fine, if lumpy, picnic table. I dug into a second portion of stone crabs, dipping the white meat into a tangy mustard sauce.

"Menippe mercenaria," Charlie said with genuine affection, spearing one of my claws. "Sweeter than lobster."

"Bad for your cholesterol, Charlie," I said, hoarding my remaining stoners.

"Don't be a spoilsport." When I signaled a waiter to bring me a beer instead of champagne spiked with vitamin C, Charlie pilfered another claw. I used to stalk stone crabs in the shallow coastal waters each winter. You can find them under rocks or buried in mounds of sand on the grass flats in the bay. Some folks use baited traps, but those attract the wily octopus, which eats your crab by sucking the meat from the shell, and leaves you with a bunch of tentacles to wrestle with. Others use a metal prober and a net, it being illegal to spear our eight-legged friends. Most people simply pay thirty bucks à la carte at Joe's for a handsome tray of the claws, but I always enjoyed catching them by hand.

You don't kill a stone crab. You grab it and rotate the body one way and the claw the other way. The claw snaps off cleanly. Toss the crab back into the water, and it will regenerate the claw. Then, next winter, do it again. Do the crabs feel pain, I wonder. And do they miss their claws?

Charlie was making slurping noises, leaving a trail of mustard in his beard. "What's new, Jake? Still handling those chicken-shit civil cases?"

"You're close, Charlie. Very close."

I told him about Chicken Prince versus Percy's Perfect Poultry, and Charlie scowled. "Arguing about the *pectoralis minor* muscle of the chicken, for goodness' sake. Who cares? Now give me a good murder . . ."

Charlie went on for a while, reminiscing about a couple of cases we had worked together—the doctor caught in a web of lust and greed, the women strangled as they played computer sex-talk games—as other dignitaries took the stage to heap praise on our host. The director of a local art museum gave his thanks for Yagamata's generous gifts, and the head of the symphony did the same.

Around us, Biscayne Bay shimmered black under a soft easterly breeze. The lights of the Collins Avenue hotels winked, and an occasional jet from M.I.A. soared overhead. It was a beautiful night filled with beautiful people doing beautiful things. As usual, I didn't quite fit in.

"Will you look at that," Charlie Riggs said, interrupting my reverie.

Yagamata stood alone on the stage. He had opened a red velvet box and withdrew what appeared to be a green and silver egg-shaped sculpture. At its base, two winged creatures stood with swords and shields raised high.

"Come closer, Jake," Charlie said, moving toward the stage.

Yagamata was speaking to his guests: "As many of you know,

I have given many gifts of art to museums both in Japan and in the United States." He allowed himself a modest chuckle. "I thought you might like to see a little something I gave myself."

The crowd tittered at the "little something." Yagamata was showing off and enjoying it.

"I love art, and I love jewelry. So the jewelry-art of Carl Fabergé is most attractive to me. When Fabergé made imperial eggs for the family of the czar, he often enclosed a surprise." Carefully, Yagamata lifted the lid of the egg and delicately pulled out what at first looked like a thick gold chain.

Moving closer, I saw it clearly, a miniature train, an engine, a tender, and five coaches of solid gold.

"The Trans-Siberian Railway Egg of 1900," whispered Charlie Riggs, who knows everything worth knowing and a lot that isn't.

"I don't know if you can appreciate the incredible detail from where you are standing," Yagamata said to the crowd. "One coach even has a miniature imperial chapel. There are tiny signs for 'smokers' and 'ladies only.' It is really quite special."

Charlie made a harrumphing sound that he sometimes uses to clear his throat and his mind.

I nudged him from behind. "What do you suppose that thing cost?"

"You couldn't buy it," Charlie replied, testily.

"I know *I* couldn't, but what do you suppose Yagamata spent?"

"He couldn't buy it, either. Not if it's the real McCoy."

"You think it's fake? Skim milk masquerading as cream?"

"Trust me, Jake. The original could not be bought. What I don't understand is how anyone could afford to copy something so intricate. It would simply be too expensive to duplicate."

Yagamata was still fondling his little gold train, and Charlie Riggs was still chewing over something I didn't understand.

"Didn't that magazine publisher buy a lot of those eggs?" I asked.

"Yes, Malcolm Forbes. But he bought them from private collections."

"So, maybe Yagamata—"

"The Trans-Siberian Railway Egg is in the Armoury Museum

in the Kremlin, and not in the gift shop, either. You can't buy it, Jake, any more than you could buy Lenin's Tomb. It belongs to the Russian Republic."

Yagamata folded the train together. The cars fit snugly together by the minute gold hinges that connected them. He put the train back into the egg, and the egg into its red velvet box. The guests began gravitating toward the dessert table, where white-gloved waiters served chocolate eggs filled with white mousse and a raspberry for a surprise. I just love theme parties.

"Sometimes, Charlie, you make life too complicated," I said to my old pal.

"I'm waiting," Charlie said, *"arrectis auribus,* with ears pricked up."

"Sometimes, things are just the way they seem."

"Meaning what?"

I seldom get anywhere quicker than Charlie Riggs, so I wanted to prolong the moment. "If Matsuo Yagamata wanted that shiny little choo-choo train and it wasn't for sale, what do you suppose he'd do?"

Doc Riggs eyed me suspiciously but didn't say a word.

"He'd just take it, Charlie. He'd steal the damn thing."

4

THE PROFESSOR AND THE PRIVATE EYE

"You smell anything fishy?" Marvin the Maven whispered to Saul the Tailor.

"Vad you say?" asked Saul, fingering the part in his steel gray toupee and cupping a hand around his ear.

"The smell," Marvin repeated, tapping his nose. "You can still smell, can't you?"

Saul the Tailor sniffed the air and nodded. "Somethin' ain't kosher in Denmark."

H. T. Patterson carried a brown bag to the clerk's table and pulled out your everyday supermarket chicken. In the pale fluorescent light of the courtroom, the dead bird was pasty white. "At this juncture, without further ado," Patterson began, in his hypnotic singsong, "the plaintiff wishes to offer demonstrative evidence, *ipso facto,* the deboning of a deceased fowl in order to facilitate the jury's understanding of Professor Pennywhistle's testimony."

Translation: A farmer with a Ph.D. was gonna cut up a dead chicken.

"Time out, Your Honor!" I was on my feet. "We've had no notice of this. They're going to perform—"

"A simple demonstration," Patterson interrupted.

"An autopsy is more like it. It serves no purpose, none at all.

Either Chicken Prince has the exclusive right to use the term 'Chickee Tender,' or it doesn't. The anatomy doesn't matter."

"Objection overruled," said Judge Bricklin. "Let's see what they've got, but move it along, Mr. Patterson."

The clerk, a young Cuban woman with dyed red hair and three-inch fingernails, wrinkled her nose and tied an exhibit tag—plaintiff's number twenty-seven—around the deceased's drumstick. The bailiff opened the door to the corridor and ushered the witness down the aisle. Professor Clyde Pennywhistle toddled to the witness stand. He was a fifty-year-old cherub, portly and round-faced with a small mouth curved in a perpetual smile. His hair was a 1950's flattop gone gray. He wore bifocals, and his eyes were slightly crossed behind the lenses.

H. T. Patterson ran sonorously through the professor's background, all the way from working on a pig farm as a kid to professor of poultry science at Purdue. Patterson opened a gunnysack and pulled out a stainless steel instrument that looked like an upside-down funnel. "The deboning cone," he told the jury gravely, as if it were the Holy Grail. On cue, the professor stepped down and walked to the clerk's table, just a few feet from the jury box. With a sharp knife and a deftness that Charlie Riggs would admire, the professor made an incision down the back, peeled the skin off, and started carving away.

"This will just take a moment," the professor said, expertly slicing through the shoulder joint, then pulling at the wing to tear the carcass apart. Then, with small precise movements, he pared some more, removing the breast. He held up a piece of the meat. "The *pectoralis major,* often called the chicken fillet . . ." Next he sliced off a strip of muscle, maybe an inch wide and six inches long.

The high-ceilinged courtroom was hot and stuffy, the ancient air-conditioning wheezing just to stir the soggy air. Even without decaying flesh on the premises, the courthouse usually smelled like a locker room after three-a-day practices in August.

I thought the professor made a mistake when he moved the deboning cone and the eviscerated chicken from the clerk's table to the rail of the jury box. Juror Number Two, a Coral Gables housewife, seemed to be leaning backward, increasing what Dr. Les Weiner would call her horizontal zone from the professor and the poultry. Number Three, a commercial fisherman, didn't seem to mind, but Number Five, an accountant in a three-piece suit, looked a tad green around the gills.

"The tenderloin, or *pectoralis minor,* pulls the wings down when the bird tries to fly," Professor Pennywhistle explained.

Wafting across the courtroom along with the tepid air was the unmistakable smell of rotting tissue, and some of the spectators began to leave. Behind me, Marvin the Maven was fanning himself with his straw hat: "That ain't no spring chicken."

"The term 'tenderloin' came from the pork industry," the professor droned on, oblivious to the odor, "then was borrowed by the turkey growers, and finally was adopted by the chicken industry, but it was Chicken Prince that gave the word 'tender' its specific commercial meaning . . ."

The professor gestured with his knife, accidentally sideswiping the deboning cone, sliding it over the rail and into the jury box. What was left of the chicken dropped straight into the crotch of the queasy accountant. All except for the liver, which squirted into the lap of the Coral Gables housewife, and the gizzard and heart, which plopped with a satisfying *splat* onto the stenographer's open-toed sandals.

"Oh, duck feathers and flapdoodle," said the Purdue professor. "Should have brought a wog."

"Haven't heard that word since *Lawrence of Arabia,*" whispered Marvin the Maven.

"Larry Oravian?" asked Saul the Tailor, leaning forward, head cocked toward the witness stand.

"A wahg?" the stenographer dutifully asked, wiggling her bare toes free of the glop.

"W-O-G," the witness explained. "Without giblets."

The professor bent down and picked up the gizzard, which the stenographer had kicked in the general direction of the bailiff. Sniffing it, his mind seemed to wander. "Wonderful digestive tool, the gastric mill."

The accountant did it first, upchucking in the front row of the jury box. As he gagged, the housewife covered her mouth, then let go, too. I had never seen anything like it. A chain reaction, four of the six losing their lunch right after the other.

"What *mishegoss,*" Marvin the Maven said, picking up his

hat. "C'mon, Saul, there's a sexual harassment trial gonna start down the hall."

The day of the arraignment and not even a paragraph about *State of Florida* v. *Francisco Crespo.* Fine with me. I've never tried my cases in the newspaper. The press always convicts.

The lack of publicity wasn't surprising. That morning's *Miami Journal* featured a quarter-page map of the county showing where each of last year's 441 homicides occurred, according to zip codes. In some cities, folks buy their homes depending on the quality of the school district. In Greater Miami, cautious citizens check the neighborhood's body count. Best I could figure, 33039 was the safest zip code. Not one homicide all year. Unfortunately, that's Homestead Air Force Base, and I'm not real good at saluting, so I continue to live in the little coral-rock cottage tucked alongside chinaberry and live oak trees between Poinciana and Kumquat in Coconut Grove. It's quiet except for an occasional police siren, and my pillbox of a house could withstand a hurricane and has. It weathered the storms of '26 and '50 and only lost a couple of shutters to Hurricane Andrew, which leveled the air force base in '92.

So it would be just another item on the clerk's computer printout when Francisco Crespo stood to enter a plea. By local standards, a warehouse brawl—even a homicidal brawl—was barely newsworthy, though in the warped world of the news media, another case was. I was eating my morning papaya with a slice of lime when I saw the *Journal*'s headline: JURORS BARF; JUDGE BARKS. Oh, the courthouse gang would have fun with me over that one.

A fine layer of dew covered the old canvas top of the convertible. Only April, but the humidity was picking up already. I headed to the criminal justice building, happy to stay out of the downtown civil courthouse. On the exit ramp of the Don Shula Expressway, a few blocks from the sheriff's department, a black Porsche Testarossa with dark tinted windows downshifted and powered past me on the right berm. Ordinarily, in that situation, I hit the horn, shout, and make a few gestures that would make John McEnroe blush. But the bumper sticker on the Porsche said, *"Honk if you've never seen an Uzi fired through a car window,"* and I already had.

There weren't any reporters in the courtroom when I pleaded my friend Francisco Crespo not guilty to second-degree murder. That's right. The plea is "not guilty." A defendant doesn't have to be "innocent." That's for the gods to decide. A jury only determines whether the state meets its burden of proving guilt to the exclusion of a reasonable doubt. If the state fails, the defendant is adjudged "not guilty," even though the jurors may believe the guy is a slimeball who hasn't been "innocent" since kindergarten.

I did the usual: waived reading of the criminal information, demanded trial by jury, and requested all the discovery materials in the state's possession. I also asked the state not to inadvertently lose evidence favorable to the defense, which prompted the prosecutor to ask if I thought he was unethical or incompetent, and I simply said "yes."

The judge set the trial for June. Stone crabs would be out of season, and rich Miamians would be headed out of state. The jury panel would be comprised of folks angry at the heat, the mosquitoes, and the person responsible for their involuntary civic duties, one Francisco Crespo.

I didn't tell Crespo any of this. We had only a moment together. He stood next to me, looking deceptively puny in an oversize pale yellow guayabera. I asked him if there was anything else he wanted to tell me, and he shook his head. I told him I wanted to talk about Matsuo Yagamata, and he gave me a sad smile that said no. He asked me to tell his mother that he was okay, and then he left the courtroom, free on bond, trusting me with his life.

I slipped from the courthouse nearly unnoticed. The only people who needled me about the mistrial were two bailiffs who flapped their wings, a probation officer who clucked an excellent *cock-a-doodle-do,* and an ex-client, shackled at the ankles, who told me not to chicken out.

Lourdes Soto tilted her head and gave me a mischievous smile. I figured it might have been my twinkly eyes or suave manner.

Then I caught sight of myself in the mirrored wall of the Versailles, a Cuban restaurant with a French name. I saw the same thing she did: an overgrown boy with a splendid guava milkshake mustache. Resisting the urge to use my shirtsleeve, I wiped my mouth with a napkin, swallowed a mouthful of my sandwich—sliced pork, turkey, and cheese with a pickle on crunchy Cuban bread—and got down to business. I've got nothing against angel hair pasta with olive oil, pine nuts, and sun-dried tomatoes. Nothing except the downtown yuppies who populate the trendy restaurants. Same thing with French water and German cars. Fine products. It's just the assholes who use them as status symbols that get me down. So I prefer lunch in Little Havana, which I suggested when Lourdes Soto called me and asked if I could use a good investigator.

"I already have one," I told her.

She knew that.

"I've used Ernie Palmer for years."

She knew that, too.

"What's your experience in homicide—"

"You just came from the justice building, didn't you?" she interrupted.

I had, but how did she know?

"I watched you pull into the parking lot coming south on Twelfth Avenue," she answered without being asked. "If you'd been driving from the courthouse or your office, you would have been headed west on Calle Ocho. There's also a layer of brown dust on your hood. They're repairing the trestles on the ramp to the interstate just south of the justice building. I'd say you parked in the shade next to the pilings where the construction is going on."

Not exactly Sherlock Holmes, maybe, but noticing details makes for a good investigator. "I'm impressed."

"Women have certain advantages as investigators," she said. "We take people by surprise."

No one would think Lourdes Soto was a PI. Not with that rare combination of jet black hair and flawless porcelain skin. It is a stunning combination you find in some of the Cuban women who trace their ancestors to northern Spain. The contrast makes the black velvet eyes even darker, the ivory skin even whiter. She had a prominent, forceful nose that went well with her strong cheekbones. She wore her hair in a short shag, and her makeup was understated, her lips brushed with just a hint of rosy gloss. Pearl earrings gleamed pure white against her dark hair. A trace of perfume, not too sweet, wafted my way. She wore a white knit dress with a fitted waist and padded shoulders. Her body was small and well-proportioned, the outline of her breasts visible beneath the knit dress.

"It's easier for women to get witnesses to talk," she continued. "Men especially. They always want to help a lady. One way or another."

She laughed and dug into her *ropa vieja,* the stringy Cuban beef in a piquant tomato sauce. She was right. Who needs another lumpy, middle-aged guy in a four-door Ford, drinking coffee and eating doughnuts waiting for the motel room door to open. If you were lucky, he got the 35-millimeter Canon up and focused before the businessman and his secretary were back on the expressway headed downtown.

"Tell me about your work," I said.

"The usual. Asset reconstruction, missing persons, surveillance, witness interviews, sworn statements in both civil and criminal cases."

She told me she had started working eleven years ago, right after she graduated from Florida State. Her first job was with a big company, Wackenhut, when it was looking for bilingual women. Then she went with a three-investigator firm in a seedy building with a flashing neon sign and a boss who kept a bottle of bourbon in his desk, just like in the movies. Recently, she opened her own shop, and now she was hustling business from semirespectable lawyers such as myself.

"I thought it would be glamorous," Lourdes said, "for about twenty minutes. My first job was sorting a guy's garbage for two months. Every Monday and Thursday at four A.M., I'd be in his driveway, substituting my trash for his."

"What were you looking for?"

"Proof of assets. He'd gone into bankruptcy to defraud creditors. Buried in the coffee grounds was a magazine for owners of private aircraft. Found a twin-engine Beechcraft under a phony name at Tamiami. Also a property tax bill from North Carolina.

We located a nicely furnished A-frame on the side of a mountain near Boone, plus thirty acres of land just off the Blue Ridge Parkway."

She smiled and speared a sweet plantain with her fork. "I love the challenge," she said. "Once I was hired by a gynecologist who knew his partner was stealing but couldn't prove it and couldn't figure where the money was going. All he knew was that the books were cooked and his partner was tired all the time. I tailed the guy home from the office. Midnight, sharp, five nights a week, he'd hit the strip joints in Lauderdale, one after another, buying magnums of overpriced champagne, slipping hundred-dollar bills into every G-string in the joint."

"You'd think a gynecologist would see enough . . ."

"That's what I thought, too, but who knows? Anyway, so much for the glamour of my job. After a week chasing the horny doctor, all my clothes smelled like cigarettes, cheap perfume, and stale beer. You'd be surprised how many men offered me money to take off my clothes."

"No, I wouldn't," I said, just as I was expected to do.

She ran a hand through the shag hairdo, then told me a few more war stories. She was a neat package of woman in total control. In the guise of friendly patter, she was letting me have her résumé one page at a time. I was supposed to be impressed with her competence, and I was. At the same time, there was that faint air of flirtation, the sidelong look, the smile that slid from friendly to provocative without crossing the border of good taste.

So what was going on here, Jake old buddy? You get a call from a lady PI who wants to have lunch and maybe work for you. She paid attention to the dust on your car, and who knows what else. She knew you used a regular investigator but thought you might switch. Why?

"One time," Lourdes was saying, "I was hired by an older man whose lover was a young man who taught aerobics."

"Your client thought his boyfriend found someone younger at the gym."

"Someone prettier. He was convinced the young guy was making it with a *woman* in one of his classes. So I signed up. Three classes a day for a month. High impact, low impact, step classes. I was in great shape."

"You still are," I heard myself say, then took a last slurp of the guava shake.

"The problem is," she said, "I always start to empathize with the subject of the investigation. I mean, the instructor had a right to his own life, didn't he?"

"Did he? I mean, with a woman."

"Two at a time. They used the back of his van in the parking lot. Right after class and without taking showers. Maybe he needed to prove to himself that he was still a man, even if he was bisexual."

"Most investigators just gather information. You analyze it."

"I like to know why people do things. The doctor I told you about was just divorced and had some emotional needs that weren't being fulfilled, so he took a walk on the wild side. Even the man who went bankrupt was responding to financial pressures he didn't know how to handle." She finished the last of the *ropa vieja*—"old clothes" in Spanish—took a sip of iced tea, and patted her lips with her napkin. "I shouldn't be telling you this, because you may think it affects my work. It doesn't, but the truth is, I feel compassion. I always see the other side."

"I have no problem with that. It's called humanity. I wish the state attorney's office had some."

She studied me a moment, her eyes dark and knowing. "I think you and I will get along well, Jake Lassiter." Then she looked away, her fine white skin coloring a bit. "Would you like to see my work?"

I smiled my crooked smile and allowed as how I would. Okay, I admit it. I try to be a modern man, treating women equally in the give-and-take of the business world. But I didn't feel like punching Lourdes Soto on the shoulder and asking, *So whadaya think of the Dolphins' draft?* I try not to regard women as sex objects, but damn it, I can't forget who they are and what they've got, and if one turns out to be beautiful and bright and knows how to laugh, no matter how professional and courteous the conversation, there's always the question lingering just beneath the surface: Is she finally The One?

Lourdes Soto reached under the table and opened an aluminum case. She pulled out a dozen eight-by-ten black-and-whites and spread them on the table. A middle-aged man, his gut hanging over his swim trunks, had his right hand on the bare breast of a superbly endowed young woman. She wore only black bikini bottoms and sunglasses.

"He's putting on the Coppertone," Lourdes said.

"From the looks of her, he'll use the whole bottle before he gets to her back."

"Augmentation mammaplasty. He paid five grand for it. I got the receipts by impersonating a State Farm auditor."

"Good work. You shot the photos from above."

"They were on the beach behind the Palace Hotel in San Juan. From the roof of the hotel, I used a Nikon 8008 with a three-hundred-millimeter autofocus lens at a twenty-two F-stop, two-fifty speed, and your basic Tri-X film."

"His wife must have loved them."

"Ordered two dozen different shots, blew them up into posters for the divorce party."

Lourdes reached into the case again and pulled out a pair of binoculars with a microphone mounted between the barrels. A wire ran from the mike to two earpieces.

"Audio glasses," she said. "From the top of the hotel, I could hear everything they said at two hundred meters. Got a handle on how much he was spending on the girl, where he was hiding his money, who his shrink was, and wouldn't his wife just die if she could see him now."

I shook my head. "Why do you suppose men tell their mistresses so much?"

"Because men are just little boys looking for their mommas." She cracked a decidedly nonmaternal smile. "Anyway, my client got the kids, the dog, the Dolphins and Heat tickets, the condo in Aspen, plus fifty percent of the business, and permanent alimony."

"How'd you know he was going to be in San Juan?"

She looked from side to side and leaned closer. The faint perfume was stronger. "I'll show you," she whispered. Again, she reached into her case. What other treasures were stored there? She pulled out a fountain pen, removed the cap, and shook out an inch-long capsule.

"A tracking transmitter," she said. "I had the wife slip it into a pen he always carried with him. The receiver is portable. It'll track up to sixty-five miles. A great help on surveillance when you take a wrong turn coming through Ponce and into old San Juan. First, I tailed him around Miami for a few weeks. I'd call his secretary and pretend to be a bunch of different people. Used the electronic voice changer to become a man with a southern drawl, that sort of thing. It's amazing how much secretaries will tell you if they think you're important business associates."

I signaled the waiter for two cups of *café Cubano.* "You didn't track him to Puerto Rico with that."

She tried not to chuckle. "No, I had some help. The wife put a voice-activated recorder on his private line. He talked in code to his girlfriend, but I knew they were headed to the airport, and I just followed."

"Illegal as hell . . ."

"But extremely effective."

She gathered up the accoutrements of her cloak-and-dagger life. I watched the fine blue veins on the back of her hands. White, tapered fingers with short, clear lacquered nails. She ran a hand through her glossy black hair and cocked her head at me again. She put the binoculars back into their foam-cushioned spot in the aluminum case. "So what took you to the justice building this morning?"

"Francisco Crespo, a murder case. Probably a reasonable doubt defense. I need a witness to put somebody else at the scene, maybe find somebody who had a grudge against the victim."

"Is that all? No signed confession from a notorious serial killer?"

I like a woman with a sharp sense of humor. Especially when she isn't afraid to aim it at me. "You're right," I conceded. "I sometimes ask for too much. Right now, I'd settle for knowing a little more about my client's employer. Crespo worked for an importer named Matsuo Yagamata. Ever heard of him?"

Her lips played with a smile, then let me have it. "Francisco Crespo used to work for my father. And my father used to be in business with Matsuo Yagamata."

Oh.

"You knew I was representing Crespo, didn't you?"

"A good investigator ought to know what's going on around town."

"Why didn't you tell me this earlier? Why the life and times of Lourdes Soto?"

"I wanted you to hire me based on my qualifications, not my contacts."

The waitress brought the check. I tried to sort it out. Lourdes Soto had information I wanted. Or she could get it. What did I have that she wanted?

"Crespo's not telling me everything," I said. "Or he's telling me too much."

"What do you mean?"

She was staring intently at me, her body perfectly still. This was happening a little too fast. I wasn't ready to entrust Francisco Crespo's future, or lack of it, to a woman I had just met, a woman who encouraged wives to illegally wiretap their husbands, and who probably knew what I ate for dinner last night. Still, I could use her.

"I need to find out everything I can about Yagamata. Why don't we start with your father? Will you set up a meeting?"

She smiled and nodded. "I guess that means I'm hired."

Back went the photos and the transmitter pen. As she slipped the pen into its slot, her hand brushed the leather divider of the case, revealing another compartment. It was visible for only a second, but I know a voice-activated tape recorder when I see one. Of course, it could have been turned off. Probably was, right?

"Glad to be on the team," she said. "Now, tell me everything you know."

That wouldn't take long, I figured, watching the little red light pulsate with each word as she snapped the case shut.

5

PREACHING WATER, DRINKING WINE

Usually, I don't show off.

Some guys blast up to the shore, carve a hard jibe, and shower a rooster tail of spray over a bouquet of bikinis. Sort of a male boardsailor's adolescent fertility rite. I'm too old for that.

Then there are the ones who rig their boards, slip into harnesses, and tune their sails until the wind dies, never getting their booties wet. Swilling brew all day and talking a good game but never playing it. I like the sport too much for that.

I just rig and go. On an April day, a steady northeasterly wind of twenty knots, the temperature a perfect eighty-one degrees, I was chop-hopping the green squirrelly waters off South Beach. Puffy white clouds scudded across the sky, darkening the water with their fleeting shadows. The windows of the high-rise condos winked at me in the morning sun. Okay, so it's not like windsurfing at Sprecklesville Beach in the shadow of Haleakala, the great Maui volcano. No ten-thousand-foot peak hidden in the mist. But it's the best we can do in these parts. Four feet of chop for jumping, a steady wind for speed, and if you are so inclined, a beach full of tourist gals from every corner of these here United States, not to mention a wide collection of Central and South American *chicas* plus some Germans and Danes thrown in on a package tour.

I was so inclined.

My board was a nine-and-a-half-foot custom-made sliver of fiberglass with a five-point-four-meter square of orange Mylar for a sail. I was bouncing over the chop, leaning back into the harness, guiding the boom with a light touch, and generally luxuriating in the beauty of the day.

And showing off. Near the shoreline, beginners climbed onto clunky floaters in the frothy surf, unsteady as rookie riders at a dude ranch. *Just why do they call this horse Dynamite?* Windsurfing is a sport with a steep learning curve, and the first few tries can be frustrating. Watching an experienced boardsailor tear through a series of bottom turns and slashbacks on the offshore waves can be inspiring to the newcomer, or so I rationalized my blatant showboating. On occasion, I could even be persuaded to teach a grateful beach bunny how to tie a bowline or a Prusik hitch knot, all in the spirit of sportsmanship, of course.

Approaching the shoreline at warp speed, I leaned a heavy foot on the rail, and the board carved into the wind. I let go of the boom and dragged my aft hand in the water, a flare jibe. In theory, the hand acts as a daggerboard and pulls the board through the turn. In reality, it's a grandstanding technique equivalent to a hot-rodder fishtailing on the asphalt. *Hey, look at me!* I finished the jibe, flipped the boom, then shot back out over the chop, the wind snapping my sail and whistling a tune like a flute through the holes in the mast extension. I squinted into the sun, jibed again, and rode heavy rollers into the shallow water near the Fifth Street beach. I shot past startled swimmers, a couple of teenage sailors in a Sunfish, and some novice boardsailors. Nearing the shore, I pulled the foot of the sail over my head as the leech swung through the eye of the wind—a flashy duck jibe—and just as the board should have started on a new tack, the tail sunk and the bow shot up like a leaping marlin. I toppled backward into five feet of surf. Served me right.

Shaking water out of my eyes and sand out of my trunks, I recognized the sound of sail crackling in the wind, somewhere behind me, moving closer. It is equivalent to hearing a trucker's horn when you are on a bicycle. I turned just in time to have a mast topple onto me, whacking my right shoulder, and I went under again. This time, I had company.

She was a tall, sunburned blonde, who hadn't seen thirty. She wore a white one-piece Lycra suit, and when she crawled back onto the board, I could see telltale scraped shins. Her hair was plastered to her skull, and she breathed heavily through pouting lips. If anyone had ever taught her to boardsail, they hadn't taught her right.

"Oh, sorry," she said, clinging to the board, which teetered in the surf. "This is so much harder than it looks."

"First time," I guessed.

"No. Yes. I mean, in the ocean. I've sailed on Lake Minnewaska. But this . . ." She gestured at the rollers.

"Lake Minnie . . ."

"In Minnesota."

She had a faint singsong accent. Swedish maybe. "It's a different sport in the waves," I agreed. "Try again. I'll give you some pointers."

Jacob Lassiter, Esq., to the rescue. Accused murderers and sopping wet damsels, walk right in. She looked at me the way they do when sizing you up. Deciding whether you're Tom Cruise or Charles Manson. I crinkled my best beach smile at her and must not have looked too lethal, because she allowed as how my assistance would be peachy, got to her feet, grabbed the uphaul, and pulled, straining to get the sail out of the water. She had some fine ripples in her triceps, but the mast stayed put, weighted down by what must have seemed like a ton of water burying the sail. Beneath the white Lycra, her nipples were perking up.

"Heavy son of a bitch," she muttered.

At first I thought she meant me.

I like a woman who curses. Makes me think she'll be honest in personal relationships. It's stupid, I know, like believing a guy who doesn't look you in the eyes is shifty, when he may just be bashful.

"Damn right," I said, adapting my lingo, chameleonlike, to my companion. "Try leaning back. Let your legs do the work. Don't be afraid. You won't fall, just keep hold of the uphaul."

Beginners have this fear of toppling over backward, so they stand straight up and do all the pulling with their arms. Gradually, she leaned back and got the tip of the mast out of the water, and the rest followed. She grabbed the boom, raked it in, and headed the twelve-foot board out through the surf.

She yelled something that sounded like "whoopee," and looked back at me over her shoulder through her flying blond hair, brave enough now to loosen up a little. "Sail with me."

Willingly, I ducked under my boom and lay in the water on my back. I propped my feet on the board, and tilted the mast into the wind. When I felt a gust, I lifted the boom gently and let the sail pick me up as it filled with air. I slid my feet into the straps, tugged the boom toward me, and followed my Minnesota friend. I pumped the sail twice and whizzed alongside her.

"Thanks for showing me the ropes," she called out. "I'm Jillian. Will you let me take you to my hotel for lunch?"

I couldn't think why not. "Sure. I'm Jake. Let's get past the surf line. I'll show you some tricks they don't know in Duluth. When we get in, I'll give you some salve for those scrapes."

Doctor Lassiter at your service; we make beach calls.

She smiled and kept sailing. I stayed upwind and behind her, watching her calf muscles undulate through the window on my sail. "Watch out for those jet skis," I yelled, pointing in the general direction of Bimini. Three hundred yards away, two machines euphemistically called "personal watercraft" were chawing away, fouling the breeze with their noxious noise. Nearby, a sleek yacht was anchored, pitching gently in the offshore waves.

What loggers are to forests, what sheep are to grass, that's what jet skis are to a fine patch of turquoise water. It's not the machine, of course, loud and irksome as it is. The yahoos who ride them, water bullies, are the problem. They ignore the rules of right-of-way, cut off sailboats, terrorize swimmers, scare the fish, and toss beer bottles into the surf. Down in Islamorada recently, a fisherman plugged a jet skier with a .22 rifle when the punk wouldn't heed his warnings to keep a distance. Only a flesh wound in the leg. Most of the locals wish the fisherman was a better shot.

These two surf jockeys were headed right for us on their black-and-white monsters, churning up the water, jumping each other's wake, and generally destroying the tranquillity of a place where the only sound is the smooth slash of water and the tune of the wind. We stayed on our tack, a close reach to the northeast. The onshore wind swept the gaseous stink across the waves. The two intruders slowed about thirty yards away. Two Hispanic men, early twenties. Both wiry, both looking at me, instead of Jillian, which any red-blooded guy would do. One of them said something, but with the sound of the damned engines and the whistling wind, I couldn't hear. A second time, louder. "Ay, you! Follow us."

I shook my head, dumbfounded.

"C'mon, asshole. Somebody wants to see you."

I luffed the sail and slowed, but at two hundred twenty-something pounds, I can't stop. If I do, the board will sink. "No thanks, have a lunch date."

Jillian sailed by and was looking back over her shoulder. Probably thinking about all the Miami horror stories she must have heard. It's one thing to be caught in the crossfire of a Colombian cowboy drug war at a shopping mall. Or to wander into a Santería ceremony sacrificing live goats to the god Yemayá. But to witness a boardsailor's kidnapping might be a new one for the folks in mid-America.

Their engines were idling, and the incoming tide brought them closer. Both had tattoos on their upper arms. The talker had a neatly trimmed mustache. "C'mon, Hector. We'll tow him."

They revved up and followed me, Hector zooming close, reaching for the bowline that sweeps back into the water as you sail. I pumped the sail and caught a gust that took me out of his reach. Except for a couple of space-age trimarans, a fiberglass board with a sail is the fastest wind-driven craft in existence. The America's Cup yachts? Spare me. The fastest boards can triple their speeds. But a sail is not an engine. I depend on nature: wind and water. Those damn motorcycles on water generate four hundred fifty pounds of thrust out a jet nozzle.

I heard the machines growling behind me, louder now. In a smooth patch of water, I carved a fine jibe, and headed the other way. They just leaned into the turn like bikers, and followed me. In a moment, they had me sandwiched. Hector reached for the bowline again, and I whipped the boom toward him with my aft hand. The outhaul tip caught him on the side of the head and nearly toppled him from his steed. His curses were drowned out by the engines.

The other one sped up and shot across open water ahead of me. Then he turned and idled, blocking my path. I could have jibed again and headed back toward Hector, who was bleeding just above the ear. Or I could imitate some of the wind fanatics from Maui and the Columbia River Gorge, gymnast-sized guys who fly over objects in their path. A decent-sized roller was coming, just between us. I had the board for it, but not the body. At my weight, you don't jump waves so much as hippity-hop them. Still, I tried to unweight, lifting my feet against the footstraps just as the wave hoisted me, pumping the sail hard.

I got airborne, all right, but only about eighteen inches. I heard him scream, saw him duck, felt the pointy nose of the board strike metal, as I catapulted forward. I didn't know my bow had hit the gas tank until a moment later. The explosion wasn't much. You don't get much of a pop from three gallons of lead-free. Besides, I was under water at the time, and it felt no worse than a tight end cuffing me across the ear holes of the helmet. Hector's pal wasn't so lucky. If his nose wasn't broken from the mast smacking him, its appearance wasn't improved any, either.

As I treaded water next to my splintered toy, Jillian sailed close, trying to figure out how to stop her big, lunky floater.

"Jeez, you were right," she said, splashing by me. "I've never seen anything like this in Minnesota."

"Would you care for lunch?" Matsuo Yagamata asked, gesturing toward a buffet table spread with cold seafood that somebody had forgotten to cook.

My social life was improving: two invitations in one day.

Yagamata didn't wait for me. He lowered himself into an orange deck chair with a canvas back, while a lean Asian man in white served him raw octopus from an ice-filled platter. We were anchored a mile offshore, the bow pointing northeast, and we had a splendid view of the Art Deco hotels of South Beach. I still hadn't said a word.

"Mr. Lassiter, you did call my office asking to see me."

I took a seat at the table directly across from him. "Most

clients simply call back, set up an appointment. They don't send two goons to scoop me up."

His look told me he was not like most clients. I glanced over the rail toward the beach. "Besides, I had other plans."

"Don't worry about your friend. My crew members saw to it that she made it safely to shore."

"Your crew members are thugs," I said. Beneath my feet, the deck of Yagamata's yacht swayed with the surge of the wind-whipped tide.

Yagamata nodded so gravely it was almost a bow. "You have my sincere apologies for the conduct of my men. They obviously did not convey my invitation in the proper manner. Had the occasion been strictly social, I could have asked your beautiful friend to join us, also."

Yagamata was wearing khaki cotton slacks and a matching short-sleeve shirt with buttoned pockets and epaulets. He looked at me from behind wire-rimmed sunglasses and tapped the barrel of the yellow, waterproof binoculars that hung around his thick neck. For the second time in a week, I thought of Pearl Harbor.

"I watched you approach her on the beach." Either he had something in his eye or he winked at me. "You can learn a lot about a man by the way he handles women. I have heard a saying in your country that all you need to know about a man is the car he drives, the shoes he wears, and the woman he marries. Would you agree?"

"My car's twenty-five years old; I go barefoot whenever possible; and no woman has ever had the nerve."

Yagamata allowed himself a brief smile. From somewhere below deck, a pump began whooshing. The clipped chatter of Japanese—two men, voices competing with the rush of the wind—came from the galley. I had changed into a dry pair of trunks that were too small for me, and I wore a terry-cloth robe with the monogram "Yugen," which was the name of the fifty-one-foot Bluewater cruiser whose deck was now pitching beneath my feet. My board and rig had been hauled aboard and were lashed to the starboard rail.

A handsome beige helicopter was tied down near the stern. An Italian model, the Agusta. The *Yugen* was a fine boat, Yagamata told me, with a modified V-hull and a flared bow, and though it displaced twenty-six thousand pounds, its draft was only twenty-three inches. So it was suited for cruising the shallows of Biscayne Bay, but here on the ocean side, in twenty knots of wind, it was top-heavy and rocked me right out of my appetite. I can windsurf in the choppiest water for hours and never feel a thing. But anchor me on a bouncing tug, I'd lose my lunch, if I had any, which I hadn't.

Whether he sensed the problem or not, Yagamata barked orders at his captain—a sunbaked man in his forties—in what I first thought was Japanese but then realized was Russian. Somewhere among the guttural sounds, I picked up the word "Intracoastal." Then, Yagamata asked again if I wanted some sushi. I had to be polite. This guy was an important client, who also went to some effort to demonstrate that a luncheon date was more a command than an invitation. I knew I could get the raw tuna down with no problem. It looked like beef tenderloin, and I'd had it before with ample quantities of Kirin. But the salmon roe and eel did not make my mouth water, and I'd stepped on enough sea urchins to know I'd rather eat porcupine quills. Besides, I've seen the sludge that pours into our waters, so I prefer my fish cooked.

When I hesitated, Yagamata tried gentle persuasion. "Perhaps some *miso ae,* a very light appetizer?"

I looked a question at him.

"Conch, octopus, and cucumbers in a miso sauce. Or you may prefer flying fish eggs and swordfish belly."

I would have preferred a cheeseburger with a chocolate shake, but I settled for cold tofu spiced with ginger and scallions. The taste was fine, though the consistency reminded me of a soggy sponge. I was washing it down with some of Matsuo Yagamata's champagne when he asked why I had wanted to see him.

"To learn more about Crespo and Smorodinsky," I told him.

His arms were folded across his stocky chest. "You received their personnel files, did you not?"

I had. There was nothing useful in them. Crespo had worked for Yagamata Imports for five years, Smorodinsky for three. Each one had been shifted around, sometimes assigned to the Atlantic Seaboard warehouse, sometimes helping at a wholesale distribution office, or on the *Yugen,* even doing chores at Yagamata's Palm Island home.

"The two men shared some work details," I said. "Did they ever argue? Did Smorodinsky do anything to provoke Crespo?"

Yagamata dismissed the notion with an economical wave of his hand. "I am not that close with my workers. Ask your client these questions."

"I have. All he talks about is an argument over eighteen dollars."

Yagamata speared a slice of squid on a fancy toothpick with a frizzy red head like Little Orphan Annie. "Men have been killed for less. Surely you know that."

"Crespo's making it up as he goes. He didn't kill the Russian."

Yagamata showed me a meager, quizzical smile. "Tell me, what does a lawyer do when he doesn't believe his own client?"

"Keeps on breathing, 'cause it happens every day."

"So your job is not to find the truth, Mr. Lassiter."

"Truth is for judges and juries. My job is to make the best possible case with whatever evidence I've got, and leave judgment day to somebody else."

"Then why do you worry so much? Take what you have and present it to your judge and jury."

"What I have stinks worse than two-week-old catfish."

I immediately regretted the reference to rotting fish, but staring at octopus tentacles doubtless has a subliminal impact. I drained the rest of my champagne, which made my head rock gently with the tide. I am not used to midday doses of the bubbly. Especially combined with sun and a swaying boat.

"Besides," I continued, "I lied."

He looked puzzled.

"I can't do it, leave judgment day to someone else," I explained. "I have to know. It isn't enough just to win or lose. Like the sign says in the courtroom, 'We who labor here seek only the truth.' My problem is I believe it. Not that the system searches for the truth. It doesn't. It only seeks *evidence,* and that can be true or false; it doesn't matter as long as it meets certain technical rules of admissibility. The truth can be excluded and the falsehoods can be admitted and polished to a fine gloss by smooth-talking lawyers. I'm looking for the literal truth. Who done it? And why? I can't help it. I just have to know."

"Regardless of the consequences?"

Now it was my turn to look puzzled.

"Isn't it conceivable that your client knows better than you how his interests are best served?" Yagamata asked.

"It's possible," I said, warily, realizing he was playing lawyer, setting me up for another question.

"So that if you thwart his intentions out of some misguided belief that you are helping him, you could actually do him great harm."

We were dancing around like a couple of boxers in the first round, feeling each other out. I said, "It's also possible he's being misled by others, and unless he levels with me, or I figure out on my own what's going on, he could be doing himself great harm without knowing it."

Yagamata's eyes were hooded by the wire-rimmed sunglasses. "And who would do such a thing to your angelic client?"

His voice was tinged with sarcasm, the words filled with challenge. Would I call his bluff? He didn't think so, and he was right. Yagamata had probably paid for the thick carpet my partners loved so much in their offices. He was also paying my client's fees. I had no proof, nothing to go on, and he knew it. "I don't know. That's why I do my best to poke around in the shadows, to turn over rocks."

"In my country," Matsuo Yagamata said, "we have an expression. If you look under enough rocks, you will eventually find a snake."

I was just this side of woozy but could still figure that one out. A warning in pleasant tones, but I got the message loud and clear. While I was thinking about it, a crewman in a white smock silently delivered another bottle of champagne and expertly popped the cork. He refilled our glasses without spilling a drop. I could take being rich if I didn't have to lie, cheat, and steal to get there.

Okay, I figured, my head buzzing pleasantly. Why not listen to the rich guy and let Francisco Crespo take the fall? He seemed willing enough to do the time. Be smart for once, Jake old boy. Go for the champagne lunches and six-figure fees. Or be a schmuck and keep turning over rocks until you grab a rattlesnake by the tail. Which would it be?

I moved the champagne glass across the table, out of my reach, but still within temptation. I always preferred beer, anyway. "I noticed several Russian names on your payroll list."

It was a question, and Yagamata knew it. It was also an answer to my own question. I thought I heard him sigh, but it might have been the wind. We were cruising at a stately ten knots, the cruiser ably cutting through the chop, headed for calmer waters.

"A lot of Russians have emigrated in the last few years," I continued. "But Miami hasn't gotten that many, and I was wondering . . ."

C'mon, Matsuo, I wanted to yell. Help me out here. Don't make me subpoena you. I'd have to commit hara-kiri if my partners found out.

He probably considered telling me to go to hell. But after a moment, he settled back in his chair and said, "As you know, I collect Russian art. I did business there even in the days of Brezhnev. It is much easier now, of course, though knowing who to bribe is a little more complex." He allowed himself a slender laugh. "I do not have the traditional Japanese antipathy for the Russians. They are a sad, yet beautiful people. Very warm, very spiritual. Lovers of high art, ballet, the finest music. Even Smorodinsky was a worldly man of culture."

I must have been thinking about the brute on the slab in the morgue, because Yagamata smiled and said, "Don't look so surprised. Americans believe that you have to live on Park Avenue and subscribe to the Metropolitan Opera to be cultured. In Russia, art has long been enjoyed and understood by the masses. Both Smorodinsky and his brother were well versed in native Russian art and had a passing familiarity with European painting. Vladimir was an intelligent man, who knew the lessons of history. There were many nights he and I walked along the River Neva debating the future of his beloved homeland. He was more than a valued employee. He became a friend."

Vladimir? Whatever happened to *I am not that close with my workers*? "You brought Smorodinsky here from the Soviet Union? You collect Russians, too."

A hundred yards off the stern, two dolphins jumped in unison, their question-mark silhouettes etched into the horizon. Yagamata's look was impenetrable. He seemed to be deciding how much to tell me. "Vladimir began as a low-level operative for one of my business contacts in St. Petersburg, when it was still called Leningrad. He spoke English reasonably well and knew how to grease the wheels in the old bureaucracy to get things done. He was a resourceful man who helped me obtain certain, shall we say, hard-to-get items."

"He was a thief, a smuggler?"

Yagamata very nearly smiled. If he found me amusing, maybe next time he'd send a limo for me, instead of two goons. "The Russians have a far kinder term. *Fartsovshchiki,* black marketeer. Religious icons, vestments, antique weaponry, a divan from Mikhailovsky Castle, silver bridle chains that may or may not have belonged to a czar, these were his specialties."

"Still, he was a criminal. If Smorodinsky had a known propensity for violence, it could help Crespo's defense."

Yagamata gave me a quizzical look, as if the furthest thing from his mind was Francisco Crespo. "Criminal," he said, rolling the word around his tongue, "is a relative term. In my country, and yours for that matter, a successful businessman who generously shares his wealth with underpaid public servants is considered a criminal. Yet, in certain Latin American countries, that is the accepted method—indeed the only method—of doing business. When there was still a Soviet Union, everyone looked for ways to circumvent a system no one but the party *apparatchiki* wanted. It was great sport to battle the government, to get the extra sausage or to steal state property from a factory. The Russians tell a wonderful political joke that is just as meaningful now as when the *verkhushka,* the Party elite, called the shots. What's the difference between communism and capitalism?"

I played along and held up my hands.

"Capitalism is the exploitation of man by man, and communism is the opposite." He laughed at his own joke. "Mr. Lassiter, do you know much about art?"

"No, I don't even know what I like."

Yagamata nodded with approval. Maybe he preferred working with a clean slate.

"Japanese art is very simple, very clear. By Western standards, the depiction is unreal, highly idealized, and there is little perspective. If a painter always has his cherry blossoms in bloom, always facing the viewer, always in full color with no shading, the art is mere decoration."

"And you find Russian art more complex and interesting."

"*European* art. Once Peter the Great came to the throne in the early 1700s, Russia left its Byzantine past behind. Its artists were greatly influenced by those in France, Italy, and Holland. The Russians know fine art and appreciate it. Have you ever been to the Hermitage in St. Petersburg?"

He didn't wait for me to say no before continuing. "The Winter Palace of the czar. Three million artifacts! Let your mind try to comprehend it. It is impossible."

I thought about it. "How do they even keep track of it all?"

"Precisely, and if you know anything about the laziness and incompetence of the Russians under the old order, you would know that they do not. Less than ten percent of these works are on display. What is in storage is priceless. What is available for viewing will take your breath away. More than a hundred forty rooms of just Western masterpieces. Monet, Gauguin, Van Gogh, Cézanne, Matisse, da Vinci, Rubens, Goya, El Greco, Raphael . . ."

Yagamata kept going, a roster of first-team All-Pro painters. I didn't relate to it. Oh sure, I could name the 1976 Dolphins roster, top to bottom, but somehow, it didn't have the same cachet.

"You know the place pretty well," I said.

He let out a little snort. "You could *live* in the Hermitage and not know it well. It is too vast. Too much of the great work is simply not to be found. Even with special privileges, even knowing Russians with *blat*—connections—they can't find half of what I wish to have."

"Have?"

He drained his sparkling champagne. "Have a look at. Unfortunately, you cannot buy them." He scowled, apparently thinking of the injustice of it. "It wasn't always so. After the Revolution, the Bolsheviks were so strapped for hard currency they sold off a number of priceless pieces. You'll find more than twenty in your own National Gallery in Washington, thanks to Andrew Mellon."

There was no doubt Matsuo Yagamata preferred it the old-fashioned way. Pay as you go; buy what you want.

"So you are left smuggling silver bridle chains . . ."

"I have business associates who take care of the necessities of exporting certain items of value," he explained in language a clever shyster could admire.

"Like the Fabergé egg with the choo-choo train."

Yagamata looked as if he suddenly regretted kidnapping me for lunch. Off the stern, an osprey with lethal talons swooped low, eyeing our wake, on the lookout for an à la carte lunch. I thought about offering some swordfish belly.

"A gift," he said.

The party at Yagamata's house. The way he had stage-managed our privileged view of his precious egg. I could have sworn he said he bought it. But I couldn't quite remember. And it would be awkward to ask who gave it to him. Still, if it had anything to do with Smorodinsky, I needed to know more.

"A generous friend," I probed.

"The Russian people are indeed generous."

He left it hanging there and I didn't know how to grab it. After a moment, I said, "The liberalizing of the economy under Gorbachev must have helped your exporting business."

"*Perestroika* was irrelevant to what I do, Mr. Lassiter. Politics is irrelevant. What was it your Will Rogers said? 'All politics is applesauce.' There was always a profit motive in the Soviet Union, at least among those who knew how to manipulate the system. Before the liberalization, the masses would say of the Party leaders: 'They preach water, but they drink wine.' It was only a matter of time before the leaders were toppled. For me, there were methods of doing business before Gorbachev and Yeltsin, and there will always be methods. You cannot stop what the Russians call *spekulatsiya,* speculation and profiteering, under any system. There was always a free market in the Soviet Union for those who knew how to push the right buttons. The failed coup, the dismantling of the Union, the destruction of the Party, it's all applesauce."

The yacht was slowing, and the water had calmed. Hard shafts of sunlight danced off the bay. "You like them for it, don't you? Sort of what you do, *spekulat* . . ."

Yagamata's brow furrowed with just a hint of surprise, like maybe I wasn't as dumb as he thought. I should shut up. It's better if they think I could be used for a blocking sled.

"I have great affection for the Russians," he said. "They have a finely tuned sense of the human dilemma. Far superior to the Japanese, I must say."

"And Smorodinsky. What can you tell me that will help my client?"

"Nothing, Mr. Lassiter. Vladimir Smorodinsky was not a violent man. And in many ways that even he did not understand, he was true to his principles and a patriot. Perhaps too much so."

"I don't understand."

We were in the quiet waters of the channel with the old Mediterranean homes of Star Island visible off the bow. The skyline of downtown Miami—built with loot from failed savings and loans—dominated the horizon. Yagamata took off his sunglasses and turned to me. The nosepiece had left little red dents alongside his nose. His eyes were black and bottomless.

"It is not necessary that you do," Matsuo Yagamata said.

6

A TROUT IN THE MILK

"Entrapment," Cyrus Horner said, his cigarette dancing in the corner of his mouth, spraying ashes on his chest. "Plain and simple. Female cops got no business working massage parlors."

I studied the A-form while Horner kept yammering away. He paced in front of my desk, banging his right fist into his left palm, cursing the police, the courts, his probation officer, and his three ex-wives. Horner was one of those scrawny guys with a potbelly. He was bald on top with pale wispy hair covering his ears. His sideburns were so far out of date they had just come back into style, and his Hawaiian shirt was decorated with pink roses, some of which had cigarette holes in the blossoms. His eyes were tiny black pebbles, his skin the color of curdled milk. Naturally, he considered himself irresistible to women.

"I been a regular at the Feather Touch for years," Horner was saying, "so I know all the girls, and they know me. Some of them, you gotta cajole a little."

"Cajole? Like with compliments?"

"No, like with Ulysses S. Grant."

Outside, a rare spring thunderstorm pelted the high-rise windows. The vultures, which circled the courthouse all winter, were no longer soaring in the updrafts. Like the tourists, they had returned to the north. The ugly birds make their summer home in

Hinckley, Ohio, where their diet probably consists of leaves and field mice. In Miami, they feast on beheaded goats from Santería sacrifices and drug lords stuffed into garbage bags.

Cindy, my secretary, stuck her headful of copper-colored curls into the office. She wore studded jeans, black shoes with stiletto heels, and a purple T-shirt emblazoned I LIVE FOR LOVE. She was chewing a wad of Juicy Fruit when she asked, "Would you gentlemen like some coffee?"

Why did she roll her eyes when she said *gentlemen*?

"Doughnuts?" she inquired. "Danish . . ."

She shot a look at Horner and seemed to make a mental note to disinfect his chair.

". . . burglary tools?"

"Cindy, scram!"

She shrugged and ducked out of the room and into her cubicle. Cindy's secretarial skills are limited—with three-inch fingernails, she does not so much type as slash at the keyboard—but she is smart and loyal. For years, Cindy has been trying to persuade me to upgrade my practice. This is hard to do when your clients are con men, real estate developers, and doctors accused of malpractice. It is sometimes difficult to tell which group has the most accomplished perjurers.

"One time, the Feather Touch gets this new girl," Horner was saying, his cigarette wagging at me, "Lucinda from Loxahatchee. And she won't do nothin'. 'Whatsa matter,' I say, 'you don't touch genitals?' She goes, 'Sure, genitals, Jews, it don't matter none, long as they pay.' "

Granny Lassiter was right; I should have been a civil engineer. Build roads, she said, something solid. Instead, here I was listening to Cyrus Horner—part-time grifter, professional whiner—bemoan the sorry state of our law enforcement community.

"Entrapment," he repeated. "I had no predisposition to commit a criminal act."

Whew. Your three-time losers sure know the lingo. I grabbed his file and spread the contents across my desk. "The room was bugged, so they have tapes and transcripts plus video and still photos. Want to see?"

I gave him a moment to add it up. Addition was not his strong suit.

"They have a warrant?" he asked.

"Didn't need one. It was their place, not yours, so you didn't have a reasonable expectation of privacy."

"I had a reasonable expectation of a blow job."

"Tell it to Chief Justice Rehnquist. Maybe you can change the law."

He flicked ashes on my carpet. "I studied some law, you know."

I figured. Our prisons have excellent libraries.

"I got a well-rounded education," he continued. "I was on the fencing team in school."

"Really, like with sabres and foils?"

"Nah, like with tires and TV's."

Why didn't I listen to Granny? "C'mon, Cy. You're avoiding the issue. We should be talking about a plea."

He kept pacing; I stared out the window. Heavy gray thunderheads hung over Biscayne Bay, obscuring the view of Miami Beach, Fisher Island, and Virginia Key. If there were any windsurfers out there, they were using their masts as lightning rods.

"All right, let's see what they got."

I opened a manila folder and poured out a dozen eight-by-ten glossies. They made me think of Lourdes Soto, lady PI and long-lens photographer. What had she come up with, anyway? And why had she scouted me out? Just looking for some new business, or was there something more?

Horner came around the desk, leaned over my shoulder, and belched, giving me a whiff of tobacco and sour mash whiskey. I spread the photos in front of him. They had been shot from a peephole in the ceiling. Horner lay on his back, wearing only a Fruit-of-the-Loom athletic shirt and black socks that barely reached his ankles. A woman in a blond wig and a camisole sat on the edge of the bed, a bottle of oil in one hand, a fifty-dollar bill in the other. If Horner had been excited, his brain forgot to tell his loins.

"Hey, that's libelous!" he blurted out.

"What?"

He jabbed the photo with a nicotine-stained fingernail. "That picture's taken out of context."

"What do you mean?"

"Jeez, shooting me all limp like that. When I get an erection, I gotta take out a building permit."

A flash of lightning streaked across the bay, striking behind the warehouse area at the port. Horner moved back in front of the desk and slumped into an old leather chair. He used a seventy-nine-cent lighter on another cigarette. I don't know what happened to the first one. He either swallowed it or tossed the butt behind the credenza when I wasn't looking. His Hawaiian shirt had flapped open, and his belly—hairier than his head—peeked out at me. A delayed thunderclap rattled the windowpane.

"You could cop a plea. Soliciting for prostitution is only a second-degree misdemeanor."

"No can do. I'm on probation."

I found the rap sheet the state attorney's office had been kind enough to provide. "I remember the B.R.C., but what's the fraud conviction?"

"Rubbertech, Inc., a franchise I promoted. Strictly legit. Sold condom machines to restaurants, convenience stores, what have you. I should have told the investors about a little problem we had with the machines."

"Stolen, right?"

"Nah, nothing like that. My ex-brother-in-law made them in the tool shop when he was doing thirty months at Avon Park. Only problem, the damn machines put a little hole in the package as it came out the slot."

"In the package?"

"Well, in the condoms, too, about two out of three. Hey, you bat .333, you're in the Hall of Fame, right?"

I flipped to the next page. I had seen longer rap sheets, but few as eclectic.

"What about the grand larceny?"

"Complete railroad job, a kangaroo court. I was selling prints of the Last Supper for four grand per set and advising customers to donate them to a church and take a nineteen-thousand-nine-hundred-ninety-nine-dollar charitable tax deduction."

"Nineteen thousand . . ."

"Yeah. If it's more than twenty grand, you gotta have an independent appraisal. This way, I give them my appraisal certificate from the Church of the Shining Sun. The rectory's in my garage."

"You're a preacher, too?"

He gave me a sly grin and let me see a matched set of yellow incisors. "They call me Brother Cyrus."

Another peal of thunder, but Horner didn't flinch. Maybe he answered to a Higher Authority. "Look at it this way," he said. "If you're in the thirty-one-percent tax bracket, I could save you twenty-two hundred on a four-thou investment. The IRS gets pissed off, and the Justice Department flips a coin with the state attorney. Tax fraud or grand larceny. The state attorney won."

I watched two raindrops race each other down the outside of my windowpane. I put my money on the juicy, oblong one, but the thin guy seemed to pick up a tailwind.

"Brother Cyrus, if you want me to try the case, we'd better prepare your testimony."

His beady eyes lit up. "Great. I love testifying. I'm very affluent, you know."

Judge Herman Gold had retired eleven years ago, but that didn't keep him off the bench. With our crowded dockets and the propensity of our criminal judges to be removed from office in the wake of bribery scandals, we need retired judges to help out. Some of the old judges have forgotten more law than most of us ever learned. That could have been true of Judge Gold, but he'd also forgotten most everything else. Hardening of the arteries had left the bulb a bit dim. There he was, perched on his high-back chair, peering into the cavern of the courtroom, a wizened bald buzzard of eighty-one, wearing his custom-made, minilength fuchsia robes, yapping at court personnel, keeping order in the snake pit.

"A *tango!*" the judge demanded.

"A *tanga,* Your Honor," replied Sally Corson, a proper young assistant state attorney in a blue suit and white silk blouse. "It's a Brazilian bikini, and it's illegal on state beaches."

She held up state's exhibit one, and if you had good eyes, you might identify a red piece of string as the bottom of a bikini. The evidence tag was at least twice as wide.

"Illegal?" the judge demanded. "Says who?"

"The legislature, Your Honor. No buttocks or breasts on state-owned beaches. Chapter eight forty-seven."

The judge was shaking his head. "*Meshuga.* Ay, Marvin, what do you think?"

In the first row of the gallery, Marvin the Maven consulted with Saul the Tailor. "If she's a *shayna maidel,* a Kim Basinger, what's the problem? If she's *zaftig,* a Roseanne Barr, I'd throw the book at her."

Judge Gold nodded judiciously. At the defense table, a young woman who was demurely dressed in a knee-length skirt and long-sleeve blouse looked from the judge to Marvin and back again. Alice in Wonderland couldn't have been more confused. At least her lawyer had the good sense to dress her for court. It's one of the first rules. If you can manage it, even a murderer should look like a choirboy. When I was a young lawyer, I once forgot to give my dress-for-acquittal lecture to a weightlifting champion charged with aggravated assault. He showed up in a muscle-T that depicted Darwin's ascent of man—an ape, a Neanderthal, and finally, good old homo sapiens moving up the evolutionary ladder. The jury thought he most resembled the ape, and he got two years to plan his next wardrobe.

The assistant state attorney cleared her throat, trying to regain the momentum before the rest of the gallery voted. "Your Honor, the defendant was observed by numerous witnesses at Keys Memorial Beach. She was playing Frisbee while wearing state's exhibit A."

"Frisbee?" the judge demanded. "Is that illegal, too?"

I waited while Judge Gold ran through the rest of his calendar. It was a typical day. A man convicted of murder wanted a new trial *and* a divorce because his wife had an affair with his lawyer sometime between opening statement and closing argument. A Hialeah homeowner faced zoning charges for building a statue of La Virgen de La Caridad in his front yard. The Biting Bandit of Miami Beach was arraigned on charges of stealing two watches and thirty dollars in food stamps, and severing three ears and one index finger. The prosecutor was careful not to stand too close when pointing toward the carnivorous fellow and intoning, "This defendant . . ."

I waited through several dozen other hearings. The clerk called a number of minor drug cases, all scheduled for pretrial intervention, just one of a number of devices to toss cases out of the courthouse. The criminal justice system does not so much dispense justice as process defendants. The prisons cannot hold the miscreants already there, much less the thousands who should be added each year. So the prosecutors, public defenders, probation officers, and various state agencies engage in a gentle conspiracy with judges—real and retired—to spit out the defendants who are swept into the maw of a system that has bitten off more than it can chew.

We think of the courts as slow, unwieldy machines with creaking parts. Not in Miami. Here, what passes for justice takes place with frightening speed, each judge sometimes ruling on a hundred cases a day, hearing motions, taking pleas, dismissing charges, and occasionally even presiding at trial.

The players in the justice game speak their own language. Rapists are treated in a program for MDSO, mentally disordered sex offenders. Sleazy street criminals who rat on their pals are CI, confidential informants. First-time offenders get bounced into PTI, pretrial intervention with CTS, credit for time served.

"Set aside the *alias capias,* and send him back to PTI," Judge Gold ordered the clerk, in a case where a drug defendant, a college instructor, finally showed up in court.

"The meter is ticking on the speedy trial rule," an anxious prosecutor told the judge, pleading for an early court date.

"We'd take a deal," the public defender offered, "if the state *nolle prosses* all but one count, agrees to CTS, in-house rehab, five years' probation, early termination on completion of MDSO."

"I'm thinking about one year incarceration," the judge mused, considering a plea bargain.

"Min man is three," the prosecutor responded, shaking her head, indicating she'd love to help, but the legislature has set minimum mandatory sentences.

Behind the bench, the flag of the state of Florida hung forlornly. The flag itself is a glorious historical fabrication. An Indian woman stands on the beach, greeting an arriving steamship with flower petals. A more appropriate state symbol would be a fat county commissioner taking cash from a condo developer with the skeleton of a rickety high-rise in the background.

Finally, the clerk called out: "State of Florida versus Francisco Crespo. Motion to dismiss."

I stood, stretched my neck out of its eighteen-inch collar, and approached the lectern in front of the bench. Abe Socolow beat me there. Credit his daily power-walking routine. He hadn't changed. Lean as a rake, mean as a snake. Black suit, black hair, white shirt, black tie decorated with gold handcuffs and prison bars. A sallow complexion, a sardonic sneer, a brooding intelligence that barely controlled his seething anger at every defendant who crossed his path. He is a rarity in today's age of get-rich-quick lawyers who pass through the state attorney's office long enough for a cup of coffee and a smidgen of trial experience before migrating downtown for the big bucks. Abe Socolow is a career prosecutor, and his career was built on being smart, tough, and nasty.

"Your Honor, this motion is frivolous, ludicrous, and utterly beyond the pale," Socolow said. "It is a misuse of motion practice, outside the bounds of Rule three one-ninety, and should be summarily rejected by the court."

Good day to you, too, Abe.

I cleared my throat and elbowed Socolow to one side. "There are no material disputed facts, and the undisputed facts do not establish a *prima facie* case of guilt against Mr. Crespo."

Socolow snorted in my ear. "Mr. Lassiter is excellent at quoting the rule. Unfortunately, he does not know how to apply it. The evidence of a *prima facie* case is here." He stabbed a finger at a stack of pretrial depositions.

Judge Gold took one look and cringed. He didn't read the newspaper unless the ponies were running at Calder. "Why don't you fellows summarize it for me?"

"The case is entirely circumstantial," I began, jostling Socolow with a shoulder and screening him from the judge's view with my height. "What proof does the state have? That my client was found in proximity to the scene of an alleged homicide.

That he had an altercation with the deceased. Where is the direct evidence of the crime?"

You can get away with that sometimes with juries, ridiculing the state's case as based on circumstantial evidence, but judges know better. A few even remember Thoreau's admonition: Some circumstantial evidence is very strong, as when you find a trout in the milk.

"Your Honor!" Exasperated now. "Mr. Lassiter sees what he wants and ignores the rest. His client's latents were all over the steering wheel of the forklift that impaled the victim."

"Mr. Crespo used that forklift every day," I replied. "It would be highly suspicious if his fingerprints were *not* there. What is significant is that the state has no eyewitness to put him on the forklift at the time of the assault. Indeed, the only eyewitness testimony, that of the paramedics, puts Mr. Crespo several aisles away and unconscious when the attack took place. Finally, other than what appears to have been a fistfight between the two men, there is no evidence of an assault at all."

I sneaked a peek at Socolow. His jaw muscles were doing aerobics. I kept going. "The forklift could have been driven negligently by a third party who simply bolted after he accidentally ran down the deceased. Perhaps there was no driver at all. It could have been a runaway forklift."

"A runaway forklift!" A touch of crimson crept into Socolow's sallow complexion. "Why not suicide? Maybe Mr. Smorod-whatever-his-name-is jumped at the moving forklift in order to kill himself. Mr. Lassiter isn't arguing the undisputed facts. He's relying on his own vivid imagination. There's a jury question here . . ."

In the gallery, I saw Marvin the Maven's head swivel as the rear door opened and a woman walked in. Marvin doesn't miss anything. He nudged Saul the Tailor, who nodded his approval as Lourdes Soto took a seat in the second row. Even under the fluorescent lights, the ivory skin was perfect, accented by the jet black hair. She wore a black jersey dress that came to midcalf and gathered itself under a wide matching belt. She carried a woman's leather briefcase, not the all-purpose aluminum model with camera, lenses, and voice-activated recorder.

Of course, the black onyx necklace might be a wire, for all I knew.

"The autopsy is consistent with an attack by a forklift traveling at maximum speed," Socolow was saying. He was waving some papers at the judge. It could have been the autopsy report or his laundry list. No matter, the judge wouldn't read either one.

I didn't need to read the report, either. It was one of those rare cases when I'd been there, a foot away from the deputy medical examiner when he did his dirty work. Crespo had called me within minutes of being arrested. The autopsy was scheduled twenty-four hours later. I had phoned Doc Charlie Riggs, and calling on an old friend, he got me into the cool crisp confines of the Last Hotel, a place where the guests sleep on wooden pillows.

The county morgue sits at Number One Bob Hope Road, just north of the intersection with Ed Newman Street. Newman used to play for the Dolphins. So did I, but the only thing they named after me was a missed sack—the Lassiter Leap—for a peculiar habit of leaving my feet at the wrong time on a blitz. As for Bob Hope, I doubt he's funny enough to wake the dead.

The morgue is nearly new, a gleaming place with a handsome waiting room of rose-colored sofas, a three-story skylight, and sturdy brick walls. It is a sad fact of city life that most of those who end up here never lived in such splendid surroundings.

"Interesting puncture wound." Dr. Bruce Harper poked at the gash in Smorodinsky's abdomen. "See a lot of knife wounds, bullet holes, once in a while a screwdriver. Even had a corkscrew through the jugular last week. Domestic dispute, of course." He held a tape measure to the wound while an assistant took photos. "Ten point two centimeters in width. Point six four centimeters in height." A lab technician wrote with a special marker on a white wall. Later, the numbers would be transferred to a written autopsy report and the wall washed down. "What'd you say did this?"

"Forklift blade," I told him.

Dr. Harper was one of the young ones, three years out of his residency in pathology, a guy who grew up not knowing whether he wanted to be a detective or a physician. Now he was both. He was of medium height and weight but with solid wrists and veined forearms. He had neatly parted dirty blond hair and wore latex gloves and a green smock. On a tray next to him, another deputy M.E. worked on the body of an enormous black woman killed in a head-on traffic accident on the Don Shula Expressway. He was whistling—it must have been the doc—the theme music from *Rocky*.

Dr. Harper went to work, grinning at the world, oblivious to his surroundings. After photos were taken of the entrance and exit wounds, he used a scalpel to make a Y incision in the chest. In one smooth motion, he sliced straight down the midline of the abdomen, then peeled the skin back, exposing a thick layer of yellow, fatty tissue and the rib cage beneath. Using what looked like your Saturday afternoon pruning shears, he cut through the cartilage of the ribs near the breastbone.

With quick, deft movements, he was inside the chest cavity, slicing away. He removed the heart and plopped it into a scale. Three hundred grams, the technician wrote on the wall. The right lung was five hundred fifty grams; the left lung five twenty-five. In the abdomen, he inspected the wound track, and an assistant took more photos.

"A clean path through and through," he said to nobody in particular. "Nicked the bottom rib, then a direct hit on the ascending colon, the right kidney, the duodenum, and then bingo, the inferior vena cava."

Dr. Harper reached into the abdomen with what looked like a soup ladle. He scooped out several portions of blood and filled two plastic containers. "The rib cartilage and bone show marks consistent with a powerful and moderately sharp instrument."

He started peeling out the large intestine, hand over hand, like a candy maker pulling salt-water taffy. At the same time, he kept up a running conversation. "I'll drain some urine from the bladder and the vitreous humor from the eye to check for alcohol, but I can tell you right now, he'd been drinking, for what that's worth."

I asked him, "How can you—"

He pointed a bloodied glove toward his nose. His head disappeared into the open cavity. What had been a body now was an empty shell. No wonder they call them canoe makers. His voice was an echo from inside what used to be Vladimir Smorodinsky. "They say your buddy Doc Riggs could distinguish rye from bourbon. Don't know what this is, but it's booze. Want to check it out?"

I took his word for it.

He kept slicing and measuring, telling his technician there was evidence of a right retroperitoneal hematoma where the blade went through. The liver was enlarged and greasy, but still not cirrhotic. The coronary arteries showed some arteriosclerotic blockage, but "he didn't die of a heart attack, sorry, Lassiter."

I made some observations myself. The fingernails were missing. The crime lab was checking for skin and blood—Crespo's—underneath the nails. They would find what they were looking for. There was recent bruising on Smorodinsky's forearms. All in all, no surprises.

"Anything else?" Judge Gold asked, glaring at the clock on the wall, if he could see that far.

Both Socolow and I shook our heads, and the judge shook his. "Motion denied. Jake, you got yourself a jury question here. Now, that doesn't mean I won't hear a motion for a directed verdict at the close of the state's case, but that's the way I see it now, and I call them as I see them."

"Thank you, Your Honor," I said, in the classic statement of the losing lawyer, acknowledging his respect for the court, even as it crushes him.

I turned to go and caught sight of Lourdes Soto in the gallery. She wasn't looking at me. Her eyes were on Socolow, and a small smile played across her lips. I was trying to figure it out when the judge stopped me. "Say, Jake, you still playing ball?"

"Not for a long time," I said.

"Ah." A look of confusion, his memory futilely paring away the years.

When I turned back, Lourdes Soto was watching me. Her dark eyes were bright, her face composed. The eyes and mouth worked themselves into a look of concern and empathy. It was so subtly done, a cocking of the head, a pursing of the lips, a gentle furrowing of the brow calculated to show just how much she cared about poor Francisco Crespo and little old me. It was so damn good it sent a chill right up my spine.

7

THE COMBINATION

I parked the old convertible under a bonsai banyan tree that had been there a lot longer than any of us and would be there long after we are gone. When the top is down on the 442, I avoid Spanish olive trees. Same for bottlebrush and a few others whose leaves, seeds, and blossoms leave stains on the ancient upholstery. Only trouble I ever had with a banyan was when a green iguana dropped from a branch as I was tooling south on Old Cutler Road. It didn't bother me, but the young lady into whose lap it fell—a humorless lass whose idea of getting close to nature was suntanning topless on her condo balcony—refused to see me again.

Lourdes Soto lived in an old section of Coral Gables just off Alhambra Circle. It was once a neighborhood of grand homes in the Mediterranean Revival style, full of columns and courtyards, Spanish tile and loggias. Many of the houses have been razed and modern concrete creations erected in their place. Oddly, though, the postmodern trendy architects are borrowing from the older Florida styles. Curved eyebrows above windows and doors are derived from the Art Deco hotels and apartment buildings of South Beach. Arches are distinctively Mediterranean. The sloping roofs with steep overhangs and deep porches recall the old Florida cracker houses of the 1800s. So the old neighborhood is a hodgepodge of styles, some combined in the same house.

Next to the Soto home, workmen were putting finishing touches on one of the new models. It was designed by a young Argentinian architect. I knew this because of the tasteful sign with his name, address, and phone number plus a history of his obscure design awards, all indicating he'd be ever so willing to perform the same feats of mishmash postmodern tropical-Deco neurotic construction on your lot, if you were so inclined. Other signs adorned the front yard, fastened there on stakes driven into the fresh sod. The grass, as well as the bougainvillea, coco plum, and sweet acacia, were courtesy of Manuel Diaz Landscaping. Burglars were kept away by Advanced Security. Bugs were gassed by Truly Nolen Fumigation, and the pool was cleaned by Sparkling Waters, Inc. While I learned all this, a black Labrador retriever was relieving himself on the mailbox post. The dog was apparently not part of the marketing plan; at least, he didn't have a sign.

The Sotos lived in one of the few remaining Spanish-style villas. By the time I rapped twice on the double doors of Dade County pine, Lourdes was there. She was wearing a baggy white T-shirt and chocolate-colored twill slacks with a web belt and lots of pockets. The brown velvet eyes seemed to warm up at the sight of me. She touched a finger to her forehead, adjusting the bangs of her jet black hair the way women do when they're taking their own inventory while in the presence of a man.

Instead of inviting me in, she guided me around back on a path of pink terrazzo. We were nicely shaded by a loggia of Roman arches, Spanish tile, and wood-beamed ceiling. We emerged in a courtyard with a tinkling fountain, molded columns with pockmarked stucco, and a rose garden surrounded by jasmine hedges.

A small, wiry man sat in a turquoise wrought-iron chair at a matching table covered with papers, clipboards, and ledgers. He wore a white guayabera and had thick black hair swept straight back and a bushy black mustache. He held a fountain pen in his left hand. There wasn't another hand. The right arm ended in a stump just inside the guayabera sleeve. The left arm was heavily veined with a ragged scar just below the elbow. An unlit cigar was clamped into his teeth. He was weathered around the eyes, his face comfortably creased and lived in.

"Papi, this is Mr. Lassiter," Lourdes said.

The man nodded but didn't stand up. He placed the pen carefully into a white marble holder, and extended his left hand. I shook it awkwardly with my right. "Mr. Soto, I've heard a lot about you." It was true. A folk hero to the Cuban refugees, Severo Soto's fame had spread through the Anglo community as well.

Soto released my hand, nodded, and removed the cigar. "I understand Francisco Crespo has finally killed someone. Not that it surprises me."

So much for a character witness.

"He's *accused* of murder," I said, taking a seat opposite him. "Lourdes tells me he once worked for Soto Shipping Company."

The dark eyes locked on mine. "Some years ago, in the freight-forwarding division. It is all in there."

The voice was remarkably free of an accent. He gestured toward a manila folder. I riffled through some meaningless payroll records and company medical exams. Lourdes Soto had teased me with the concept of inside information. In the week since we first met, she had given me three written reports that didn't tell me anything new. If she had something useful, she was keeping it to herself. At the same time, she plied me with questions about my progress and strategy. I told her everything I knew, which was nothing, other than my suspicion that Crespo wasn't nearly as guilty as he claimed to be.

"Could Crespo have been involved in any anticommunist groups?" I asked.

"Crespo is a peasant," Severo Soto said, "too young to remember Cuba *antes de Fidel.*"

"Did he have any political leanings?"

"Of course, he was against the *comunistas*. But was he active? Not that I am aware."

Lourdes placed a hand on her father's forearm. "The man he killed—"

"—Allegedly killed," I reminded them. We all know about the presumption of innocence; we just don't believe it.

"—was Vladimir Smorodinsky."

Soto raised his eyebrows but didn't say a word.

"You knew him," I said.

"A Russian who worked for Yagamata. We have met."

"Yagamata apparently got him an exit visa."

Soto nodded. "Yagamata could do that. He has made much money with the Russians. He would do business with the devil if the price was right."

"He did business with you," I said evenly.

Soto took a moment to consider whether I had intended *el insulto,* or whether I was just clumsy at conversation. His eyes were placid. After what he had endured, he had all the time in the world. *"Lo hecho, hecho está.* What's done is done. I did not realize that the man's only principles were in his wallet. *Claro,* I did business with him. We had, Lourdes, what was it, not a partnership, an adventure?"

"Joint venture," she helped out.

"We shipped cargo for him from Helsinki to Miami. It was supposed to be Finnish wood products, textiles, furniture."

"But it turned out to be smuggled Russian artifacts," I chimed in.

Soto appraised me. Who was it who said I wasn't as dumb as I looked?

"I do not make a habit of speaking of these things to strangers." Severo Soto looked toward his daughter.

"It's all right, Papi. My loyalty is to Mr. Lassiter."

That was news to me, but I nodded my approval.

"I have spent years building the reputation of my firm," Soto said. "My honor as a businessman is paramount. My relationship with customs, all my import licenses were jeopardized by Yagamata."

"How?"

"It took me a while to understand just what he was doing. He began his dealings while there was a Soviet Union, prospered through Gorbachev's *perestroika,* and now continues with the Commonwealth under Yeltsin. Principles don't matter. Not when the almighty dollar is your god. With a wrecked economy and political turmoil, his business thrives. Chaos and conflict are honey and wine to Yagamata."

I waited for him to continue. Sometimes silence is the best question. Overhead, a meadowlark was singing its spring song. I hoped Severo Soto would keep talking.

"He had an entire network inside Russia," Soto said finally.

"Museum curators, bureaucrats, customs officials, members of various ministries and the Supreme Soviet. Hardliners, reformers, it didn't seem to matter. For hard currency, his contacts would have dismantled the Kremlin and sold it by the brick."

"And Smorodinsky?"

"His *aprendiz de todo.*"

"Jack of all trades," Lourdes translated.

"Yagamata didn't tell you Smorodinsky was just a laborer, did he?" Soto asked me.

"No. He said the Russian was a man of culture and a patriot."

Soto allowed himself a humorless laugh. "Smorodinsky and his brother ran Yagamata's Leningrad operation. Artifacts would be gathered from all over the Soviet Union and stored in safe houses they arranged. Then somehow—and this was their genius —they managed to ship the goods in small boats from Leningrad across the Gulf of Finland to Helsinki. It is not, I assure you, like sailing from Miami to Bimini. How they were able to bribe enough officials to avoid capture by the police, the military, and the KGB is something that always baffled me. Even with Yagamata's contacts, it was still an impressive feat."

A wooden door creaked open and a short, swarthy woman in a colorful print dress appeared, carrying a tray that held a silver pot and three espresso glasses.

"Then why bring him here? What good could a Russian do at this end of the operation?"

Soto shrugged. "That is for you and my daughter to determine, though I don't know what it has to do with your client killing . . . *allegedly* killing the man."

"It might help explain why Yagamata seems willing to have an innocent man convicted of the murder," I said.

The woman left her tray, and Lourdes poured the hot, syrupy drink for each of us.

"About that, I have no idea," Soto said.

While the sugar and caffeine were jump-starting my dead batteries, Severo Soto told me about his business and his life. It was a story I already knew. When they were both students, Soto and Fidel Castro were friends with similar ideals. Together, they plotted the doomed July 26, 1953, attack on eastern Cuba's Moncada Barracks. Soto spent two years in prison, but it did not shake his will. Again he joined Castro and they stood side by side during the revolution, until he became disenchanted with Castro's brand of socialism. "I did not plan for my country to be the bastard child of the Russians," he told me.

He commandeered a Cuban patrol vessel and fled to Key West and then to Miami, where he became a major in Brigade 2506 and returned to Cuba, landing on the beach at the Bay of Pigs in April 1961. The betrayal and cowardice of the United States had stranded him and his men without air support. His friends died around him, bleeding into the sand. He was wounded, captured, imprisoned, and tortured by Castro's *matónes*. "I did not see the sun for three years," he said. "The only sound was a high-frequency wail broadcast into my cell twenty-four hours a day at a volume that broke both my eardrums. They gave me *comunista* propaganda, which I tore up and ate and gave back to them as *mierda*."

Lourdes's mother didn't know if her husband was dead or alive. Then one day Severo Soto was picked up by a Coast Guard cutter, drifting north on a raft of inner tubes in the Gulf Stream due east of the Fontainebleau Hotel. It had taken four years to claw and chew through a limestone wall in his cell. His teeth were reduced to nubs, but he clambered through an eighteen-inch hole and made his way to the sea.

When Soto showed up again on Calle Ocho, Lourdes was five years old and did not know her father. Her mother worked as a seamstress. Before long, Soto was gone again, leading Alpha 66 on its fools' mission to stir up an anti-Castro rebellion. Captured in the Escambray mountains with grenades and automatic weapons, he was again imprisoned, the most famous of the *plantados*, the political prisoners.

When he was finally released and joined his family a final time in Miami, Soto was a legendary hero in Little Havana. Cuban millionaires, burdened by their guilt and awed by Soto's steely determination, set him up in the shipping industry. With business funneled his way, it did not take long for him to prosper.

"You know the stories of our *exilados*," he told me. "The lawyers who spoke no English and began here pushing brooms in your banks . . ."

"Then ended up owning the banks," I added.

He nodded. "The Cubans are an industrious people. But dreamers, too. We dream of a *Cuba Libre.*"

I didn't think he meant a rum and Coke.

"Papi is president of the Cuban Freedom Foundation," Lourdes said. I knew that from the newspaper. The Foundation was a middle-of-the-road organization, not as liberal as those *diálogueros* who would begin negotiations with Castro, not as fanatic as those Omega Sevens who would stick nitroglycerine in Fidel's cigar if they could. "If Castro falls . . ." Lourdes caught her father's sharp glance. "*When* Castro falls, the Foundation will likely be installed as the first free government in Cuba. Since Papi is president of the Foundation . . ."

Soto dismissed the idea with a modest wave of his hand. "It will not be a position to be coveted, Mr. Lassiter. Cuba is in a state of complete economic collapse. The country faces what Fidel calls the zero option, now that the Russians can no longer furnish sufficient fuel and food. All consumer goods are rationed. So many of the industrious people have escaped the island, who is there left to rebuild? My friends all vow they will return. But will they? Like me, they are old men. And what of their children? Are they ready to forgo their shopping malls and their cable TV? I assure you, the president of a free Cuba will have his hands full."

Soto sipped the rest of his *café Cubano,* then pushed his iron chair away from the iron table. When he stood, I figured it was time for me to go, but he didn't seem in a hurry.

"I am proud of what I have accomplished here, Mr. Lassiter. And I will keep my vow to return to a free Cuba. But on my own terms and in my own way. The Cuba of my past is gone forever. The job of rebuilding will be a massive undertaking."

"Our government will surely help," I said.

He scowled. "We cannot base our recovery on American largesse. The politics are too uncertain. Who is to say who will control the White House and the Congress when the time comes? Who can forget the treachery at the Bay of Pigs? The Americans can never be counted on. They have allowed the butcher to remain in power for more than thirty years. We must be self-sufficient and prepare for every eventuality."

With that he motioned toward the loggia and we began circling the house once again, this time with Soto leading the way. Before we turned the corner, he stopped and pointed to a small freestanding building in the shade of two live oak trees. At one time it would have been maid's quarters. "Would you like to see my study?" he asked.

"Papi," Lourdes moaned. "Mr. Lassiter is a busy man."

Papi didn't care. "Indulge an old man. I want to show your friend something of beauty besides my only daughter."

The building was a one-story wooden box with pink Bahama shutters. Soto fished in his pocket and produced a key ring. It took three keys to unlock the door and a three-number combination to turn off the panel alarm inside the door.

Twelve, thirty-one, fifty-eight.

I don't know why I watched him do that and immediately committed it to memory. Maybe it was something about the number. Or maybe I was a cat burglar in another life.

It was just one room, dark and cool. An old window air conditioner wheezed in the corner. A brown leather chair, its hide cracked, sat at a mahogany desk. A crystal decanter of cigars was perched on a matching credenza. The desk was cluttered with papers and photographs in brass frames. One was in black and white, a much younger Severo Soto and a slender, pale woman with full lips who had been kind enough to bequeath her complexion to her daughter. Next to it was a color shot of a teenage Lourdes in what looked like a prom dress. Her hair was longer, her smile innocent and hopeful.

"My *quince* party," she said, catching me spying.

"Over here," Soto said. He flipped on a light switch and pointed toward the wall facing the desk.

It was an oil painting of a nude man, practically featureless, bent over a nude woman on all fours, who was trying to crawl away. The man's hands were large and grasping, the woman's head bent in shame. The colors were vivid, the grass a deep green that seemed to stain the woman's bare feet, the sea a rich blue. "Do you know much about art?"

No, I thought, but I'm learning. I shook my head.

"What does the painting say to you?" he asked.

"I don't know. It's very powerful. Almost frightening in a way. I just don't know enough to judge its quality."

"It is a very well-known work, Mr. Lassiter. One of my favorites, in fact, by—"

"Papi!" Lourdes practically stomped her foot. "It is not like you *presumir.*"

"Forgive me. I am *indiscreto,* and I embarrass my daughter." Severo Soto stared hard into the canvas. "What is important is the art itself, what it says, what we can learn from it. To me, the man in the painting is Russia. The woman is Cuba. And every day of my life, Mr. Lassiter, I force myself to watch what he is about to do."

8

I HATE BUDWEISER

The ramshackle building sagged in the middle and slouched on weathered pilings in the soft earth alongside an Everglades canal. An aging frump without makeup or girdle, Mississippi Jack's was jammed with workers from the limestone pits, an Anglo-Hispanic-black crew that may have lived in segregated neighborhoods but drank more or less together in a place where you could feel, and occasionally hear, the dynamite blasts from the nearby rock pit.

I had pulled my ancient but amiable convertible into the muddy parking lot and found a spot next to an oversize Dodge Ram pickup that was hauling an airboat. I wore old jeans, boots, and a shirt that celebrated the joys of eating oysters raw.

The "L" in the neon Schlitz sign was dark and had been for as long as anyone could remember. Faded photos of the winners of the latest turkey shoot hung haphazardly inside the door. The jukebox rumbled with "Honky Tonk Woman" followed by "If It Don't Come Easy." Fishing corks plugged bullet holes in one wall and the hide of a sixteen-foot alligator decorated another. There was one pool table, the green felt stained from decades of spilled beer. The waitresses were sturdy sedans no longer on warranty and wore jeans, sneakers, and T-shirts tied around ample waists. The bartender paid off winners of a stud poker video game with two six-packs or a sawbuck—take your choice—and if the boys from the state beverage commission didn't like it, screw them.

The bongs and clangs of a pinball machine competed with the twang from the jukebox. The voices were husky southern drawls, but pockets of the room erupted in occasional bursts of rapid-fire Spanish and inner-city jive. A gray haze of cigarette smoke drifted toward a ceiling of unpainted two-by-fours and kept the termite population to manageable levels. On the men's room wall, above a machine that dispensed condoms for a quarter, a poet had scrawled, "Encase your porker before you dork her."

There were no ferns. Or guys with white-on-white shirts, power ties, and red suspenders. Or talk of Aspen, tax-free municipals, or selling short.

Mississippi Jack's was not the Harvard Club.

The waitress wiped our table with a wet towel, then stood, head cocked, hip shot, and smiling. About forty, she had a round face and a headful of bleached yellow curls that made her look like a happy poodle. "You'all here for the catfish fry or the gator hunt?"

"The beer," I said. "Pitcher. Whatever's on tap."

"How 'bout some swamp cabbage to go with that? Got a vat simmering in the back."

So that's what I smelled. "Plain or fried?"

She raised an eyebrow. I didn't mean to sound like Chef Paul, just wanted to know what I was getting into.

"Any way you want it. We cook it with salt pork and milk, a dash of pepper. Personally, I like it plain in a cup, but you want it fried up with fritters, you got it. You want it another way, go talk to the cook after he sobers up."

I turned to my drinking buddy. "Francisco?"

He was shaking his head.

"Maybe we'll just stick to the beer," I told her.

I have nothing against eating the boot of the sabal palm tree. In a little bottle at the French grocery, soaking in vinegar, they call it heart of palm. It's not as elegant hereabouts, but it's the same raw ingredient.

She brought Budweiser. American beer is weak and watery, and like network television, is calculated to appeal to the most folks while offending the fewest. It's the lowest common denominator of brew, and like so many of our products, competes not on its quality, but on its image as created by Manhattan video slicksters. Best I can tell, there's no beer that will help me dunk a basketball or attract a bushel of beach bunnies, so I go for the taste when I have a choice. Not that I'm a beer snob, which is an oxymoron rivaling "honest lawyer."

Still, the Dutch beer Grolsch is my all-around favorite for savoring full flavor. I like it at forty-two degrees, not out of the ice chest. Americans drink their beer too cold and too light. The Yankee brews are laced with rice malt or corn malt, bland substitutes for barley. There are exceptions. Brooklyn Lager with its burnt amber color and molasses aroma is strong enough to go head-to-head with the spiciest chili. The wheaty, oaky Anchor Steam from San Francisco can hold its own with barbecue. Boston's Samuel Adams has a bittersweet hoppy taste that washes down peanuts and jalapeños. But that's about it for the American beers. The only time I'll go for a light beer is with some broiled red snapper or other delicate victuals. Then I'll choose one of the German *weiss* beers made from wheat. With a steak, I'll try a Dos Equis if there's no Grolsch around. Tsing Tao, the sweet Chinese beer, is fine for Szechuan or Hunan food, and a Guinness stout with its nutty hop aroma and burnt-oak flavor goes well with dessert.

Today, though, the talk was more important than taste, and after turning down the swamp cabbage, I didn't want the waitress to consider me a citified sissy:

"Hey, Jim Bob, feller out here wants to know if we serve beer from Holland."

"No, but if'n he wants, I'll stick a tulip up his ass."

Crespo drained his first glass without taking a breath. If he was feeling any heat from the upcoming trial, he didn't show it. *"Diez años?"*

"That's the offer now. A plea to manslaughter. Ten years, you'd be out in three."

He poured himself another beer from the chipped pitcher. Budweiser was fine with him. I fished some boiled peanuts out of a bowl. From *Jaw-ja,* the waitress told us. You were supposed to scatter the shells on the floor. I did what I was supposed to. "Of course, you'd have to cooperate."

Crespo looked at me with wary eyes. His face had healed

nicely with only traces of scars on his leathery skin. Small and ferret-faced, he still managed to look dangerous. You wouldn't be surprised to see him pull a switchblade from an ankle sheath.

"You'd have to tell them who killed the Russian," I continued.

He shook his head. "I could do the time. *No problema.* But I'd have to live that long."

He just let it hang there.

"Want to talk about it?" I asked.

Over at the jukebox, Randy Travis was singing a song I didn't know. At the next table, a guy in a University of Florida baseball cap was telling a pal how much money he would make snaring alligators during the thirty-day hunt. "I figure I get my limit easy. That's fifteen gators at, say, average of ten feet." He did some arithmetic with a pencil on a soggy napkin. "Close to seven thousand for the hides at forty-five dollars a foot. And that don't include the meat."

"But you're not figurin' expenses," his friend argued. The guy wore Army fatigues and was no wider than your average Buick. He sounded like a cracker C.P.A. "Don't be fergittin' your costs. License, tags, gasoline. And your time. Figger it out, boy."

I moved closer to my client. Dr. Weiner would have said I was closing the horizontal zone. I just wanted Crespo to trust his faithful mouthpiece, somebody who had known him a long time, but maybe didn't know him at all. "Francisco, you want to tell me about it. Who's threatening you?"

His eyes darted across the room and back to me. But the mouth stayed closed.

"Is it Yagamata? Because if it is, I've got a real problem here. I don't care if he's a big client of my firm. I can't let him manipulate you."

"I am grateful to Señor Yagamata for looking after me."

"That's *my* job!" I banged my beer glass on the table, slopping some of the anemic brew. The alligator hunter stopped computing and glared at me. "Look, I promised your mother I'd take care of you, and I promised myself, too. This is a murder charge, Francisco, not another A and B in a bar."

That made him smile, just a little. "I've gotten away with worse."

Of course. I just wasn't used to him bringing it up. "That wasn't murder, Francisco. Justifiable homicide all the way. Even I could have gotten you off."

"No, you couldn't. You would have been a witness." He smiled again. Two in one day was a new world record. "Except you couldn't identify the killer, so nobody was ever arrested."

"I thought the physical description I gave was pretty creative. You remember what I told the homicide detective?"

"*Sí.* A tall, husky Anglo with red hair in a brush cut and a tattoo of the American flag on his forearm."

"I'd nearly forgotten about the tattoo. A nice touch, wasn't it? Specifics always add a touch of reality."

We both sat there thinking about it, the link between us that spanned the years, the spilled blood that made us the unlikeliest of brothers. My debt to him could never be repaid, so he wanted to cancel it. I couldn't let it go.

"The coaches always told us to stay out of bars," I said.

Crespo shrugged, then looked away. He was finished talking about it. He could banish the thoughts. I couldn't. I always asked what I could have done differently. I could have listened to the coaches, for one thing.

Now I sat looking at Francisco Crespo in another bar. This time, ten years later, it was his life on the line, or at least his freedom. "Your mother's worried to death, and so am I."

"I will survive. I always do."

"We're the ones who care about you. Not Yagamata. Do you understand that?"

"He is taking care of my fees, *verdad*?"

"Yes, but I don't care who's paying the freight. I don't answer to Yagamata, or anyone else. My loyalty is to you. I don't know what Yagamata's agenda is. I only have one, and that's to give you the best defense possible. I can't do that if you're compromising your own case on orders from Yagamata. Do you understand what I'm saying?"

He looked straight into his beer.

"Francisco, I need you to help yourself. Show as much care for yourself as you did for me on a hot Sunday night a long time ago."

"Jake, *mi amigo,* it is not your concern. I will handle it."

"Wrong. It's my concern. Even if I didn't feel the way I do about you and your mother, there's something else involved. It's called ethics."

Crespo furrowed his brow, and the little scars grew pinker. He didn't seem to understand. That's all right. A lot of guys who've hung out their shingle wouldn't either. That's not to say I've always walked the straight and narrow. The ethical rules are a hundred fifty pages of mush. Mine are shorter and simpler. I won't lie to a judge, steal from a client, or bribe a cop. And I won't bed down a wife in a divorce. Until the case is over.

"C'mon, Frankie baby," I implored him. "Tell me what happened in the warehouse. Why did you attack him? Who put you up to it? Who killed Smorodinsky?"

Silence.

"Who are you protecting?"

He helped himself to the beer but stayed quiet.

"Will you talk to me?"

"No sé. Maybe later."

"We pick a jury tomorrow. If Socolow likes the panel, he'll withdraw the offer."

"What would make him like the jury?"

"Six people who've got cops for cousins or who've been victims of crimes, or don't like *Marielitos.* A bunch of hard cases who feel superior to you, who think you wouldn't be in court if you hadn't done something shitty. Mean-spirited people who won't hold the state to its burden of proof and won't cut you an even break."

Our waitress appeared with a second pitcher of beer. "You boys want to try the chicken wings?" I waved her off.

"But we might get a jury he doesn't like, *verdad?"* Crespo asked.

"Sure, half a dozen open-minded people with a healthy mistrust of authority and a feel for the underdog. It can happen, but don't count on it."

"If it does happen, this Mr. Socolow might offer an even better deal."

"Maybe, but whatever it is, your cooperation will be a condition of the plea. You'd have to tell him who else was involved. You understand?"

Before Crespo could answer, we were interrupted. *"Hola,* lawyer! Ay, where's your little sail?"

Them again. Hector and what's-his-name. Yagamata's goons. Wiry guys in muscle shirts to show off their stylish tattoos.

"And the blond," Hector said. *"¿Donde está la rubia?"*

I felt the little surge of adrenaline our knuckle-dragging ancestors must have known. The fight-or-flee response. But I'm a lawyer, so I had another alternative: talk. "Tell your boss if he wants to have lunch, he can come here for some swamp cabbage and chicken wings."

"He don't wanna see you, asshole. It's your friend here. He's worried about him."

"Me, too. We're getting ready for trial, and we appreciate your kind help, but—"

"It's okay," Crespo interrupted, getting to his feet. "I'll go."

"Sit still, Francisco," I ordered. "We're not finished here. And this time, let me handle the problem."

"Jake, it is all right. If Señor Yagamata wishes to see me, I will go."

"Bueno," Hector's buddy said, a humorless smile curling his lips. "We don't like *hacerle daño,* to hurt nobody."

"Good thing," I said, "because it would take another dozen just like you."

Hector looked surprised, but then, the time of day would surprise this guy. "What you mean by that?"

I was still in my chair, and they had moved, one on each side of me. In the movies, Arnold Schwarzenegger would just reach out and grab each one by the neck, bang their heads together, and calmly finish his beer. Try it sometime, and you'll get bopped upside the head by two guys who have leverage and mobility on their side. A smart guy would just call it off. Who was I to play knight errant when the damsel had a mustache and was willing to take a ride with the dragon? But I was steamed at Matsuo Yagamata, who had bought himself some trinkets and some people, while he was at it. He owned Francisco Crespo and two petty thugs and maybe me, too. So here I was, expiating a decade of guilt by spitting in the dragon's eye, because mad as I was at Yagamata, I was enraged at *me,* and short of banging my own head against a wall, I didn't know what else to do.

"What I mean, dirtbag, is that you guys are two-bit sacks of shit with brains smaller than a mouse's asshole. You're a couple of candy-assed errand boys who need both hands to find your own dicks."

It takes years of forensic training to become so eloquent. At the next table, the gator hunters stopped talking and turned to listen to our sophisticated colloquy.

Hector cracked a malicious grin. He liked this. His buddy started bouncing on the balls of his feet, excited and expectant.

"And your friend here is so scared his asshole's whistling Dixie," I concluded.

"Jake," Crespo said. "It is not necessary. Please. I will see Señor Yagamata and meet you in court in the morning. Tell Mr. Socolow we go to trial."

"You're a good man, Francisco," I told him, "and even if you weren't, you're my brother because of what happened in a place like this. So don't worry. I can handle Hector. He's shaking like a dog shitting peach pits."

There are times when a man's got to act like a man, and other times like an adolescent.

"Cagado cabrón!" Hector snarled. I didn't know what it meant but figured it wasn't *Have a nice day.* He picked up a handful of peanuts and dropped them into the beer where they sizzled happily. Then he picked up the pitcher and poured it over my head.

At the next table, I heard someone say, "Shee-*it,"* and I heard chairs scraping against the planks of the wooden floor, veteran spectators giving us room to arbitrate our grievances. Hector placed the pitcher on the table. Peanuts stuck in my hair. The beer stung my eyes, soaked the front of my shirt, and dripped, icy cold, into my crotch.

"Hector," I said softly, "I *hate* Budweiser."

And then I slipped a hand under the table, grabbed it where the base met the top, planted both feet, and pivoted, swinging the table hard into Hector's crotch. I dropped the table but continued the movement, swiveling two hundred seventy degrees and getting to my feet, expecting a first punch from his buddy and taking it, a glancing right hand off the side of the skull. I squared up, and snapped a left jab that he ducked. I followed with another that missed, and then feinted yet another jab and came across the top with a right that he tried to avoid by turning his head. He had good quickness, but I still caught him solid on the ear. I felt the jolt all the way to my elbow, and his cerebellum must have been dialing 911, because he folded neatly in half and crumpled into a carpet of peanut shells, unconscious before he hit the floor.

I didn't have time to give him the mandatory eight-count because Hector took that moment to smash a pool cue across the back of my head. The wood broke with a hellacious *cr-ack,* but it didn't hurt my head. Not a bit. Then he ricocheted what was left of the cue stick off my shoulder, and again, same thing. No pain. Those chairs they smash over the cowboys' heads in B westerns must be made of cue sticks.

I was starting to feel invincible, a celluloid cowboy, snapping long-distance jabs. Since I was taller and stronger, I wanted to maintain what the experts call an outfighting range, keeping Hector from getting inside with quick punches or kicks. But Hector knew what he was doing. He had some hand speed and understood how to retreat, then come back with a flurry. When he counterattacked, I covered up with the double forearm block. It isn't pretty, something like Floyd Patterson's peek-a-boo style. It leaves you with bruises on both arms but protects your dimpled chin and semihandsome face.

I had stalked Hector halfway across the bar, around the pool table, and up against a cooler, but he spun away. He kept leaping in and leaping out, a flurry of punches, and then a retreat. He knew something about martial arts, his style similar to the White Crane method of kung fu. A crane can defeat a gorilla, simply by spinning out of its grasp and counterattacking with furious beats of its wings, beak, and claws. But it takes patience, intelligence, and timing. The bird must continuously circle the beast, changing position and attack angles, retreating time and again until it can attack and peck away at the gorilla's eyes or otherwise discourage it from continuing the fight.

Hector had landed enough rat-a-tat-tats to raise some welts on my forehead, and the back of my skull, where the cue stick had landed without immediate effect, was starting to ache. Pain is like that, sometimes creeping up on you. I'm not exactly immune to pain, but I've grown accustomed to its pace. I played ball when a lot of guys got intimate at halftime with the Caine Brothers—Novocain and Xylocaine. It was expected. You played hurt or you didn't play at all. I resisted the needle until a game against the Bills when I took an elbow through the face mask on a kickoff, and my nose went east and west where it used to be north and south. If we hadn't been so thin on the special teams, they would have sent me to the locker room, but you don't tackle with your nose, so you can play—compound fracture notwithstanding—if you control the pain. With the offensive line huddled around me on the bench to block the view of the cameras, the team doc put a shot of Xylocaine right between my eyes, and damned if I didn't recover a fumble on a kickoff in the fourth quarter. After that, it was Darvocet for a separated shoulder, cortisone for turf toe, and an occasional jolt of my buddies, the Caine Brothers, for assorted twists and sprains.

Now I moved in again, and Hector caught me in the chest with the front snap kick they call *Mae keage* in karate. Then he spun to his right and tried to connect with the *Yoko keage,* the side snap kick. His timing was off, and he missed, leaving himself off balance, still spinning toward my left, his body open.

From somewhere in my peripheral vision, I was aware of the faces at the bar, intently watching us. They seemed to be smiling. The jukebox had switched gears, and Paula Abdul was in a rush for a guy who kissed her up and down.

I pivoted from the hips and stepped forward with the left foot. I hit him square in the solar plexus with a left hook that had everything I've got behind it. I heard the air wheeze out of him, and as he gasped for breath, I unleashed a right uppercut that started near my shoelaces and ended on the point of his unshaven chin. The punch lifted him off the floor and stretched him out on his back, feet twitching.

Francisco Crespo had gotten up and now stood at the bar, watching without expression. He hadn't helped them and he hadn't helped me. He was a good soldier who didn't want to cross the general. I wondered what he would have done if I'd been in real trouble. But then, I already knew that.

I was aware of some murmuring at the tables, and in a moment, everyone was drinking and talking as if nothing had happened.

I was breathing hard when I paid the tab. I threw in twenty bucks for a broken cue stick and a fifty to cover renting the place as a boxing ring. Another twenty for the waitress, who asked us to come back real soon and bring our friends.

In the parking lot along the canal, an ugly Bufo frog the size of a double cheeseburger burped hello. Or was it good-bye? Some extremely unbalanced druggies are known to lick the Bufo, which secretes a milky hallucinogenic goo. I could never help wondering what bozo discovered this pharmaceutical phenomenon by first putting tongue to toad.

The knuckles of my hands were split and beginning to swell. I sank stiffly into my old convertible and looked at my maniacally macho self in the rearview mirror. Angry knots were already popping out of my forehead. A judge once told me that, based on my trial strategy, I must have played football too long without a helmet. Now I looked the part. Maybe that was good for my buddy Crespo. The trial was two days away, and when the jurors filed into the box, they wouldn't be able to figure out which guy was the felon.

9

THE LADY IN RED

A tractor-trailer had collided with a bus on Tamiami Trail, snarling traffic on the way back into the city. A light rain was falling, and it was growing dark. An ambulance sat on the soggy berm alongside the canal where the bus was jammed nose-first into the shallow water, its rear wheels angled into the air. Raindrops slithered down my windshield, glowing blood red with each revolution of the ambulance's flashing light. From the east, I could hear a siren drawing closer. I know a personal injury lawyer who loves the sound. Whenever he hears an ambulance, he turns to his partner and says, "They're playing our song." The same lawyer branched out into divorce work and had a new business card printed: "Broken bones and broken hearts." And my brethren at the bar wonder why they're considered bottom-feeding gutter rats.

Eventually, the traffic cleared, and I headed into town, passing Sweetwater, home to several thousand Nicaraguan refugees, heading into Little Havana, then south on Ponce de Leon, through the Gables, and into Coconut Grove. My head was clanging by the time I downshifted into second and pulled onto Kumquat Street. The neighborhood was quiet, except for the buzz and crackle of insects and the warbling of a mockingbird in the marlberry bush in my front yard. By this time of night, most birds were nuzzling their mates and telling whoppers about the fat, juicy night crawler that got away. But here was my mocker chirping midnight melodies. He sang his own song, then a few he picked up during the day from a yellow-billed cuckoo, and if I could whistle "Raindrops Are Falling on My Head," he'd give that a try, too.

Mimus polyglōttos, Charlie Riggs calls my feathery friend. Mimic of many tongues. I like him because he's a tough bird who chases away crows and cats and even an occasional German shepherd. Charlie says he's a bachelor, just like me. They're the only birds who sing at night, crooning their own Personals ad. *High-flying male mocker with stunning white wing patches seeks sleek mate for dining, gliding, and more.* So far old Mimus hadn't had much luck. He was still serenading the crickets, but then, who was I to gloat?

My neighborhood is what the guidebooks would call eclectic, if they called it anything, which they don't. To me, it's just weird. Not fancy enough for the *crème de la* crumbs, real estate developers and drug dealers, it is home to a collection of what I call soloists, men and women who reject marital and suburban bliss.

In the blank marked "occupation" on the census form, my neighbors are all "other." Geoffrey, who lives in the stucco house behind the poinciana trees, is a free-lance cameraman who works the wee hours and peddles videos of late-night car crashes and drug busts to the local TV stations. On the other side of the limeberry shrubs, Mako is esconced in a wooden tree house reachable only by rope ladder. He trades custom-made hammocks for Florida crawfish with Homer Thigpen, a lobster pot poacher down the street. Phoebe with the bright red hair hosts swingers parties complete with nude diving contests in her swimming pool. And Robert and Robert—art gallery owners—keep to themselves behind the hibiscus hedge. All of which makes me the most bourgeois of the bunch.

My parking spot in the gravel under a chinaberry tree was occupied by a red BMW convertible. On my front porch, a lady in a red leather mini and white silk blouse sat in Granny Lassiter's cherrywood rocker. Granny used to rock while sipping from a Mason jar filled with liquid propane she called home brew. Now the Lady in Red sat there holding a supermarket bag. A loaf of

Cuban bread stuck out the top. "You hungry?" Lourdes Soto asked.

In the glow of a three-quarter moon enhanced by the misty light of the mercury vapor anticrime lights, Lourdes appeared as an apparition, her creamy complexion in soft focus. Her slight smile had the peacefulness of a Madonna, and for a moment I thought maybe I'd been hit harder than I realized. When I got close enough for her to see my face, she let out a low whistle. A fine and dandy lady whistle. "Is this what you downtown lawyers do on weekends? Flex that Y-chromosome, burn off some testosterone?"

"I was working."

She sniffed at the air and didn't smell frangipani. "You sure you weren't runner-up in a beer-guzzling contest?" She showed me a wide smile, giving me a good look at scarlet lips and white teeth. "Maybe I should put something on those scrapes," she said.

I gestured toward the groceries. "After you cook some dinner."

"Cook? What do you think, I came here to make paella and *boniatos*? I'm not one of those traditional Cuban girls, convent schooling, black beans and rice with Mami, waiting for the men to come home. That went out with chaperones. We're having sandwiches, Jake."

"Okay, okay. Sandwiches are fine."

I put a shoulder against the humidity-swollen front door and gave a good shove. It groaned open and I chivalrously allowed Lourdes to enter my palace. She surveyed the surroundings and remained graciously silent. In decorating, I have spared great expense.

Lourdes didn't blink an eye at the coffee table made of a sailboard propped on concrete blocks. She didn't fuss at two weeks of newspapers spread across sofa and floor. She ignored a rusty scuba tank, a wetsuit that had dripped itself dry into a potted geranium, now comatose with saltwater poisoning, and she didn't comment on my architectural skill at building a giant house of cards out of empty cartons of home delivery pizza.

I flicked on the lamp with the translucent rotating Dolphins helmet for a shade. She looked at me in the orange-and-turquoise light and gently touched my forehead with what I took for sisterly concern. "You have any hydrogen peroxide?"

"You gonna nurse me, or you planning to burn this place to the ground?"

"Forget it. Your head is so hard, a few dents and scrapes won't do any damage." She put a hand on my shoulder and steered me toward the stairs. "Why don't you shower? I may tidy up a bit."

"You sure? I don't want you to violate some feminist manifesto."

"Don't be a jerk. Go!" She ran a hand through my beer-sticky hair, then paused, a puzzled look crossing her face. "Is it my imagination or is that a peanut in your ear?"

I showered and slipped into blue nylon running shorts. The occasion didn't seem formal, so I skipped the shirt, socks, and shoes. I found her in the kitchen. The living room had been rearranged, dusted, and sorted out. "What I assumed to be garbage, I stacked in the corner by the door," she said. "The cans and bottles are in separate bags, the newspapers tied in bundles for recycling."

"Thanks. Those sneakers with the missing tongue and flapping soles were my favorites, but I can live without them. And that's quarter-inch outhaul line around the papers."

The coffee cups and cereal bowls that had filled the sink were now in the dishwasher, which had come out of retirement and was happily chugging away. The countertops had been wiped clean, and the floor mopped. And I always thought the kitchen tile was gray.

I gave her a look. "What was that speech about not being the domestic type?"

"You exceeded even my limits of tolerance."

"I guess the place could use a woman's touch."

"Or even a human touch," she said.

She rooted around in a drawer and came up with a hammer, a screwdriver, some matches, a deck of playing cards, and some plastic gizmos that were once attached to some appliance or another. "Don't you have any flatware, or do you just use your hands?"

"The *flatware,*" I informed her, "is with the *al fresco* utensils." I opened a drawer filled with paper plates, paper cups, and plastic forks, spoons, and knives.

"Environmentally unsound," she said.

"I reuse the forks and spoons," I replied, defending myself against charges of pillaging the earth.

"I can see that." She was inspecting a fork for toxic scum. After some sudsing and rinsing, she made sandwiches of roast turkey, cream cheese, and strawberry jam on Cuban bread. I watched her slender hands moving quickly. I watched the muscles in the calves of her legs as she moved across the small kitchen. I watched myself watch her and wondered what was going on.

"You know Cubans have a weakness for sweets." She added an extra dollop of jam to her bread. "This one's yours." She slid a plate across the counter to me. It contained a thick sandwich, a garnish of fresh pineapple, and a pile of banana chips. "Beer?" she asked.

"No, thanks. I filled my quota today. Besides, the combination . . ."

She shrugged, opened the fridge, and found some milk that didn't predate the Carter Administration. We ate standing up at the counter, looking at each other, contemplating the situation. At least that's what I was doing. What *was* going on here? After a moment of silence, I said, "We sure needed the rain, huh?"

She looked at me as if I were a complete fool, which of course I was. There is that peculiar mating dance for the species that doesn't sing songs or lock antlers to win its mate. We paw the earth and shuffle and smile and chat about everything and nothing and send out little coded signals. I decided to dispense with the meteorological insights. She touched her ebony hair and smoothed it back over an ear. She cocked her head and looked at me from under dark eyelashes. I responded by taking a bite of my sweet turkey sandwich and leaving a glob of cream cheese stuck in the corner of my mouth. When it comes to *savoir faire,* I come up a little short.

"Let me," Lourdes said, with a come-hither look. She moved close enough for us to breathe each other's air, and she scraped up the cream cheese with the ruby red fingernail of a pinky. Then she stuck the fingernail in my mouth. And then the whole finger. When the finger came out, her tongue went in. We stood there, kissing soft and slow, pressed against each other, my hands running from her shoulders to her buttocks. She arched herself into me, running the tips of her nails across my bare back, full lips caressing mine. I cupped my hands under her leather-clad bottom and lifted her off the floor, bringing her to my height. She wrapped her legs around me, and we stood there, motionless except for the grinding of loins.

"The bedroom's upstairs," I whispered.

"Here's fine," she said.

And it was. I stepped out of my shorts. She wriggled out of her mini and pulled the white silk blouse over her head. Underneath she wore lacy white panties and matching bra. From somewhere she produced a foil-wrapped condom. She opened the foil with her teeth, smoothing the condom on me with steady fingers. She slipped out of the panties and bra with no help from me and was left in her red stiletto high heels. The shoes stayed on as I lifted her again, feeling her moist heat pressed against me. My hands flowed over her, from the shoulders through the smooth valley of her back to the silken skin where her hips flared into that wondrous sweep of womanhood.

"I want you," she breathed into my ear.

"Whatever the lady wants."

Our engines hummed along, the fires building. She raised her breasts to my mouth, cradling them in each hand. Her nipples were taut and erect, startling in their darkness against the creaminess of her skin. I lifted her buttocks higher and pressed into her. As she took me into her sweet soft vise, her body stiffened and her eyes widened, nearly fearful. Then she exhaled a slow warm breath, closed her eyes and locked onto me. There was a perfect meshing of gears, temperature rising, cadence matching. When my pace increased, hers matched stride. When my breathing deepened, hers followed. Our tempo built to a crescendo, she dug her nails into my back, wailed some entreaty in Spanish I had never heard, threw her head back, and tightened her grip while spasms shook us both.

"Good Lord," I said, at last.

"Ay, Dios mío," she breathed in my ear.

Later, upstairs in the bed under the paddle fan, her head cradled in the crook of my right arm, she said, "I nearly forgot why I came to see you."

"It wasn't to cook—sorry—make sandwiches?"

"No."

"Or to clean my kitchen?"

"Hardly."

"Or to fix my clock?"

"That just happened. *Yo no planee."*

Uh-huh.

"Want to talk about it?" I asked. Lately, I've become sensitive to a woman's needs. I'm not sure why, but it seems only fair. My rules are simple: I say what I feel, and I never pretend, mislead, or say *I love you* unless I mean it, so the words have seldom been heard. After an encounter, I try to talk, and not about the recent narrowing of the goalposts in college football. Some years ago, in the dentist's office, I picked up one of those women's magazines with a bosomy woman in a low-cut dress on the cover. I took a quiz on my lovemaking skills and made Dean's List in technical proficiency but flunked the part about postcoital cuddling and conversation. So I read some of the other stuff, too, about connection and communication. Now, I've picked up the buzzwords about how men and women misunderstand each other. Men speak the language of power and independence; women speak of closeness and intimacy. Men *report* what they do; women *reveal* their feelings. So here I was, a former varsity member of the AFC Eastern Division All-Star Party team, master of the one-night stand, lying entangled with Lourdes Soto with lots of me touching lots of her, trying to make sense of it all.

"Talk about it?" she responded.

"Like what just happened. What it means."

She chuckled into my ear. "You mean, will I call you tomorrow?"

She was mocking me, just like *Mimus polyglōttos.*

"I was just surprised, that's all. I wasn't expecting this."

"So you want to analyze it?"

"No. Yes. I don't know. I just thought that, as a woman, you might want to talk. . . ."

"Hey, big guy, just lean back and enjoy it."

She was tracing figure eights on my chest with her manicured nails. And then the eights moved south to my stomach. And then lower still. Soon her lips took over the movements. I gave up and did what I was told to do.

"I have some news for you about the Crespo case," Lourdes Soto said, her head resting on my chest.

"No business now. Let's enjoy the moment."

"*Good* news."

"Whatever it is can wait."

"Okay, but I've got sworn statements from two witnesses that the Russian threatened Crespo on several occasions and once attacked him with a knife."

"What? Who?" I sat up so quickly Lourdes nearly slid off the bed.

"Tomas Rivera and Lazaro Soler. They're on your witness list."

"Sure they are. I listed everybody who worked for Atlantic Seaboard, just to cover all the bases. But I've interviewed them, and they didn't see, hear, or know anything."

Lourdes propped herself on an elbow and ran a fingernail across my thigh. "Maybe you didn't smile when you asked the questions."

I wanted to believe her. And when we want to believe, we sometimes do. But Francisco Crespo never told me about being attacked. "Crespo told me he owed Smorodinsky some money, and they argued about it, but he said nothing about a knife."

"I'll give you the written statements. The Russian tried to slice Crespo's throat with a survival knife. You know, like Rambo used. Three rows of saw teeth, a hollow handle, and a spear point. Took Soler and Rivera to stop him, had to threaten him with a gun. Of course, you'll need their live testimony, and they're willing to come forward."

Three rows of saw teeth. The best lies are crammed with details, like the redheaded Anglo with the American flag tattoo I'd invented ten years before. "The police didn't find a knife, not at the scene or in Smorodinsky's belongings."

"They didn't *report* any," she corrected me. "A knife like that, maybe a cop slipped off with it. Maybe another worker did." She pushed me back into the pillows. "It happens."

Outside, the rain had stopped, but the mockingbird was still singing up a storm. He sounded like a bobwhite. My windows are open because I choose not to have central air. I don't want to live in a hermetically sealed tomb. I like the breeze and the smell of mango trees and the sounds of burglars in the bushes. I listened to the mocker and the rhythm of the paddle fan, *whompety-whomp*ing its endless circles. "If the two guys saw the attack," I said, after a moment, "we can get that into evidence, but I don't know about the threats. All hearsay, unless they're considered *res gestae* or excited utterances. How long before—"

"Three days. The Russian attacked him April thirteen. Then on the sixteenth, it happened again. Only no Soler and Rivera to stop it or witness it."

It was neat. All wrapped up like a Christmas package and delivered by one of Santa's elves. A naked elf who at this moment was resting her right breast on my forearm. A smart guy would shut up and take it all. He would conveniently forget that his own client admits attacking the Russian without provocation.

"I was going to keep Crespo off the stand and try it as a reasonable doubt case. Plant the seed that maybe somebody else came along and killed the guy. Now you're telling me the Russian attacked Crespo. Now, it's self-defense."

"Looks that way."

The bird quieted down. From across the hibiscus hedge, I heard a radio with a late-night talk show, Larry King interviewing a Hollywood starlet whose book discussed the sexual equipment of numerous leading men. Larry announced that Ross Perot was the next guest, but I didn't think the two segments were related.

"It'll work," I said, "if Crespo corroborates it."

"I think you'll find he will."

"What do you know that I don't but should?"

"Trust me."

How do you tell a naked lady you wouldn't trust her to change a ten into two fives?

You lie.

"I trust you all right, Lourdes, but I don't trust Yagamata. Somebody besides me is handling Crespo's defense, and it's got to be him. Yagamata's sending in the plays. I'm just supposed to call the numbers."

"What if he is? If he found the witnesses and told them to talk to me, why not—"

"Found? Paid is more like it. Let your star witnesses take a polygraph. If they pass, I'll use them."

She slid a hand up my leg, cupping it against the part of me that has a mind of its own.

"Why do that? Why look for reasons not to win?"

"It's one of my many flaws. I want to win, but I want to win fair and square."

"If you don't know whether or not they're lying, it's not unethical to put them on the stand, is it?"

"No. It's up to the jury to decide."

"And if you know they're lying . . ."

"I can't use them."

"So, forget the polygraph. Just let the jury decide. You have an obligation to your client."

More than she knew. A two-generation obligation. Emilia Crespo had been there for me and only asked one thing in return. *Protect my son.* Francisco Crespo had put his life on the line for me. Now I was being handed a way to make the first installment on my debt to both of them.

So easy.

Kill two burdens with one stone.

Maybe three. Yagamata would be happy, too. I'd made such a fuss about defending Crespo and not rolling over that Yagamata came up with a way to get him off. It's called suborning perjury. Maybe there'd be a bonus for my crafty work.

So why didn't I just take the ball and run with it?

Because I have an obligation to me, too. Sometimes I just need to know. I need to know the truth. It isn't supposed to be part of my job, and usually it's better not to know. But it just doesn't work for me. I wanted to know who killed Smorodinsky.

Why was Crespo willing to take a fall? And what was Yagamata covering up? There were just too many questions and too few answers.

"I can't do it, Lourdes."

"Why on earth not?" There was genuine astonishment in her voice.

"It's hard to explain. I just live by a code that isn't written down anywhere but tells me to do what I think is right. I make compromises like everybody else, and I sometimes break the rules, but usually only the little ones. I try to go through life doing the least damage possible. I drop quarters into tin cups and feed stray cats. I don't lie to the court or let witnesses do it. It may sound old-fashioned, but I don't cheat to win. As for Francisco Crespo, I'm not going to tank the case, and I'm not going to win it with perjured testimony, either."

No one applauded, and best I could tell, no bands struck up the national anthem. So I shut up and waited for my bedmate to show me her beatific smile, draw me to her bosom, and tell me how proud she was of my moral fiber.

Lourdes sat up and seemed to be looking for her clothes. The last I had seen them, they were scattered on the kitchen floor. She stood and turned away, leaving me watching the smooth, naked expanse of her flank. "You're just an overgrown Boy Scout, aren't you?"

I didn't answer and she continued, a tinge of sadness in her voice. "You want a merit badge and a pat on the back. You want to be told just how wonderful and decent you are. Okay, here it is. You're honest and noble and virtuous. You have principles and scruples and morals. You're all that and more."

"More?"

Her bare feet were already padding down the stairs as she called to me over her shoulder. "You're also a goddamn fool."

10

TO SPEAK THE TRUTH

Judge Herman Roth adjusted his eyeglasses, ran a hand over his shiny skull, and peered in the general direction of the twelve warm bodies filling the jury box. "Does each of you understand that a defendant is not required to prove his innocence or to furnish any evidence whatsoever, and that this right is guaranteed by the Constitution?"

Twelve heads bobbed yes.

"And does each of you promise not to hold it against this defendant if he chooses to exercise his constitutional right not to testify?"

The double negative notwithstanding, on cue, all the sheep baaed.

Sure, I thought. They've all heard of the Fifth Amendment, some technicality used by wily lawyers to keep racketeers out of jail. Jurors want to follow the law, they really do. And they'll answer all the questions correctly in *voir dire.* But behind the closed door, whether it's said openly or not, the thought is there. *Dadgummit, if I was innocent, I'd just get right up there and say so. What's that fellow hiding?* Every lawyer knows this, but there are simply times you cannot subject a client to cross-examination. It is often the most important decision a lawyer will make in a criminal case.

With Francisco Crespo, it was easy. If Crespo took the stand and told the story he had recited to me, he would convict himself. No doubt about it. So my original plan was to keep him sitting at the defense table looking frail and innocent while I took a whack at the state's witnesses and tried to ferret out some reasonable doubt. That morning, I had asked him whether he had forgotten to tell me about Smorodinsky threatening him with a knife three days before the fatal fight.

"Ay, el cuchillo. Three rows of saw teeth."

Those teeth again. At least they had their stories straight. "And on the sixteenth. Did he come at you again with this knife?"

"Would it get me off if I said he did?"

I like someone who thinks before answering.

"Maybe. But you never mentioned it to the cops and nobody found a knife. If the jury thinks you're lying, you'll be convicted for sure."

"Veintecinco años."

"Right, without parole, and it would be a damn shame, Francisco, because you didn't kill him. If you'd only tell me what happened . . ."

He shrugged and his neck disappeared inside the dress shirt I had just bought for him. I got him a new suit two sizes too large and a white shirt with a collar that would fit me. When Crespo dozed off during the judge's preliminary statement to the jury, his chin disappeared inside the shirt collar.

Emilia Crespo sat in the first row of the gallery, directly behind me. She gave us moral support plus a bag of homemade guava pastries. In the corridor that morning, she kissed Francisco and hugged me, but without the strength I remembered. Then she whispered a prayer in Spanish, crossed herself, and said again, *"Protégeme a mi hijo."*

I hugged her back and promised I would. I looked into her eyes. She had gotten old without my noticing it. Dark shadows clung to the folds below her eyes. Along the jawline, the skin was no longer taut. She moved slowly and seemed to have lost weight. A robust woman when I first met her—she carried *my* suitcase into the house that day years ago—she had shrunken with age.

Now Judge Roth was holding up a blue-backed document and waving it at the jury. "Does each of you understand that this piece of paper called the information is not evidence. It carries no inference of guilt."

Twelve heads nodded in unison. *But where there's smoke, there's fire. That sumbitch didn't get here by helping little old ladies cross the street.* Sometimes, I wonder why we even bother. Just round up the first six people you find and sit them in the box. Our juries wouldn't be any better or any worse.

Abe Socolow sat at the state's table, furiously taking notes, recording observations about each prospective juror on the twelve-square grid he had drawn on his legal pad. He was also trying to memorize each name before he began his questioning. All lawyers do that. *How about you, Mrs. Ferbergooble? Can you give the state a fair trial, Mrs. Ferbergooble?* We all love to hear our own names. If you don't believe it, you haven't been imprisoned in an eight-foot-square cubicle with a car salesman.

Socolow was good. He was always prepared, and once he worked with them, so were his witnesses. Once, when I was new at this and he was still handling misdemeanors, I defended a DUI case where my client caused an accident that didn't hurt anybody but ruptured his own car's radiator. Socolow's main witness, the investigating officer, testified that he smelled alcohol on my client's breath.

"Isn't it possible," I asked on cross-examination, "that what you smelled was antifreeze?"

"Sure," the cop replied, not missing a beat, "if that's what he was drinking."

Judge Roth was reciting his litany, asking if anyone had served on a jury before, if there were any policemen in the family, and if each juror would base his or her verdict solely on the testimony and the law. He received what he sought, mindless agreement. The judge droned on, hunched over the bench, a wizened old bird who liked running a courtroom better than poling for bonefish or whacking a little ball out of the sand or any other sane activity. He asked whether they would be more likely to believe testimony of police officers, and they all solemnly said no. Funny, I whispered *yes* because cops are the best liars.

I kept waiting for my favorite question as did Bill the Bailiff. Bill is a retired postal worker who's even older than Judge Roth and skinnier than Abe Socolow. We had a standing bet on the victim-of-crime question. I took "over"; he took "under." Although we only needed to seat six jurors plus two alternates, there were twelve prospects sitting in the box at all times. If more than six raised their hands, I would win the over, and Bill would bring me a quart of his homemade *cerviche,* bay scallops marinated in lime juice with onions, peppers, and cilantro. It's my one exception to the no-raw-fish rule. If fewer than six jurors raised their hands, I would bring him a lug of Saigon mangoes I would steal from neighborhood trees. An even six, and the bet would be a push.

"Any of you ever been a victim of a crime?" Judge Roth asked. Bill the Bailiff tugged his suspenders and winked at me.

Eight hands shot up, then slowly a ninth, a computer systems analyst for a department store chain. "Does it count if my car was broken into but not stolen?" he asked.

Judge Roth considered the question as if it were of momentous gravity. "Nothing stolen, you say?"

"Well, my gun, of course. A Colt Combat Commander .45 taken from the glove compartment."

Two other jurors nodded and murmured something about their guns being stolen in home burglaries.

The judge let out a low whistle and shook his head. "Never leave a gun like that in your car. Too valuable. Personally, I prefer something lighter, but not too small." He pulled up his fuchsia robe until it covered his bald head. We were now treated to a view of a sweat-stained armpit and a shoulder holster with a small pistol. With a palsied hand, the judge drew the gun, squinted one eye shut and aimed in the general direction of Francisco Crespo, who sat about two feet to my right. I leaned the other way but decided not to raise an objection.

"Colt Mustang 380," Judge Roth announced, using a two-hand grip now, the barrel bouncing up and down as if he stood on a pitching boat. "Only five rounds, but packs four times the knockdown power of the 25 ACP automatic."

A middle-aged woman juror—a registered nurse at Mount Sinai Hospital—raised her hand. "I think firepower is overrated, Your Honor. I just carry a Beretta 25 semiautomatic. Seven rounds and only weighs twelve ounces. Fits in my purse."

The judge nodded judiciously. "Light weight's an advantage,

no doubt about it, but with a twenty-five millimeter, you'd better hit the perp in a kill spot."

At this point, half the jurors were exchanging views on handguns. The court clerk, a black woman with a well-groomed Afro, told the stenographer she kept a Sig Sauer 230 in her gym bag to keep interlopers out of her spot in aerobics class. The stenographer was too busy typing to answer.

Bill the Bailiff looked gloomy as he moped over to the defense table to congratulate me. He hadn't won an under bet in two years. "A little less onion this time, Bill," I told him.

Finally, sensing that matters had careened off track, Judge Roth cleared his throat and plunged ahead. "Does any of you have a physical impairment that would keep you from serving on this jury?"

Nothing worse than your hardening of the arteries, I thought.

Eleven heads wagged no. "I got a pretty fair case of hemorrhoids," answered an airline mechanic in a blue work shirt.

"The bailiff will find you a pillow," Judge Roth said, dismissing the notion that an itch can keep you home. To get a medical excuse, a juror better qualify for last rites. There are just too few folks willing to spend a week with smart-alecky lawyers who ask nosy questions and try to trick them into believing that a degenerate slimebag is a misunderstood choirboy.

Finally, it was Abe Socolow's turn. Before he stood up, a middle-aged man in a gray suit and wire-rimmed glasses walked from the gallery to the prosecutor's table, leaned over, and whispered something in Socolow's ear. The state gets all the help. I only had my client, who was sound asleep, and my secretary Cindy, who sat behind me and selected jurors by their astrological signs. Marvin the Maven was still miffed with me and was spending the week in Divorce Court.

Socolow unfolded his long, lean body from the carved wood chair and approached the jury box. He wore his trial suit of undertaker's black, a white button-down shirt, and a black tie festooned with silver handcuffs. His sallow complexion had a hint of color today, and not from the sun. The start of a trial, the adrenaline flows, the heart picks up the pace. With Abe, it was an insatiable desire to win. Me? I just try not to embarrass myself.

"May it please the court." Abe bowed deferentially to Judge

Roth, who waved a liver-spotted hand signaling Socolow to begin. "This is the part of the trial known as *voir dire.*" Somehow Abe gave it four syllables, *voy-eur dy-ar.* "That's a fancy foreign phrase meaning 'to speak the truth.' Judge Roth has asked some preliminary questions, and now it's my turn, and then Mr. Lassiter's. Each of us wants you to simply speak the truth. Now, why do we ask these questions, some of which can be quite personal. To embarrass you? No. To get a jury biased in our favor? No. We merely want a fair and impartial jury . . ."

Maybe you do, Abe, but I once seated a blond flight attendant for the simple reason that she wasn't wearing a bra.

". . . a jury that will decide the case solely on the evidence and free from any prejudice that may result from their backgrounds."

Abe took up the rest of the morning asking everybody's occupation, whether any of their kinfolk had run-ins with the law, and whether they believed in the grand old American jury system. "Mr. Bolanos, you heard the judge tell you that, to adjudge the defendant guilty, you must find that the state proved its case beyond and to the exclusion of a reasonable doubt."

A hesitant nod. He knew there'd be a follow-up.

"And Mr. Bolanos, do you understand that beyond a reasonable doubt does not mean a shadow of a doubt, a fleeting doubt, an imaginary, illusory, or fanciful doubt?"

Bolanos nodded his profound agreement.

"To be a reasonable doubt, it must be . . ."

Reasonable, I figured.

"Solid, substantial, real—"

"Objection!" I was on my feet. "Counsel for the state is rewriting the jury instructions before our very eyes."

"Overruled. But that's quite enough on that issue, Mr. Socolow. Move along."

I sat down. I had lost the objection but won the point as Judge Roth ruled in the time-honored fashion of not offending either lawyer.

When it was my turn, I decided to be brief. I stood up, reintroduced myself, and shuffled my two-hundred-some pounds over to the rail. I ran a hand through my shaggy hair, showed my friendly grin, looked at the clock on the wall, and said, "Well, it seems the judge and the state attorney have asked all the good questions, and since it's a few minutes until noon, I just want to know who's ready for lunch."

I got a dozen raised hands and just as many smiles.

11

ONE POTATO, TWO POTATO

We empaneled a jury in the afternoon, and Judge Roth gave us the next day off so he could attend a judicial seminar, and we could polish our opening statements. I still didn't know what I was going to say. There was Crespo's original story, which was a lie and would convict him; there was Lourdes Soto's sequel, which was a lie but might acquit him; and there was the truth, which so far had managed to elude me. With nothing better to do, I tried to catch up on office work. My desk was covered with bulging files of undone chores, piles of unanswered mail, and various interoffice memos from the managing partner castigating me for failing to collect bills from our deadbeat customers whom we generally refer to as our angelic clients.

It was lunchtime and my partners at Harman & Fox were nowhere to be found. That is only partly accurate. They were not to be found on the thirty-second floor of their gleaming office building hard by Biscayne Bay. But if you checked the posh College Club, Metropolitan Club, or Downtown Club, you would find them feasting on Florida crab cakes with avocado butter, or fresh grilled swordfish with mango and black bean salsa, perhaps a sweet ginger flan for dessert.

I sat at my desk with a bacon cheeseburger growing cold and greasy inside its aluminum foil. Droplets of moisture had formed around my Styrofoam cup of iced tea and were leaving a perfect circle on my oak credenza. The credenza already was adorned with an Olympic symbol of old watermarks and was now working on abstract designs.

I took a bite out of the cheeseburger and left an oleaginous glob on my chin. I grabbed three files based on their proximity to my iced tea and went to work. There was the case of Coupon Carla, who started her career scavenging Dumpsters for canned sausage rebate slips, then ended in jail for a counterfeit kitchen coupon scheme. There was the pending appeal in the Russian Roulette case, where I represented a widow against a life insurance company. I lost when the judge determined that her husband's game became suicide after the third *click*. And there was the medical malpractice case of the stripper against the plastic surgeon for allegedly using silicone implants of two different sizes in her breasts. He denied liability and claimed the defect was an optical illusion. I was studying the photos—hey, somebody's got to do it—when Cindy buzzed.

"El creepo on line *dos, el jefe.*"

"What?"

"Crespo on line two, *su majestad.* I sure wish your clients had more class. Why can't you represent rock stars instead of chicken farmers and hoodlums?"

"Why can't you spell judgment with one 'e'?"

She bleated something at me, and I picked up the phone.

"Jake, you were always my favorite player on the team," Francisco Crespo said, "even though I knew you weren't very good."

I thought about saying thank you, but it didn't feel quite right.

"You always treated me well. Not like some of the ones making the big money. Never a 'Hello, Francisco.' Most of them never knew my name."

"Don't take it personally," I said. "Star athletes have been pampered so long they think the whole world exists to hand them towels and do their laundry."

"What I mean, Jake, is that I have respect for you. My mother loves you. She wanted me to be like you, and that was very hard to accept. For a long time after I came to this country, I was jealous of you even as I respected you. So, instead of trying to be you, I did just the opposite. I got into trouble here, just as I did in Cuba. But now, I want your advice. You are the finest *abogado* in all of Miami."

"That's flattering, but I'm not even the best on this floor."

"I'm going to listen to you, not Señor Yagamata."

"Then you'll have to tell me the truth."

He paused, and I heard a television game show in the background. The announcer was gabbing away in Spanish, and the audience was cheering.

"Maybe there are some other things I remember now," Francisco Crespo said.

I headed the convertible west on Luis Sabines Way, which used to be called Seventh Street, and headed into Little Havana. I passed Pedro Luis Boitel Avenue, General Maximo Gomez Avenue, and Luis Medina Munoz Marin Avenue. Then came Ronald Reagan Avenue. I don't know, so don't ask me.

Seventh Street turned into Eighth, Calle Ocho, and I hit every stoplight for thirty blocks. The heat rolled up in waves from the pavement and pressed down at me through the black canvas top. Maybe it was the blistering day that made me remember. Maybe it was the country music station I found while twisting the old AM radio dial. Or maybe it was because I was on my way to see Francisco Crespo, and he always brought back the memory of a night that would last forever.

It was a hot Sunday in September after a home game, a one-point win over the egg-sucking Oakland Raiders. Clem's was a tough country music place on Okeechobee Road between the airport and Hialeah. Half a dozen of my teammates were there, tossing darts, playing pinball, dropping quarters into the jukebox. But they all left early. Not me. Monday was a no-pads day, and tonight was for celebrating, so what's the rush? I had two tackles on special teams and set an Eastern Division record for Gatorade consumed by a reserve linebacker in the second half, and now was having too much fun and too many beers. Three long-legged, fluffed-hair escapees from secretarial school had captured me, and I was demonstrating the swim move—or was it the snatch?—for getting around an offensive lineman on a blitz.

Which is when Big Mouth started yapping. A beefy, sunburned, greasy-haired guy in jeans, cowboy boots, and a tank top. He'd been at the game, and he was goddamned tired of all the faggot Miami Dolphins, half of 'em jigaboos, who never covered the spread, then come waltzing in here, talking big and waving their dicks around like they owned the place.

I ignored him, which only made him angrier. He stepped closer and breathed down the neck of one of the would-be secretaries, a redheaded kid from Pensacola with electric blue eye shadow and Clearasil-covered zits, who was clearly frightened of the big sloppy guy smelling of beer and sweat. I didn't say a word until he ran his hand over her backside.

"Hey, pal, ease off," I told him, as low-key as possible.

"You gonna make me, you bench-warming, second-string cocksucker?"

"Extremely clever riposte," I told him. "Unfortunately, bench-warming and second-string are redundant, so you lose points for creativity."

"Fuck you and the horse you rode in on."

"Ah, a regular Cyrano de Bergerac in the wit department. But judging from your looks, pal, you know more about horse fucking than I do."

"What's that supposed to mean!" He was even uglier when he tried to think.

"Come on now, this is ridiculous," I said. "Tomorrow morning, you're going to wake up and feel like a shithead."

He shoved the girl aside and stepped into my space. "Who you calling a shithead?"

"Nobody. Look, you're making everybody uncomfortable."

"Too fucking bad."

Still looking at me, he reached out and grabbed the redhead's breast. She jumped away, and he laughed. Around us, people were backing away. Big Mouth turned to little old me, as gentle a guy as ever walked into a bar, and I smiled, then popped him one, a straight left hand that didn't have enough hip behind it. The punch bounced off a cheekbone made of granite. He blinked and backed up a step but didn't fall or yell for his mama. Then he came at me with a saloon swing, a lunging roundhouse right. I could have read the comics waiting for it to arrive. I blocked it with my left, knowing I'd have a bruise on the tricep tomorrow, then tried to nail him with a straight right hand. This time I caught him on the forehead, doing more damage to my hand than his head.

He spit and cursed at me, then turned and scooped a Budweiser bottle from a table, held it by the top, and smashed off the bottom on the back of a chair, just like in the movies. Then he came at me, jabbing the ragged bottle in front of him.

I backpedaled, and he kept coming.

Where the hell were the bouncers, the police?

I brushed up against a table and nearly fell over backward. He took a long, looping swipe, and as I whipped my head back, the jagged edge just passed in front of my eyes. I backpedaled some more, then stepped to my left, picked up a chair, and slung it at him. Instinctively, he raised his right arm. The chair knocked the bottle out of his hand, breaking the glass. He yelped, cursed my ancestry, and licked at blood coming from the webbing between his thumb and forefinger. "You cocksucker!"

"You thumbsucker," I said.

He bent over and reached into his boot. Either his feet were bothering him, or he was grabbing at something. His hand came out holding a gun.

It was a small gun.

Probably a .32.

But it didn't look small pointed at me.

The gun, blood dripping onto the butt, was four feet from my sternum. No one made a sound. Except for the Doobie Brothers on the jukebox, everything was quiet.

The song.

Now, I forced myself to remember the words, something about what a fool believes. I summoned up the tune. That's how I chased the memory away, blanked it out. Let the image of the gun fade into a melody. It always worked.

Except at night.

In dreams, that's always where the memory began.

Francisco Crespo lived just past LeJeune Road in a trailer park tucked between a rent-by-the-hour motel and a cemetery. Across the street was a full-service gun shop—sales, service, and paramilitary fashions. Tamiami Sunset Park is not home to the double-wide, king-size bed variety of modern mobile homes with microwave kitchens and cable-ready built-in TVs. It is a collection of rusted-out trailers propped on concrete blocks. Torn screen doors hang cockeyed on sweltering metal boxes jammed shoulder to shoulder on a lot with no trees or shrubs, and even the weeds are parched and trampled.

The only open spaces are filled with dilapidated lawn chairs, discarded mattresses, and sofas whose springs had long since sprung. An occasional clothesline crisscrosses from trailer to telephone pole. In a hurricane, the air would buzz with metallic vibrations, and the trailers would be torn loose, bashing each other like so many bumper cars. In a storm the caliber of Hurricane Andrew, which hit twenty miles south of here, they would be torn apart, turned into chunks of shrapnel mowing down everything in their path.

I parked the car and picked my way between trailers, listening to babies crying, televisions blaring, and a drunken couple arguing in slurred Spanish. It was one of those South Florida days with no clouds and a brutal, relentless sun. Our midday sun is a firestorm that jars the senses, and combined with the humidity, drains the life from folks who cannot escape to cooler climes. Today, not a breath of a breeze worked its way this far inland. I had left my suit coat in the car, and paused long enough to loosen my tie and roll up the sleeves of my blue oxford-cloth shirt.

I wended my way among the trailers, new home to immigrants from Caribbean islands and Central American countries, all trying to carve out a piece of the pie for themselves as so many had done before them. Some of the men bag groceries during the day and wait tables at night. Their wives work as domestics and take in laundry, and their kids pick up English and graduate from high school. Some will study business and law and medicine at the university. Others will hang out on street corners and bum smokes and deal crack. Others will just get along, making neither waves nor headway. In short, these folks soon will be just like everybody else.

I ducked under a soggy white slip and panties, hanging limp on a clothesline. It took a few minutes, but I found Crespo's trailer, one of those old models that looks like a thermos jug. I found it by staring right at its shiny aluminum side and having the glare of the sun nearly blind me. I closed my eyes and watched a parade of red and blue dots march across my eyelids. The trailer sagged onto deflated tires. Two folding chairs with torn straps sat under a red-and-white awning out front. Curtains were drawn on a side window. The front steps were two concrete blocks which led to a screen door. Inside, a dragonfly buzzed and snapped against the screen.

I thought there was movement inside the trailer when I banged on the door, but it could have been my imagination. I put my face to the screen, but it was dark inside. Sweat began to trickle down my neck.

"Francisco, it's me, the best *abogado* in town."

Nothing.

Suddenly, a radio was turned on inside. The tinny sound of a Cuban talk show, turned up too loud.

". . . para opinar sobre lo que dijo la señora esa que llamó hace un ratico para protestar sobre las fincas que ella perdió en Las Villas, que se las quitó Fidel a sus abuelos en 1961."

I called his name again.

". . . es que todo eso es 'lo que el viento se llevó.' Hay que 'hacer borrón y cuenta nueva.' Si no, nos vamos a quedar aquí treinta años más."

"Francisco. Are you in there?"

Still nothing. I listened some more. On the radio, the deeper voice of the *comentarista. "Yo estoy de acuerdo. Además, aquí en Miami dicen que si Cuba en realidad hubiera tenido tantas fincas como las que los exilados dicen que les fueron confiscadas por Fidel, que Cuba tendría que tener el tamaño de los Estados Unidos . . ."*

Then what sounded like a *pop-pop,* but it could have been the radio.

I let the dragonfly out and myself in.

It took a moment to get used to the darkness.

"Francisco."

The living room had a small sofa and cheap mica coffee table. A twelve-inch TV with rabbit ears sat on the floor. Yesterday's issue of *Diario Las Americas* was on the table, open to the sports page. The talk show was coming from the galley kitchen where a portable radio sat on the counter. But no one was there. I walked to the counter and turned off the radio. Two Key limes sat in a basket and half a dozen potatoes were soaking in a sinkful of water.

The only sounds now came from outside, the blaring of a television from across the row of trailers, the midday news in Spanish. The announcer competed with the voice of a woman in a nearby trailer, then silence, then her voice again, talking with someone on the phone. A dog barked, one of those small *yip-yap-yappers* that make you think the Vietnamese have the right idea. From somewhere on Tamiami Trail, a police siren wailed.

The door to the bedroom was partly open. Sweat rolled down my back, chilling me. It was no more than three steps to the bedroom. I took them slowly, listening for movement. The only sound from inside the trailer was the creak of metal under my feet.

I slowly pushed the door open, took a half-step into the room, and saw Francisco Crespo on the bed, lying on his back. Two blackened holes stained the front of his T-shirt. I had stepped on something that squished under my shoes, and I looked down at the floor. As I did, the door snapped back, smacking me a glancing shot on the shoulder and a solid *thwack* on the forehead. I heard something crack and hoped it was the paper-thin door. I had been hit harder by skinny wide receivers who know how to throw a crack-back block. But still I staggered backward, from the blow or the surprise, I didn't know which.

A shape rushed past me, a man dressed in brown or black who was either tall or short, young or old. He passed eight inches in front of my face, and I never got a look at him. I have always been dumbfounded at witnesses who give such god-awful descriptions to police when they're really trying. And now here I was, unable to focus on who just bashed me on the head and most likely put two holes in the chest of Francesco Crespo. I had only an instant to think about the wiry guy who used to bring me

Gatorade, who once put his life on the line for me, and who most recently trusted me to protect him. There was the flash of shame, the realization I had let him down, and worse, that somehow I had led him to his death.

I heard the screen door bang, realized I should do something, and took off. I skipped the concrete block steps and jumped to the ground, just catching sight of him from behind, weaving his way around an old Chevy slouched onto cinder blocks and a splintered wooden dinghy that sat on the ground. He *was* wearing brown, or maybe khaki, work pants and a matching shirt.

He looked stocky, but he didn't run stocky. Gliding steps. Coaches have a word for it. Fluid. No wasted motion. The head stays still, the arms pump but not too high. There's a word for my running style, too. Herky-jerky. All arms and legs, grunts and groans, working hard, getting nowhere fast. I was the slowest linebacker on the team, but not the dumbest. I made up for a lack of natural ability with decent instincts and a lot of hard work. I studied film till my eyes blurred, learned tendencies of offensive linemen and receivers, and generally knew a split second before the next guy where the play was going. I wished I had a playbook now.

The man in brown was a decent broken-field runner. He did a nifty job avoiding an overturned tricycle, a hibachi, and a woman in curlers with coppery red hair. I remembered the agility drill with the tires as I hopped the tricycle and hibachi but didn't try it with the woman, though she was nearly short enough. Ahead of me, the man ducked between two trailers, heading toward the outer boundary of the lot.

When I turned the corner, there was just a streak of brown, turning left between a pink-and-white trailer and a canal that separated the lot from the cemetery. I kept my eyes on the trailer and picked up my pace. Coach Shula always started summer practice with the twelve-minute run. Not a jog, a run, and in the ninety-degree heat, ninety-percent humidity, a lot of my teammates left their breakfast on the practice field. I may not have led the pack, but I never hurled either.

I made the turn and saw him scrambling on all fours near a live oak tree that bordered the canal. It occurred to me then what

I was doing. Here I was, without even a stick, a stone, or an Italian leather briefcase, and I was chasing a guy who had a gun. And had just used it. Yes, Abe Socolow, you're right. Sometimes circumstantial evidence is *very* persuasive.

I didn't know what I'd do if I caught him. He was thirty yards or so away when I saw him duck as he neared the tree, then . . . *whoosh* . . . my feet were swept out from under me. My body was jolted upright, my feet were off the ground, continuing their running motion like Wile E. Coyote, and I wondered who had crushed my Adam's apple. No one threw a flag or blew a whistle, and I crumpled to the ground, looking up to see the clothesline humming like a guitar string.

The sweat was pouring off me when I got back to Crespo's trailer. I gingerly walked into the bedroom, felt a squish beneath one foot, and looked down to see a potato splattered in pieces across the floor. It made no sense to me.

I was trying to swallow but couldn't. In football, a forearm across the throat is called a clothesline, for obvious reasons. As a linebacker, I had lots of chances to level receivers coming across the middle that way. Never did it intentionally, so why aren't the gods kinder to me?

I looked toward the bed. I half expected the body to be gone, like something from a Hitchcock movie. *Now, Mr. Lassiter, you say you saw Mr. Crespo with two bullet holes in him. Really, had you been drinking?* But Crespo was still there, lying on his back, hands beneath him. I rolled him over. The hands were tied at the wrists with baling wire. I felt for a pulse. Not a flicker. As I held his wrist, I saw a metallic glint in Crespo's palm. I pried open the fingers, and something fell out, rolling across the bed and onto the floor. I found it among the potato pieces—a gold rabbit holding an egg of what looked like brown glass flecked with gold. A loop that would have held a thin chain was fastened to the bunny's head. Somehow, I doubted that the gold rabbit was part of Francisco Crespo's personal jewelry.

I picked up Crespo's phone with two fingers and called the police, Abe Socolow, and Charlie Riggs. The cops were there first,

Abe next, and Charlie last, but he had to interrupt a med school lecture on figuring date of death by the extent of insect larvae in the corpse.

I was sprawled on the sofa holding my throat when Socolow came in. He took a look at the body and said, "Looks like somebody saved the state some money."

"Abe, do you try to be an asshole, or does it come naturally?"

"Oh, excuse me, counselor, I forgot. This was one of your minions. Presumed innocent until proven an asshole." He looked at the red welt forming on my neck, did a double take, and smiled. If I'd been shot, he'd probably bust a gut laughing. "Somebody doesn't know you, Jake, they'd say you struggled with your client, then shot him."

"Somebody doesn't know you, Abe, they'd say you were a supercilious son of a bitch. In fact, somebody who knows you would say the same thing. So, before you shoot off your mouth anymore, let me tell you something. Francisco Crespo was more than a client. He was a friend, and you keep it up, the only arrest you'll make today is for assault on a state official."

"Okay, okay, keep your cool. Don't be so touchy." He wiped his forehead with a handkerchief and turned to a uniformed cop. "Must be the weather. Makes everybody crazy."

An assistant medical examiner opened the door, followed by Doc Riggs. A homicide detective came in, then the crime scene investigators, then a man in a gray suit who looked familiar, but I couldn't quite place him. Maybe he was a homicide detective I didn't know. Cops like to travel in flocks, stand around and shoot the bull, reminisce about other cases, and gossip about who's screwing the new divorcée in communications. One of the lab technicians was shining a laser at every nook and cranny in the trailer, trying to pick up invisible fingerprints. Another was using a portable computer to draw the crime scene.

"What the hell was he doing, making potato salad in the bedroom?" Socolow asked nobody in particular.

Charlie Riggs scratched his beard. "A silencer," he said.

Socolow wrinkled his forehead. He didn't enjoy someone else figuring out something first. The man in the gray suit whispered something to Abe Socolow, and then it occurred to me. He was the guy in the courtroom who came up to Socolow during *voir dire*. Now Socolow was listening attentively. Something in Abe's body language showed deference, a trait for which he was not well known.

"The gunman used a potato for a silencer," Riggs continued. "Or two potatoes, actually, one for each shot."

"A potato silencer?" Abe Socolow repeated, incredulous.

"Messy, but effective," Charlie said.

Somewhere in my mind, a children's rope-skipping rhyme was singing to me. *One potato, two potato, three potato, four . . .*

The man in the gray suit walked to the sofa where I was sitting. He had a lean leathery face and walked on his toes. He wore wire-rimmed glasses, and his body gave the impression of rangy strength underneath the baggy business suit. His hair was short, dishwater brown, and had a cowlick at the peak of his forehead. A vein protruded from his neck as he spoke to me. He asked me to tell my story, and I did. He tossed a pad and pen on the sofa and pointed with an index finger. "Would you write it out and sign it," he said. He didn't make it sound like a question. The lawyer in me said not to do it. But now I was a client, and I knew I didn't kill Crespo, so I scribbled a statement, going through it step by step, then signed my name, putting an "Esq." at the end of it, which sounded more impressive than ex-linebacker.

When he asked whether I could identify the assailant, I told the truth for once. When he asked whether I had left anything out, I lied. Then it was my turn. I asked his name, and he handed me a card.

Robert T. Foley and a phone number, area code 703. No gold stars, embossed titles, or even an address. I've known some heavy-hitting businessmen like that. Maybe you're just supposed to *know* who they are. That might work with Galileo or da Vinci, but Robert T. Foley didn't mean anything to me.

Socolow was scowling. Silencers meant assassinations, organized crime, or Colombian cowboys. Not just a murder of a nobody in a trailer park. Even worse, a potato silencer was screwy enough to interest the newsboys. Socolow looked straight at Charlie Riggs. "You can buy a silencer on the street for a hundred bucks. Why would anyone use a potato?"

Five potato, six potato, seven potato, more.

"Maybe he wasn't going to kill Crespo," Charlie said, "at least not here. Maybe he wanted to talk to him, didn't like how it was going, and made a hasty decision. Maybe Jake spooked him by coming to the door. Or maybe it was just a botched robbery."

Socolow looked around the tiny trailer. "What would you steal from this place?"

Nobody answered him.

"Jake, you know anybody who would want to kill your client?"

I shrugged. Inside my pants pocket a gold bunny rabbit was growing warm. "Maybe Vladimir Smorodinsky had a friend."

"My thought exactly," Socolow responded. "Maybe just a revenge killing, one slimeball's pal knocking off another slimeball. Crespo tell you anything we ought to know?"

"I don't know any more than you do, Abe." I'm not sure why I didn't tell Socolow and his gray-suited friend about the gold rabbit. Part of it had to do with Emilia Crespo. She had trusted me to protect her son, and I had failed. I was responsible. Part of it was Francisco Crespo. He had trusted me, too. He took my advice, and my advice killed him. I had owed him something—everything—and I let him down. Now, it seemed, I owed him even more, and I needed to set things straight on my own.

Finally, part of it was my natural suspicion of authority. I remembered the reporter's line from Graham Greene's book about the French-Indochina war. Something about not giving information to the police because it saves them trouble.

Socolow turned back to Charlie Riggs. "Doc?"

"Who knows? Maybe it was the weather. It's well known that violent crime goes up seven to ten percent during a heat wave."

"C'mon, Doc. You can do better than that."

"Sapiens nihil affirmat quod non probat."

Socolow squeezed his eyes shut. He looked like he had a migraine.

"A wise man states as true nothing he cannot prove," Charlie translated.

"Good advice for opening statement," Socolow agreed, "but I'm looking for some leads here."

Charlie shrugged and Socolow turned away to speak to one of

the cops. Before opening his mouth, Socolow swung back to Charlie Riggs. "Where?"

"Where what?" Charlie asked.

"The potato silencer. Where was it used before?"

"Why, Russia, of course," the bearded wizard said.

12

ART HISTORY 101

Charlie Riggs shoved an oversized book in front of me, tapped the cover with a pudgy forefinger, and leaned back in his chair, chewing a cold pipe.

"Not another one, Charlie. My eyes are bleary, and I need a beer."

"Perhaps if you'd had a well-rounded education, this wouldn't be necessary."

"Hey, I studied every linebacker's assignment in the split six and knew every cheerleader by the shape of her thighs, so give me a break."

Charlie *tsk-tsk*ed his chagrin at the decline of the liberal arts. We were on the second floor of the downtown library, huddled into a corner with every book Charlie could find on Russian art museums. After five hours, everything looked alike. Still, I worked, looking at pictures and turning pages like a robbery victim scanning mug shots.

I had told Charlie that Soto's painting looked "sorta, I dunno, modern." Charlie regarded me skeptically, then gave me a crash course on Russian art at the turn of the century—Korovin, Vrubel, Konchalovsky, Mashkov, and a bunch of other names that were meaningless to me—but that was only the beginning. The Russians were great collectors. Prior to the Revolution, Charlie told me, the nobility had gathered the finest artwork from throughout Europe. So here I was, leafing through books I had successfully managed to avoid in pursuit of more or less higher education. We had finished the Italians, Dutch, Germans, English, and Spanish, and were halfway through the French. I had overdosed on winged horses, Madonnas, and naked women who obviously never took high-impact aerobics.

"If you were able to describe the painting with any degree of particularity, I could identify it, and I do not pretend to be an expert. Even a basic class in art history—"

"Friday afternoons from three to six," I said.

"What?"

"Art History 101. Fall semester, every Friday from three to six P.M. Conflicted with road trips and Happy Hour chugging contests. Also kept out the guys who just wanted to meet coeds, which was the primary purpose in the days when we figured a woman's chastity could be determined by her major."

"No?"

"Sure. Art majors did and business majors didn't. Petroleum engineering, no way. Elementary education, maybe, but you had to talk marriage first. The gals in creative writing would, especially during their Anais Nïn phase."

Charlie slipped his pipe into a buttoned pocket of his blue chambray shirt, harrumphed, and removed his crooked eyeglasses. He fiddled with the fishhook that held them together, breathed on the lenses, wiped them off on his shirt, and slid them absentmindedly on top of his bushy head. His eyes were weathered, the crinkled face a tanned hide, and he was starting to show his age.

"You miss your nap today, Charlie?"

"I can still outfish and outwork you, and don't forget it."

Outthink me, too, he could have said.

Charlie Riggs was as close as I had ever come to having a father, and my look must have betrayed some of the feelings I usually tucked deep inside, because he turned away and slid the glasses back down. Charlie limited his emotions to a healthy academic inquiry, and it wouldn't do to give him a hug and get misty-eyed over personal feelings. But the truth for me was simple. I loved my Granny who raised me after my father was killed and my mom took off, and I loved Charlie who taught me just about everything worth knowing.

Clearing his throat, Charlie adjusted the reading lamp, tilting the shade so that the light shined directly on a slightly musty copy of the book, *French Paintings from the Hermitage.* If I didn't get anything else from the book, I could bench press it a few times and have a healthy workout.

"Don't you have the Cliffs Notes version?" I pleaded.

"Read," the doctor ordered.

I groaned, stood up, did a few spinal twists and some deep knee-bends, then dropped to the floor, and just to get the blood flowing, powered through twenty-five one-armed push-ups with each arm. Except for my breathing, I didn't make any noise, so the librarian didn't say boo.

Then I sat down, groaned again, and opened the book. I'd already pored through directories of the Pushkin Museum, the State Picture Gallery, the Museum of Modern Western Art, the Gorky Museum, the Tretyakov Gallery, the Russian Museum, and the Petrodvorets Palace. I had seen gloomy paintings of ships on a stormy sea by a Dutch artist, some dead birds entitled *Trophies of the Hunt* by an artist from Flanders, which must be a place I missed in geography, more virgins with child than I could count, and some fine Italian noble ladies with graceful necks and melancholy pusses.

I studied portraits of generals from the War of 1812, handsome bemedaled chaps with generous mustaches and muttonchops. I looked at Monet's *Boulevard des Capucines,* but couldn't remember it fifteen minutes later. I saw *The Madonna and Child* by da Vinci and listened to a fine lecture by Charlie Riggs on the High Renaissance style.

"Doesn't the Madonna's tender gaze reflect the humanist dreams of the ideal man and a harmonious life?" he queried.

"Took the words out of my mouth," I agreed.

Now I was looking at a bunch of stuff by Van Gogh, Gauguin, and Toulouse-Lautrec, but I still didn't find the painting I was looking for.

"What style was it?" Charlie asked for the umpteenth time. "Try to describe it more completely."

"Green."

"Green?"

"Like a lawn. And two figures, a man with large hands about to grab a nude woman. That's all I remember. The faces were not well defined, sort of crude. Like I told you, Soto was going to say more about it, the name of the painter maybe, but Lourdes stopped him."

I was leafing through some haystacks by Monet, some ripe women by Degas, some still lifes by Cézanne, and a bunch of Tahitians by Gauguin. Still, no husky guy about to pounce.

I stretched my arms over my head, intertwined the fingers of each hand, and cracked my knuckles with the clatter of a cue ball on a break. "Damn, I'm tired," I announced, a tad too loud, and a young woman in a ponytail working at a nearby carrel gave me a grad student's indignant glare.

Charlie didn't notice. He was gazing into the stacks, his eyes unfocused. "The ugliness of murder and the beauty of art." He sighed.

"What?"

"The irony, Jake, that the clue to man's brutality may be buried in such works of beauty." He pointed his empty pipe at the pile of books. "When I see all this, my first thought is how far we've come. Five million years ago, our ancestors were tree-dwelling apes in tropical rain forests. The strongest males ruled by either killing or banishing their rivals. When the climate cooled, the apes came out of the trees, stood erect, and foraged for food, mostly seeds. Still, the largest and fiercest controlled the others by force. Another two million years or so later, the climate cooled again, and the australopithecines developed. They were meat eaters, and despite their evolution and loose society, they were still violent toward one another."

I wasn't sure where Charlie was going, but between his discussion of hungry apes and images of Cézanne's fruit platters, I realized my stomach was growling. "I'm sure there's a point to this, Charlie."

"They are the forebears of our genus, Homo. They developed into man."

Charlie withdrew a packet of cherry-flavored tobacco from a

buttoned shirt pocket and tamped a wad into the bowl of his pipe. "We've come so far as a species," he said. "We've built bridges and machines that fly out of the solar system. We compress a billion bits of information onto an infinitesimal wafer. We produce ageless works of beauty, such as you see before you, and yet . . ."

I was starting to catch on. "We still kill each other. That's what you mean, isn't it, Charlie?"

My old friend didn't say a word, so I must have gotten it right. I thought about Vladimir Smorodinsky and Francisco Crespo, two men descended—like all of us—from Charlie's tree-dwelling apes. I thought of Francisco's body lying face up, bound and bloodied, on the bed. I was the one to tell his mother, hold her as her knees gave out, sit with her as she cried, and listen all night as she remembered Francisco as a *niño* in Cuba, when the air was still sweet with future promise.

"Can you find who did this to my son?" she had begged me.

I told her the truth. I didn't know, but I could try. I showed her the gold rabbit. She had never seen it before.

Now I thought of Smorodinsky, too. Somewhere, did he have a mother crying in the night? Or a *brother.* What was it Matsuo Yagamata had said? Something about Smorodinsky's brother being well versed in Russian art. And Severo Soto knew something, too. He told me the two brothers ran Yagamata's St. Petersburg operation.

Only he had used the old name, Leningrad. An operation that had to do with art. Then Soto proudly showed me a painting his daughter didn't want to talk about.

Which is why we were in a library looking at pretty pictures.

Because you have to start somewhere.

"Do you think, Charlie, that your line of work has made you cynical?"

"Why? Because I have concluded that evolution of our species stopped somewhere short of true civilization?"

"That, for one thing."

Charlie Riggs produced an old-fashioned wooden match maybe six inches long and flicked it with a brown thumbnail. The tip burst into a flame of red phosphorous, and Charlie lowered it into the bowl of his pipe, while drawing air through the stem. Nearby, the grad student raised her head and squinted at us from above the top of her carrel, a turtle peeking out of its shell.

"Really!" she whisper-shouted. "You're not allowed—"

"The smoking ordinance doesn't apply to him," counseled the lawyer who lurks inside of me. "He's grandfathered in."

Charlie exhaled a cloud of sweet tobacco and said, "We kill, and like the apes, not only for food. We kill our own kind. We kill for greed and anger and lust. Five million years of evolution, and the beast is still within us."

"C'mon, Charlie. Don't be such a curmudgeon. Enjoy what we have. Life's too short."

He smiled and jabbed at me with the bowl of his pipe. "Hippocrates said it first," he told me.

"Said what?"

"Ars longa, vita brevis. Then Longfellow picked up the expression." Charlie dropped his voice into a deep rhythmic chant:

" 'Art is long, and time is fleeting,
And our hearts, though stout and brave,
Still, like muffled drums, are beating
Funeral marches to the grave.' "

I was just about to applaud when a shadow crossed the table.

"I'm going to report the both of you," the grad student hissed at the county-approved decibel level. "Talking *and* smoking! Why don't you go to a tavern?"

"Excellent idea," I agreed.

She huffed off, clutching a book to her breasts, and Charlie puffed on, oblivious, still thinking about homicidal apes and the brevity of life, I supposed.

"Hey, Charlie. We can't solve mankind's problems. Let's just figure out who murdered Francisco Crespo."

The old wizard's eyes cleared. *"Cui bono?* Who stands to gain?"

"Somebody who couldn't let him reveal who ran that forklift through Smorodinsky, and why."

"And what is there that links Crespo and Smorodinsky?"

I walked through it. "Both men worked for Yagamata, a guy who likes Russia and collects priceless art. Crespo attacked Smorodinsky, but somebody else finished him off. Somebody killed Crespo using a fairly ridiculous Russian method of silencing the gunshot. A lady P.I. with black hair and molten eyes offers her help and her body without the usual preliminaries . . ."

Charlie raised his bushy eyebrows. *"Mores,"* he sighed, shaking his head.

I'm not the kind of guy to kiss and tell, but in retrospect the loving of Lourdes seemed more business than pleasure. "The P.I.'s father is Severo Soto, who also employed Crespo and happens to be a Russia-hater. So Crespo is linked to both Yagamata and Soto."

Charlie beamed. When a student passes his oral exams, the teacher is pleased. "What conclusions have you reached?"

"None yet. You're the one who taught me not to jump too fast. The wise man keeps his trap shut, et cetera, et cetera."

He nodded happily, and I kept thumbing through the book of French paintings when I stopped at two naked men on a lawn. The same green, the same muscular build with few facial characteristics. The men were rolling balls across the grass. "Charlie, there's something about this one. It's the same artist, I'm sure."

"*A Game of Bowls* by Henri Matisse," he said. "Part of the French collection at the Hermitage."

I scanned the next few pages. Some nudes, a red room, a blue tablecloth, a bouquet of bright flowers. All by Matisse. And then there it was. The man, oversize hands extended, reaching toward the naked woman who tried, futilely, to crawl away.

"*Satyr and Nymph,*" Charlie Riggs said, studying the page.

"Russia and Cuba," I told him.

Charlie ordered his hog snapper broiled and well done. I chose yellowtail sautéed with a mess of onions and green peppers. We were at Tugboat Willie's on the Rickenbacker Causeway, halfway between the city and Key Biscayne. The fish was fresh, the beer cold, and a breeze riffled the palm trees as we sat on the front porch, the sun a forest fire setting in the west.

"We could tell Socolow," I suggested weakly, hoping Charlie would veto the idea.

"Tell him what?"

"What we know from our research."

"Which is what?"

I had drained my first beer and was working on the second. "The artwork, Charlie. Matsuo Yagamata shows off a gold choo-choo train inside an egg that's supposed to be in a Moscow museum. It's probably worth more than two million, based on the sale of the Pine Cone Egg for a million eight at Christie's in Geneva a couple of years ago, and the train is funkier. Then there's Severo Soto, one of our town's most famed anticommunists. He keeps a priceless painting by Matisse in his study. Only problem, the painting is owned by the Russians and, last time anyone checked, it was in the Hermitage in St. Petersburg. Francisco Crespo, whose idea of jewelry is a Timex watch, dies holding a miniature gold rabbit, which you say was made by the same artist who made Yagamata's egg—"

"Carl Fabergé."

"And was worn as a pendant by an empress . . ."

I reached for one of the books Charlie had checked out of the library. He had marked the page. There was a photo of a small gold bunny holding an egg made of flecked aventurine. It was an Easter gift to Empress Alexandra in 1913. I was convinced that Crespo was not the empress's distant cousin to whom the bunny would have passed.

"So what does it all mean to you?" Charlie asked patiently.

"It's confusing. All this Russia stuff. Two men dead. Famous art popping up all over. I don't know. It doesn't add up."

Charlie sipped at a glass of wine. For the occasion, he had chosen something white, light, and French, believing, I supposed, that Matisse had joined us at the table. Between sips, he dug into his dried-out fish and asked, "Who's in charge of the Crespo investigation?"

"Socolow. You know that."

"Then, who was the gentleman in the trailer to whom Socolow showed such deference?"

I love Charlie, but he can be a pain. Never comes right out

and tells you anything. Always a bunch of questions, dragging it out of you. "I don't know. He gave me his card." I fumbled inside my wallet and found it. "Foley. He's from out of town."

Charlie raised his chin, scratched his beard, and peered at me through the bottoms of his bifocals. I answered the question that wasn't asked. "You're right. We ought to find out who he is."

Tugboat Willie's is not the kind of place to whip out a cellular phone at your table. It would interfere with the banjo music and peg you as an insufferable yuppie. I got up from the table, skillfully avoided two stray cats that hang around the porch, and made my way to the pay phone by the kitchen. I was greeted by steamy garlic smells and the clatter of pans. I studied the card again. Printed, not embossed. Black ink on white paper. Nothing fancy:

ROBERT T. FOLEY
(703) 482-1100

It was after six o'clock. If it was an office, I might get the answering service. I dialed the number, putting the charge on a credit card. Where the hell was 703 anyway?

"Good evening," the sweet-voiced lady said. "Central Intelligence Agency."

13

THE RABBIT JUMPED OVER THE MOON

I spent all day Monday interviewing new clients, but my heart wasn't in it. Some lawyers are great at bringing in business. Schmoozers and self-promoters, they are our rainmakers. They have an ability to terrify and mollify clients in the same conversation. First, in somber tones, they magnify the gravity of the harm if expert legal counsel is not immediately retained in this most complex and perilous of legal matters. Then they confidently explain how Harman & Fox recently extricated another wretched soul from a similar predicament, and for a small fortune, could work the miracle once again.

A good lawyer is part con man, part priest—promising riches, threatening hell. The rainmakers are the best paid among us and have coined a remarkably candid phrase: *We eat what we kill.* Hey, they don't call us sharks for our ability to swim.

Bringing in business is not my strong suit. I have a small network of jailbirds, hospital interns, and bail bondsmen who send cases my way, but generally, I work for the firm's clients. Like Atlantic Seaboard Warehouse and the legal problems therein. This morning, though, I was making a halfhearted attempt to build my own practice. Joaquin Evangelista, an ex-client who took a fall for grand larceny—parrot theft—had referred a young couple to me about a civil suit. A nice favor from a guy who was doing time, but Joaquin didn't blame me for losing the case.

After putting my virtuous client on the stand to swear that he'd never seen any cockamamie cockatoo, the prosecutor brought the bird into the courtroom for rebuttal. "Hello, Joaquin Evangelista," the feathered witness announced brightly.

Today I was staring out the window at a foamy three-foot chop curling across the reef at Virginia Key and pretending to take notes as Sheldon and Marilyn Berger told me they wanted to sue their rabbi. Sheldon owned a pet store, which probably explained how he knew Evangelista, who called himself an aviary consultant, rather than a bird thief. Sheldon was in his early thirties and had dark hair in that trendy short, brush look. He wore cordovan loafers with no socks, white slacks, a polo shirt, and a blue sport coat. Marilyn Berger, his bride of seven weeks, had streaked blond hair done in the wrinkled look. She let a cigarette dangle from the corner of her mouth, but she didn't remind me of Lauren Bacall. I watched the cigarette flap up and down as she told me the story. As I listened, I drew two stick figures, a man and a woman, on my yellow pad.

"The *schlepp* was an hour and a quarter late for the wedding," Marilyn explained. "It was *sooo* embarrassing. I mean all our friends were just wondering, like was Shelly getting cold feet."

"I was getting drunk," Sheldon said with a sly smile.

"So were half the guests," his bride chimed in. "Daddy calculated that, at the prices the country club charged, the rabbi cost us an extra five hundred twelve dollars in liquor."

"Plus the band's overtime," Sheldon reminded her.

"Of course, darling." She patted his arm as you might a puppy. "The band had to stay an hour longer. Another three fifty."

I drew a picture of a Beretta nine-millimeter semiautomatic. "Why was the rabbi late?"

Marilyn leaned forward in her chair as if to share a secret. "He says we told him two o'clock, but I know we said one, because I told Sheldon to tell him one. If you ask me, the rabbi had another wedding at one. He just stacked us up, like the gynecologist."

I managed to draw fifteen miniature bullets streaking from

the gun barrel toward the man and woman. "Anything else?" I asked. "Any other damages besides the liquor bill and the band?"

Marilyn looked at Sheldon and exhaled a gray stream of smoke into his face. "Well, of course, it gave me a case of stress and severe mental anguish," she said.

"Of course," I said sympathetically.

Marilyn leaned toward me again. "I've read that stress can cause everything from wrinkles to bad breath."

"You don't have wrinkles," I said.

Sheldon was fidgeting, crossing and uncrossing his legs. "It practically ruined the honeymoon."

"Cancún," Marilyn said.

I scribbled some more, drawing sombreros on each of the bullet-riddled stick figures. "Did you get off?" I asked Marilyn.

"What?"

"Your wedding night? Didja come?"

The color drained from her face. Her mouth dropped open. The cigarette stuck to her lower lip. Bright red lipstick covered the top of the filter.

"I see this as a lost consortium case," I announced gravely. "Now, if you couldn't get off on your wedding night, or if Shelly here was so bummed out he couldn't get it up, I see some big bucks."

Sheldon grabbed both of his wife's hands. "Honey, that's what it might have been. . . ." She dipped a shoulder and shook him off like O. J. Simpson shedding a tackler.

"We'll get the best expert witnesses," I continued. "Now if we're talking the whole honeymoon, or better yet, continuing to this very day, we'll get you into therapy, counseling, sex surrogates."

"Sex surrogates?" Marilyn Berger cried out, crushing her cigarette in a Miami Dolphins commemorative plate, circa 1973.

"Sex surrogates," Sheldon repeated, hitting a high note, nodding in my direction. Here was a man who understood the legal process.

"You didn't videotape, by any chance?" I asked.

"The ceremony?" Marilyn asked, still dazed.

"No, the honeymoon, if you get my drift. A lot of newlyweds

these days get a camcorder as a gift and find a real quick use for it. But not too quick, eh, Shelly?"

Marilyn Berger was straightening her dress and shooting sideways glances at her husband. "Darling, I think we should leave now."

He seemed to want to discuss the case further, but he stood up a split second after his bride.

"Sheldon," I said, pointing at him, "you might want to keep a bedroom scorecard if you're serious about this."

"Scorecard?"

"Balls, strikes, errors, that sort of thing."

"Sheldon!" she commanded, and he followed her out the door.

I could have used the work, but I prefer cases that I believe in. Best is to have a client you like, a cause that is just, and a check that doesn't bounce. Two out of three and you're ahead of the game. There are a lot of frivolous suits these days, and I didn't need to add to the bunch. I used to think that the courthouse was the little guy's haven, the place where the multinational corporation stood on the same footing with Joe the shrimp fisherman. In the past, lawsuits have righted some wrongs. Product safety, civil rights, and consumer protection cases have all expanded individuals' rights. But the pendulum has swung the other way. An inmate who killed five people including his two children sued the state for denying him rehabilitation after lightning knocked out the satellite dish that carried public television. He claimed the programs on commercial channels were too violent. Then there was the man who sued his father for failing to attend his grandson's communion. He asked for one hundred million dollars for anxiety and depression. Parents whose seventh-grader came in second in a school spelling bee sued, claiming she had correctly spelled horsy, or is it horsey? And, in the time-is-of-the-essence department, concertgoers sued Latin heartthrob Julio Iglesias, claiming he was two hours late taking the stage. Maybe Julio and the rabbi were having drinks together.

The courts are not equipped to handle all of society's problems. They have enough trouble with a simple breach of contract to sell a hundred widgets from the Acme Corporation to the Zebra Company. So when I have a choice, I try not to add to the mountain of silly suits. Besides, today, I had a dinner date.

I was dipping the crunchy Italian bread into the olive oil when he sat down, drew a vinyl notepad and a ballpoint pen from his suit pocket, and started talking.

"Do you have it with you?" Robert T. Foley asked.

"The antipasto is very nice," I answered. "I'm particularly fond of the cold eggplant."

"Where is the rabbit?"

"The veal porcini, too, and the pasta is very good. But no rabbit on the menu."

"Don't jerk me around, Lassiter. Where is it?"

I laughed and took a bite of the oiled bread. Foley removed his wire-framed glasses and cleaned them on the napkin. He was still wearing the gray suit, or its twin brother. Maybe they're standard issue for federal agencies. He was in his late forties and looked in shape, a lean body and a creased, outdoorsy face. He stared hard at me. "The rabbit," he repeated.

"The rabbit jumped over the moon," I said.

"Do you find this funny?"

The waiter brought the menus, but Foley waved him off before he could tell us the specials. I said, "You're a spy, right? Like in the movies. A spook? And here we are at Domenico's in Coral Gables, but the waiters are speaking Italian, so maybe it could be some place in Rome, and you ask, 'Where is the rabbit,' like it's some code. So I answer . . . Oh, never mind."

Foley didn't crack a grin. Maybe it wasn't that funny after all.

"I'm not a spy," he said with apparent boredom. "I compile reports on subjects of concern to national security."

"Like a *Marielito* killed in a trailer park?"

"I am not at liberty to tell you the parameters of the investigation."

"And I'm not at liberty to show you my gold bunny rabbit."

The waiter returned and I ordered the antipasto and the veal with mushrooms and pine nuts. Foley asked for coffee, black. When the waiter left, Foley lowered his voice. "You're withholding evidence in a homicide."

"Out of your jurisdiction. That's Socolow's problem."

"I'm going to be *your* problem, pal, if you don't cooperate."

"I'm willing. I just want to know what's going on. That's why I called you, and that's why I told you about the rabbit."

He gave a little snort that was supposed to be a laugh. "That's *all* you want? Information is my stock in trade."

"Okay, so deal with me. Who killed Crespo?"

"Who gives a shit?"

"I do. And so do you, or you wouldn't have shown up at the scene."

He shrugged. "Crespo murdered a Soviet national we'd had under surveillance. It relates to an ongoing investigation of an international criminal conspiracy." Foley grudgingly peeled off a piece of Italian bread and took a dry bite. "That's all I'm going to say, got it?"

"Crespo didn't do it. He was set up to take the fall, and for a while, he went along. When he didn't—"

"Not my jurisdiction, remember? Go tell Socolow."

"But Crespo was innocent. Somebody else killed your Russian. Doesn't that interest you?"

The waiter brought the antipasto and Foley's coffee. I sliced a piece of buffalo mozzarella that was relaxing on a sliver of juicy red tomato.

Foley sipped at his coffee and said, "I'm more interested in what he was doing while he was alive."

"Then you should be investigating Yagamata. He called the shots. You've got to know that."

Foley looked at me over the rim of the cup. "Like I said, I'm through talking. You have something for me, give! If not, I've got other things to do."

I was nibbling at the marinated mushrooms when it dawned on me. "I get it. You *are* investigating Yagamata. That's what you can't tell me, right?"

"I can neither confirm nor deny the existence or nonexistence of an ongoing investigation."

"Then I can't tell you about the bunny rabbit . . ."

"Suit yourself."

"Or," I said, dropping a line into the water, "the priceless artwork that should be in Russia but is showing up right here in Mia-muh town."

They may train them not to show emotion, but the central nervous system doesn't always listen. His eyes gave a little blinkety-blink behind the glasses. "What art?" he asked, a mite too delicately.

"A Fabergé egg that's supposed to be in Moscow, not in a mansion on Palm Island. A Matisse that's in the Hermitage according to the guidebooks, but is hanging in an *exilado's* study in Little Havana. Not to mention the trinket I told you about, the gold rabbit once worn by an empress."

He screwed up his face, adding some new lines. He drained his coffee. "Okay, Lassiter, let's take them one at a time. Did Crespo give you the rabbit pendant?"

In a manner of speaking, he handed it to me, I thought. "Later. First, tell me what's going on."

He sat there thinking about it. Finally he said, "You know anything about art?"

Now where had I heard that before? "Sure, I've been taking a crash course."

"Yeah, well, it better include some arithmetic."

I gave him my big-dumb-guy look. It isn't hard to do.

"Dollars, Lassiter. Very major dollars. At Christie's in New York not long ago, a Japanese industrialist named Ryoei Saito paid eighty-two million dollars for Van Gogh's *Portrait of Dr. Gachet*. A few days later, at Sotheby's, he bought Renoir's *At the Moulin de la Galette* for seventy-eight million. Do you understand what I'm saying?"

"Yeah. Vinnie and Pierre must really be pissed."

"Two paintings, Lassiter. A hundred sixty million dollars! And legitimate sales are just the tip of the iceberg. You know anything about the international trade in stolen art?"

"Only what I read in the papers. There was a story about a guy on a tour in a Paris museum who cut a Renoir out of the frame, rolled it up, and walked out. Then, there was that soldier from Texas who picked up the German stuff during the Second World War."

"Child's play. I'm talking about the organized theft and distribution of two billion dollars a year in art and antiquities."

"Billion with a 'b'?"

"Everything from a Roman sarcophagus that was on loan to the Brooklyn Museum, to the Decadrachm Hoard, two thousand Greek coins that date from 500 B.C. Plus classical paintings by the masters."

"Who would buy that kind of stuff? It doesn't sound as marketable as a stolen CD player or a set of steel-belted radials."

He looked at me as if I had cut a few too many classes. I had.

Foley said, "The museums buy stolen art all the time. Sometimes, they know. Sometimes, they close their eyes. Once in a while, they even give stuff back. The Getty did it recently with a sarcophagus of Hercules. The San Antonio Museum was loaned a marble statue of the goddess Demeter that was smuggled from Istanbul to Munich, which is the headquarters of the stolen art trade. Private collectors like Yagamata don't care where they get the stuff, as long as it ends up in their house."

"I still don't understand the CIA's involvement," I said. "Why isn't it the FBI, like with stolen securities?"

"When a foreign government asks for our help . . ." He let it hang there.

"You're not talking about Roman antiquities here, are you? You mean the Russians."

He managed to smile without breaking his face. "One of the ironies of the liberalization in the Eastern bloc is the increase in Western-style crime. Before, with travel restrictions, smuggling was virtually impossible. Now, Karl hides priceless paintings in his suitcase when he goes from East to West Berlin to visit his cousins. There are criminals with shopping lists from Western collectors. Do you know *Table with a Goblet* by Picasso?"

"No, but if you hum a few bars . . ."

"A couple of months ago, thieves broke into the National Gallery in Prague. The security there was laughable, simply no experience with sophisticated, organized crime. Anyway, the wiseguys made off with four Picassos, estimated value thirty million. In Czechoslovakia, there were over five hundred burglaries of churches in the first twelve months after the Communists fell. Chalices, paintings, candlesticks, Stradivariuses, everything that wasn't nailed down. In East Germany, it's just as bad. You're probably not familiar with the sixteenth century statues of saints at the Church of Saint Nicholas in Prenzlau."

"Not intimately."

"Well, don't go looking for them, because they're gone. Same thing with the bronze nymph and seahorses from the gardens of Sans Souci in Potsdam."

"Russia," I reminded him. "What about Russia?"

Foley looked around the restaurant. If there were any KGB agents, I didn't see them. Just the usual suspects—expense account lawyers, overweight accountants, and real estate developers entertaining members of the zoning appeals board. Foley seemed to be trying to figure out whether to say anything else. Finally he sighed and said, "The biggest enchilada of them all. With the market economy, some of the new Russian capitalists are petty thieves, and some not so petty, including a helluva lot of government officials. After the failed coup, then the fall of the Union, it got worse. Corrupt old bureaucrats were replaced by corrupt new bureaucrats who didn't fear the KGB anymore, now that it's been reorganized and renamed, and morale is worse than the Pentagon's after 'Nam. The new regime looks good on paper, but it's no controls, no holds barred for the wiseguys.

"In the past, the Soviets had five main exports. Oil, weaponry, gold, platinum, and diamonds. Now, some smart Boris figures there's hundreds of museums stuffed to the rafters with uncountable fortunes in artwork. The museums are run by low-level functionaries who can be bribed with a set of snow tires for their Lada. You wouldn't believe what they've got—classical Russian stuff plus all the Western art that was accumulated before the Revolution and whatever they could steal during the war. Plus, of course, precious gems, sable pelts, church icons, and historic treasures. They're being stolen and smuggled into the States and Japan. They slip past customs without paying duties, so the federal government has jurisdiction even if we didn't want to do the Ruskies any favors."

"But you do. Our government is doing what the Russian government can't."

"If word got out—the piracy of Russia's precious art—it would be a major embarrassment to the reformers and the new republics. So as a favor from the highest level of our government, we're tracing the goods back to their source. It's not much different from what the DEA does with drugs from foreign countries. What you've done, Lassiter, is get in the way. You've stepped on some toes. Matsuo Yagamata has been under investigation for a long time. So has Severo Soto. They pose as respectable businessmen, but they're both dirty and ruthless. If you have a problem with either of them, it could be serious, and we're not in a position to protect you."

I dipped a piece of crunchy bread in olive oil and took a bite of the veal. "Who killed Francisco Crespo?" I asked.

"Who do you think?"

"I don't know, but whoever murdered the Russian murdered Crespo to cover it up."

Foley shrugged. "It's possible."

"Because Smorodinsky knew something. He was your informant, wasn't he? A whadayacallit, a mole?"

"Lassiter, this is way out of your league. Go back to your torts and contracts, okay?"

"Okay," I said. I knew I was lying, but did he?

"The rabbit," he said.

Oh, I almost forgot. I reached into my pocket and drew out the pendant. It rolled around in my hand until Foley plucked it out. From his shirt pocket, he produced a small plastic bag with a ziploc top. He dropped the bunny into the bag.

"Hey," I said. "Just lookee, no keepee." He ignored me and started to put the bag in his pocket. I reached across the table and caught him by the wrist. I have a good grip. There's nothing more embarrassing than having a skinny wide receiver pull out of your grasp, so I always worked hard on forearms, hands, and wrist. And now I was squeezing Foley until his fingers unclenched. So I never saw his other hand slip cleanly inside his jacket and go beneath the table.

"A Glock nine-millimeter semiautomatic is aimed directly at your balls," he said quietly.

Various intimate portions of my anatomy tightened, shriveled, and tried to make themselves invisible. "The Model seventeen?"

"No, the Model nineteen Compact. Fits easier under the jacket."

I nodded. "Watch that pressure on the trigger." I let go of Foley's wrist and sat back in my chair. "Perhaps I should donate this unique piece of jewelry to my government," I said. "Do you think I'll get a deduction for a charitable contribution?"

He scooped up the rabbit, replaced the gun, and stood. "Watch your ass, Lassiter, and stay out of my way. Your problems have nothing to do with me."

He walked out of the restaurant, leaving me sitting there, wondering whether I should have the *tiramisu* for dessert.

14

RIPTIDE

I dialed a number on the cellular phone, and a gruff voice answered, "Alpha here, over."

"Where are you, Alpha?"

"Identify yourself, over."

"Hey, Charlie, we're on the telephone here. This isn't Operation Burma."

"Security violation, over and out." Click and dial tone.

Damn.

I dialed the same number. "Alpha here, over," Charlie said again.

"Baker here, you cantankerous old goat."

"Alpha traveling north on Ponce, subject vehicle turning east on the Trail."

"Good job. I'm stuck in traffic on Salzedo. Stay with him."

It's not easy tailing a guy when you're driving a Dodge pickup with slabs of Everglades mud protruding like frozen slush from the wheelwells. But Charlie Riggs was doing the best he could and having a blast. I had stayed behind at Domenico's to have dessert, figuring Foley might have somebody watching me watching him. So Foley had a ten-minute head start by the time I reached my Olds 442, which was parked at a meter on Aragon. Now, headed north toward Tamiami Trail, I looked in the rearview mirror. Best I could tell, no one was following me while I followed Charlie while he followed Foley.

When the cellular phone rang, I pushed the right button and gave a friendly "Yeah."

Silence.

Okay, okay. "Baker here," I said.

"Alpha here. Subject headed north on Twelfth Avenue."

Toward downtown. He could be returning to the federal building on Flagler Street. The CIA maintained a small office there. But it would be quicker to stay right on Tamiami Trail, then take the I-95 flyover. Where was he going?

It had turned dark, and a breeze from the bay brought temperatures down to manageable levels and also blew some of the mosquitoes back toward the Glades. I had the top down on the convertible and listened to the sounds of salsa as I drove east along the Trail—Calle Ocho—in Little Havana. I passed city parks where old men hunched over their domino games sipping espresso. And I thought about Robert Foley and the little gold rabbit I had begun to think of as mine. What I didn't stop to consider was exactly why I was doing this. To fulfill a promise to Emilia Crespo, or to mend a broken one. To prove something to myself, maybe. Just as I decided to ponder all of that, the phone bleeped again, and after the obligatory preliminaries, Charlie, a/k/a Alpha, told me Foley had turned his four-door Chrysler northwest onto South River Drive.

Then I knew. Atlantic Seaboard Warehouse.

"Charlie, peel off, old buddy. I got him covered."

A tractor-trailer with a supermarket logo on the side was pulling out of the gate when I walked up. I had parked the car in an empty lot a block away. With any luck, it would be there when I got back, hubcaps and aerial still attached.

I was feeling good. I knew the territory from preparing Crespo's case. There would be two security guards, one on the river side, the other on the loading dock facing the parking lot. They worked twelve-hour shifts four days a week, seven guards rotating so that the place was always protected. I had interviewed all of them.

The asphalt of the parking lot shimmered green under the mercury vapor lamps. Foley's gray Chrysler was in the lot. So were a black Mercedes and a white Cadillac. I took the steps two at a time to the concrete loading dock.

"Hey, Carlos," I greeted the guard. If he wasn't collecting social security, it was only because he'd been paid under the table for the last thirty years. He was stubby and emaciated, with a narrow face that had run out of room for its fleshy nose. He wore a white shirt with epaulets, gray trousers with a black stripe, and a .357 Magnum on his hip. The trousers kept sliding down from the weight of the handgun. He had white hair swept back, and a bushy white mustache tickled his oversize nose.

"Doctor Lassiter. *El jefe* is in the traffic office if you're looking for him."

"Thanks, Carlos."

I walked straight through the open front door, which was the exact width of a tractor-trailer. The traffic office sat on an orange steel catwalk thirty feet off the floor of the warehouse. Metal stairs led from the floor to the catwalk. The traffic office was divided into two rooms. You walked into an open area with metal desks, old typewriters, and a couple of new computers. During the day, three or four clerical workers sat there, pushing paper, keeping track of inventory and shipments. A conference room with a walnut table and eight chairs was tucked inside. I had conducted my interviews there.

What appeared from the floor to be a mirrored wall of glass on the outside of the office was a window looking out from the conference room. I couldn't see in, but whoever was inside could see out. I ducked into the first row, which was marked *Foodstuffs*. Canned tomato paste from Italy and pickles from Poland were stacked twice as high as an NBA center. From behind me, I heard a buzzing. A worker on a forklift whizzed by me into the next row, swinging the wheel hard. He deftly touched a lever, and the fork dropped to just a few inches off the floor. I watched the blade. Three-inch-thick steel at the base where it was bolted to the lift, tapering to maybe a quarter inch at the tip. The driver slid the blade under a pallet of fertilizer bags, shifted gears, backed the lift out, wheeled around, and whirred toward the loading dock and a waiting trailer.

I stayed put, wondering what to do now that I was here. Who was in the office overhead? Foley and Yagamata, *el jefe,* for sure. Why? Was the CIA buying a load of Polish pickles? The catwalk surrounded the office on three sides; the conference window only faced the front, but that ruled out going up the stairs. If I did, I would be in plain view from the office window. I needed to get to one of the sides.

I looked at the stack of containers on the side facing me. Not high enough. Even if I climbed to the top and stood on my tippy-toes, I'd be several feet too short.

Outside, an air horn tooted three times. The Second Avenue Bridge was going up over the Miami River. Inside, workmen were beginning to drift toward the dock, removing their gloves. I looked at my watch. Nine P.M. End of a shift. Twenty yards away, a forklift sat empty.

Why not?

When I turned the ignition, there was a whoosh of propane and the little motor jumped to life. How hard could it be? I fooled around with what looked like a gearshift and stepped on the pedal that should have been a clutch. I hit the gas, found myself in reverse, and crashed into a stack of hundred-pound dog food bags. I found the forward gear, hit the gas again, turned the wheel, and whirled three hundred sixty degrees like Dorothy Hamill on the ice. Damn thing steers with the rear wheels.

After a couple of minutes, I could drive semistraight. So there I was, an ex-football player, ex-public defender, ex-a-lot-of-things ricocheting a forklift around a corner and trying to get the blade into position to lift a ton of applesauce ten feet off the ground. After several tries, I figured it out. I slid the fork under the pallet and lifted it cleanly, locking the blade into place. Then I climbed up the pallet, and standing on top, reached the floor of the catwalk with my hands stretched over my head. I hoisted myself up, swinging first one leg then the other to the floor. In a moment, I was on the catwalk, out of view of the conference room window.

I looked down at the warehouse. No workmen were visible. I eased around the corner, ducked underneath the mirrored window, and made it to the front door. I listened for voices but heard none. Quietly, I turned the door handle. Inside, the outer office was dark. The door to the conference room was cracked open, the light spilling out. I duck-walked inside and closed the door behind me. A metal counter split the office in half, with clerks' desks on either side.

I heard voices now but couldn't make out the words. In the movies, your Indiana Jones types are always sneaking up on the Nazis and eavesdropping from a hundred yards away. It doesn't work like that. You've got to be within spitting distance to understand anything, unless you're equipped with sophisticated gear like Lourdes Soto carries in her aluminum case. I didn't even have a pencil. I waddled closer to the open door, keeping my back pressed to the counter. I tried to breathe slowly, my brain telling the rest of me not to sneeze, fart, or sing the national anthem. My various body parts obeyed, all except my right knee. Three feet from the door, it *cra-cked,* the sound of a dry twig snapping in two. I convinced myself that it sounded loud to me because, after all, it was my knee. I waited a moment to see if my elbow or ankle answered. Sometimes it happens that way, a symphony of sympathetic bones: snap, crackle, and pop. But they stayed quiet, and I held my breath, listening some more. I couldn't see into the room, but now I could hear.

". . . shameless exhibitionism. Carelessness. Inexcusable leaks."

I recognized Robert Foley's voice. He grew louder and angrier with each word. "What the hell is the Matisse doing in your —what the hell is it—your garage?"

"My study. You would not understand. To me, the painting is very symbolic." A faint Cuban accent. Severo Soto. Oh, brother. What was going on here?

"Symbolic! Jesus H. Christ, we're not talking art appreciation here. You guys are skimming. You're treating the product as your own personal property. Security risks, both of you."

Then another voice, at first too faint to understand. Then, ". . . but I take full responsibility. It was my decision." A foreign accent, someone who had been taught the language by a Brit.

"And speaking of exhibitionism!" Foley again. "At a goddamn public party attended by half of Dade County, you showed off some goddamn gold train that wasn't made by Lionel."

"Lionel?" Matsuo Yagamata sounded puzzled.

"Never mind!" Foley shouted savagely. "If you two guys are the brains of this operation, I'd hate to see—"

"Please show me the rabbit again," Yagamata said, quietly and politely.

It grew silent. I pictured them passing *my* little bunny around the table.

"An interesting piece from the House of Fabergé, probably the work of Fedor Afanassiev or Henrik Wigstrom," Yagamata said. "Not especially valuable. Perhaps inspired by an egg-shaped pendant worn by Catherine the Great and stored in the treasury of the Hermitage at the time Fabergé's artisans were at work there. So they could easily have been influenced—"

"Who gives a flying fuck! How did that shitbucket Crespo get his hands on it?"

No one spoke, and I imagined a series of shrugs. "See what I mean?" Foley continued. "We knew the Russians couldn't keep records to save their ass. Completely incompetent. Give me the Germans, any day. Christ, they always knew where every bullet was stored. Great record keepers. But the Russians. Drunken, lazy bastards. It doesn't matter if they're commies or democrats or Rotarians. We expected inefficiency and pilferage at their end, not *ours*. It's bad enough you guys are dipping into the trough, but now you got minimum-wage *Marielitos* running around with the crown jewels . . ."

Crespo's not running anywhere, I thought.

". . . Can you imagine the flak if Geraldo Rivera got hold of this? I gotta tell you, if word gets out, you guys are on your own. Common criminals. We wash our hands of the whole fucking lot of you."

"A trinket, nothing more." Yagamata again. "I have allowed various operatives to keep mementos of our successful activities."

"Mementos!" Foley was screaming now. "*Evidence* is more like it!"

"Why do you worry so much?" Yagamata asked, calmly. "We have other, more pressing concerns."

"*El abogado,* what about the lawyer?" Soto asked.

"He doesn't know shit," Foley said. "I told him the government is trying to help stop the theft of Russian artwork."

I heard a laugh but couldn't tell the source. "Isn't that just like government everywhere?" Yagamata chortled. "A lie that is so close to the truth."

"You have a problem with that?" Foley again.

"To the contrary," Yagamata responded. "I applaud every aspect of your Operation Riptide. Until recently, I believed myself to be a master of deceit. But I am—what do you call it here —a small fish . . ."

"Small fry," Foley said.

". . . compared to the cunning of civil service employees in polyester suits."

"Matsuo, you're being too modest," Foley said. His voice faded. I had the impression he was walking around the room. ". . . fact remains that the lawyer knows too much, even if he doesn't know what it means." The voice grew stronger and I heard the shuffle of his oxfords against the tile floor. "I'm gonna leave the lawyer up to you, but let me make something clear. You have no sanction to terminate him . . ."

Terminate? Why did I think he wasn't talking about firing me as a legal eagle?

". . . none whatsoever."

Maybe I should thank my new buddy Foley. Okay, maybe he had pointed a gun at my crotch. But now . . .

"Do you forbid it?" Yagamata sounded peeved.

"We sanction nothing. We forbid nothing."

Thanks a lot, buddy.

Just then, a new voice startled me. "It would not be discreet." That sweet voice with just a trace of an accent picked up at *quince* parties and from giggling friends at the St. Christopher School for Girls. "First the Russian, then Crespo, now the lawyer. Do you really believe this would escape the notice of the prosecutor and the grand jury?"

That's my Lourdes. Arguing for my life because it would be imprudent to kill me. At the same time, I wondered if her reasoning was influenced just a bit by the memory of the slow rhythmic grinding of our loins. *Spare the infidel, and fetch him to my chambers.*

There was murmuring at the table that I took to be agreement. There were also the sounds of chairs moving and people stirring. I thought it might be an appropriate time to put some distance between myself and four characters who were deciding if my demise was more trouble than it was worth. I duck-walked back to the door without tearing ligaments or knocking over any typewriters. I made it to the catwalk and turned the corner to get out of view of the window.

Damn. Someone must have decided that a fifteen-foot stack of applesauce violated a housekeeping rule. The forklift and my makeshift ladder were gone. I could risk it and try to get down the stairs. Or I could—

". . . Tomorrow, then," Foley said.

They were coming out the door. In a moment, they would turn the corner and face me on the catwalk. I ducked under the railing, dropped my feet over the side and hung there, my hands gripping the cool steel, my feet swinging gently below me. I did not feel like Cathy Rigby.

"This Kharchenko," Foley said, "can he be trusted?"

They were directly above me. The catwalk swayed slightly with each step.

"Completely," Yagamata answered. "He is not as intelligent as Smorodinsky, but perhaps that is to our advantage. He follows orders without thinking about the consequences."

No one was moving. My arms ached.

"When will he arrive?" Foley asked.

"Tomorrow from JFK. He is carrying a cardboard tube with a rather colorful poster of Temppeliaukio Square in Helsinki."

"And?"

"Inside the poster is Matisse's *Girl with Tulips,*" Yagamata said. "Even as we speak, he is on the train, the St. Petersburg Express. He will be in Helsinki in two hours."

For some reason, I thought of *Dr. Zhivago,* and an old Russian steam engine belching smoke into a wintry night, red flags crackling in an icy wind.

"I'm only going to say this once, Matsuo. Any more slipups, the whole operation will be scuttled."

Yagamata replied, but a factory whistle blasted twice, and I couldn't make out his words. Between the blasts, I heard a name. "Sue Molaynen" maybe. Yagamata's voice became stronger.

"She supervised the loading of the freighter in Helsinki last week and will pick him up at the airport here."

"Freighter?" Foley sounded irritated.

"A Polish freighter under lease to one of my companies."

"What are you doing, stealing the whole damn Hermitage?"

"In due time." Yagamata laughed. "Perhaps a hundred years. For now, several trailer-size containers of *objets d'art,* the most we have ever transported. What did you think, Mr. Foley, that we are still carrying baubles inside Matryoshka dolls?"

"I don't like it," Foley said. "You take too many risks, and you exceed all authority."

"Like all bureaucrats, you worry too much."

My shoulders were on fire.

"I'm not kidding, the strictest inventory control on this shipment," Foley said, sternly.

"Of course," Yagamata said.

"I mean it."

"Of course you do."

"You are a real piece of work, Matsuo baby."

"Thank you."

"Boys," Lourdes pleaded. "Please stop. We must work together. One misstep and—"

"Ouch!"

Her stiletto heel dug deep into the flesh between the thumb and forefinger of my right hand. Suddenly I was hanging only by my left hand, my body swaying as if in a breeze. For some reason I pictured a paratrooper caught in the trees, the enemy about to spray him with automatic weapons fire.

Commotion above me. "What the hell!" Foley shouted. Severo Soto was yelling at someone. He leaned down and looked at me. *"Maldito!"*

This time it was a man's foot, and it hit hard, crunching the fingers of my left hand. And then I fell.

I missed the applesauce jars and landed on the fertilizer bags with a thud. I didn't break, sprain, or twist anything. It was no worse than getting blindsided by the tight end. I just clambered down and started for the loading dock. I wasn't running. There would be something scaredy-cat about that. But I wasn't walking either. It was more like the stiff-legged jog we used coming out of the locker room for pregame introductions. Almost a swagger to the gait.

Then the air horn blasted. Over the speaker, I heard Yagamata calling the security guards. Then, it was Severo Soto's voice, saying something in Spanish I couldn't understand. In a moment, I saw Carlos doing his best imitation of a cop, gun held in two-hand grip, edging his thin body along a pyramid of tomato paste cans, his back plastered to the wall. What had they told him, *BOLO for fast-talking shyster, presumed flippant and dangerous*?

I flattened myself to the floor and watched Carlos straining on tippy-toes to see on top of the pallets. A moment later, I heard the ominous rumble of the steel doors, lowering from overhead. Both loading docks—riverfront and parking lot—were sealed off. We were going to be spending some time together, my art-loving friends and me.

Carlos turned a corner, raising and lowering his gun with arms locked straight in front of him as he doubtless had seen on TV. He had his left hand cupped under his right, rather than in front of it, where each hand could neutralize the other, steadying the gun. I started moving the other way. I doubted Carlos could shoot straight but would rather not test my theory.

The warehouse had no windows, and best I could tell, the only doors were locked tight. But the building was huge, and they had to find me first. I was near a raised cubicle at the intersection of two walls. A stenciled sign said: INVENTORY AND MERCHANDISE CONTROL. I took my own inventory. Nothing useful on the desk, not a telephone, not even scissors. What looked like a janitor's closet was nearby. Maybe I could fight them off with a mop.

The door was unlocked.

Inside were wires and switches, the electrical controls for the building. I grabbed a handful of wires and yanked them out of their little sockets. On the wall was the circuit breaker panel. I opened it, reached in, and popped all the breakers. The heavy-duty air-conditioning wheezed and clunked to a halt. The lights blinked off; I was in total darkness.

Footsteps echoed on concrete, but in the cavernous warehouse I could not tell the direction. Yagamata would try to find the electrical room, so I kept moving. I tiptoed cautiously into the blackness, taking care, trying to remember the tomcat stalk an outdoorsman once taught me: high slow steps, heel down first, roll onto the ball of the foot. I was doing fine. I didn't wake any sleeping bears or fall into any rushing streams. But then I smacked into something.

"Cono!" the something yelled. It was Carlos, tumbling to the floor. I didn't move. He couldn't see me, because I couldn't see him. A nerve-shattering *cl-ick* warned me that he had cocked the hammer on his .357 Magnum. My breathing sounded like a locomotive in my ears. Silently, I reached into a pocket, took out a quarter, and tossed it into the darkness. It landed with a *ping* on the concrete, and Carlos fired a shot that made my ears ring. The flash from the barrel was just below me. He was sitting on the floor at my feet. With the noise still echoing, I took off the other way and turned what I thought was a corner, but slammed into a metal rack, banging my bum knee hard. I backed up, tried to figure where the middle of the aisle would be, then started moving slowly, my arms in front of me, feeling the air.

A soft noise.

A buzzing.

Louder now.

Two small headlights swung around a corner. In the blackness, the lights blinded me. I was caught in their glare, frozen like a startled deer. The lights grew in size, the forklift closing the distance. I turned and ran, chasing my shadow, which loomed twenty feet in front of me.

Thirty miles an hour. That's how fast Crespo told me they went. Me, I never ran an hour in my life. On my best day, it took me four point eight two seconds to run forty yards. On this day, rapidly shaping up as my worst, I may have trimmed half a second off my time.

The lift closed on me, someone shouting from behind. I looked back over my shoulder. It hung there five yards away, then closed the gap. We were coming to an intersection of rows. Let's see how that baby corners. I faked left and took the corner right like a wide receiver on a deep post, trying to make a hard L-cut. My turn was a little flabby around the edges, but it was better than the guy behind me. The lift banged into a metal rack, sending sparks into the darkness. It stopped, backed up, and started again. I had gained twenty yards but was losing steam. With the air-conditioning off, the air went stale and the warehouse was a sweatbox. I was having trouble with my breathing, and there it was again, behind me. I thought of Smorodinsky, impaled on the wall. I thought of Cary Grant in *North by Northwest*, being chased by the crop duster. If I got out of this, I was going to buy Lourdes Soto a drink and ask "how a girl like you got to be a girl like you."

Slanting to the right, I tried to calculate how much room there was on either side of the forklift. I couldn't outrun it, but maybe I could pivot out of its way, reverse my field, and take a poke at the driver as he went by. It was probably no more difficult than kicking a ball through the uprights, then running and catching that sucker before it hit the ground.

More yelling behind me. No more time to think. I planted my left leg and pivoted. I heard the *snap* before I felt it, the knee giving way. I spun into a pallet of bottled barbecue sauce, my hands gripping the wooden frame to keep from falling. My back was pressed against the pallet, my arms outstretched, my knee throbbing. The forklift growled past me, braked hard, spun around, and came back. It stopped three feet in front of me, its headlights bleaching me in their malevolent glare. I heard the hydraulic whoosh of the lift and saw the blade raise to my chest level. Then the ugly machine moved forward, at first slowly, then with a charge. I raised my arms as the blades slashed into the pallet on either side of my rib cage. Behind me, bottles shattered, and what I hoped was barbecue sauce ran down the back of my legs. My chest was pinned to the front of the forklift, my back to the splintered wood pallet.

The driver turned off the ignition, leaving the headlights on. My lungs wanted oxygen, but the lift was crushing my ribs in a mechanical bearhug. I watched the driver dismount, peel off a pair of gloves, and walk into the twin shafts of yellow light.

"My father was right about you," Lourdes Soto said, softly. "You are the kind of man who touches a stove to see if it is hot."

15

THE POISON IS IN THE TAIL

"But I don't like Washington in the summer . . ." I said.

Robert Foley didn't seem to care.

". . . or the rest of the year, for that matter."

He sat on the vinyl sofa, reading a newspaper, ignoring me. His tie was at half mast, and his white shirt wrinkled. His creased face was pale and drawn. Maybe baby-sitting for me was a tiring job. Around us, a potpourri of government agents went about their tasks. There were customs inspectors in uniform, DEA agents in plainclothes, one with a German shepherd, and a variety of federal employees wearing photo ID badges and toiling at various secretive tasks in that governmental tempo that is somewhere between slow motion and a dead halt. In the center of the room, a dozen cubicles each contained eight miniature television monitors. Bleary-eyed women scanned the screens, occasionally whispering into their headsets. We were deep in the bowels of the airport in a restricted federal area. The sign on the door said simply, SPECIAL SERVICES.

I was watching the inside of the door when Foley said, "You don't have to go with me. Leave now if you want. I'll get you a cab."

"Uh-huh. Only the cab driver has a different kind of license, right?"

"What?"

"A license to kill."

"Lassiter, you see too many movies. We haven't done that sort of thing in years. At least not domestically."

On the wall was a panel with numbers one through fifty. Four or five numbers were blinking at once. Another lighted panel showed arriving and departing international flights with a matching number from one to fifty.

"Okay, I think I'll leave now," I told him. "I need to put some ice on this knee."

Foley went back to his newspaper.

I stood, straightened my bum leg, and said, "Well, I guess this is good-bye. Next time you're in Miami, do me a favor. Don't call me."

"Oh, you'll be seeing me at the trial."

"What trial?"

Foley put down the newspaper, creasing the folds as if it were the flag at Arlington. "Yours, pal. For the murder of Francisco Crespo."

The board showed a flight arriving from Bogotá. Three numbers started blinking. Had I heard him right? He couldn't have said what I thought he said.

"Your prints are all over that trailer, Lassiter. You tell us a cock-and-bull story about a man dressed in brown running away. There were a hundred people in that park, and nobody saw your mystery man."

"A hundred people from south of the border, but not one green card in the bunch. *Of course* nobody saw anything."

Foley beamed. He looked genuinely happy. "Oh, I wouldn't put it that way. Three witnesses saw you go into Crespo's trailer and heard two muffled popping sounds maybe a minute later."

"Bullshit! It was the other way around. I went in after—"

"That's not what the witnesses say."

I sunk back into the sofa. My knee throbbed. "I take it back. There'll be three green cards in that park by next week."

"Sorry, Lassiter, but you'll be indicted for second-degree murder. As the English say, a nasty bit of business."

"You prick! You bastard! You scum-sucking pig!"

Around us, various civil servants stopped to watch. Or did they just slow their tempo another nanosecond? The German shepherd padded over and sniffed my leg for contraband, or maybe just to see if I was edible.

"Why would I shoot Crespo?"

"Ah, yes, motive. Hard to get a conviction without one, but why should I tell you your business? Some dispute over fee splitting. Crespo wanted a bigger cut of the cases he sent your way. You brushed him off. He threatened you with exposure and disbarment. You warned him once. He persisted. You offed him."

"You bullshit artist! I never split a fee with Crespo or anybody else."

"Then how do you explain the letter written in your own hand?"

"What letter?"

He opened a thin briefcase and removed a one-page photocopy. "Exhibit A," he announced.

I grabbed it. My handwriting all right. A curt little note telling Crespo to lay off or he'd regret it. And my signature at the bottom, a forgery so good even I couldn't tell it wasn't real.

I balled up the note and tossed it back at Foley. "That's why you had me write out a statement, you fuckhead."

He took an identical copy from his briefcase and admired it. There seemed to be half a dozen copies. "The exemplar was quite useful, I admit."

"Who's going to believe this? What kind of asshole would write a letter like that?"

He smiled and put the letter back into the briefcase. "I believe that's what you lawyers call a jury question."

"I ought to kick your ass."

"Go ahead. Assaulting a federal officer is pretty tame stuff compared to the trouble you're in." He smiled again and leaned toward me. "Of course, I could help you out. I could see to it that Socolow never gets this letter and those wetback witnesses all end up working in the Post Office in Corpus Christi."

"Who do I have to kill?"

"Don't be so melodramatic. All you have to do is sign a confidentiality agreement. Not a word about Operation Riptide to anybody, ever."

"That's all?"

"That's all."

"Why not have your handwriting guy just sign it for me, save the trouble?"

"Not for this one. We'll go to the Farm at Langley, videotape the signing, have you state for the record you're not being coerced, that sort of thing."

"What makes me think you've got the statement all typed up and neatly bound in blue-backed paper inside your government-issue briefcase?"

He opened the case and beamed. "Because you recognize efficiency and grudgingly admire it."

He handed me a three-page document, which, by golly, was stapled to a blue backing with a gold government seal. I skimmed it. "You prick, Foley. This isn't a confidentiality agreement. It's a confession to the murder of Francisco Crespo."

"Best confidentiality agreement I know. It goes in the safe in Langley. It'll never see the light of day as long as you keep your mouth shut. You talk, or do anything contrary to our interests, the confession will be in Socolow's hands quicker than shit through a goose."

"Or the next Socolow, or the one after that. There's no statute of limitations on murder. You guys would have something over me for the rest of my life."

"Hey, nobody promised you a rose garden. I'm just trying to help you out here. So think about it." He looked at his watch. "Flight leaves in ninety minutes."

I asked Foley if I could use the phone to call my secretary. He grunted an okay and told me I was free to call the Prince of Wales if I wanted. I used an unmanned desk out of Foley's earshot and caught Cindy at home.

"What is it, boss? I'm late for ladies' night at the Crazy Horse."

"Sorry to make you miss the Chippendales."

"Nah, it's the lifeguards from Daytona Beach, all those tan lines." The line buzzed with faraway static as she paused. "Whadaya mean, *miss . . . ?*"

"You remember how to write a writ?"

"Now?"

"C'mon, Cindy. I need a writ of prejudgment attachment under Chapter Seventy-six, and I need it quick."

"Courthouse is closed, *el jefe.*"

"Call Judge Boulton at home. Prepare a short complaint, emergency motion, and affidavit. You swear to it. If you're indicted for perjury, I'll get you a good lawyer. The property to be attached is a one-page document belonging to me. At least, it seems to have my signature on it. An original and some copies, I don't know how many, so plead it broadly. The document is a letter with no monetary value, so we don't need to post a bond. The tortfeasor, one Robert T. Foley, is about to flee the jurisdiction, which gives us the statutory basis for prejudgment relief. Unless we secure the property now, the normal process of the court will be for naught, blah, blah, blah. Get it?"

"Yeah. The usual bullcrap boilerplate."

"Good. Get the writ signed by the judge and hustle it to Concourse F, gate eleven at the airport, and I mean quick. Better bring the biggest process server you can find. Maybe one of the guys who used to repo Harleys from that Broward biker gang."

I hung up and walked back to Foley, who sat placidly, hands in his lap, watching me. "Well?"

"I'm yours," I told him.

"Good. I'll file a report. Then we'll head to the gate."

He moved to one of the empty desks, worked quietly on a computer for half an hour, printed out a multipage document, and used an intercom to ask a young woman to fax it to Langley. Then he came back to where I was sitting. "Let's go, counselor."

An elevator took us to Concourse F for the Delta flight to Dulles. I was still limping as we passed through the X-ray machine and then the neutron explosive detector. It scans for gamma rays, an indicator of high-density nitrogen. We didn't ring any bells, so I assumed Foley was neither armed with his Beretta nor carrying TNT in his Jockey shorts.

We sat at the gate until a loudspeaker announced that cattle with coach tickets were now being herded to the rear of the aircraft. Anyone within flushing distance of the aft lavatory should begin boarding. So should expense account first-class types, if they so desired. Foley stirred and stood up. I didn't move.

"I need a drink," I told him.

"What?"

"Always have one before a flight. Sometimes two. Calms my nerves."

"You can get a drink on the—"

"No, need it now. It's a ritual."

The bar was twenty paces away. Airports may be big and noisy, sterile and dehumanizing, but the best ones use every spare inch for taverns with cushioned barstools and televisions tuned to the sports channel.

"Okay," Foley said, "but make it quick."

I ordered a Jack Daniel's on the rocks, changed it to a double, and made myself comfortable on a high stool. Foley stood next to me, pulled a pack of Camels from his coat pocket, and lighted one. They called the flight a second time. Passengers in the middle rows who would get trapped by the food carts should begin boarding. I sipped at my drink, and Foley crushed his half-smoked cigarette in an ashtray. "C'mon, Lassiter."

I drained the drink and motioned the bartender for another. "Lots of time," I said. "They probably haven't gotten the pilot out of the detox center yet."

When the second drink arrived, I swirled the glass, watching the auburn liquid crash into the ice cubes like waves against a rocky shore. I usually stay away from hard liquor, and now I already felt a spreading warmth that moved from my stomach to my chest and, if given half a chance, would spread to my toes.

"Final boarding call for Flight three-seventy-six to Washington-Dulles," a voice announced. They used to just say "Dulles," but a lot of passengers headed to Dallas ended up on the wrong plane.

"C'mon!" Foley ordered. "We're on our way."

I stood, stretched, reached into my wallet, and found a fifty. "Gotta get my change," I said, sliding the bill across the bar. We waited for the bartender to put the fifty under what could have been an electron microscope. Next he dribbled some blue chemical on the bill and showed it to the manager, who seemed to memorize the serial number before autographing it. Finally, I had my change. Deliberately, I calculated a tip, peeled off five dollar bills as slowly as possible—counting them three times—thanked the bartender for his outstanding service, and finally wished him a good day in English, Spanish, and Serbo-Croatian. Then I joined an impatient Robert Foley for a short walk to the gate. As I did, I took a peek up the concourse toward the terminal.

No Cindy.

No bullnecked process server with a writ.

Lots of harried tourists with bulging shopping bags and salesmen with briefcases and career women with hanging bags and go-to-hell looks. And one sawed-off, bandy-legged bearded guy in a suit that hadn't been out of the closet since Ike was in the White House. He hustled past a sunburned family carrying boxes of duty-free liquor from the islands.

"Mr. Foley," he called out. *"Sistere!* Stop!"

Foley turned and scowled. It took him a moment. "You're that retired canoe maker, aren't you? What the fuck do you want?"

Doc Charlie Riggs was out of breath. "The documents in your briefcase," he said, puffing, "the ones bearing Mr. Lassiter's signature." Politely, Charlie handed Foley certified copies of the complaint, motion, affidavit, and writ. It was pretty impressive, if legal jargon impresses you. "You are under court order to forthwith deliver to the plaintiff—" Charlie cleared his throat, *ahchem,* "—Mr. Lassiter here, the original document described herein and all copies, pending a subsequent hearing to be duly noticed by the court."

Foley's reply was not learned in Civil Procedure I. "Go shit in your hat."

"Dear me," Charlie said. "Judge Boulton would not appreciate that. Indeed, once I report to her that you were served with process just as you were about to leave the jurisdiction, *in flagrante delicto,* while the crime was blazing, and that you ignored a duly issued court order, she'll—"

"Tell her to go fuck a duck."

From behind Charlie, two uniformed airport policemen appeared. "This him?" one asked.

Charlie turned and nodded.

"If he's giving you any trouble, Officer Riggs, we can take him in," the other said.

"Officer Riggs!" Foley was turning pink. "This old fart's a quack, a retired sawbones. What the fuck's going on here?"

"We know exactly who the gentleman is," said one of the cops, a trim black man with perfect posture. "When the Eastern L-1011 went down in the Glades, Doc Riggs was on the scene within fifteen minutes. He happens to be an honorary police officer, and we give him all due respect." The policeman's eyes narrowed. "On the other hand, we don't know you from a lump of gator shit. Now, if there's a problem complying with a court order, we can go downtown . . ."

"That won't be necessary, officer," Foley replied through clenched teeth, opening his briefcase and pulling out a sheaf of documents. He wheeled toward me. "We've still got the witnesses, Lassiter."

"Fine. When they crumble on cross-examination, maybe some folks will want to know why government agents are suborning perjury."

Foley thrust the documents at me. "You can run, but you can't hide, Lassiter. This isn't over."

"No. Not for you and not for me. But for Francisco Crespo, it is."

I hobbled off, my arm around Charlie Riggs, who was muttering something about missing one of the better episodes of *Quincy* in order to run this errand. In the main terminal, we took the elevator to the bar in the airport hotel. It has a fine view of planes taking off and landing.

I ordered a beer to chase away the bourbon, and a bowl of conch chowder because I was hungry. The chowder was tomato-based the way I like it, heavy on the conch, light on the vegetables. I poured a few drops of sherry into it and munched some saltines while we talked.

"What now?" Charlie asked.

"A Russian named Kharchenko is coming to Miami tomorrow. He's bringing a stolen painting with him, another Matisse. Plus there's a freighter that left Helsinki loaded with stolen art."

"Freighter?" Charlie's bushy eyebrows arched toward the mirrored ceiling.

"That's what Foley said, and just that way, when Yagamata told him. Like, 'holy cow.' "

Charlie whistled. "They're getting greedy. Even a valise filled with precious objects could be worth millions.'' He was quiet a moment, his forehead furrowed in thought. ''Did you say Helsinki?''

''Yeah.''

Charlie scratched his beard, then his head, warming up those brain cells. ''Makes sense, geographically. Take a look.'' He pulled out a pen, grabbed a cocktail napkin and began drawing what I took to be a map of Russia's western border. ''Here's St. Petersburg,'' he said. ''It was Russia's Window to the West during the time of Peter the Great, and it still is. Helsinki can't be more than what, two hundred to three hundred miles due west across the Gulf of Finland, right here at the sixtieth parallel.'' Charlie made a horizontal line connecting the two cities. ''When Yagamata's people get the art out of Russia, they've got to take it somewhere, a storage and distribution point, preferably in a Western country with a free flow of tourists and easy border crossings.''

That reminded me of something. ''Severo Soto told me that Smorodinsky and his brother used Finland as an intermediate point.''

Outside the windows, a 747 was lumbering off toward a runway. Charlie nodded. ''Russia is Finland's largest trading partner. It wouldn't be unusual to ship goods in that direction. Then the art could be hidden in shipments from Finland to the States. I'll wager that the manifest shows glassware and wood products. There's a great deal of trade going on with items about the right size for hiding contraband. There shouldn't be much trouble with U.S. Customs. It's not like getting goods from Colombia or Peru. Nobody expects anything illegal from Scandinavia.''

''So what do I look for?''

''In cauda venenum, the poison is in the tail.''

''What?''

''Watch out for the part you can't see. Whoever shot Francisco Crespo was part of something much bigger than some art thefts, no matter how much money is involved.'' Charlie dipped a spoon in my chowder, took a sip, looked appreciative, and ordered a bowl of his own. ''There'll likely be an interlocking network of Russian and Finnish nationals, a real international cast of characters if they're using other countries for shipping.'' Too hungry to wait for his chowder, Charlie slid my bowl toward himself and spooned out meaty chunks of conch. Between slurps, he said, "What else is there, Jake? What else do you know?"

"There's a woman picking him up. Sue Molaynen, or something like that."

After a moment Charlie said, *"Suomalainen?"*

"Yeah, you know her?"

"Jake, a *suomalainen* is a citizen of *Suomi,* or what we call Finland."

Oh. Where does he learn this stuff? I felt like I was being sent into a game, and I didn't know the plays. It was starting to overwhelm me.

"Look, Charlie, if anything happens to me, you know that graphite spinning rod of mine you've been admiring for a long—"

"Hush! *Quaere verum.* Seek the truth and do what you have to do. When this is over, Jake, we'll go fishing together."

I could have gone home. Charlie would have given me a ride, or I could have taken a cab. But I didn't go. I said good-bye to Charlie, took the elevator back to the terminal, ducked out an "Airline Personnel Only" door, and limped across the tarmac, weaving between a 727 about to taxi out, and a DC-9 easing up to the jetway. A guy with two flashlights and protective eargear gave me a dirty look, but I kept going. The door was open at the foot of Concourse E, and I went up the stairs.

I put some coins into a machine and bought the local newspaper. I sat down at a departure gate and buried my head in the sports section. Baseball and golf. What a lousy time of year. The pro football draft was history, but the league's summer camps hadn't opened yet. Not a word about the Dolphins. Sports was so boring this time of year, I might be forced to read the business section. Why not? I had lots of time.

The airport is a sort of high-tech prison with air-conditioning and souvenir stands. It has its amenities, a decent raw bar in the terminal, countless taverns and ice cream stands, rest rooms and telephones. You can buy T-shirts with funny slogans as gag gifts or battery-operated toys that will never work at home. The airport is designed to make agonizing waits, if not pleasant, at least tolerable, while relieving you of the contents of your wallet. It is a modern way station between anywhere and home.

I wasn't leaving town, and I wasn't going home. The egress road from the airport is one-way headed east. A mile from the terminal, you can swing south onto LeJeune and head into Coral Gables, or take the expressway to Miami Beach. Go west, and you're aiming for the Everglades. Take LeJeune north, and you'll hit Hialeah. But it would only require one police car at the ramp to stop every car leaving the airport. I wasn't leaving, not for a while. I wasn't giving Foley a chance to come up with another stunt to get me out of the way.

Even if I made it out of here and buried myself somewhere, I'd have to come back to the airport tomorrow, anyway. As in Edgar Allan Poe's "Purloined Letter," maybe the best hiding spot is the most visible one.

Over the loudspeaker, a man named Milligan was being paged, and it gave me an idea. I had all night to think about it. So I settled back into the molded plastic chair by a Delta Air Lines gate and let my mind drift. I closed my eyes and wondered, first, what a man named Kharchenko was up to, and second, what the son of a bitch looked like.

The gun was pointed at my chest. A little gun that could punch little holes straight through my chest and out my back. Blood dripped onto the butt from the big man's torn thumb. Silver, luminous smoke drifted toward the ceiling.

No one said a word. Not the beefy, beered-up lout with the gun. Not the open-mouthed patrons who drifted in a semicircle around us, eyes glistening with excitement. Not the young woman whose honor I defended and who now backed away, her shoes scraping the floor.

And not me. Jake Lassiter, reserve linebacker and second-string dragonslayer, was too scared to talk. Big Mouth was sneering, baring his teeth, daring me to make a move.

I didn't.

Petrified. Each foot weighed a ton. My breathing was labored, my chest constricted. On the jukebox, the Doobie Brothers were singing, but no one was listening.

Finally, Big Mouth said something, the sounds dense and ponderous like a tape recording played a speed too slow. I strained to hear, the words echoing. "Who . . . who's . . . gonna help you now, asshole?"

I tried to answer but was mute. I tried to move but was frozen. Then I saw him, silent as a shadow, moving toward the big man. Was he real or did I conjure him up? I hadn't seen him in the crowded bar, but he'd seen me, and now, there he was, a guardian angel without wings or halo.

But with a knife.

Francisco Crespo.

For a second I lost sight of him, but then he materialized again a step behind and just to the left of Big Mouth. As the man's fat thumb pulled back the hammer of his gun, I heard the *cl-ick*, and simultaneously, Crespo flicked his wrist, and a six-inch steel blade flashed out of a black onyx handle. Big Mouth heard the blade whipping into place, and his eyes widening, he wheeled to his left, the gun swiveling toward Crespo.

Crespo drove his hand forward, straight and hard, with no wasted motion. The blade struck between the sixth and seventh ribs and plunged straight into the man's heart. His mouth opened, a startled look, and his eyes shifted from Crespo, to me, to the blade jammed in his chest. Crespo pulled out the knife with a wet, sucking *plop*, then watched the man crumple to the floor.

No longer an apparition, Crespo was a small, wiry agent of doom, his face devoid of expression. He leaned over, wiped the knife on the man's shirt, straightened, folded the blade into its handle, nodded to me, and walked out. The bar patrons scattered as he left.

Then I saw it again, just as always, this time at dreamscape speed, the gun pointing at me, Crespo appearing in the crowd, and I heard the sounds again, the man's raspy voice, the wailing jukebox, the *cl-ick* of the hammer, the snap of the blade, and the *plop* of punctured tissue. Over and over, slower and slower, until I chased the foggy ribbons out of my head and shook myself awake, realizing where I was and how long ago it had been.

Now I checked my watch. Three-thirty A.M. I stood and stretched. My shirt was clammy, my back stiff. I curled up again in the molded plastic chair created by a noted designer who was a distant cousin of the Marquis de Sade. As I groped for sleep that eluded me, the rest of it emerged from deeply etched memory.

Two patrolmen were there in seven minutes, the homicide detective in another twenty. Everyone in the bar suffered from either myopia or amnesia. Except me, and the best I could do was recollect a six-foot-five, husky Anglo with a knife, a guy with short red hair and a flag tattoo. Looked like a marine, I told the cops.

The day began with the roar of floor polishers moving down the deserted concourse. My head was filled with sand and my back needed half a dozen spinal twists to work out the crinks and knots. I bought a toothbrush, toothpaste, and a ninety-five-cent razor in the sundries shop, rinsed my face with cold water, and went to a counter to borrow the Official Airline Guide, international edition. Sure enough, a Finnair flight would arrive at JFK nonstop from Helsinki just after noon. I switched books to the national edition and tried to figure the connecting flight.

Easy. American Airlines had a two o'clock nonstop, JFK to Miami. Enough time to clear customs in New York and climb aboard. The clincher. Finnair and American shared terminal space. No need to hop the bus and go round the horn from terminal to terminal.

I had the day to kill, so I bought a couple magazines, a Travis McGee paperback, and a bag of jelly beans. When a Metro policeman eyed me at midday, I sat still until he passed, then changed concourses.

The American flight from JFK was an hour late. The plane was supposed to do a turnaround, and the gate area was crowded with angry folks who couldn't board because the aircraft wasn't here yet. Some businessmen in suits, ties loosened, already dreading yet another delay. Tourists with bawling children going home, carry-ons stuffed with presents and mementos. A blond boy of about seven was playing with one of those remote-control cars, zooming it across the tile, banging into walls, getting the hang of the steering. Nearby, a few tourists lingered at the magazine stand. A young couple shared one chair. Newlyweds, probably, or maybe they always groped each other at airport gates.

I tried to blend in with the crowd. Finally, a scratchy public address system announced the arrival of the flight, and a few minutes later a 727 pulled up to the jetway. I walked across the corridor to a pay phone that had clear line of sight to the arrival gate and dialed the airline's number. After a "Please hold," and "I'll transfer you now," and then a repeat of both messages, I told the clerk my problem and asked for a teensy-weensy favor. Then I hung up and waited, watching the counter.

Passengers were already disembarking, but nothing happened. The counter clerk, a young man with a frizzy mustache, seemed preoccupied with a family of six who must not have liked their seat assignments. More passengers streamed out, a mix of tourists and businessmen. I watched a middle-aged gray-haired man in a blue suit. Did he look Russian? A body-builder type in blue jeans and a leather jacket walked out. Was that Kharchenko? A round-shouldered man in wire-rimmed glasses could have been an art expert. No one was carrying a cardboard tube, but it might have been in the luggage. Then again, maybe this was the wrong flight. I looked down the concourse at a mass of humanity, realizing the difficulty of my task.

A moment later, the counter clerk lifted the microphone, pushed the button, and solemnly announced, "Arriving passenger, Mr. Kharchenko. Please report to the counter and pick up the red courtesy telephone."

I waited some more, aware I was staring, catching a few curious glances back from the passengers. I picked up the pay phone again and pretended to talk to my Granny, complaining loudly about the sorry state of bass fishing in Lake Okeechobee.

The plane must have been nearly empty by now. Again, the clerk picked up the microphone. "Arriving passenger, Mr. Kharchenko . . ."

The man stopped dead, but just for a second, his head swiveling left and right. Then he resumed walking. A thick-necked, burly man in a brown suit, beige shirt, and brown knit tie. He carried a soft leather bag that could have held a cardboard tube. He was one of those toe walkers, not bouncing along, but gliding, his heels never touching the floor. The man had graying short hair and was close to six feet, and though the suit was baggy, I could see the outline of broad shoulders.

". . . Please report to the front counter and pick up the red courtesy phone, Mr. Kharchenko."

He never stopped. He walked right by the counter. Just as he did, the little blond boy's race car turned a corner and headed right for the man. When it was nearly at his feet, he skipped over it.

It was an odd sight, the sturdy man giving a little hoppity-hop over the car, without breaking stride, landing on his toes. It took a second for me to figure it out, why it seemed so peculiar. He hadn't been looking down. He had been scanning the gate area and the concourse and the bank of phones where I stood pretending to talk to my Granny. He'd been watching everything around him, his eyes fixing on me momentarily as he covered the expanse of the concourse, the magazine stand, the duty-free shop, the soft-pretzel stand, the candy wagon. He gave the impression that his every sense was primed and alert. He was cautious and agile and strong, and as I laughed at some imaginary joke, I knew it was him.

He didn't answer the page because he had been trained not to. His ticket probably was not in the name of Kharchenko. No one would call him here, at least no one he wanted to speak to. But I had found him just the same, and as he turned the corner and headed toward the terminal, I was busy congratulating myself. Falling in behind him, staring at his broad back, I realized that I had seen him before. I had never seen his face, or if I had, it hadn't registered. But I had seen *him*. I had chased him through a trail of lawn chairs and hibachis. I had watched him duck low and scramble effortlessly under a clothesline.

Sure, Kharchenko, I know you. I just missed seeing you kill Francisco Crespo.

16

RENDEZVOUS

Kharchenko toe-walked the length of the concourse, stopping once at a water fountain. It gave him a chance to look back to see if any bozos were following him. Best I could tell, there was only one.

I kept walking, passing him at the fountain, but slowing down just a bit. Then, I stopped at the newspaper machines, studied the front pages of the Miami and Ft. Lauderdale papers, then opted for *The Wall Street Journal* to check on my ten shares of I.B.M.

My delay let Kharchenko leapfrog me, and I fell in step again. At the juncture with the main terminal, passengers streamed toward us through the metal detectors. Behind glass doors, waiting friends and relatives craned their necks, peering down the concourse, eyes searching for familiar faces.

Kharchenko wended his way past a horde of South Americans wheeling Sony TVs and Mitsubishi CD players toward their flights. He passed by the escalator that would have taken him down to baggage claim and headed straight toward the exit on the upper level. Carrying his soft leather bag, he stepped outside. I followed, a blast of warm air greeting me, the glare of the late afternoon sun making me wince.

He grabbed the first taxi in line, and I hustled toward the second, elbowing past a family with three kids and Mickey Mouse stickers on their luggage. "Can you follow that cab?" I asked the driver.

"Sure, mon." He was a thin black man who sat on a beaded cushion and kept his radio tuned to a Creole station.

We headed east, taking the expressway above the streets of Liberty City, crossing the bay on the Julia Tuttle Causeway, a high, looping six-lane bridge built on landfill and pilings and lined with towering palm trees. The sun was behind us now, glinting orange sparks off the windows of the oceanfront hotels on the Miami Beach side of the bay. The causeway, jammed with taxis from the airport, hits Miami Beach just north of the Sunset Islands and dumps traffic onto Arthur Godfrey Road. After touching the shoreline by Mount Sinai Hospital, Kharchenko's taxi swung right and headed south on Alton Road along the municipal golf course. Some late-afternoon hackers were still out, flailing away.

Near Convention Hall, at the intersection of Dade Boulevard and Meridian Avenue, Kharchenko's taxi slowed, then pulled into a diagonal parking place between two tour buses. A stream of Japanese tourists poured out of one bus, heading toward the Holocaust Memorial. My driver, Jean-Claude Saint Martine, according to his photo ID, stopped, too. I paid him, gave him an extra ten to keep him there, grabbed my newspaper, and fell in with a group of well-dressed, middle-aged Japanese couples. I was as inconspicuous as a moose among kittens.

Ahead of me, Kharchenko crossed a walkway of rough-hewn Jerusalem stone. The setting sun was a fireball that shot sparks across the semicircular black granite wall. The reflecting pool seemed ablaze, as if flaming oil had been poured on the water. The Japanese were peering at the wall, which was etched with photographs of the horrors of the Holocaust. I followed Kharchenko slowly around the exhibit, walking under wooden trellises laced with white bougainvillea vines, aware of the contrast between this peaceful garden and the tortured exhibits, which so fascinated the tourists.

Kharchenko paused to read the words etched into the granite. I couldn't tell if he was waiting for someone, or if he was genuinely interested. I examined the etchings, too, recoiling at the photos of emaciated bodies in the death camps, reading the familiar inscription by Anne Frank: "In spite of everything, I still believe that people are really good at heart." I passed two bearded men dressed in black suits and black hats, their heads bent, their lips moving in silent prayer.

I followed Kharchenko through a narrow tunnel with a lowered ceiling, a claustrophobic place that displayed the names of Auschwitz, Dachau, Buchenwald, and the others. Then I came into the open where a towering bronze sculpture of a tattooed arm reached toward the sky. Clambering up the arm were tormented bronze figures of parents and children, the aged and infants, all crying out in pain and despair, portraits in misery. An outstretched hand at the top of the sculpture seemed to represent both despair and hope. This was a piece of art I understood, at once exquisite and heinous, a nightmare that was reality.

I saw her before he did. She stood near the lily-covered pool, watching the reflection of the towering arm in the rippling sun-tinted water. The long platinum hair peeked out from under a white hat with a broad brim and a black velvet band on which was fastened a black velvet rose. The A-line skirt was knee-length and white with black snaps down the front. The snaps were undone to midthigh. The matching top had long, puffy sleeves and the same black snaps down the middle. Her shoes were black with stiletto heels, and lifted her to an even six feet, give or take an inch. Black wraparound sunglasses shielded her eyes, and a black leather bag hung on a strap from her shoulder.

Kharchenko walked toward her. She didn't nod, toss her arms around him, or kiss him hello. Neither said a word. The Russian simply moved to her side, and they strolled to a nearby concrete bench and sat down.

I took up a position behind them, where I could read the names on the memorial wall and watch the back of Kharchenko's head at the same time. He leaned close to the blonde and whispered in her ear. She nodded, glanced to one side, reached down, opened her bag, and handed him an envelope. He slipped it into his inside coat pocket without looking at it. From the other pocket, he removed a document and gave it to her. She placed it in her purse. Then Kharchenko opened his carry-on bag, reached inside, and removed a cardboard tube. He seemed to offer it to her, but she shook her head. He shrugged and replaced the tube in his bag.

She touched her hand to the side of her face and pushed her long straight hair back under her hat, and her head turned my way. She seemed to be scanning the area. I got a quick look at her profile—fair skin, an upturned nose—as I lowered my head and raised my *Wall Street Journal.* I turned a couple of pages. Pork bellies seemed to be doing very well. When I looked up again, Kharchenko was standing. He grabbed his leather bag, said something that might have been good-bye, then turned and headed back toward his waiting taxicab.

Which left me with a choice.

Follow the Russian or follow the blonde. Which wasn't much of a choice after all.

She didn't take a taxi or get into a car. She walked. She had a fine, tall-lady walk. I stayed twenty-five yards behind, and she never looked back. She kept up a good pace, heading south on Meridian toward Flamingo Park. Soon, my knee throbbed. Spending all night cramped in an airport chair was not the recommended therapy. I kept my position behind her, thinking about a hot whirlpool, remembering twin cheerleaders a dozen years earlier who thought it would be fun to dump bubble bath into the tub. It was.

I could hear the soft *thwock* of tennis ball against racket as we approached the park. Then she turned left on Espanola Way, and I followed, staying a bit closer, admiring the muscular curve of her calves, undulating under the white skirt. She crossed a street against the light. She ducked behind a produce truck that was headed toward the Ocean Drive restaurants. I picked up my tempo again. She kept up a good pace. The lady had done some walking in her time. Maybe some sports, too. I watched the bag swing on her shoulder. Whatever Kharchenko gave her was in there.

At the corner of Espanola and Washington Avenue, a small crowd milled through a dozen stands at an outdoor farmer's market. The blonde lingered in front of a wooden box of yellow and orange mangoes. I came up beside her, reached into the bin, and pulled one up, bringing it under my nose. A rich and lusty fragrance, the skin yielding to the touch. "Nearly ripe," I said.

She turned and peered at me over the top of her sunglasses. From her expression, she might have been looking at a two-hundred-twenty-six-pound cockroach.

"Better than peaches, if you ask me," I said.

"I didn't," she replied, turned, and walked on.

She passed up the avocados, lychee nuts, and carambolas, and so did I. She crossed Washington, heading toward Collins and the ocean, then turned abruptly into a cramped alley behind a Thai restaurant. I thought for a moment I might lose her, so I broke into a jog and turned the corner, the fragrance of ginger sauces heavy in the air. Then I stopped dead, not six inches from her. She stood near a Dumpster, facing me, hands on hips, scowling.

She said something in a language that sounded like loud snoring. It had a lot of *k*'s and *t*'s and, whatever the tongue, probably was the equivalent of, "What kind of asshole are you?"

I didn't respond. I just looked at her. Pretty. Pouty lips. Blond hair spilling out of the white hat. She looked familiar, but behind the sunglasses, I couldn't place . . .

"Kusipaa!" she yelled at me. *"Idiootti!"*

She took a half-step toward me and snap-kicked a knee into my groin. The pain was a spear straight through the spine. I doubled over, and she let fly a fist that came from her hip in a half-circular movement, the *mawashi-zuki* in karate. This time I saw it coming and pivoted the other way, twisting my bad knee. The punch glanced off my temple but I was off balance, and a second later, I was flat on my back in a puddle of foul-smelling water coming from the Dumpster. I looked up at her with my best choirboy demeanor. "Okay, so you don't like mangoes."

"You son of a bitch!" she yowled, with a tiny lilt of a singsong accent. She moved back a step and peppered me with three or four kicks in the ribs. The ribs might have hurt if my crotch hadn't claimed an exclusive on agony. I got to my knees, reached out and grabbed a slim ankle that was attached to a foot that was trying to kick my brains through my ear. I yanked hard and down she came, right on her nicely tailored rump. The hat spun off her head and the sunglasses slid down her nose.

"Alypaa!"

"Ali-Baba," I said.

I kept hold of the ankle and yanked again, as she tried kicking me with the other foot. I dragged her toward me and gave the ankle a twist until she yelled. Then I hopped on top, straddling her, pinning her arms to the cool stones and sitting on her rib cage. Her pale hair was swirled across her mouth, and she looked at me with very blue, very angry eyes.

"Get off me, you big slug!"

"I believe the expression is *big lug.*"

"Paskianen! You weigh a ton."

"And you kick like a mule."

I heard a door bang open and looked up to see an Asian man in a kitchen smock staring at us from the rear of the restaurant. "It's okay," I said. "We're married."

"I would rather be dead," she spat, and the man ducked back inside.

She was breathing hard, so I eased a little weight off her. As I did, she tried to buck me off. I kept both hands around her wrists, and pushed her back down. She struggled again, and I dug my right thumb into the ulnar nerve of her left forearm. Wincing, she fell back.

She shook her head, tossing a long strand of hair out of her face. Then I saw it, a gold pendant on a necklace. A rabbit holding a red egg flecked with tiny diamonds. I looked up from the necklace to her full lips, and it was slowly coming back to me. A blonde in a white bathing suit. "Jillian from Minnesota! What are you doing here?"

"It's Eva-Lisa from Helsinki. I'm a Suopo agent."

"Sue-poh?"

"The Finnish Intelligence Agency, you moron."

"I don't believe this. I thought you were a sunburned tourist who wanted a windsurfing lesson."

"A lesson! From you? *Toope!* I won the Scandinavian freestyle championship three years in a row. Tell me, what makes men so vain and stupid?"

Practice, I thought.

I stared into her arctic blue eyes trying to figure it out. A windsurfing lass from Finland frolics in the water off Miami Beach, pretending she needs a lesson. Now, she's playing games with a Russian who most likely held a potato in front of the gun that shot Francisco Crespo. Small world, isn't it?

"Jillian . . . Eva-Lisa, whoever you are, what are you doing here?" I asked, and not for the first time.

"I told you, I'm on assignment. I am working. What are *you* doing here?"

I didn't answer her. I couldn't. I didn't have a clue.

17

TEARS OF REINDEERS

"You work for Yagamata," I said, dusting myself off, my voice an octave higher than an hour earlier.

We had untangled, said mutual apologies, and were walking toward Ocean Drive. She shook her head. "For the Finnish government under contract to Yagamata, who in turn works for your government."

No wonder I couldn't tell the players without a scorecard. "What are you, some kind of spy?"

That made her laugh. "I am little more than a clerk."

"What were you doing with Kharchenko?"

"Making him a delivery boy for Yagamata."

"I don't get it."

She looked at me from under the white hat and dark glasses. Though I couldn't see her eyes, I thought they were appraising me. "I am not sure I can trust you."

"Funny, I was thinking the same thing about you, or if I wasn't, I should have been. The way I figure it, you're part of a conspiracy to steal Russian art."

"Nothing is as simple as it seems," she said, and I wondered if Charlie could put that in Latin for me.

"Tell me about it. Tell me why an old friend of mine got killed and why I'm getting set up."

"Give me some time," she said. "Maybe we are on the same side." We stopped in front of the News Café on Ocean Drive, and she motioned me toward a silver Saab parked at the curb. I let her unlock my door, and I settled into the seat, buckling the shoulder harness.

Eva-Lisa got behind the wheel, turned the key in the ignition, and asked, "Do you know what tonight is?"

"Sunday," I said, "June twenty."

"Seuraasaari. Midsommareldarna. Midsummer's Eve, a national holiday in my country. It is the way we welcome the longest day of the year. In Helsinki tonight it will be cool and clear, and it will not grow dark. The sun will seem to set, but it will hover at the horizon, casting a most beautiful glow. Then it will slowly rise again."

Of course, Finland, land of the midnight sun.

She swung the car into traffic, heading south past all the trendy sidewalk cafés. "You probably know of the Finnish community in Lake Worth." When I nodded, she continued. "My father has a house there. It is reminiscent of our home in Tapiola. Very Finnish, made of stone and wood, an authentic sauna on the edge of the lake. We Finns try to keep up our traditions. My family is in Spain on holiday, and I was going to spend the night alone. If you would like, you may be my guest at the festivities tonight. It is really rather simple. Just a bonfire, some folk songs, and dancing, but we can talk there about Yagamata and Kharchenko if you wish."

It sounded better than being chased by Robert Foley, so I said fine, and we turned onto Fifth Street, which led us to the MacArthur Causeway. The ferry to Fisher Island was just pulling out, taking home all the rich folks who need a moat to protect them from the realities of life. We passed the real estate developers' dreams of Star Island and Palm Island, dredged landfills transformed into million-dollar lots. On the Miami side of Biscayne Bay, we swung onto I-95 and headed due north. Lake Worth is a few miles south of Palm Beach, a straight shot on the expressway. If I were looking for me, it would be the last place I would look. But then, I wasn't looking for me. Somebody else was.

Despite its substantial Finnish population, Lake Worth is not Helsinki. At midnight, the sun was not hovering on the horizon. The air was not crisp and cool. There was no lemon glow across the water. Instead, mosquitoes hummed around the mercury vapor lamps on the patio behind the large flagstone house. Still, it was pleasant enough, a quiet, placid place unlike Miami. Beyond the patio, a lawn sloped toward a lake. A three-quarter moon hung in the eastern sky, casting a pearly glow on the dark water. A hint of a breeze kept the temperature tolerable, though the air was soggy with tropical humidity. From the rear of the house, a stone path led down the lawn to a small building made of pine. The building sat at the edge of the lake on a wooden dock, and a chimney poked out of the roof. The sauna, my hostess told me, pronouncing it *sow-na.*

She looked across the water toward a small island. A band played what I took to be Finnish folk songs. Children's voices carried across the bay. On an outcropping of rock at the island's shoreline, dozens of trees were lashed together in a pyramid. A dinghy was tied on top, fifty feet above the water.

"It is almost time for the bonfire," Eva-Lisa said. She had changed into khaki shorts and a matching blouse, and was reclining in a chaise lounge made of light wood and covered with a blue cushion. I sat in a matching straight-back chair looking at her pale, muscular legs.

She told me her father, Reino Haavikko, was in Finnish intelligence, an expert on what used to be the Soviet Union. Then she gave me a quick history lesson. Since the end of World War II, living in the shadow of the Russian bear, Finland has walked a tightrope. It was a Western democracy toeing a line of neutrality while paying homage to its massive, dangerous neighbor. She said something in Finnish and then translated. "The only good thing from the east is the vodka." The Finns scorn the Russians for their inefficiency and laziness but dread their armaments and temperament. "Finlandization" became a catchword for the way to get along with the Soviets when the U.S.S.R. was a fearful entity. When the Union broke apart, Finland and the other Scandinavian countries were the first to recognize the independent Baltic states. Now, after more than forty-five years of tiptoeing around the Russians, Finland was ready to profit from them. Along with the rest of the West, the Finns were queuing up to build factories and apartment buildings, to sell tractors and hamburgers and VCR's to a nation starving for decent shoes, microwave ovens, and Nintendo games.

She poured a red drink from a pitcher. I took a sip. Syrup with a kick. *"Poron kyynel,"* she said, hoisting her glass.

"Cheers," I returned.

"No. What you are drinking is Finlandia with lingonberry juice. We call it *poron kyynel,* tears of reindeers."

Earlier, she had fed me a platter of four different kinds of herring, a Finnish favorite, plus salmon soup with vegetables and a casserole of potatoes, ham, eggs, and anchovies. Sturdy country fare. While I ate, she apologized again for practicing her place-kicking against my ribs. I had looked vaguely familiar, a Russian perhaps, someone dangerous who hadn't been bought by Yagamata. When I asked what she meant, she clammed up. She seemed to be bursting with the desire to tell me what I wanted to know and more, but something was holding her back.

I had showered and changed into a pair of her father's gray pants that were too big and a white short-sleeve shirt that was too small. The drink was too sweet but bearable. The company was attractive but evasive. I wasn't getting anywhere except slightly potted. I like to think of myself as an astute questioner. I can be deft and subtle, can parry and thrust. But sometimes I just wade right in.

"Okay, Eva-Lisa, I'm getting different stories about what's going on, so how about setting me straight. What were you doing in Miami, and what's happening here? Who's behind the theft of Russian art and what's Yagamata really up to? What's Kharchenko doing here, and what's arriving on the freighter? Why did Kharchenko kill Crespo, and why am I being set up for his murder?"

She looked genuinely puzzled. "I don't know any Crespo. . . ." If that's all she didn't know, what she knew could fill a book. "As for what is arriving on the freighter," she continued, "the manifest says Finnish lumber."

"And what do you say?"

She smiled enigmatically. "I will answer your questions if you will answer mine."

I nodded.

"What is on the freighter is the most valuable collection of artwork ever assembled in one place. Ever! It is from the Hermitage and other museums in Russia. My job was inventory control in Helsinki. Today, Kharchenko gave me the bills of lading showing what arrived here. An exact match, the paintings, the jewelry, the historic artifacts. No pilferage, no damage. I always did my job well, except when Yagamata stole a little something here and there, and I had no control over that." She looked toward the island. The sound of children singing drifted across the lake. "Tell me about Mr. Crespo."

"He used to hand out towels in a locker room, and lately he'd been working in a warehouse owned by Yagamata. First he gets charged with murdering a Russian named Smorodinsky, then—"

"Who?" She spilled a drop of her blood-red drink.

"Another guy who worked for Yagamata. Smorod—"

"Vladimir or Nikolai?" she asked. Her voice cracked.

"Vladimir."

She sighed and bit her lower lip. Across the bay, I heard what sounded like accordion music.

"Is it a sin," she asked softly, "for me to be happy that a good and decent man is dead?"

"I don't understand."

"Nikolai is my lover. He works for Yagamata in St. Petersburg. Or at least, he did. He is with us, now. Vladimir is his older brother."

"I'm sorry. I mean, I'm sorry for Vladimir. I'm glad it wasn't your—"

"Exactly. It is a tragedy, but not really mine." On the island, hundreds of people gathered around the pyramid of trees. Excited shouts of children mixed with the music. "You think Kharchenko killed your friend?"

"I saw him there. At least I think I did. Yagamata has gone to a lot of trouble to make it look like Crespo killed Vladimir. When Crespo was about to tell who did, he was shot."

She looked across the water, shimmering silver and black in the moonlight. She seemed to be considering how much to say. When she spoke, it was quietly, almost to herself. "Yagamata must have killed Vlad to protect the operation, and if he did, Nikki is in great danger, too."

"Where is Nikolai now?"

"On his way here. He should be in Miami Beach tomorrow."

Everybody's coming to town, I thought. No wonder Foley wanted me out of the way.

"Nikki wanted to stop the thefts," she said, "and when that became impossible, to gather the evidence against those responsible. I must alert Nikki to the danger, but I do not know where he will be staying. He is so afraid of telephones. There is a Russian saying, 'Never trust anyone but your pillow.' That is Nikki, so very suspicious. All he said was he would find me when he got to the place of the fish."

"The fish? Like a dock, a boat?"

"Or a hotel. Are there any hotels named after fish?"

"I don't think we have a Hotel Herring, but I'll look into it."

On the island, an orange torch flared at the foot of the bonfire. A second later, the trees caught fire, and the flames slowly worked their way to the top. The scent of scorched pine carried across the calm water.

"Eva-Lisa, tell me what's going on. Everything."

"How do I know you don't work for Yagamata now?"

"Me?"

"The last time I saw the two of you, it was lunchtime aboard the *Yugen,* and you were eating his caviar. Doesn't he pay your legal fees, too?"

"Look, I was trying to save somebody's ass. Francisco Crespo was a guy who never amounted to much, but he didn't deserve to die. He saved my life once, and I had a chance to return the favor but muffed it. Today you were playing post office with the man who put two bullets in him. I'm the guy they're trying to frame for the murder. I need to bring Kharchenko in. There are witnesses who got a look at his face. Put him in a lineup, and maybe I could get him indicted for murder. Especially if I can show a link between the two deaths."

"Meaning what?"

"Motive. To know why Crespo was killed, I need to know why Smorodinsky was killed. You've got to tell me what Yagamata and the brothers Smorodinsky were up to."

She kept her eyes on the island. "You really do not know, do you?"

"All I know is that my government is trying to stop the theft of art treasures from Russia. Something about our protecting the reformers from being embarrassed."

She laughed. "Who told you that?"

"Robert Foley. He's with the—"

"CIA. I did not think Mr. Foley had such a delicious sense of irony."

"I don't get it."

I hadn't finished my first one, but she topped off the glass with the potent drink and gave herself one, too. "There is something very sweet about you," she said, softly. Before I could thank her, she added a footnote. "But something so naive, too. Our job is not to *stop* the thefts."

"No?"

"Of course not, Mr. Lassiter. We are the thieves."

I had put away two more glasses of the red stuff when Eva-Lisa told me she would cut the *vaihtaa* if I would chop the wood. She grabbed a machete and disappeared into the overgrowth at the side of the house, while I contented myself swinging a short-handled hatchet at some birch logs that had never hurt anybody. I luxuriated in the weight of the hatchet, the stretch in the muscles of my arm and back with each swing, the satisfying *thwack* of steel on wood. I chopped enough to keep the Haavikko clan toasty all winter, at least a Florida winter. A few moments later, Eva-Lisa walked out of a stand of pop ash trees. She was carrying a handful of leafy branches, maybe three feet long.

She came up to me, shook the leaves in my face, and smiled. "It is a shame the white birch tree doesn't grow here. Its branches have just the right amount of give for the *vaihtaa.*"

I looked at her, not fully understanding.

"You'd be surprised how some gentle switching can heat you up."

Actually, I didn't think I would be surprised at all.

I carried the wood into the sauna. The interior was light pine, sparkling clean. An anteroom contained a shower, wooden pegs in the wall to hold our clothes, white fluffy towels, and benches carved from ash trees. I found some old newspaper for kindling and a box of foot-long matches. The fire began slowly, the dry wood crackling with flames under a pile of gray volcanic rocks. Eva-Lisa filled a bucket with cool water and brought it into the sauna, closing the door tightly, letting the heat build, while we sat in the adjacent changing room. Another bucket contained bottles of Finnish beer, *olut,* on ice. A horse frolicked on the label. The beer was for later. Good, the coach always told us to replace our bodily fluids.

We sat on a bench studying each other. She started unbuttoning her blouse. "Do you believe the naked body is beautiful?"

"I have a suspicion yours is, but mine has railroad track scars across both knees, a crosshatch over my rotator cuff, and one toenail that's permanently purple from turf toe."

"In America, they believe we have sex in the sauna," she said evenly.

"Oh?"

She had slipped out of the blouse and loosened the web belt on her khaki shorts. "But we don't."

"No?"

She let the shorts slide down her long legs, kicked them off in a graceful motion, and hung them on a wooden peg with her blouse. "No, it is far too hot. Besides, the sauna is a spiritual place. The heat will cleanse the body and the mind." She unfastened her bra and tossed it aside, her creamy breasts tumbling free. She stepped out of her panties and smiled at me.

I could feel the warmth from the other side of the pine walls. At least, I think that's where it came from. In a moment, my clothing was crumbled in a corner of the room. I was ready to partake of the heat. I wasn't sure about my body, but just then, my mind needed a good cleansing.

We were sitting on mats that covered the wooden benches inside the sauna. The fire glowed white hot. Eva-Lisa used a ladle to pour water on the rocks, sending waves of steam toward our faces. Each breath scorched the inside of my nose, each burst of steam seemed to melt my fingernails. But if she wouldn't cry uncle, neither would I. A small window overlooked the bay. Outside, the orange flames of the bonfire glittered off the smooth surface of the black lake. The moon ducked behind silvery clouds.

"I don't understand why the CIA would be in the business of stealing Russian art treasures," I said, exhaling the words in gasping breaths. "And why are they doing business with a crook like Yagamata?"

She looked toward me, cheeks rosy, but vital signs apparently within normal limits. "Yagamata is a broker between your government and various Japanese and German millionaires who purchase the artwork." She ran a hand through her sweat-streaked hair. "Originally, the plan was to eradicate the old hard-line communists, to assure that the reformers have complete control. What was it Foley used to say? 'To drive the coffin nail into the godless heart of communism.' "

"Sounds like J. Edgar Hoover. But that stuff's out of date now."

"It started a year or so before Yanayev and his friends attempted the putsch. The CIA never believed that *perestroika* would work. The old guard—the Party, the military, the KGB—would wait for near chaos, then overthrow Gorbachev and crack down. Operation Riptide was intended as a preemptive strike against the hard-liners so that the reformers could create a capitalistic state subservient to the U.S., Japan, and the European Community. Before it could happen, however, the eight little dwarfs tried their takeover."

"So the CIA was right."

"Sure," she said, "except they never figured the coup would fail. In three days, those old Reds accomplished what the West couldn't do in seventy years. They destroyed the Party, dissolved the Union, and freed the republics."

"I still don't see what stealing Russian pictures has to do with politics. To me, it just looks like a burglary."

"You are missing the subtlety of it. The museums, the ministries of culture were appendages of the Party, which every Russian knew to be corrupt and self-serving. Long before Gorbachev resigned as General Secretary, your CIA was trying to discredit the Communist Party. What do you think an aroused populace would have done when they learned that the Party elite and their appointed bureaucrats were on the payroll of the West?"

My look must have told her she had lost me, so she continued. "How do you think we get the icons, the Fabergé eggs, the French paintings, the diamond-studded artifacts out of Russia?"

"Federal Express?"

She whacked the *vaihtaa* across my shoulders. The blood rose to the surface. If I kept sweating, I could box bantamweight by morning.

"Bribery, of course," she said. "What the *verkhushka* didn't know is that it was a gigantic sting operation. Some of the bribes got paid in cash, but the really large sums were deposited into numbered Swiss accounts. The accounts could be traced to government leaders, everybody from local officials in St. Petersburg and Kiev to bureaucrats in nearly every republic, to hard-liners who used to have lunch with Gorbachev. All the CIA operatives were wired. Vladimir and Nikolai, Kharchenko, even Yagamata. They videotaped money changing hands, just like your . . . Amway."

"Abscam," I said.

"It went so close to the top you wouldn't believe it. Does the name Pugo mean anything to you?"

"A French car assembled in Yugoslavia?"

"Boris Pugo was Gorbachev's Interior Minister."

I remembered the stories. "Right, one of the clowns who took part in the coup. Didn't he commit suicide?"

"Now do you understand the significance of this?"

I let out a whistle. "It ain't borscht."

"But do you *understand*?"

"Wait a second, are you saying some commie in the cabinet committed suicide because he was caught selling golden eggs, not because of the failed coup?"

She looked at me with some tenderness. "You're getting warmer."

Of course I was. Sweat was running down my face and dripping onto my chest. "The coup! You're telling me these guys tried to grab control because Gorbachev found out they were on the take. He was going to have their heads, so they had to take power and cover it up."

She smiled conspiratorially, and my mind kept racing. I stood up and paced, two steps one way, two steps the other. I kept banging into the hot walls. "But the hard-liners are gone. Gorbachev is gone. The republics are free. The CIA operation should be over."

She shook her head and sweat dripped from her chin. "But it is not. It is no longer a surgical operation to discredit certain hard-liners. Now Foley and Yagamata aren't interested in just bringing out a few paintings and icons. They want it all. They have discovered how easy it is to steal, and they just can't stop. They already know how to bribe the lower functionaries, who are still there, and they don't need the higher-ups anymore. Even if the leaders of the republics know what's going on, they are powerless to stop it. They must cover it up because they are responsible now, and what's happening is so big and their governments so fragile, it could topple them. That's why Nikki and Vlad wanted to blow the whistle. They can't let Yagamata and Foley rape their country, steal the legacy of the Russian people, and redistribute it to millionaires in the West. There has never been a burglary, as you put it, on this scale before."

She tossed the *vaihtaa* onto the floor.

I thought I saw a shadow pass by the small window. When I looked up, it was gone. The clouds had scudded away, and pearly moonlight streamed through the window. "Why did you get involved?"

"Just like Nikki, I was fooled in the beginning. I had no idea of the scope of the operation. Now, everything is out of control. It will come out, the thefts, the deception. There is a proverb: 'In Russia, everything is a secret, but nothing is a mystery.' The people are used to official corruption, but nothing like this. Selling their birthright, disowning the motherland, treason at the highest levels, the continued pillaging under the reformers. The Russians take such pride in their art, even when their cupboards are bare. When this story breaks, with the new freedom of the press and expression in the Soviet Union, what do you think will happen?"

"People will be pissed," I guessed.

"Complete anarchy. Maybe not if everything else was stable. But it will be fueled by the economic crisis, by the reality that democratic reforms do not make life luxurious, that a change of government does not automatically eradicate corruption. There will be violence. The army will attempt to crack down, but it will not work. My father estimates desertions will run between thirty and forty percent. The borders will be opened, and the cork will be out of the bottle. Fifty percent of the population will try to flee to the west, untold numbers into Finland. Moscow itself is less than eight hundred kilometers from Helsinki. Imagine the consequences. Millions of impoverished Russians will overwhelm us. Many will want to travel to the U.S. or Israel or who knows where. But they will have no money, no prospects. The first ports of call will be the last for so many. Finland is a small country. Only five million people, fewer than in the city of St. Petersburg. Already, with the easing of the visa laws, we have criminals coming from Estonia. They smuggle everything from vodka to Kalashnikovs on the black market. Estonian prostitutes fill our streets on the weekends. But that is nothing compared to what is coming. We will drown in the dregs from the east."

She stood up, and rivulets of sweat trickled between her breasts and down over her flat stomach. Outside the window, the bay again had turned to a black silk sheet, clouds covering the moon, before flitting by, leaving the calm water drenched in ivory light. It was impossible to determine the time. Sometime between midnight and dawn. I was exhausted from the tension of the last forty-eight hours, from the scorching heat, from the growing knowledge that this was more complex than anything I had imagined. I leaned back against the wooden wall of the sauna, closed my eyes, and let my mind wander.

I remembered a lazy night in a Boston Whaler, anchored beneath one of the bridges in the Keys, drinking bourbon and fishing all night with Charlie Riggs. Just before five A.M., the eastern horizon lit up with what I thought was a new day.

"Sun rises early down here," I had told Charlie.

He laughed. "Just zodiacal light, my boy."

"Huh?"

Charlie bet me twenty bucks it would be pitch black again before the sun came up. Of course, I took him on, and a few minutes later, it was so dark I couldn't see if I was handing him Andrew Jackson or Ben Franklin.

"False dawn," Charlie said, pocketing the money.

"Say what?"

"The orange glow you saw to the east. Particles of meteors reflecting the light of the sun that hasn't risen yet. It's called false dawn."

Charlie said some more about the *gegenschein,* or counter-glow, and something about the F-corona of the sun, but I forget it now. What I remember is Charlie spouting one of his Latin expressions, something about *non teneas aurum* something-or-other, which he translated as "all that glitters is not gold."

"What are you trying to tell me?" I asked him.

"The first light is not always the dawn, Jake. Often it's the reflection of something not really there at all."

I stood and left an outline of sweat on the bench. "You're not going to get any sympathy from me for the plight of your country in all of this. You're part of it, you're responsible—"

"Until today. I gave Kharchenko a letter to take to Yagamata. It's my resignation."

"Your what?"

"You heard me. As you Americans say, 'I quit.' "

"Look, I don't know anything about this, but it doesn't sound to me like you've got a Civil Service job that you can just—"

"It is a concern, surely, especially in view of what happened to Vlad. I know far too much. But Yagamata understands that my family is too highly placed to attempt anything that could risk his operation. Yagamata is a cautious man and a brilliant one. I am counting on that. As for Kharchenko, he is actually quite fond of me. He asked me to accompany him to the ballet tomorrow night."

Kharchenko at the ballet? It didn't quite compute. Eva-Lisa seemed to be reading my mind. "Like most Russians, Kharchenko loves his culture," she said.

"Yeah, but that doesn't make him civilized. Maybe it's my imagination, but you seem as if you're trying to convince yourself that you're not in danger."

She shrugged her naked shoulders. She looked so vulnerable, standing with arms folded beneath her full breasts, slick with sweat. I took a step toward her, the floorboards squeaking under my feet. I put my arms around her, and she closed her eyes and rested her head on my chest. The floorboards squeaked again, which was strange because neither of us was moving. She cocked her head toward the door, eyes open and suddenly fearful. I started to ask something when the door burst open, a blast of light behind a bulky figure, framing him in silhouette.

I pivoted instinctively and went for him, ducking below a raised arm and slamming a shoulder into his chest. It drove him into the wall, which shuddered, and we stood there, jammed against each other. He snarled something guttural I didn't understand, and I looked him straight in the eye.

Kharchenko.

He got a hand under my chin, and shoved me off. I collided with Eva-Lisa, who lost her footing on the sweat-soaked floor and slipped to one knee, crying out in pain or surprise, I couldn't tell which. I was just getting my feet planted, ready to throw a punch, when I saw the hatchet.

In the incandescent glow of the reflected moonlight and orange flames, the blade glinted with lustrous sparks. It moved in a downward arc toward my head. I dodged to the left, and it missed. I thought of Vladimir Smorodinsky playing tag with a grappling hook. Before Kharchenko could bring the hatchet up again, I came at him, shoulders square, knees pumping, ready to wrap him up and bring him down. I was never fast, but my form was always right out of the diagram. It should have been an easy tackle. The sauna was the size of a condo closet. There was nowhere for him to go, but he slipped to the side, turning gracefully as I charged. I still had a chance, one of my arms catching him by the shoulder. But I had no leverage, and my hand was slick with sweat, so I went past him, my shin banging the bench as I crashed into the wall headfirst.

Little black dots floated across my eyeballs. Behind me, I heard a scream. I turned and saw Eva-Lisa grinding a hot lava stone into Kharchenko's face. She had used the mat to pick it up, and her face was contorted, the heat searing her hands, even through the thick cloth. Kharchenko's eyes were closed, his mouth frozen in agony, the stone crushed against his cheekbone.

But he never dropped the hatchet.

A crazy thought. Thinking about Charlie Riggs just then in the split second that I had to react. Almost as if I weren't there, just watching these demented strangers trying to kill each other. I wanted to ask Charlie how a man blinded by pain could still hold a weapon. Charlie would probably tell me something about the synapses and neurons and the involuntary nervous system, and maybe even a prehistoric survival instinct that affects muscular reflexes.

My own reflexes were fine. I lunged for Kharchenko, reaching toward the hand that held the hatchet by the short wooden handle. I caught him by a thick wrist. He tried to shake me off. My other hand went above his on the handle. That gave me two hands to his one on the hatchet, which meant he had a hand free. I discovered this when he hooked me in the ribs with his left. I held on, jerking at the hatchet, nearly tugging it free until his left hand arrived with reinforcements. We stood there, our four hands covering the length of the short handle, like kids choosing sides with a baseball bat. We each used the strength in our legs to get leverage. I was taller and maybe heavier, but he was powerful, and had a low center of gravity like a noseguard. I was pushing the hatchet toward his neck, leaning close, smelling the scorched skin of his face when he lifted a leg and brought his shoe down on my bare instep. I howled, lost my grip, and looked up to see the blade coming in a roundhouse right aimed at my chest. I jumped back, flattening against a wall, and it smashed the pine wall, sending chips flying. He yanked the hatchet out of the wall and came for me again.

This time, Eva-Lisa grabbed him from behind, raking his face with her nails from over his shoulders. It slowed him down but left her midsection exposed, and he whirled effortlessly on his toes, the hatchet held at his hip, blade up. I lunged for his wrist, but missed. His fist was an uppercut filled with steel. The blade caught her just below the navel, dug in and caught. He had two hands on the handle and brought it up, tearing through her stomach and diaphragm, rupturing the aorta, snapping the sternum, embedding in her chest. Bending his knees, using the strength in his back and legs, his hands still on the handle, he lifted her off the floor. Then he spun and tossed her at me, a blond rag doll gushing red. I slipped to the floor wrapped in a jumble of limbs, and fell, face-first, into a puddle of warm blood. I was vaguely aware that the door had opened, and he was gone.

I lay there a long moment before standing up, holding her lifeless body, pulling the blade from her chest. Blood spurted from the wound, spraying onto the rocks. Steam rose from the hot stones, pink and sticky sweet. I carried her out of the sauna and into the anteroom. I turned on the shower, letting the cold water cleanse her. I put her body on a wooden bench and covered it with a towel. Then I sat there, letting the water pour over me, silent and alone, just before dawn on the longest day of the year.

18

CHERRY BLOSSOM IN THE SNOW

I called Charlie Riggs from a pay phone on Hypoluxo Road just east of the entrance to I-95.

I had only said hello when he asked, "What's wrong, Jake?"

"Can't talk now. I need some help."

How many times had I used those words over the years? But it was always true. Whether I needed Charlie to solve a dilemma in a case or to sort out my personal life, he was always there for me. Like I should have been there for Francisco Crespo.

When he was younger, Charlie used to ride the graveyard shift with homicide detectives. As a result, he knows the county like a mapmaker. He knows how to find Avocado Drive in Homestead and Satinwood on Key Biscayne. If you ask him to meet you on Anastasia Avenue, he'll know it runs along the Biltmore Golf Course in Coral Gables. He knows Sedonia Road from Segovia Street, Paradiso Place from Paradelo Court. So, he was the one to ask about the place of the fish.

"Now if it was a bird, there's the Flamingo Hotel, the Pelican Place Apartments, and of course, the Meadowlark Motel," he said.

"Fish, Charlie."

I heard his friendly growl over the line. It meant he was thinking. "There's Snapper Creek Apartments, but that's out in Kendall, and all long-term rental," Charlie said. "Fish, fish, what else can there be? Can't imagine a hotel named after a grunt or hogfish. I do remember a Hotel Pompano in Surfside, but that burned down in fifty-seven."

"C'mon, Charlie, this is important."

"Fish," he repeated. "I recall a dismembered body once at a place in South Beach. There was a marlin mounted in the lobby. Now what the heck was the name?" He thought about it some more. "The Blue Marlin. Rough place, even the palmetto bugs carried guns. Can't say I'd want to stay there."

"Maybe you would," I said, "if you didn't want anybody to find you."

I got back into Eva-Lisa's Saab and headed south on the expressway. Squeezed into one of Reino Haavikko's diplomatic gray suits, I felt as anonymous as Robert Foley. In Miami, I took the flyover to the MacArthur Causeway where I got stuck at the drawbridge while a wooden sloop used its motor to *put-put* through. When the bridge came down, I headed toward South Beach, looking for Nikolai Smorodinsky.

Hoping Kharchenko hadn't found him first.

The morning sun was playing hide-and-seek with heavy rain clouds, and the clouds were winning. A light sprinkle gave the causeway a silvery glow.

Which made me think of St. Petersburg. Just as in Helsinki, it never got dark there this time of year. What was the name for it?

I couldn't remember. My brain was fuzzy from the endless night. I fought to keep my eyes open as I swung south on Alton Road south of Fifth Street. I yawned. I must have been operating on adrenaline and strong coffee ever since . . .

I pushed it away again. My mind was slogging through the muck of a dozen haphazard thoughts, struggling to think of anything but . . .

Try not thinking of a brick wall.

Eva-Lisa.

I had tried to push her out of my mind. She was still there, of course, tucked away in one of the dark corners, the sensations of heat and fear, the smell of the hot, sticky blood.

Now, on the way to deliver hideous news to a man about his brother and his lover, I thought about it all. I tried to summon the right emotions. They wouldn't come.

Just dead, dumb numbness.

It hadn't registered yet, watching a woman gutted in front of me, seeing the life ooze out of her. I had been there, had tried to stop it, and had come up short.

But had I tried to save her or me? I didn't know. I just did what comes naturally: I hit somebody. But when it counted, I missed, and a young woman was dead. I hardly knew her, but she was flesh and blood and brains and possessed of the great conceit of the young—an imagined immunity from harm. She had played a very rough game with some characters with too much to lose. Characters who found her expendable. She was one of the courageous, idealistic breed, risking all for her lover and her country. In the end, neither returned the favor.

As usual, I hadn't called the police. What could they have done, besides detain me for questioning and foul everything up? "You say the killer was a Russian who shot your friend?"

I could see their cynical cop faces. The locals would call Miami, and who knows? Maybe Foley already had Socolow dancing to the tune that I killed Crespo. Palm Beach County would fight Dade County to see who would provide me room and board.

White Nights. That was it. The phrase came to me through the haze in my skull.

White Nights. It was a movie with Mikhail Baryshnikov. He was a Russian defector who ended up back in the U.S.S.R. after a plane crash, and he had to dance his way out. Something like that.

My mind was dancing, too, playing a game of free association. Names and faces kept popping into my head. Charlie Riggs. Thanks for the help, you old coot, but it's up to me now.

Lourdes Soto. Her beautiful liquid eyes. The way she wheeled that forklift around, she could have killed me if she wanted to.

Robert Foley. Where do you fit into this? Whose side are you on?

Kharchenko. I have tasted the blood you spilled. We will meet again.

The Blue Marlin Apartment Hotel was jammed between Commerce Street and an alley in a dingy neighborhood of South Beach that has yet to see the benefits of either restoration or redevelopment. In earlier times, it would have had a flashing neon sign with a couple of missing letters. Now that neon is trendy, it just has a painted sign that once could have been blue, but that was before years of sun and salt-laden air blanched it. A few blocks away is prime oceanfront real estate. Here, where a kid with a strong pitching arm could hit the cruise ships plowing through Government Cut, the neighborhood is a minighetto of recent Russian immigrants sharing a few run-down buildings with Cuban *Marielitos*.

To say the Blue Marlin was drab would be to exaggerate its charm. The building was a three-story brownish square box with not enough paint left on its hide to be considered peeling. Rusty air conditioners poked out of windows like boils on an unwashed back, oozing moisture and noise. A stuffed blue marlin minus its sword hung cockeyed in the lobby. There was a darkened staircase to the second floor and a single elevator that didn't work, or so said a hand-lettered sign in English, Spanish, and what I took to be Russian, Cyrillic characters and all.

A sallow-complexioned man of perhaps sixty sat in a blue haze of cigarette smoke behind a scarred counter. He wore a stained white T-shirt and was drinking what smelled like cheap whiskey from a Styrofoam cup. The clamor of a baseball game squawked from a black-and-white portable television on the counter. I asked him about Nikolai Smorodinsky. He squinted at me through the smoke, stared at my suit coat that wouldn't button, and hacked up a wad of phlegm.

"Friggin' Ruskies, who can tell one name from another?" A southern accent, Tennessee maybe. He spit into a metal waste can. "All commies and spicks here, never seen nothing like it. They sign the book, I cain't even read it, and I read good. Spick writes down 'Jose Delgado Diaz,' somebody comes asking for Señor Delgado, I say he ain't here. An hour later, Jose comes down from his room, all pissed off, but I figure it ain't my fault they cain't tell their daddies from their whore mommas. The Ruskies, they just bark at you and go up to their rooms."

"I'm looking for a Russian man named Smorodinsky," I repeated. "Maybe thirty. He would have checked in today."

"Couple of hours ago, one of 'em came in."

I waited.

"Talks English as good as you. Looks like a gypsy, but he's a Rusky. Room two-twelve."

He was hacking again as I made my way to the darkened staircase. There were three steps to a landing. I felt along a wall, found a light switch, and flipped it on. A bulb of maybe twenty watts went on overhead, and a slow ticking started. There was graffiti scrawled on the wall, Manuel boasting about his conquest of Rosa. I listened to the wail of a radio, one of the Spanish-language music stations. Somewhere overhead, two children were squabbling with an astonishing command of four-letter words. The light went out. It must have been on a thirty-second timer. By then, you should have completed your business. I climbed the stairs to the second floor, pushed another button, and was granted another half-minute of light. I climbed more stairs, finally emerging through a splintered door on the third floor. Here there was the smell of disintegrating plaster and steaming cabbage. Voices, two men, two women, who may have been playing cards. I headed toward a door at the end of the corridor.

I knocked three times before getting a response. It sounded like a question, the voice deep and melodious, the words foreign.

"My name is Jake Lassiter. I'm here to see Nikolai."

Nothing.

"It's about Yagamata."

"Do you work for him?" The words flowed easily and seemed to carry, like an actor on stage.

"No."

"Whom do you work for?"

I didn't know whom.

After a moment, I said to the door: "No one." It sounded like a lie, even to me.

"Did Yagamata send you?"

"No. Eva-Lisa sent me. It's about your brother. It's about Vladimir."

I heard a bolt slide, a chilly sound like the action on a Mauser thirty-ought-six. The door opened with a squeal, and I was looking into the face of an olive-skinned man in his early thirties. Nikolai Smorodinsky looked nothing like the corpse I had seen in the morgue. Unlike his brother, he had prominent cheekbones, a black mustache, and long, almost feminine eyelashes. He wore a black linen shirt open at the collar and regarded me suspiciously with piercing dark eyes. He had a strong neck and was wiry beneath the oversize shirt.

"Please come in." He extended an arm in a graceful motion to smooth my entry and held the door for me. He didn't move back to let me in. I had to scoot in sideways, and as I did, the arm that had welcomed me so graciously swung around hard, driving a fist deep into my stomach. It was a right hook, and a helluva sucker punch. My gut was relaxed when it hit. I doubled over, gagging, and he grabbed a handful of my shaggy hair and yanked me to the floor. Then he spun behind me, dropped a knee into the small of my back, and pinned one of my arms against my spine in a half nelson. He had one hand against the back of my head and was using it to grind my nose into a hardwood floor that stank of oil.

"Who are you?" He yanked my wrist higher, locking the half nelson even tighter. He was strong. "What's happened to my brother?"

I had a feeling that the truth could break my arm. "Let me go. I'll tell you everything."

"Where is he? Why hasn't he contacted me?"

I was kissing the greasy floor and my shoulder was just about to pop out of its socket. Through the pain, I pictured Vladimir Smorodinsky on a cold metal tray.

"He's dead," I said, my teeth scraping the wooden slats, a trickle of blood oozing from my lip.

After a moment, Nikolai released the pressure on my arm, took the knee out of my back, and stood. I rolled over and rubbed the back of my shoulder.

"Are you certain of what you say?" he asked.

I remembered the young assistant M.E. tugging out Vladimir's intestines, hand over hand. "I'm sure."

He let out a sigh and buried his head in his hands. "I knew. I just knew." Then he looked back at me, his eyes asking the question.

"I'm a lawyer. I represented the man accused of killing your brother. But my client didn't do it. Yagamata had your brother killed, and I think you know why."

Nikolai studied me but didn't say a word. "Yagamata said something to me after your brother was killed, something about Vladimir being a patriot true to his principles. Too much so. That's what he said, that your brother was too much the patriot." Nikolai was nodding, taking in every word. "Vladimir was trying to stop Yagamata, wasn't he?"

Nikolai extended a hand, offering to pull me up. I'd had enough of his neighborly gestures. I got to my feet all by my lonesome. He gestured toward an opening. The kitchen. A narrow passageway with an ancient stove, a waist-high refrigerator, and against a wall, a wooden table with three chairs. I sank into one of the chairs. There was blood on my face, and my shoulder throbbed.

Nikolai stood over me. He didn't answer my question. "My brother loved the Hermitage," he said finally. "Have you ever seen it?"

"I've never been to Russia," I admitted.

"The Winter Palace of the Czars, more than a thousand rooms in just one of the buildings, all filled with irreplaceable art. Think of the magnitude of it."

I remembered what Yagamata had told me. *Three million artifacts. How do they even keep track of it all?* Or was that his point?

"The czars could build great monuments," Nikolai said, "but could not feed the peasants. Not much different from the communists or our new democrats, eh?"

"The art," I said, licking my torn lip. "That's why Vladimir was killed. When he figured out what really was going on, who was getting the money, how much of your national heritage was being stolen, he wanted to stop it, and so did—"

I never heard the footsteps in the hall. The voice came from behind me. "As usual, Lassiter, you're half right."

I whirled around, nearly falling out of the chair. Standing there in his gray suit and white shirt, black tie knotted at the neck, was Robert Foley. He looked like a man who would rather be anyplace else. "But it's the other half," Foley said, "that'll get you killed."

Nikolai looked up, stunned. "Mr. Foley, what are you—"

"Shouldn't leave your door open, kid. Who knows what'll come in. Goblins, spooks, half-assed lawyers." Foley glared at me. "You tell him yet? Or should I?"

"He told me." Nikolai answered for me. "But, deep in my heart, I already knew. We had a system. Vladimir could get messages to me through an Aeroflot pilot who flew to New York. Every other Sunday, he would—"

"Not talking about your brother, kid." Foley's voice had softened. Behind his rimless glasses, his eyes were tired and sad. He grabbed a wooden chair, swung it around, and straddled it backward, placing his forearms on the chair's back. He looked like a cowboy in a gray suit. "We tap Yagamata's phone. Hell, all his phones. We scan his cellulars, bug his home, his office, his boat. The son of a bitch is under twenty-four-hour surveillance. Yesterday, I'm in Washington, the Miami bureau picks up a call from Miami Beach to Yagamata's home. A male voice: 'The Finnish bunny has flown the coop.' And Yagamata says, 'What a shame to lose a bunny with such pretty fur.' The caller asks, 'Lose?' And Yagamata says, 'Lose like a cherry blossom in the snow.' "

Nikolai's voice echoed his disbelief. "They killed Eva-Lisa?" He slumped into a chair.

Foley said, "In Miami, my people thought it was just another bullshit code about the artwork. Some agent just out of training even asked what artist painted bunny rabbit pictures. It took the better part of the day for the tape to be transcribed and faxed to me in D.C. By then, I was at a reception at the Polish embassy. Nobody in D.C. understood the importance of the transmission, either, or they would have gotten me out of there. I get home late and call the night desk. It's an old habit, and they read me the fax. I'm yelling to get somebody to the girl's apartment on the Beach. They do, and there's no sign of her. Another crew heads up to

Lake Worth, but it was too late.'' He opened his palms on the table in a gesture of helplessness. He did not look at me. ''I'm sorry. As soon as I heard, I caught the next flight to Miami.''

Nikolai's face was white with anger, and tears glittered in his eyes. ''You swore you would protect her. You knew what she was like. So impetuous. So young.''

So dead, I thought.

''She didn't follow instructions,'' Foley said. ''I assume from the message to Yagamata that she was bailing out. She never even warned us.''

''Who did it?'' Nikolai asked, his voice cracking. ''How was it done?''

''Why don't you ask Lassiter?''

I didn't like the way he said it, his tone changing from mournful friend to sarcastic cop in the blink of an eye. When I didn't say anything, Nikolai turned toward me. A vein throbbed in his neck.

Foley said, ''We checked every police report yesterday in Miami Beach. Yesterday afternoon, a restaurant worker called the cops about a scuffle in an alley. Seems like a guy was tussling with a woman, may have hit her. By the time the cops got there, the couple was gone. Our people showed photos of Lassiter and Eva-Lisa to the worker. Positive ID on both of them.''

I couldn't believe what I was hearing. ''Foley, what kind of bullshit is this?''

''Shut up, Lassiter.'' He turned back to Nikolai. ''We've gotten some help from Palm Beach County homicide, too. Eva-Lisa was butchered in the sauna behind her parents' house. A short-handled hatchet did the job.'' I sensed Nikolai shifting in his chair, angling toward me. ''They picked up latents all over the place. The wooden benches, the hatchet handle, even one on her shoulder using the methyl methacrylate test. We faxed Lassiter's prints to them. A perfect match. If you look on the inside pocket of Lassiter's sport coat, you'll find the initials 'R.H.' If we scraped under his nails right now, we'd find . . .'' He grabbed one of my wrists and turned my hand over. ''. . . a speck of dried blood, and I'd bet you a hundred bucks DNA testing would match up with the decedent.''

I tore my hand away. ''You bastard, Foley! You know I didn't kill her. Tell him!''

"You tell him, asshole."

Before I could respond, Nikolai's hand came up. In it was a stainless steel push dagger that must have come from a sheath on his leg. He pressed it hard against my neck, forcing me back in my chair.

I hate a knife.

When I spoke, I felt the tip of the blade pierce the skin. "I didn't kill her. Foley, goddammit, you know it."

"Who killed her?" Foley asked.

The knife pressed harder. "Kharchenko. You know that. He called Yagamata when she tried to quit. Your office picked up the call, you said so yourself." Warm blood trickled down my neck. "Why are you doing this?"

Foley shook his head. He seemed genuinely sad. "I don't know any Kharchenko."

"Of course you do! He works for Yagamata. You were there in the warehouse when Yagamata told you about him."

"What's he look like? Where is he now?"

Too weird. I was about to have my throat cut, and Foley was taking a statement. It didn't make sense. Or did it? I was arching backward, trying to escape the knife. If my chin went any higher, I'd snap my cervical vertebrae. Nikolai didn't seem to mind.

"What's with you, Foley? I thought this was your operation."

"So did I," Robert Foley said. "Now, what's he look like, this Kharchenko?"

"You *really* don't know him?"

"Christ, Lassiter, if I knew, I wouldn't have asked for your detailed statement at the Crespo scene."

"I thought that was a trick to get my signature."

"That was a bonus," he said, "like having a big-boobed secretary who can type."

I let out a breath and tried to relax. Foley wouldn't let Nikolai kill me. At least not yet.

"I know Kharchenko when I see him," I said, lowering my head enough to look at Foley. "And I know where to find him tonight, but if Nikolai slices me, you won't learn a thing."

His eyes dismissed the notion as irrelevant. "He cuts your jugular, I'll clamp it shut with my hands. Make a hell of a mess, but give you another two minutes to live. For those two minutes, you'd tell me your mother's darkest secrets and your father's fondest dreams."

"I never knew my mother," I said. It was true, though it sounded ridiculous just now. She was a platinum blonde who waited tables in Key West and ran off with an oil worker from Galveston. "And my father was killed in a barroom brawl."

Killed with a knife.

I shifted my gaze to Nikolai, whose face was a dark mask. "Don't you see what he's doing? He can't kill me. Against regulations or something. But he could let Yagamata do it. Or you. And he wants to make a quinella out of it." A flicker of puzzlement crossed Nikolai's face. "He wants to get the information he needs, then have you kill me."

I felt a bead of sweat trickle down my cheek. The pressure of the knife eased just a bit. Foley's palm slapped the table. "Half right again, Lassiter. Sure, I want information from you, but I don't want you dead. I just figure you deserve to piss your pants a little after that trick you pulled at the airport. Just answer my questions."

I was having trouble breathing. A lump of rage was stuck in my throat. "First, you tell Nikolai the truth, you bastard. Tell him they found another set of prints in the sauna. Tell him you don't know who Kharchenko is because the prints don't match up with anything you've got. Tell him how Yagamata took your nice little Operation Riptide and made it his own." I licked my lips, salty with sweat. "Tell him I didn't kill Eva-Lisa."

Foley shrugged his shoulders. "The lawyer's right," he told Nikolai impassively. "He didn't kill her."

The knife clattered to the floor. With a strangled sob, the young Russian pushed away from the table and stood at the grimy window with his back to us.

Foley's eyes tried to apologize. "I'm sorry, kid, but this is a lot bigger than you are." He said it as if he believed it. Then he turned to me. "Okay, Lassiter, let's you and me kiss and make up." I didn't care much for the phrase but figured it was better than *bury the hatchet.* Foley gave me his snoop's imitation of a friendly grin. "Where do we find Kharchenko?" he asked.

"At the ballet," I said.

19

ART FOR WHEAT

I didn't move in time, and a woman the size of Larry Csonka, but not as attractive, stomped on my feet and plopped into the seat next to me, elbowing me in the ribs. Foley on one side of me, a Russian *babushka* on the other. Welcome to the Bolshoi Ballet, at least the touring version. The audience was an eclectic mix of South Florida society and Russian émigrés. Foley and I were sitting in the balcony with the Russians. I was wearing a rented tux with an undersized shirt collar that felt like a garrote.

Foley owned a formal outfit, or was it government issue? He was practicing his Russian by silently reading the bilingual program. I tried to get his attention. "First, you said our government was trying to stop the art thefts, help out the reformers."

Foley didn't look up from his program. He was tracing under the words, moving his lips slightly, but he was reading Russian, and that's more than I can do.

"Then, I learn you're really behind the thefts. You were trying to get the goods on the hard-liners, protect the Yeltsin crowd, help make the country a colony of the West, or something like that. What's your expression, 'drive a coffin nail into the godless heart of communism.' "

"That was for the benefit of Soto and the Finns. Christ, Lassiter, do you believe whoever talks to you last? Don't you have the ability to reason for yourself?"

"Yeah. All by myself, I figured you're a lying scumbag, because now I know you're the thief. You and Yagamata are stealing the art."

Ordinarily, I am much more polite in ornate surroundings. But I doubted that many of our newest immigrants bustling into the gilded red velvet balcony of the Performing Arts Center would care, even if they could understand my poison-tipped whispers.

"Look, Lassiter, you don't even know the players, much less the rules of the game." Foley folded the program neatly and placed it in his lap. He leaned close enough for me to smell the tobacco on his breath. "Severo Soto is a rabid anticommunist. He's crazy as a bedbug. All he cares about is overthrowing Castro. He figures that if the Russians can't subsidize the bearded one, the Cuban government will fall. He wants to be the first president in a democratic Cuba, or maybe it's a fascist Cuba, who the hell knows. Everybody hears what they want to, and Soto heard me talk about nailing communism. The Finnish girl, too."

"So what the hell *are* you doing here?" I demanded. "What's the U.S. interest in Russian art?"

"What I told you was true at one time. A couple of years ago, the Russians let us know they were starting to lose valuable artworks, primarily from churches, but then some of the less valuable artifacts from the museums were missing, too. It was part of the crime phenomenon all through Eastern Europe, once travel restrictions and other controls were eased. All the Russians wanted was a little help on our end, trace where the stuff was being sold in the West, make some arrests, get people to talk, and find the source here that was funding the flow."

I used a finger to get some breathing room between my neck and my shirt collar. "Sounds like drug interdiction."

"Same idea. Anyway, we help them out, pick up a stolen Rubens at an auction house in New York, track it back to some semiorganized crime types in Minsk who have Party ties, and everybody's happy. But then, somebody at Langley's talking to somebody at State about how *perestroika* is stuck, and the *nomenklatura* are getting itchy because Gorby is cutting off their caviar, and suddenly, everyone's scared shitless there'll be a coup. So, with the reformers' blessing, we take the initiative. We target some of the real assholes in the army, the Foreign Ministry, the KGB, and set them up for a sting. We're paying off these guys in return for some valuable pieces from the museums. We're taping the transactions, tracing their deposits into foreign accounts, and pretty soon, we have enough evidence to send some important commies to Siberia for treason. It would have gotten some of the real hard-liners out of the way. Then, all of a sudden, way more art is coming out of the country than we need to hold the top Reds' feet to the fire."

"Yagamata," I murmured.

"You got it. Stuff starts turning up in private collections in Japan, and KGB agents there get word back to their masters in Moscow. So our cover is blown, and—"

"Gorbachev gets a short vacation in the Crimea, all expenses paid by the guys who got caught."

Foley finally looked at me. "Lassiter, you're not as dumb as you look."

I didn't tell him I'd had a Finnish tutor. "But the coup fails, and you go into business for yourself with Yagamata."

"Wrong! I spoke too soon. Just listen. After those bozos fuck it up—hey, they let Lesley Stahl interview Yeltsin when Parliament was surrounded—everybody at State is so happy they're walking around with hard-ons. If you know anything about history, you know that when the Russians are unified—no matter what form their government takes—their neighbors aren't going to get any sleep. It's in the West's interest to break down the Union into individual republics with no strong central authority. What the hell does Estonia have in common with Tadzhikistan, anyway?"

I didn't know, but Foley wasn't looking for an answer. "The trick, Lassiter, was to separate the republics from central authority without fostering civil war. It wouldn't do to have the Russian army in Georgia tossing nuclear warheads at rebel troops in Azerbaijan. We have to support the reformers, the nationalists in each of the key republics. They don't need tanks and mortars. They need food for their people. Central planning kept the country from feeding itself. Jesus, you wouldn't believe the inefficiency and corruption. There's a city on the Volga called Astrakhan. The biggest industry is fishing—huge sturgeon from the river, excellent caviar. But you couldn't even buy a stinking herring in the city. The central planners ordered it all to be shipped elsewhere."

Below us, the orchestra was tuning up. The strings and the horns seemed to be at war with each other. "So send them foreign aid," I said. "Send them some of our surplus wheat."

"Not that simple. Who gets to distribute it, the old incompetent bureaucrats or the new incompetent bureaucrats? And how will they pay for it? They have no hard currency."

"Gold," I suggested. "They have stockpiles. I've read about it."

"*Had.* A few years ago, their reserves were probably thirty-five hundred tons. If they have two hundred tons left, it'd be news to us."

"Where'd it go?"

"Some was traded for credit with the West, some for dollars and pounds and marks that ended up in Swiss accounts of Party bigwigs. Hey, we'll never know. The last two Party treasurers, Pavlov and Kruchina, threw themselves out windows before anybody could ask them questions. Lassiter, the fact is, their goddamn country is *broke.* So what's our government to do? Give them easy credit? Forget it, might as well give the money away, but that'd never fly in Washington."

I was beginning to understand, but I didn't know if it was true. How could you tell with Foley? I said, "So instead of going through diplomatic channels, our government supports a bunch of burglars, just like Watergate, only on a bigger scale. You borrowed Yagamata's idea. You steal the Russians' art, sell it to Japanese and German collectors, and use the money to send Wheaties back to Moscow. Is that what you're telling me? Instead of arms for hostages, art for wheat?"

The lights were beginning to dim, and the music came up. Foley chuckled. "An oversimplification, and I would object to your characterizing us as burglars. Russian officials with the appropriate credentials authorize the *sale* of the art. We can be considered legitimate brokers. Look, Lassiter, we're not bad guys. We're doing the reformers a favor. We're feeding their people and keeping them in power. Of course, it's all surreptitious, and we spread some dollars around, but that's a cost of doing business with the Russians, always has been. Under the communists, everyone who could swing it was *vzyatka,* on the take. Why should it change now? Besides, it suits our purposes."

"What purposes?" I asked.

He didn't answer. But he didn't have to. I was catching on. "You're doing the same thing again, aren't you?"

Still, he was silent.

"Do the new bureaucrats in the republics know you're setting them up, too? Do they know you're wired when they make the deals?"

"What we do is in the American national interest. We have bought a certain amount of loyalty there, and we take precautions to assure that our friends stay that way."

The curtain went up, and on the stage, some European peasants in a colorful village were dancing up a storm. "You've bought the whole country," I said, "just like you used to do in Latin America and Africa and Asia and anyplace else that was for sale. You've turned the Soviet Union into just another banana republic."

From behind us, a loud "Shuush!" I turned around and smiled at a large woman who was slicing a salami and wagging her finger at me.

On the stage, a guy in a brown vest and tights seemed to have a thing for a pretty village woman in a blue dress. "So what went wrong?" I whispered.

"Yagamata got greedy."

"Again! Why were you still using him?"

"All was forgiven. As it turned out, the coup attempt was the best thing that could have happened for us. So Yagamata was sort of an inadvertent hero, and we needed him as the middleman for the Japanese buyers. But the bastard wasn't satisfied with his broker's commission, and with the country in chaos, he smelled an opportunity. He started skimming the artwork, making his own deals with the Russians for unauthorized pieces, selling to collectors who are security risks."

"But you're helping him! I heard you back in Yagamata's warehouse."

Foley dropped his voice to a conspiratorial whisper. "I had to find out what he was up to if I was going to stop him. Now that the operation's been canceled, my job is to terminate the transfers by any means possible and get the stuff back to Russia before any more damage is done."

I was trying to watch the ballet and listen to Foley at the same time. After a while, I figured that the guy in the brown vest was really a nobleman traveling incognito. Unfortunately, he forgot to tell the village gal that he was engaged to a babe dressed in scarlet with a feather in her hat. The fiancée made quite an entrance, what with the blaring of horns and the approach of the hunters. At the same time, the nobleman had some competition from a local guy, a dude in Philadelphia Eagles green. While they were debating who gets the girl by doing some agility drills and pointing their fingers gracefully at each other, Foley leaned close. "Do you have any idea how much money is involved?"

"I've heard a billion dollars tossed around."

He snickered under his breath. "A couple years ago, some amateurs walked into the Gardner Museum in Boston and used knives to slash a bunch of paintings out of their frames. They left behind Titian's *Rape of Europa* and the best works of the Italian Renaissance. But they got Rembrandt's *Storm on the Sea of Galilee* and some other first-rate work. It was a lousy thirty-minute heist. It was worth two hundred million."

I let out a short whistle, and behind me, the large woman smacked my head with her forearm, or was it her salami?

"Peanuts, Lassiter. The Hermitage has hundreds of rooms, each more valuable than the entire Gardner collection. Add to that all the other museums in all the republics and figure what I'm talking about. Even with a discount if they glut the market, figure ten billion, twenty, nobody knows."

On the stage, the scam was up. The brown-vested nobleman had left his fingerprints—actually his coat-of-arms—on a royal sword. The village girl didn't care for the deception or the nobleman's fiancée, so she committed hara-kiri with the sword. It made me think of Yagamata.

"What's Yagamata want?" I asked Foley.

"Everything! He's stripping the damn country bare. He makes Robert Vesco look like a shoplifter at K mart."

The curtain fell, and the lights were coming up. "Halftime," I said. "Let's get a hot dog and a beer."

We had arrived at the theater early. I had stationed myself at an angle to the main entrance with Foley standing in front of me, his back to the door. It was supposed to look as if we were in deep conversation. In reality, I had a clear view over his shoulder of everyone entering the theater, while I was barely noticeable. I stood there in my striped pants and shiny black shoes, my strangling collar, my eyes darting back and forth looking for the stocky Russian.

We stood there, talking about the Dolphins, the Heat, and the new baseball team, the Marlins. Foley told me it was hard to keep up with sports, as he'd been stationed in Panama, Grenada, Managua, Guantánamo, and more recently Helsinki in preparation for Operation Riptide. I looked at him closely, the creased face, the stony eyes behind the rimless glasses. About forty-seven, forty-eight maybe. "I figure you were in the military during Vietnam," I said.

"You can call me Major Foley, except Foley isn't the name, of course. But you're right. Army intelligence. I had a couple dozen VC working for me out in the bush. Troop movements, enemy strength, that sort of thing. Know what my cover was?"

"Stand-up comedian?"

"World Health Organization gynecologist. Really. I wanted to be a dentist, but we didn't have the tools. Someone in the Saigon station came up with a whole set of OB-GYN tools, or at least enough for me to keep in the pocket of my smock. You know, you could take somebody's eye out with the speculum."

"Don't tell me you delivered babies."

"Nah. I'd do a cursory exam, nothing I hadn't seen before, then let the nurse figure the rest out. When we moved the operation to Pleiku, I ran a whorehouse. Built a secure room for interrogations and made a profit for the Company."

As I listened, my eyes scanned the sidewalk. I watched as the locals queued up, tickets in hand. I was looking for a brush-cut, husky Russian partial to brown suits. I didn't see him. The patrons were turned out in what Granny Lassiter would call their Sunday best. On opening night, many of the locals wore their formal duds. Others, the trendy Miami Beach crowd, favored black leather, or black capes, or black silk. It didn't seem to matter as long as the color was black. The Russians, many of whom worked in the new restaurants and clubs, were freshly scrubbed but not as flashy. I studied the crowd pushing toward the theater. No Kharchenko.

"Was it true what you said back at Nikki's place?" Foley asked, as we kept up the patter.

"About what?"

"Your father was killed when you were a kid."

"Yeah. I was raised by my Granny. She taught me how to fish, drink, and curse. Went up north on a football scholarship, saw mountains and snow the first time in central Pennsylvania, then made the Dolphins as a free agent. Hung on as a second-stringer and special teams player for a few years before I got into night law school."

"My father was killed in Korea," Foley said, his voice trailing off. "All I ever wanted to do was serve my country. Never thought I'd be breaking and entering museums. There he was fighting the communists, and here I am buying them off. At least they used to be communists. It's getting confusing out there." He moved closer to me. "You know what they do when you graduate from spy school?"

"Spy school?"

"Well, Foreign Studies School."

"Give you a cyanide pill to put in the heel of your shoe," I guessed.

"They hand you a diploma, just like getting your B.S. in phys ed, or whatever you studied . . ."

"Theater."

He raised his eyebrows. "Except when you walk off the stage, you give it back. An agent takes all the diplomas, puts them in a trash can, and they burn them all. We are anonymous workers for democracy and our way of life, Lassiter. We're the goddamned last best hope for mankind."

I would sleep better knowing that.

"Intermission," Foley told me, as the lights came up. "Not half-time. A theater major should know that."

I knew. We continued our reconnaissance starting at the snack bar at the rear of the mezzanine. An attendant was selling little bottles of champagne and cellophane-wrapped shrimp cocktails. I followed the line of patrons to the end. No Kharchenko. Maybe if they sold borscht . . .

"We should try downstairs," I said.

Foley's face was screwed up in secret spy thoughts. "In Russia, Kharchenko was one of the *verkhushka*. He'd get special treatment."

"So what?"

"He would never have come in the front door. Even now, some Ruskies are more equal than others." He grabbed my arm and motioned me back toward our seats. "On a foreign tour, he would have gotten his tickets from the Ministry of Cultural Affairs. He probably came in the stage entrance with the cast and crew. In Russia, he'd be in a reserved box. He would have made similar arrangements here."

By the time we got to our seats, the orchestra was playing again. As the lights dimmed, Foley reached into his inside coat pocket and pulled out a pair of opera glasses. At least that's what they looked like. He adjusted the focus, pushed a button, and handed them to me. Then he gestured with his head in the direction of the boxes at the mezzanine level to the right of the stage.

Below us, the curtain had opened, and the dead lady was in her grave, wearing white. I raised the binoculars and looked into the darkened boxes. Wow! Infrared. Power plus acuity. I could see them, but they couldn't see me. A weasel-faced man had his hand on the bosom of a well-endowed woman. Two men snoozed in the next box, their wives chatting away, oblivious to the stage. Nearby, a skinny woman sipped greedily from a champagne glass. An empty seat came next, then a thick-necked man in a brown suit. I looked closer. A white bandage covered one eye, and his face looked as if a cat had dragged its claws across his cheek.

Bingo!

I handed the binoculars to Foley and gave him directions. He nodded and took a look.

"Stankevich!" he exclaimed.

"Gesundheit," I replied.

Foley didn't thank me. He withdrew a small camera from his other coat pocket. He screwed a telephoto lens into place, aimed, focused, and clicked off half a dozen shots at a slow shutter speed.

Below us, as the music swelled, the lady's girlfriends, looking like angels in white, swirled around and raised her from the grave. Foley said, "When he was the number three KGB goon in Afghanistan, his name was Boris Stankevich. C'mon, let's go."

"Now?"

"Now." Foley stood and motioned me to do the same. "Wherever he's going, we're following, and I don't want to be stuck here when it's over."

"Damn, the show's just getting interesting."

The angels had tossed one of the guys into the lake and were after another one. I reluctantly stood and started down the aisle, tromping on toes, drawing curses in guttural Russian. Sure, I wanted to follow Kharchenko. But I wanted to stick around until the end, or at least until I figured out which one was Giselle.

20

PEARLS BEFORE SWINE

The mansion was done in the 1920s Mediterranean Revival style. It sat at the end of a brick circular drive trimmed with blooming hibiscus and bottlebrush trees. The walls were pink stucco, the roof mission tiles. You entered an interior courtyard through a loggia flanked by twisted columns. The floor was glazed ceramic tile, the exterior walls adorned with terra-cotta ornaments. There were wrought-iron grilles and wood brackets and casement windows shaded by pink-and-white awnings. There were arches everywhere, some flat, some pointed, some with Moorish elaborations. A second-floor balcony lined with balustrades overlooked the bay.

I had been here before.

There had been a party that night, too.

Only that time, I had been invited.

Foley and I had followed Kharchenko's taxi from the theater. Once on the causeway, I knew where he was headed. I just didn't know there'd be a crowd.

Matsuo Yagamata was playing host to his usual collection of political and social animals, some artist and writer types, plus a Russian cultural delegation and the cast and crew of the Bolshoi Ballet. The dancers would be along later. But Kharchenko was here now.

We pulled into the drive behind a line of limos and

Mercedeses with an occasional Lexus thrown in. Not a Lada in sight. Foley's government-owned Plymouth drew a look from the valet. For once, I was glad I had dressed up. Nobody stopped us; nobody asked to see an invitation. We entered the courtyard, passed through a segmental arch wide enough to accommodate a herd of buffalo, and came to the pool deck. Once, a thousand years ago or so, Yagamata had stood there and showed off an egg filled with a golden choo-choo train.

The scene on the patio reminded me of a famous party on a balmy February evening just down the street from here. I wasn't there. I hadn't been born yet. That night, arriving guests were searched by men with rifles. Miami's politicians and social elite drank champagne and ate canapés, figuring it was just another Valentine's Day party. The celebration was more meaningful, however, to the host. While the festivities were in full swing on Palm Island, seven members of Bugs Moran's gang were gunned down at a garage in Chicago. Newspapermen later speculated that the party was intended to celebrate that event, since Bugs Moran was a bitter rival of the party host, Al Capone.

I wondered what Yagamata was celebrating tonight.

A gentle breeze wafted across the patio, flickering the torches. A string quartet strummed quiet music, guests milling about, ooh-ing and aahing at the sheer delight of being here. Bars were set up every twenty yards or so to save on the shoe leather. In the center of the patio was a buffet table no longer than an average NFL punt.

"Stick with the *zakuski,* the appetizers," Foley ordered. How clever. Yagamata, the perfect host, was serving a Russian feast. We loaded our plates with red and black caviar, sturgeon, cucumber-and-tomato salad, and pickled mushrooms. A server handed me a tiny silver pot covered with melted cheese.

"Griby v'smetanye," Foley said. "Mushrooms and onions in sour cream."

I washed everything down with a double shot glass of ice-cold Moskovskaya vodka, then did it all again. The training table was never like this. Finally, I went back for blinis with sour cream and caviar.

By the time most of the guests had arrived, I was pleasantly stuffed from the food and warmed by the vodka. Foley hadn't touched a drop of the liquor. We kept scanning the crowd. Half a dozen Russian officials in baggy suits were lined up at the buffet table, loading their plates as if it was their first meal in a week. Maybe it was.

"Think these guys are happy to be in the West?" Foley asked. "You can't buy a decent sausage in all of Russia, but look at this. Sometimes you civilians don't appreciate what we've got."

"Don't start waving the flag," I responded, "without acknowledging that this isn't America. This isn't real. This isn't the housewife stretching the food budget with peanut butter for dinner. This isn't cocaine dealing a few blocks from the White House."

Foley gave me a nasty look. "Let's cut the bullshit and go to work. Time to earn our supper." He nodded in the direction of the quartet. Matsuo Yagamata was working the crowd, moving slowly but steadily, granting each guest a precious twenty seconds or an even briefer hello-how-are-you-so-pleased-to-see-you-again. He wore an elegant tuxedo and smiled graciously at each stop on his way to the buffet table. Over the violins, I could hear him laugh politely at some remark as he gestured with a champagne glass and speared smoked salmon hors d'oeuvres from passing trays.

Foley used the cocktail party shuffle to edge between a woman in a white gown and Yagamata, who caught sight of him, then me. Our host registered surprise, then smiled evenly.

"What an enchanting development to see my government friend and my lawyer friend," he announced loudly, his eyebrows raised. The woman in the white gown shot us a hostile look.

"Hello, Matsuo," Foley said. "How's tricks?"

"Tricks? You and your slang. Should we speak Japanese, so I can have the upper hand?"

"I didn't come to banter. We need to talk business."

"At a reception? And violate our protocol? The Russians would be offended." He shot a look around the patio, and so did I, but I didn't see Kharchenko anywhere. "Come now, Mr. Foley. Let us teach our new trading partners how to enjoy the spoils of true market economy, or at least, the part that a few can savor." His voice was tinged with sarcasm as he clamped a hand on Foley's shoulder, looked around as if afraid of eavesdroppers, and spoke in a stage whisper: "In Russia, the workers used to say of the *nomenklatura*, 'They preach water—'"

"'And drink wine,'" I said, remembering our conversation on Yagamata's boat.

"Precisely. Could not the same be said of American and Japanese politicians? Mr. Foley, you cannot abolish class distinction with either communism or capitalism." With that, Yagamata drained his champagne glass and signaled a passing waiter for another.

"Under any system, Matsuo, you would be in it for yourself," Foley said.

The laughter rattled in Yagamata's throat. "And who would not be? In the old Soviet Union, was there ever a butcher, a doctor, or a shopkeeper not tainted by *gryazny,* the pursuit of profit? Was there ever a Party Secretary who did not relish his seaside *dacha,* his access to pleasures of the West? There is a Russian epithet that expresses the people's disgust with their officials." Yagamata thought a moment and said something in halting Russian that made Foley smile. It was not a pretty sight.

Foley turned toward me and translated, "Let him live on his salary."

"Precisely," Yagamata said. "Communism failed because it was based on principles contradictory to human nature. Japan succeeds because it is based squarely on the principles of competition, profit, growth, exploitation of markets and resources. Your own country founders because it cannot decide whether it is a welfare state or an industrial power. As for Russia, it is nothing but a decrepit third world country. Mr. Lassiter, do you know why Russian watches are the best in the world?"

"Sure, they're the fastest."

Yagamata chuckled. "Perhaps in the free market, the quality of the products will improve. To survive, they will Westernize. Did you see that *Pravda* held a fund-raiser, just as public television does here? No longer subsidized, the newspaper raffled off rugs and washing machines. What would Lenin say?"

Foley shrugged, and Yagamata concentrated on me. "As Mr. Foley knows, *Pravda* means truth and *Izvestia* means news. Unfortunately—"

"There was never any news in the *Truth* or truth in the *News,*" Foley added.

"Ah, you two have heard all my jokes."

Yagamata was still chuckling at the stolen punch line when Foley grabbed his forearm and jerked him close. "This time, Matsuo, you've gone too far." Yagamata's smile froze in place. "You can't steal all the fucking art from the Baltic to the Pacific."

Yagamata pulled away. His face was white with anger. He smoothed the sleeve of his tuxedo. "And why not?"

"You're raping the country, Matsuo," Foley said.

"Stealing state property was the national pastime under the communists. I have merely raised it to an art form." He laughed again. "Art form. That is a pun, is it not?"

"Where's Kharchenko?" I asked.

Yagamata frowned. "Ah, the business with the girl. Perhaps your Yankee sense of manhood compels you to seek revenge. Those of you raised on John Wayne movies have such an outdated sense of chivalry. Instead, you should have the good sense to be thankful that you were spared. For that, I might add, you should thank me."

"You're out of your mind." I turned to Foley. "Did you hear this? He just admitted—"

"I heard him. Look, Matsuo, it's over. Everything's changed. You've exceeded your authority. Langley thinks you're out of control, and I'm under orders to take possession of the new shipment. Everything's going back to Mother Russia, including Kharchenko. You'll be paid for your trouble, and paid well. If you refuse to cooperate, you'll be charged with conspiracy, racketeering, smuggling, and about a hundred other things the boys in Washington will lose a lot of sleep thinking up."

Yagamata blinked twice, his eyes darting from Foley to me and back again. "And my personal collection?"

"Anything you've taken for yourself you can keep. It'll be written off."

"Including my new Matisse, of course. *Girl with Tulips.* I have coveted it for years. The girl is Jeanne Vaderin, and—"

"Yeah, yeah, including your new Matisse. You know, you're really a little over the top about the art, Matsuo. It affects your judgment."

Yagamata wasn't listening. "And the works by Fabergé, of course. I must keep the Trans-Siberian Railway Egg of 1900."

"Yeah, the eggs, the paintings, whatever you've skimmed off

before selling to your buddies in Kyoto. Christ, we're talking about international politics here and you're concerned with a few pieces of art?"

"Aren't you?" Yagamata asked.

"I don't give two shits about the art."

"Then you are a fool."

Foley shook his head. "Okay, I'm an ugly American, a *déclassé* barbarian. Happy? Now, do you want the money or do I start reading you your rights?"

Yagamata seemed to think about it. "How much? How much for my trouble?"

"Fifty million."

This time Yagamata didn't blink. "I could make a hundred times that by selling the art."

"You could get a hundred years in the can. I'll use the forfeiture laws to confiscate every asset you have, right down to the last tin of caviar."

Across the patio, a woman's laugh tinkled like wind chimes on a balcony. "What is the timing of such an arrangement?" Yagamata asked.

"First, I take delivery of the shipment. Within twenty-four hours, you'll be paid."

"Are you authorized to make such an offer?"

"From the highest possible authority."

"How do I know . . ."

"Have I ever breached a commitment to you?"

Yagamata shook his head. "No. You are consistently dishonorable and therefore immensely trustworthy. You always eschew principle and reward venality."

"So what's it going to be? We don't have all night."

"Ah, the well-known impatience of the Americans." Yagamata tried to put some midwestern corn pone into his voice. "Let's cut to the chase. What's the bottom line? Is it a done deal, baby?"

"Matsuo, you're getting on my nerves."

"All right. I agree to your terms. What are the logistics?"

"Give me the location of the shipment. I'll provide tractor-trailers. We'll use your workers. We'll start tomorrow at 0900. Fair enough?"

"Oh, perfectly fair. Unfortunately, however, I have no idea where the shipment is."

Foley appeared stunned. "Why not?"

"It is not yet under my control. Kharchenko will release it to me after he has been paid and the goods repackaged to resemble cartons of pottery from Peru. As you can imagine, my outlay is many millions of dollars. Ordinarily, I would wire the funds to the Swiss accounts of Kharchenko and various Russian functionaries who made all this possible. Obviously, I do not intend to make the payment if you are going to appropriate the property."

"You're telling me you don't follow the goods once they're off-loaded. You don't know the warehouse Kharchenko uses. You don't place agents along their route, bribe the drivers—"

"It's not my concern. He always delivers when promised."

Foley was incensed at Yagamata's lack of professionalism. "Have you gone soft?"

Yagamata reached for a blini from a passing tray and dipped it in sour cream. "Maybe so, or maybe I just enjoy waking up each morning. You don't play both sides of the Volga with Mr. Kharchenko."

"I'll deal with him," Foley said, anger in his voice.

"Then, perhaps we should go inside," Yagamata said. "There is something I would like you to see."

"Yeah, what?"

"A little display I have put together from my personal collection. I call it the Treasure of the Czars exhibit. Furniture, artifacts, icons. It really is suitable for a museum. It's in my gallery, and so is Comrade Kharchenko."

"Let's go have a look," I suggested, "before he steals it all."

The floors were white marble, the columns green malachite, the cornices leafed in gold. Real gold. The ceilings were high, the lighting subdued. The gallery was quiet, almost churchlike. The only worshiper was a thick-necked man with a bandaged face.

Kharchenko stood next to a jade pedestal on which stood a gold vessel filled with what looked like white marbles. Yagamata raised his hand as if to signal Kharchenko not to be alarmed.

Yagamata bolted the door behind him, and we crossed the room together. Enameled saddles shared space on polished wooden frames with silver bridle chains. Antique weaponry—rifles with ornate fretwork of silver beasts—was attached to the walls, along with intricate Russian needlework. Golden chalices laced with rubies and emeralds shared space with decorative military breastplates. A mannequin of a nobleman was dressed in eighteenth-century finery, its vestment encrusted with precious gems. Closer to the jade pedestal, I could see the gold vessel contained pearls—hundreds, the same size and lustre.

As we approached, Kharchenko pointed to a nearby painting of what looked like a holy man, head bowed in prayer. In excellent English, he said, *The Measure Icon*. Ivan the Terrible honored the birth of his son by commissioning a painting of the boy's patron saint. Twenty-seven years later, Ivan murdered his son in a fit of rage." Kharchenko watched us for a reaction, his dark eyes alert above the white bandages.

"Your history is like that," Foley said. "Works of great beauty, acts of great horror."

"Is it so much different from yours? We had our Gulag, you your lynchings."

Yagamata cleared his throat. "Politics is so boring compared with business, and in any event, your histories are about to merge. With the free market, soon you will not be able to tell the difference between the streets of Boston and St. Petersburg."

For some reason, I thought about the Hermitage going condo.

Yagamata was fondling a gem-studded egg that he had picked up from a marble-topped table. The egg was covered with a map of Russia engraved on silver. Two gargoyle creatures with shields and swords stood at the base of the egg, protecting Mother Russia, I supposed. Yagamata lifted off the top of the egg and withdrew what looked like a gold chain. "My favorite piece," he said, unfolding a miniature train of solid gold, "the Trans-Siberian Railway Egg. I sometimes carry the train with me, just to draw it out of my pocket and enjoy the sheer pleasure of it. Have you ever seen such workmanship, such love of detail combined with whimsy?"

"Whimsy," Foley said, barely suppressing a sneer. "It's just a *thing,* Matsuo. It's just an object to be bought and sold like everything else."

Yagamata folded the train back into the egg. "No, Mr. Foley, it is not. Some 'things' are too valuable to simply be bought and sold. Some are more valuable than life."

"Enough talk," Foley said, his eyes seeming to narrow behind his glasses. He turned toward the Russian, who hadn't moved. "Your face looks like shit, Kharchenko. Tell me, did a woman really do that to you, tough guy?"

"You cannot provoke me," the Russian said. "I have my instructions, and I will carry them out."

"There's been a change in plans. I'm taking charge in the field. You're to turn the shipment over to me."

Kharchenko's smile revealed a missing front tooth. He pointed a finger at Foley and said, "I don't take my orders from you."

Foley's hand shot out with frightening speed. He grabbed the jabbing finger and pushed it backward. Hard. The *crack* echoed off the marble floors. Kharchenko let out a high-pitched wail, and Foley twisted the finger, left then right. *Crack, crack.* Three clean breaks, one at each knuckle. Kharchenko was on his knees, tears filling his eyes.

Foley never let go of the finger, but used it to yank the Russian's right arm behind his back. His movements were so smooth, so quick, I never saw the clear plastic handcuffs come from his pocket. In a moment, Kharchenko's hands were bound behind him. The Russian rocked back and forth, still on his knees. He gave the impression of being in painful prayer.

Foley's eyes darted around the room. On an ornate desk was a gold wicker basket filled with lilies of the valley. Foley motioned for me to get it.

"Now? You want flowers now?" I asked.

Yagamata sensed something I didn't. "You wouldn't," he pleaded with Foley, a tinge of fear in his voice. "Please. I abhor violence and detest the destruction of beautiful things. That is Fabergé's first flower study, a gift to Empress Alexandra—"

"Lassiter! Give me the goddamn basket. That's a direct order."

"Hey, I never joined up."

"Goddammit! You're an American, and I'm calling on you by the power vested in me by the President."

I didn't know what he was talking about, but it sounded impressive. I walked over to the desk and picked up the basket. These lilies didn't need water, and the only scent was of unlimited money combined with incomparable artistry. I am, in the main, untutored in the world of art and artifacts. I do not go gaga over a fine jade doodad; I do not wax ecstatic over a Ming dynasty vase; but even my rough-hewn self could appreciate this. I had never seen such beauty in a man-made object.

The moss was spun gold. The delicate looping stems were solid gold rods, the flowers were pearls encircled with diamonds. Who was it who said that diamonds are a pearl's best friends? I gently touched the green leaves.

"Nephrite," Yagamata said.

"I've never seen anything like it."

Yagamata laughed. "There is nothing like it, anywhere in the world."

"Gimme!" Foley barked.

I walked toward him, and Foley tore the basket from my hand. He leaned over Kharchenko, who was silent now. "Where is the shipment?"

Kharchenko muttered something in Russian. Foley grabbed him by the collar of his brown suit coat and yanked backward. He roughly pulled one of the flower stems out of the golden moss. "Let's see how much you love art, Kharchenko."

There were perhaps ten pearls on the stem, tiny ones at the tip, growing larger toward the base, where each one was tipped by six rose-cut diamonds. Foley put a hand to Kharchenko's bandaged face, then pressed hard at the jaw muscles, forcing the Russian's mouth open. Then he jammed the stem in and let go of his jaw. "Eat! Savor every morsel."

Kharchenko let the pearl-laden stem sit in his mouth but did not move. Yagamata looked away. He seemed to be memorizing every detail of a colorful tapestry. Foley crouched down, grabbed another of the Russian's fingers, and bent it back again until it cracked. Pain shot across Kharchenko's face, and he involuntarily crunched down. I heard the stem break between his teeth.

"Be a good boy and chew every bite. You don't want your tummy to hurt."

Slowly, Kharchenko worked his jaws. Tiny cuts appeared at the corners of his mouth. Foley leaned over him. "Swallow! Swallow, you greedy Russian pig, or I'll break every bone in your fucking body, one at a time." He picked up another golden stem and rammed it in. "Eat, you big cow! Eat your country's precious art."

Blood flowed in rivulets down Kharchenko's chin, staining the gauze bandages, as he chomped down again and again. A tooth broke with a sickening crack.

"Now," Foley asked, squatting close to the Russian, "where is the shipment?"

Kharchenko spit a bloody fragment of gold into Foley's face.

With an angry hiss, Foley straightened, paced around the room, and stopped in front of the vessel filled with pearls. "Lassiter, a Western visitor attended one of the czar's parties in the Hermitage where the guests ate their weight in caviar. Do you know how he described the Russian nobility?"

I shook my head.

"He said they were 'dripping pearls and vermin.' Hey, Kharchenko, we'll provide the pearls. You probably have your own vermin."

Yagamata stood silently, hands clasped behind his back, eyes closed. Foley was relishing this. But I wasn't. I was thinking about it, reading my moral compass. Kharchenko killed Crespo and Eva-Lisa, and if anybody deserved to die, he did. But it's one thing to declare a man's guilt and another to execute him. It gnawed at me now, watching him tortured, my standing there doing nothing, my silence deafening.

"Foley, I don't think he's—"

"Shut up, Lassiter. You did your job by finding him. Let me do mine."

Foley grabbed the gold vessel from its pedestal. He waved it in front of Kharchenko's face. "Neither cast ye your pearls before swine." Foley laughed. He yanked Kharchenko's head back again, forced his mouth open, and poured the pearls into it. They rattled against his teeth and filled his mouth and throat. The Russian coughed and choked, spitting out as many as he could. I saw his Adam's apple bob, the muscles of his neck contract, his throat thicken.

"Where!" Foley demanded.

Kharchenko was gagging, spitting up blood and yellow phlegm, but trying to talk, too. Foley leaned close, listening. Kharchenko's lips moved. Foley smiled and patted the Russian affectionately on the top of the head. Then he stood, hitched up his formal black trousers, drew his right knee to his chest, then kicked Kharchenko flush on the temple, toppling him sideways. By the time the Russian hit the floor, a purple stain had appeared beneath the skin where his meningeal artery had ruptured. Quickly the stain spread under his ear and across his face.

The room was silent except for a faint *ping*ing as Empress Alexandra's pearls dropped, one by one, from Kharchenko's bloody lips and rolled merrily across the gleaming marble floor.

21

A CZAR'S RANSOM

The street was dark, the pavement potted with craters. Overhead, a jet whined on final approach to Miami International Airport. It was an area of warehouses, loading docks, freight-forwarding companies, and import-export firms servicing Latin America. In the middle of the night, the buildings were dark as tombs, locked and shuttered.

We looked for a warehouse painted army green with a sign that said simply, Inter-American Casket Company. Maybe the name was Kharchenko's little joke. Was he burying communism here, or merely discouraging thieves? Foley drove the Plymouth with Yagamata in back and a dog-tired me riding shotgun. Without a shotgun. Foley kept swinging the car over the curb, shining his headlights on the darkened buildings. Finally, he spotted something, hit the brakes, and killed the lights.

Foley was out of the car first, running his hands over a corrugated metal door secured by a padlock. That was it. No guards, no alarm system. Just a padlock I wouldn't trust to keep my Schwinn from being kidnapped at Bayfront Park.

Foley opened his trunk and dug out a flashlight and tire iron. He popped the padlock, and I pulled up on the handle. The door rumbled open, and a blast of cool air hit us. Pitch black. From somewhere inside, the whirr of a massive air-conditioning system.

Foley shone a flashlight on the wall, found a switch, and hit it. Overhead, bright lights blinked on, blinding me. I jumped when I heard the sound behind me, but it was only Foley closing the door.

Along one wall were wooden cartons of various sizes, sheets of Styrofoam packing material, rolls of twine and brown wrapping paper. Lettering in Spanish indicated the cartons contained Peruvian pottery. Some of the cartons were already filled, others open and empty. Waiting.

The rest of the warehouse was a jumble of colors and textures, gilt and glitter. It was filled from floor to thirty-foot ceiling with gold and silver, paintings and artifacts, statues and coins, icons and gems of all descriptions. The treasure spilled out of boxes and overflowed onto the floor, in cartons, on the walls, and on makeshift tables made of sawhorses and plywood. A czar's ransom in riches.

"One of my favorites," Yagamata said, pointing at a painting. "Cézanne's *Lady in Blue.*" He stepped closer and spoke to it. "Why are you so sad, pretty lady? Don't you want to return to the homeland?"

"How many trucks will it take?" Foley asked.

Yagamata ignored him. He was studying a painting of dusky-skinned women eating fruit by a lake. *"Sacred Spring.* Gauguin offered it for sale in Paris, and no one would buy it, not for twenty francs. Foley, have you ever been to Tahiti, or is there too little mendacity there to interest you?" He chuckled and walked slowly along a table where paintings lay scattered like brilliant playing cards. "Perhaps this is more to your liking." He gestured to an oil painting of dead, bloodied birds, surrounded by riding gear. *"Trophies of the Hunt* by Hamilton. On the other hand, for my taste, there is nothing lovelier than a full-bodied nude." He pointed again, this time to a dim, greenish painting of a woman toweling off a bare, ample hip. *"After the Bath,* by Degas. Contrast that, for example, with *Three Women* by Picasso."

Foley looked at the Picasso dispassionately. "I like my babes a little rounder," he said. "I'll take the Degas."

Yes, you will, I thought.

Yagamata roamed across the warehouse, touching this and that, talking mostly to himself. "Look what the fools have done.

They've mixed the French with the Russians. Malevich's *Flower Girl* next to Matisse, and Goncharova's *Laundresses,* about to be packed with a Chagall." He clucked his disapproval and moved on. "Foley, do you know what Khrushchev said the first time he saw the avant-garde art of the modern Russian painters? That was thirty years ago, and there was the tiniest breeze of liberalization blowing through Moscow. At an exhibition in the Manezh, the czars' old riding school, Khrushchev spat at the paintings. 'Dog shit,' he called them. 'A donkey could do better with its tail.' Ah, how long ago it seems. The dark ages. Do you know that Gorbachev was the Russians' first leader since Lenin to have a university education? A lawyer by training."

"I'll bet Gorby never watched a chicken autopsied in a courtroom," I said.

Yagamata looked puzzled. "Perhaps not, but he and Yeltsin carved up the bear, didn't they?" His laugh seemed full of regret. "I shall miss my trips there. I could spend a month just touring the Hermitage and never grow tired."

"Then you decided to bring it all here," Foley said.

"Yes, I think I did, without quite knowing it." Yagamata stopped in front of a small painting propped against a metal rack. A woman in a red-and-blue robe stared with adoration at a naked baby in her arms. "Da Vinci's *Madonna with Child,* one of his early works. Do you sense that the perspective is off, the child far too large?"

Foley grunted. He seemed to be taking inventory. Yagamata moved on, and we followed him through the cavernous room. On the floor, jewelry filled a huge, dark pot. Emerald bracelets, diamond pins, gold cuff links and chains, pearl buttons, ruby brooches jumbled together. "What is more valuable," Yagamata asked himself, "all these trinkets or Tamburlaine's bronze cauldron which holds them?"

Yagamata stooped to study the writing on a box. "*Tauride Venus,* Russia's first classical statue. A gift from the Pope to Peter the Great. The Hermitage alone has twelve thousand sculptures and a million coins. Do you know I still get lost there? I never enter the buildings without a compass. Foley, even if we tried, none of us could live long enough to steal it all."

Nearby were half a dozen other sculptures not yet boxed.

Yagamata ran his hand over the smooth white stone of one, a man and woman embracing. "Rodin's *Romeo and Juliet.* Frankly, I prefer his *Cupid and Psyche.* Ah, there it is."

He walked past the statues and picked up a solid gold dinner plate from a long table. The plate was on a stack with perhaps twenty others. Boxes of gleaming flatware sat under the table. "From the banquet hall at Petrodvorets, the White Dining Room. Gold dinnerware to serve four hundred."

Stacked on a wooden platform was a variety of jewelry. Lockets of enamel and gold, a clock of different colored golds, a desk set of rock crystal. Small animals carved from agate, others shaped from nephrite and silver. Pendants and necklaces, rings, and pins, filling boxes three feet deep.

And then the eggs.

Inside a glass egg, a rider on a horse. Yagamata saw my expression. "Fabergé's Alexander the Third Equestrian Egg," he said. "Nice, but compare it to the Fifteenth Anniversary Egg made the next year to celebrate Nicholas's accession. Here's the Madonna-Lily Egg and the Winter Egg, which everyone thought was lost during the Revolution. Good Lord, Foley, have you ever seen such beauty?"

Foley was still measuring the room with his eyes. "Eight trailers should do it. Maybe nine. C'mon, let's go. This ain't a museum tour."

The trucks were from a rental company, arranged for by Foley. I asked him why he didn't use the U.S. Marshal's Service, but he waved me off. The workers belonged to Yagamata. Some Russians, some Cubans, they were tight-lipped, dull-eyed, sullen-faced men who moved as if they were paid by the hour. There was little bantering, and the only bellyaching I heard was when Yagamata ordered one man to put out his cigarette.

The packing took most of the day and into the night. When it was done, the cartons filled eight trailers and part of a ninth. I stood there watching everything boarded and boxed, thinking about the nobility who commissioned the priceless cache, and about the peasants on whose backs the nobility walked. I wondered about the fate of these inanimate objects, given more value than that of human life. How many peasants died so the Romanovs could enjoy their gilded eggs and diamond-crusted snuff boxes? How many more would die even now to protect the art, or to steal it?

I thought of Smorodinsky, Crespo, and Eva-Lisa. And Kharchenko. He was dead, too. I took part, at least by omission. I was—how would Abe Socolow characterize it?—a coconspirator. I had stood silently and watched Foley kill the man, brutally and efficiently. I could have stopped him, but I didn't.

Didn't even try.

And now I thought about it. I wasn't repulsed by the horror of it. I was fascinated by the cool, competent administration of pain by someone good at the job. It occurred to me then that Foley enjoyed the task. His creased face became flushed, his eyes hot behind the glasses. Yagamata had turned away from the cold-blooded torture and murder, trying to lose himself in the artwork hanging on the gallery wall. But I watched, my pulse quickening, and now I knew that, like Foley, I enjoyed it, too.

I pushed the thought aside and remembered how it all began. Francisco Crespo. My debt was not repaid, never would be. But someday I would tell Emilia Crespo that the man who murdered her son was dead, and had died hard. What did it say about my character that the thought gave me a warm glow of pleasure?

Knowledge of self is a precious commodity, dearer than the finest gemstone. The mirror I held before me now was not laced with gold filigree. It was cold and flat and bared every shadow on my soul.

No, Foley, I didn't stop you. I merely watched in feigned horror, and now I have only one regret. I wish I had killed the bastard myself.

It was after midnight when Foley and I got into the cab of the lead truck with a driver who had not recently encountered deodorant soap. Foley was flipping through a folder of papers, reviewing the inventory, smiling to himself. The driver had a hard time clanking from first gear into second, but he finally got it after several Spanish curses and a tug-of-war with the shift. We rolled off into the night to points unknown.

I was just about to ask Foley where we were headed when he told the driver to pull over and pointed toward a Plymouth sedan sitting at the curb near the intersection of LeJeune Road and the Airport Expressway. The driver tugged at the wheel, the truck's brakes squealing in protest.

"The keys are under the mat," Foley said. "You're outta here."

I started to protest, but he hushed me. "It's gonna get dangerous from here on out."

"Really, what's it been up to now, a day at the beach?"

"Lassiter, you've done a good job, better than I would have thought. But you've already seen and heard too much. You don't have security clearance for this. Leave the rest to the Company. Go back to your torts and contracts."

"Where are you going?"

He put a finger to his lips. "State secret. Hey, almost forgot. Yagamata wanted you to have this." He reached into his coat pocket and handed me something metallic. I held it up to the light of an oncoming car.

"Opera glasses," I said. They were heavy. I looked closer. Solid yellow gold with what looked like white gold lacework.

"Belonged to Czar Nick. Matsuo thinks they'll help you see the truth. Go ahead. Take a look."

When I hesitated, he laughed. "Go on. It doesn't give you a black eye, and there aren't any girly pictures inside."

I held up the solid gold binoculars and looked at the waiting car in the glare of our headlights. Nothing but a blur. "I can't see a thing. They don't work."

"How about that?" Foley said. "Isn't that just like old Mother Russia?"

22

WRONG-WAY LASSITER

I approached the witness stand and politely asked, "Isn't it true that you bit into a finger cot, and not a condom, Mrs. Schwartzbaum?"

She pointed toward the defense table. "That's what *they* say."

"You're not disputing the evidence, are you?"

Sylvia Schwartzbaum was fifty and not all that pleased about it. The frosted hair was lacquered into place, and if she turned too quickly, her immense silver earrings could cause whiplash. "All I know is when I bit into my endive, I chewed something rubbery, and when I spit it out, I thought it was a condom. That's why I screamed. That's why I spilled the soup in Harry's lap, the poor dear." She paused for effect and looked into the gallery, giving her husband a small, tragic smile. "And that's why I have a severe case of mental anguish."

"But now you know it wasn't a condom, correct?" I was going to hammer away until she admitted it.

"At the time, it felt like a condom, and it looked like a condom."

I wouldn't be doing my job, such as it is, if I didn't ask a follow-up question. "Did it taste like a condom, Mrs. Schwartzbaum?"

She gave me an icy stare. "Not being a pervert, I wouldn't

know about that." She looked toward Harry, who nodded his approval.

Judge Dixie Lee Boulton leaned forward in her chair and peered at me through her bifocals, which dangled on a chain of imitation pearls. "Mr. Lassiter, I suggest you move it along. I've heard just about enough of this line of questioning."

I hadn't wanted to defend another restaurant case. Last year I lost the case of the flaming dessert. Bananas *flambé* cost the plaintiff his expensive toupee and my client, Le Parisian Eaterie, twenty-five grand. But win or lose, a trial lawyer gets typecast. Next, I was hired to defend the Calle Ocho cafeteria where an elderly man slipped and fell on an oil slick of spilled flan. Then I fought off the Consumer Protection Agency for the allegedly kosher Cuban restaurant that served *frijoles con puerco.*

Now I was dealing with the case of the rubber-in-the-rutabaga, as Marvin the Maven insisted on calling it. Every morning before court, I had to stop in the corridor as Marvin and Max (Just Plain) Seltzer told me fly-in-the-soup jokes, all of which I had heard before.

"Jacob, I got a new waiter joke for you," Marvin said earlier today. "Direct from the Catskills, which, as you know, are the Jewish Alps. Two ladies are having lunch. The first orders the borscht, but the waiter says, 'Take my advice, have instead the chicken soup.' The second lady orders the pea soup, and the waiter says, 'No, take the barley.' They do as they're told, and the first lady compliments him: 'Best chicken soup I ever had.' So the second lady asks, 'Why didn't you recommend *me* the chicken soup?' The waiter says, 'You didn't ask for the borscht.' "

Marvin and Max were still laughing as I hauled my trial bag into the courtroom. My partners had insisted I handle the case after I had missed a couple days of work. Been lollygagging long enough, the managing partner said. Taking off without warning, leaving young associates to handle motion calendars and prepare cases for trial. The litany of complaints was piling up. So my punishment was the mental anguish suit of Sylvia Schwartzbaum, plaintiff from hell.

"Your expert witnesses have examined the rubbery object, plaintiff's exhibit one, have they not?" I asked.

"They *better* have, after the bill I got."

"And they told you that the object was not a condom, correct?"

"Objection!" H. T. Patterson was on his feet, poking a finger in my direction. "Hearsay and irrelevant. The report speaks for itself, and it doesn't matter what my client thinks about it."

"I think it cost too much money," Mrs. Schwartzbaum told the judge and jury.

"Your Honor," I pleaded, "the report's in evidence. I'm merely eliciting evidence that will establish the plaintiff's state of mind. It's relevant to the damage issue."

Judge Boulton pulled a pencil out of her 1950s bouffant, made a note on a legal pad, and allowed as how the objection was overruled.

I looked at the witness and waited.

Mrs. Schwartzbaum shrugged her shoulders. "Sure, they said it was one of those little whatchamacallits . . ."

"Finger cots?"

". . . so they don't slice their filthy fingernails into your salad with the cucumbers."

"And you learned this within days of the incident, did you not?"

"Yeah, so what?" Suspicious now.

"So, in the restaurant, when you screamed at the top of your lungs that you were going to catch AIDS from . . ." I riffled through the transcript of the previous day's proceedings even though I knew the line by heart. " '. . . from the grimy Haitian wetback who jerked off in my salad,' you were obviously mistaken."

"I don't know which island the kitchen help comes from, if that's what you mean," she said.

"What I mean is you now are secure in the knowledge that you will not contract a disease from eating at Norma's Natural Food Emporium, correct?"

"I wouldn't go back there for a million dollars."

Funny, a million bucks was her settlement demand. I turned to the judge. "Your Honor, the witness is not being responsive."

Sylvia Schwartzbaum sighed. "That's what Harry says. Ever since they poisoned me, I've not been responsive. Now, we don't even have relations. It's his lost-consorting claim."

"Consortium," her lawyer, H. T. Patterson, piped up.

"In that case, Harry should pay my client," I stage-whispered a tad too loud.

"Mr. Lassiter!" Judge Boulton was seldom awake long enough to get involved in the proceedings. But now Dixie Lee was steamed, and my old buddy Patterson was not doing me any favors, prancing around, demanding a sidebar where he accused me of multitudinous sins.

"Atrocious and abominable, disgraceful and dastardly," Patterson began in the singsong he had perfected as a one-time preacher at the Liberty City Baptist Church. "Impudent and insolent, an utterly appalling, barbarous breach of ethics to make such a shameful statement in front of the jury . . ."

Oh, I don't know. A couple of them had nodded their heads with appreciation and one laughed out loud.

"Despicable and defamatory, disgusting and detestable, vile and vulgar, repulsive and repugnant." Patterson was on his toes now, chin thrust forward, strutting his stuff. I knew it was an act, and I would have to wait it out. Patterson did have an unfortunate habit, however, of bouncing close and spraying me with saliva as he worked himself into a frenzy. It reminded me of a recent study, which concluded that male trial lawyers have more testosterone than their brethren who practice real estate, tax, or corporate law. The psychologist learned this by testing saliva, a few globs of which were now affixed to my Italian silk tie. I always thought Patterson's pugnaciousness had more to do with being five feet five than overdosing on male hormones.

He was still going. "Calumnious and . . ."

"Contemptuous," Judge Boulton helped him out. "Twenty-four hours in the county stockade, Mr. Lassiter."

I like quiet contemplation. A day and night behind bars was neither novel nor particularly unsettling. In a trial a few years ago, a judge ordered me not to ask a cop if he was under investigation by Internal Review. I persisted, and the judge warned me that one more question and he'd send me to a place I'd never been.

"Already been to jail," I told him.

"Not jail," the judge said. "Law school."

I was even held in contempt once for telling a good-natured joke to a judge who had just ruled against me.

"What do you call a lawyer with an IQ of fifty?" I asked.

The judge shrugged.

"Your Honor," I answered.

I don't mind some time away from home. I don't have a dog to walk, a bird to feed, or grass to cut. No feminine companion awaits me at the door, a duck roasting in the oven. The women come and go, and life stays the same though their faces change. There were stewardesses when they were still called that, a real estate broker with a penthouse condo, more than one South Beach model with tales of Milan and Paris and how our humidity is hell on the hair, a nurse who held my hand when I tore ligaments in a knee, a statuesque literature professor from Yugoslavia who could outcuss Granny Lassiter and didn't disparage Hemingway, a Dolphin cheerleader to whom every new experience was either "far out" or "queer," and who left me for a commodities broker with a yacht. And there, too, was the sportswriter I let down when she needed me to protect her. Since then, I hadn't let anybody need me.

I always take a good book and my first baseman's mitt when I get sent up. I never apologize, post bond, or seek rehearing. I'm not sure why, but it may have something to do with the stubborn streak I inherited from my granny.

The stockade is not so bad, even if the food tends to the starchy side. The prisoners are no more reprehensible than most of my partners and more forthright about their chicanery. There's a good set of weights and a decent softball field. I like playing first base because there's plenty of action, and you don't have far to run.

So now I stood on the field in shorts and sneakers, a Marlins cap and dark shades. I had just fielded a bunt and flipped it home trying to nip a cat burglar on a squeeze play. He had quick feet, and the catcher, a sago palm thief, had bad hands, so the run scored.

"A day late and a dollar short," someone said behind me.

I turned around to find Abe Socolow. Squinting into the sun, the state attorney wore his customary funeral suit, a cigarette locked in his lips. "Want to take a turn at bat, Abe? We need a designated killjoy."

"*You* need a lawyer."

"Not me. Done my hard time. Getting out at two o'clock, thirty minutes off for good behavior."

I was trying to hold the runner on the base and banter with Socolow at the same time. Complicating the task was my awareness of the runner's vocation as a pickpocket. I didn't like him behind me.

"We gotta talk." Socolow dropped his cigarette and ground it into the base path. He looked out of place on a ballfield. In fact, he looked out of place anywhere but under the sickly fluorescent lighting of the Justice Building. He belonged there with the vaguely institutional smell, the incessant din of official commotion. He brought order to a disordered world, and did it as if he alone had the power. Sweat beaded on his high forehead, and in the sunlight, I could see his dark hair was thinning on top. "I got a call from Washington this morning. Someone asking a lot of questions about you."

The pitcher, a con man who had perfected the pigeon drop and the week-late lottery scam, used a windmill windup, then threw a change-up. The batter was so far in front of the pitch he twisted himself into a pretzel on his follow-through.

"Don't tell me," I said. "I'm about to be nominated for the Supreme Court."

"You're about to be charged in the largest art theft in history."

The con man's fastball fooled the batter, who swung late, grounding a soft three-hopper right at me. I swiped at it, but never got the glove down. Sheesh. They teach you how to do that in Little League. I watched the ball roll between my legs and into right field.

"Fix! Fix!" The second baseman, a three-hundred-pound bookie and bolita operator, was screeching at me.

"What are you talking about?" I asked Socolow.

"You and that renegade CIA agent, Foley. I figure he's the mastermind. Anybody who knows you would realize that. You're the accessory, and probably an incompetent one. But Foley's missing, and so are a few billion dollars of arts and antiquities, and you're here. There's a team from CIA, Justice, FBI, and State on their way. I'm your baby-sitter, Lassiter."

Traffic was backed up on the way to the Justice Building. This time it wasn't a shoot-out between drivers bickering over the right-of-way. It wasn't an octogenarian with cataracts going the wrong way on the interstate. It was a leaky toilet on a jet.

Two lanes of the expressway exit that spanned the Miami River were closed while workers filled a crater caused by a jet engine that dropped off a 727 during the night. A tractor-trailer carrying twenty thousand pounds of live tropical fish sideswiped the engine, veered to the right, and overturned. The concrete guardrail sliced through the trailer's roof like a can opener. Which is how thousands of angelfish, sea horses, and parrotfish came to be dumped into the river that pours into the bay, which opens into the Atlantic and theoretically gives the fish a chance to swim back to the Bahamian reefs from which they were so recently kidnapped.

The fish were happier than the airline P.R. people. They issued press releases explaining that a leaky toilet had caused the lavatory water to escape onto the fuselage of the 727, where it formed a huge blue chunk of ice that broke free and cleanly knocked the tail engine off the plane.

Traffic eased and then clogged again near Government Center. By order of the city commission, workers were hat-racking the black olive trees that shaded the street. Our local politicians somehow believed that street drug dealers would cease doing business if threatened with sunstroke. Next they'll try draining the ocean to prevent shark attacks.

It took Socolow another ten minutes to find a parking spot. The Justice Building was surrounded by Santería worshipers carrying lighted candles and bowls of animal blood. They were apparently displeased with the arrest of one of their priests on animal cruelty charges after he sacrificed a dozen goats and chickens on the median strip of Biscayne Boulevard during rush hour.

"I used to think New York was weird," Socolow said, as he nudged the county-owned Plymouth into a compact space six inches from a defense lawyer's candy-apple red Porsche.

We took a series of escalators to the seventh floor, passing the usual cast of characters in the circus they call criminal court. Spit-and-polished uniformed cops, unwashed defendants in shackles, their mothers and girlfriends teary-eyed or indignant, harried probation officers, pretty young court reporters, deal-making prosecutors and public defenders, and the occasional judge, black robes flowing, on the way to or from chambers.

"I love this place," Socolow said, almost wistfully. "Jake, I remember when you were an assistant P.D. We had some good times, didn't we?"

"*You* had good times. You had a ninety-five-percent conviction rate."

"They were all guilty of something, even if we charged them with something else."

"And even if the cops lied in suppression hearings," I reminded him. " 'Yes, Your Honor, I observed the cocaine in plain view on the dashboard. Yes, Your Honor, the subject consented to a body cavity search.' C'mon, Abe, it's just a game you're very good at."

The receptionist behind bullet-proof glass buzzed us into the State Attorney's office. "You were on the wrong side, Jake. You burned out because you were working for the bad guys."

"I burned out because I couldn't tell the difference."

Inside Socolow's office, we had company. My bearded friend sat in a corner, huddled over a book on forensic odontology. A small, dark, mustachioed man in a white guayabera didn't stand or offer his one hand. His daughter stood and ran to me. "Jake, are you all right?" Lourdes Soto asked, a tremor in her voice. "I've been so worried."

Still in his chair, Severo Soto muttered something in Spanish. From his position in the corner, Doc Charlie Riggs never acknowledged me. Eyes still on his book, he allowed as how he's seeing fewer café coronaries, restaurant patrons choking to death on chunks of meat, now that people are eating more fish and pasta.

I took Lourdes in my arms and looked into her moist dark

eyes. She smelled of a rich perfume. "I'd be better if the governments of two countries plus the state of Florida didn't want to prosecute me for crimes I didn't do."

"What you did," Severo Soto said, "was *hacer el tonto.* You played the fool."

"Papi, please!" Lourdes unwrapped herself from me and sat down again.

"But it is true," her father said. "I know that, you know that, and Doctor Socolow knows that, *verdad*?"

Abe Socolow seemed to like being given the Spanish title of respect. He nodded graciously in Soto's direction, then turned to me. "Jake, I've known you a long time. You're a little rough around the edges, and your sense of ethics is flexible, to say the least." He looked at Soto. "Jake here once robbed a grave to get evidence, and he's been known to taunt a witness into a fistfight just to prove a propensity for violence."

"I was younger, then," I said, sheepishly.

"Errare humanum est," Charlie Riggs added, without looking up.

Why didn't anyone speak English to me anymore? I plopped into a chair between Lourdes and her father. Socolow sat down behind his green metal state-issue desk. "The point is that you're unorthodox, and you play by your own rules, but I believe your story. You're not a thief. Of course, the feds don't know that, and here's the way it's coming down. Foley is off somewhere arranging for private sales of the best stuff you guys ripped off from an ex-KGB man."

"Hold on! I didn't rip off anything. Foley recovered the art from Kharchenko, who—"

"Hold on, Jake, you've got everything fouled up." Abe Socolow tapped a cigarette out of a pack on his desk. He took his time lighting it, his body language telling me to calm down, this would take a while. "In the beginning, Foley and Yagamata were doing exactly what our government ordered. Tracking down the art thefts, hushing them up, getting the stuff back. Then somebody decides the thefts have political value, so the CIA starts getting the goods on the old hard-liners who are taking bribes. It was a hell of a sting that led to the failed coup. Later, under the reformers, our two governments were supposed to—"

"Trade art for wheat," I interrupted.

"Huh?"

Now it was my turn to show off. "The CIA was helping the Russians by selling the art and turning the proceeds into food for the people. Yagamata got greedy and started selling the art and keeping the money after splitting it with Kharchenko and his pals. Foley stopped them and got everything back."

"That's what Foley told you."

"Yeah."

"And you believed him?"

Oh, shit.

Socolow sighed. "I guess Foley didn't tell you the Russian reformers vetoed all that art-for-wheat business."

"What!"

"It was on the drawing board, all right, but Yeltsin rejected it, said they'd tough it out without selling off their national treasures. Yagamata goes bat shit. He knows the nuts and bolts of how to get the stuff out of the country from his experiences with the hard-liners in the bad old days. He'd had a taste of it, and it's all there waiting to be taken. He just couldn't resist. When the stuff keeps disappearing, the Russians squawk to the CIA, which now has to reverse its policy. The smart guys at Langley figure it was a mistake to interfere in the internal affairs of a sovereign nation. They've got to restore the status quo. Foley draws the assignment, and it takes him about thirty seconds to figure who's behind it, so his job is to bring down Yagamata and get back the stuff. Instead, he beards Yagamata with a scam that the government will pay him for his cooperation, kills Kharchenko, and takes off with the art."

"But Foley said—"

"Listen up, Jake." Again, Socolow turned toward Soto and nodded with deference. "Señor Soto has been associated with the CIA since before the Bay of Pigs, and was there to keep an eye on Yagamata under the guise of providing shipping. When Yagamata started dealing for himself, Señor Soto alerted Langley, which told him to keep quiet and find out everything he could. Then all hell broke loose. These two Russian brothers—"

"Vladimir and Nikolai," I said.

"Yeah. They figured out what was going on, too, that Yagamata was stealing every ashtray in the country. Vladimir worked for Yagamata, so he was easy enough to dispose of. They used Kharchenko to knock off Crespo because Crespo knew who killed Vladimir and was starting to crack. Kharchenko also killed a Finnish agent—"

"Eva-Lisa Haavikko. She was slaughtered in a sauna. I was there."

"Eva-Lisa?" Lourdes repeated, her eyebrows raised. "In a sauna?"

"She was a Suopo operative who helped out when they were using the art to set up the hard-liners," Socolow said. "When Yagamata kept up the flow of goods after CIA policy changed, she tried to back out. But her employer had changed without her knowing it. Yagamata wasn't working for the CIA anymore, and what used to be the KGB, the new Russian Agency for Federal Security, tossed Kharchenko out on his ear. Her new bosses were international outlaws even nastier than the folks in Langley and Moscow, and it got her killed." Socolow shot a sour look at me. "Meanwhile, CIA figures out what Foley is up to and gets Señor Soto involved to try and recover the art from Yagamata. But it was too late once you and Foley pulled off the heist."

My head was spinning. Just like the old days. I never could tell the good guys from the bad.

"So, Jakie, to put it bluntly, you fucked up. You went on the road and suited up for the wrong team. You turned over the goods to the wrong side. In short, you're Wrong-Way Lassiter again."

I hate it when somebody calls me that. One lousy play a thousand years ago and they never forget. We were leading the dog-ass New York Jets by ten with a minute to go, and I was doing my best to get some grass stains on my jersey when the ball squirted out of the pile and took a neat end-over-end bounce right into my hands. Okay, so I got turned around—it could happen to anybody—and tore off in the wrong direction. The only touchdown of my NFL demicareer, and it had to be for the guys in green-and-white. We still won the game by three points, but most of my drinking buddies had taken the Dolphins minus five, which was all I heard at the Gaslight Lounge for the next few weeks. It was my most embarrassing moment on the playing field, unless you count the time I blocked a punt—*our* punt—with my backside, but that's another story.

"Where's Foley now?" I asked.

"CIA figures he's looking for experts to attest to the loot's authenticity. As you can imagine, he doesn't have documentation, and if you're going to ask ten million dollars for a painting, you gotta have some proof. The art world is filled with some incredibly good fakes."

That brought Charlie Riggs out of his book. "Jake, you're probably familiar with the Greek *Kouros* purchased by the Getty Museum."

"Intimately," I muttered. I was still trying to figure out who was on whose side.

Charlie waggled a cold pipe at me. "A marble statue of a young boy. The museum spent nine million dollars for it almost a decade ago, and despite the most sophisticated tests—electron microscopy, thermoluminescence, and carbon-14 dating—nobody knows if that statue was carved twenty-five hundred years ago on the island of Thasos, or fifty years ago in some forger's basement in Turkey."

"Anyway," Socolow said, sounding bored, "even without Yagamata, Foley will probably try to make the first deals with Japanese billionaires for selected pieces in the five- to twenty-million-dollar range. Japan's where all the money is. Plus they have a delightful law that gives clear title to the buyer of stolen art unless the lawful owner puts him on notice of the theft within two years. So, all the guy has to do is keep his egg or painting or whatever under wraps for a couple of years, then haul it out at a birthday party or the opening of a new Lexus dealership."

"What are you guys doing about Foley?" I asked. "Why aren't you after him?"

Socolow smiled, if that's what you call it when a barracuda spots a guppy. "That's where you come in."

"I don't know where he is," I said quickly, "and I don't know where the art is. Your buddies from Washington can beat me with rubber hoses, and I still won't know."

"With *your* head, Jake, they'd use lead pipes. We know where he is, and he's got the loot with him. We need you to deal with him."

"Me? Why me?"

"You're the only one we know who can get close to Foley."

"Close to him! He used me. Like Señor Soto said, he played me for a fool. I led him to Kharchenko. He had me believing I was following orders from the President."

Soto stirred in his chair, then stood up. The movement made his empty sleeve billow. "Foley should have killed you but he did not. He knew you would be taken into custody here and interrogated, that you would likely reveal everything that happened, but he wanted you around for some purpose."

"What purpose?"

Socolow lit another cigarette. "Even the boys in Washington couldn't figure that one out, until Foley called."

"Called?"

"Yeah, called. Like on the phone."

"Why?"

Again, he showed his predator's smile. "C'mon, Jake, think about it. It's what we used to call dropping the dime, or these days should we say, the quarter? Foley wants to cut a deal. He wants you to be his lawyer."

23

SUN, RUM, AND SEX

Who besides the government buys Detroit's full-size, four-door sedans with blackwalls? That's what I wondered as we rolled out of the Justice Building parking lot, neatly avoiding a demonstration by Liberty City residents against the Palestinian owners of the area's convenience stores. A federal marshal drove the first car, a navy-blue Plymouth. His passenger was an FBI agent with round glasses and an advanced degree in art history. We were next in line, Socolow driving his county-owned car, a cigarette dangling from the corner of his mouth. I rode shotgun; Lourdes Soto and her father sat in back. Behind us, another federal marshal drove a CIA agent, an assistant to an under secretary from the State Department, and someone from the Justice Department who wouldn't give his name and said he wasn't really here. Your tax dollars at work.

I don't know why we needed a caravan. Best I could figure, no one would assassinate me on the Don Shula Expressway. The only threat came from a skinny, barefoot guy who cursed in Creole when Socolow wouldn't let him clean our windshield at a traffic light on LeJeune Road. As we turned into the airport, I couldn't help asking, "Anybody want to tell me where we're going?"

"You'll find out soon enough, Jakie," Socolow said.

Ah, a quiz. They told me to pick up my passport along with my duffel bag, so I already knew we weren't going to Disney World. "They speak English there?"

"About as much as on Flagler Street downtown." Socolow kept his eyes on the road.

"In that case, I'll need an interpreter."

From the back seat, Lourdes said, "That's why I'm along, Jake."

Okay, a Spanish-speaking country. If it had been ancient Rome, Charlie Riggs would have drawn the assignment. "Never been to Costa Rica," I ventured. "Hear the fishing's great."

Socolow cranked down his window—no power accessories for the cost-conscious agencies—and flipped his cigarette butt onto the asphalt. "You're the one who's fishing, Jake."

"So tell me, already. You can't just shanghai me."

"You tell me, Jake. Where would you go if you had a few billion dollars' worth of stolen goods to sell, and you knew that every civilized country in the world would imprison you or extradite you?"

"I don't know. Some outlaw nation. Libya, maybe."

"Qaddafi may not take kindly to an ex-CIA agent, even for a hundred-million-dollar tip. And Allied jets might find you with a smart bomb."

"North Korea?"

The first car pulled off the outgoing-flights road and stopped in front of a chain-link fence. The driver showed identification to a uniformed guard, who swung open a gate and let our parade of Plymouths onto the tarmac.

"Too cold. Besides, if Moscow has any influence left in Pyongyang, you might lose your little cache of goodies as well as your head. Think about it, Jake. Somewhere neither the Ruskies nor the Yanks can reach."

"Brooklyn," I said.

The lead car stopped in front of a DC-9 that was being refueled. Vista Air was painted on the fuselage. It meant nothing to me.

"Señor Lassiter," Soto said from behind me, "on the Malecón, there is a billboard which says, *'Esta tierra es cien por ciento Cubana.'* "

Now what was he talking about?

Soto went on: "It is a lie, of course. It would be more correct to say that the land is one hundred percent Fidel. He no longer has the Russians to prop him up. Cuba is in the period of Zero Option, complete self-sufficiency. And the country cannot do it. Other than the *diplotienda* stores for foreigners, there is no clothing to buy, little food to eat. They ration bread, eighty grams a person a day. Even eggs, ironically called *salvadores,* saviors, are scarce. Castro, too, is like an egg." He turned toward his daughter. *"Cómo se llama el cuento infantile?"*

"Humpty Dumpty," she said.

"Sí, Humpty Dumpty is ready to fall. But several hundred million dollars, perhaps a billion, can get him through this time of crisis. Your State Department has always underestimated Fidel. They sneer at him for continuing to wear his fatigues. I personally heard one of the under secretaries say Fidel looked like an aging bellboy in that uniform. Have any of your bureaucrats lived in the mountains and fought guerrilla warfare?"

I figured some have wintered at Aspen and skied Buttermilk, but that probably didn't count. "So you have a certain grudging admiration for Castro, even after what he's done to you."

"What I have is disgust for your foreign policy. You Americans believed that the Embargo Act and the Assets Control Regulations would bring Castro to his knees. Instead, you drove him to Moscow, and now, you force him to stand on his own feet. The signs in Havana, *'Socialismo o muerte,'* are not just slogans to Castro. They are his reason for living. But there is an even more important sign these days: *'Patria o muerte.'* Fatherland or death. It is the crucial time for the survival of the regime. Even now, they are restoring hotels and building new ones in partnership with European companies. The Pan Am games brought thousands of *turistas,* and Europeans are beginning to flock to Cuba for cheap holidays. Japanese companies are preparing joint ventures with the Cuban government in biotechnology and medical supplies. There are ongoing ventures with twenty-nine countries. Cuba has opened its doors to foreign investment. And most important of all, Cuba's *Union del Petroleo* has begun to explore oil reserves off the north coast in a venture with a French consortium. It is expected to yield a major strike. Still, those new ventures take time, years for new hotels and factories to be built, even longer to drill for oil. Fidel needs hard currency now."

I refrained from thanking Soto for the lesson in geopolitics. We were getting out of the car when I turned to him and asked, "Very interesting, but what's that got to do with Foley and the stolen art?"

Even as I said it, I knew the answer. I'm like that sometimes. The information reaches my brain a split second after the foot lodges in the mouth.

Abe Socolow was looking at me as if he doubted I could change a buck into four quarters. "Hey, Jakie, where did Robert Vesco go after stealing a couple hundred million dollars? Where is it warm and you can pick coconuts from the trees and *señoritas* from the streets? Where can you drink the best rum and smoke the best cigars?"

"Okay, okay," I said. "Cuba. We're going to Cuba."

The passengers were mostly *exilados* visiting ailing grandparents in Cuba. A few Cuban citizens lucky enough to get visas were returning home after visiting relatives here. The woman in the row ahead of me wore three pairs of socks, men's shoes, a winter coat, and enough costume jewelry to stock a small shop. Soto explained there was a forty-four-pound limit on luggage that Cuban citizens could take home. Other than the families, there were the three of us: an ex-political prisoner turned CIA informer, a lady PI with jet black hair and dark liquid eyes, and me, an overgrown ex-jock turned mouthpiece who was always a step too slow.

It was a forty-minute flight. Just like going to Orlando, but the destination bore less a resemblance to the Magic Kingdom than to the Evil Empire, as Ronald Reagan, that old Cold Warrior, once called the now defunct Soviet Union. The customs inspector looked hard at the visas provided by our pals in the caravan, looked hard at us, then let us in.

We squeezed into an avocado-colored Lada taxicab that fishtailed through the wet streets of Havana. The radio played salsa, and in the back seat, Lourdes moved her hips to the music until we were touching. The air was hot and humid as we drove along the Malecón, the wide boulevard that runs along the shoreline. Youngsters carried truck-tire inner tubes on their shoulders toward the beach. I wondered if they were going for a swim, or trying to cross the Florida Straits to a new world. We passed the United States Interests Section where the windows overlook a huge billboard with a cartoon Uncle Sam growling toward a rifle-toting Cuban who shouts, *"Señores imperialistas, no les tenemos absolutamente ningún miedo."*

"It is true," Soto said, looking at the sign and smiling, "the Cubans have absolutely no fear of the United States. The irony is that they fear their own leader. They are afraid to protest the intolerable living conditions, the human rights abuses. But they know how the West lives. Their televisions pick up the Miami channels. They listen to Radio Martí. And yet, it must get even worse for them to pick up stones and hurl them at the barricades. It must become a situation of total hopelessness for the Army to turn against Fidel."

The sun was setting, casting a pink glow over the peeling, pockmarked buildings of *Habana Viejo.* Brakes squealing, the Lada stopped in front of the Inglaterra Hotel in Old Havana. After we got out, I said, "If it happened in Romania . . ."

"Sí. Señor Lassiter, we are at the precipice of history in this country. It can go either way, and that is why our mission is so important."

The old hotel had a faintly baroque look with curved dramatic lines, and a Spanish flair for wrought-iron railings and pale stucco. We checked in and gathered in a restaurant with a dark wooden bar and a polished tile floor. Around us, a group of German tourists noisily drank their Cuban beer. Lourdes ordered three *mojitos,* a sweet drink of rum, soda, sugar, and fresh mint leaves. Above the din of the tourists was the beating of drums from an adjacent show bar where an Afro-Cuban dance show was underway.

After the second round of drinks, Soto began talking. "I was with Fidel at the University of Havana when he ran for student office. I was with him on July twenty-sixth, 1953, in the attack on the Moncada military barracks. They threw us both in prison."

I studied Soto's lined face, his sad eyes. His mind seemed elsewhere. In the mountains maybe, leading the guerrillas. In prison, perhaps.

"Fidel was so idealistic," he said.

Lourdes patted his hand. "You both were, Papi." She was wearing a black cotton mini with a matching sweater jacket almost as long as her skirt. Under the cocktail table, she had kicked off her sandals and was stroking my leg with the ball of her foot.

Soto drained his sweet minty drink and declined a third, asking the waiter for a beer. "We took Havana on New Year's Eve, December thirty-first, 1958, firing our weapons into the air, celebrating the new year and a new Cuba, the coward Batista fleeing with his jewels. He was a pig who sold out the country to the Americans who wanted nothing more than a place for sun, rum, and sex."

Three of the four essentials of life, I thought, figuring football wasn't that popular on the crocodile-shaped island.

Soto's eyes were moist. He was staring into the past. I tried to imagine what it was like for the proud revolutionary, arm in arm with his friend Fidel, both brimming with the vigor of youth, the promise of the future. Then something came to me. "New Year's Eve," I murmured. "Twelve, thirty-one, fifty-eight. That's the combination for the lock on your studio."

Soto looked at me and smiled. "It was the high point of my life, a day to remember *para siempre.*"

After that it was all downhill, I thought. But where else is there to go after reaching the peak? Maybe now, after all these years, having sacrificed his body to a revolution and then a counterrevolution, this was his way of climbing the mountain again. Bring down the last revolutionary, and let him know it was you from so long ago. To the rest of us, Castro was titanic, one of the century's legendary figures. A monster to some, a visionary to others, either way his impact would be stamped in the history books forever. But to Severo Soto, he was something else. Soto knew Fidel before the whiskers and the fatigues. Two sharp-witted youths quick of gait and strong of limb. Their future was forever, their potential infinite. But Fidel was a boyhood confederate turned archenemy. With Soto, I thought uncomfortably, it wasn't political, it was personal.

After one more drink, we settled into our rooms. My window looked out over Old Havana, and I watched as ancient buses, crammed with workers, belched black smoke into the early evening air. Gas rationing had emptied the streets of cars, but thousands of bicycles streamed each way on the boulevard in front of the hotel. The room was spacious and neat, and the plumbing worked, though not without whining about it. Later, I joined Severo Soto and his daughter in the dining room downstairs.

Over a dinner of *calabaza* soup and paella with giant shrimp, Soto kept talking, and Lourdes resumed stroking my leg. The latter impaired my ability to fully appreciate the former.

"Your State Department, what geniuses they think they are. *Estúpido!* They thought Fidel could be forced to change, so they gave orders. Do this, do that. Don't fraternize with the Russians. Like a man who stupidly mistrusts his wife, the U.S. drove Cuba to another man."

Later, after sweet rice pudding served in half a coconut shell, we had *café Cubano.* Soto was still talking. "And what has the embargo accomplished? Has it brought Fidel crying to Washington? No, it has made him more resolute, even as the country has sunk into poverty. The Cuban people watch the Americans sell wheat to the Russians, even before reforms, and give Favored Nation status to the Chinese who crush students with tanks. So why does Los Estados Unidos refuse to sell pickup trucks to a country ninety miles away, or buy its sugar? Does this make sense?"

"Papi, do you think Jake is interested in all of that?"

He seemed to consider the question. "No. Like most Americans, he surely is not interested in the arrogance of his own government. For over thirty years, the American leaders lectured Cuba: Don't you dare follow the Soviets. Now, all of a sudden, they point to Moscow and say: *Now,* follow their example. Liberalize. Hold elections. Embrace capitalism. Do as the Russians do. Don't you find that curious?"

"I don't get it," I said. "You're against American interference. You're against Castro. You were against Batista, so what are you for? What's the answer to Cuba's problems? What is its future?"

He drained the last of his *café Cubano.* "When we succeed

here, Señor Lassiter, you will know the answer to those questions."

Soto stood and bid us both good night. He pecked Lourdes on the cheek and slapped my shoulder, then headed for the elevator.

"What did your father mean by that?"

She shrugged, then took my right hand in both of hers. The look in her eyes said that political talk was out.

"Lourdes, tell me. What's your father's agenda?"

"Whatever the CIA tells him to do."

"I don't buy that. I doubt your father's ever done what he's been told."

She smiled and tickled my palm with a red, sculpted fingernail. "Don't listen to an old man prattle on about how he would have changed the world. Maybe he would have, but he spent the better part of his life locked up in Combinado del Este. I love my father and wouldn't say this to his face, but now he's an errand boy for Washington. He's to accompany you as a representative of U.S. interests in any negotiations with Foley. But he has no authority. He will merely transmit messages back and forth between here and his superiors."

With that, she leaned closer, put her hand behind my head, and pulled me to her. Her lips touched mine. I tasted the sweetness of the sugary dessert mixed with her warm breath.

"My room has a view of the Capitolo," I said.

I was stretched out on my back on the lumpy bed, watching the breeze swirl the lacy curtains into the room. Lourdes was sleeping, her head on my chest, purring contentedly, when the phone rang. It had a jarring, metallic twang that startled me. Lourdes stirred as I reached for the receiver.

"Hello, Lassiter," Robert Foley said. *"Bienvenidos a Cuba."*

24

FINDER'S FEE

"How much money does one man need?" Robert Foley asked. "A million dollars, ten million, a hundred million?" He gestured to the waiter who silently refilled his champagne glass. "How much lobster can one man eat?"

Apparently, quite a bit. Foley was squeezing lime juice onto the tail section of his second grilled Caribbean lobster. Above us, the palm trees swayed gently in the nighttime breeze.

"How many women can one man screw?" he asked, between bites.

Now there was a purely theoretical question as far as I was concerned.

Foley turned to the young woman—maybe twenty, maybe not—whose chair was pushed up against his. Cocoa skin, shoulder-length black hair, she sipped at a daiquiri, keeping one hand draped on Foley's shoulder, occasionally showing him an adoring smile. Either our conversation bored her, or she didn't understand English. He hadn't bothered to introduce us and scarcely seemed to notice her.

"This is the issue in my life, Lassiter. How do I want to spend the next twenty years?"

"How about breaking rocks at Leavenworth?" I suggested, helpfully.

He kept going as if I weren't there. "I've been anonymous my entire life, and I like it that way. Army intelligence, then the Company. Do I really want my picture on the cover of *Newsweek,* the guy who pulled off the biggest heist in history?"

I hadn't been subjected to this much Socratic questioning since night law school. "With that notoriety, you'd be stuck in your hacienda here for the rest of your life. That's what you're saying, isn't it? What good is all the money in the world if you don't really have your freedom?"

Foley whispered something to the young woman, handed her a wad of bills, and patted her arm. She rewarded him with a dazzling smile, stood up, and headed inside toward the powder room or wherever Foley told her to go. Overhead, a three-quarter moon glistened behind the swaying palm fronds.

"That's part of it, sure," he said. "I'd rather be in Switzerland or France, a dozen places. Lassiter, I've been all over the world, and believe me, this place isn't in the top ten. You ever ride a Harley through the Alps in August?"

I allowed as how I hadn't, having spent many summers doing three-a-days on a swampy practice field.

"Ever sail your own sloop through the Greek Isles?"

"No, but I've foot-steered a nine-foot sailboard in the shadow of the Virginia Key sewage plant."

He looked around the outdoor nightclub. Colored lights spelled out *"Tropicana"* on a torch-lit upper stage. At the table next to us, half a dozen German diplomats were arguing boisterously about the *baseball-spiel* they had seen that afternoon at José Martí Park. The rich aroma of expensive Cuban cigars wafted our way in the evening breeze.

"This is pleasant enough for a few weeks," Foley said. "A few months maybe, but forever?"

"You'd be the world's richest prisoner," I agreed, "a captive of your own success."

The tables were beginning to fill. Above us, I could see the silhouette of dancers backlit behind a flimsy curtain. "And what if Castro falls?" I asked. "What if the next government is run by Severo Soto, which really means by Washington?"

He removed his rimless glasses and wiped them on a napkin. He wore his gray civil servant's suit—old habits die hard—despite his new status as an international thief and potential billionaire. "Soto's brains were fried a long time ago, but you're right about one thing. I'd be crazy not to consider the political situation here. What if Castro pulls a double-cross? Takes his fifteen percent commission, then makes a deal with the West to ship me back in exchange for some tractors. Or what if he dies and the next head Red doesn't like the way I part my hair? The Politburo just bounced Carlos Aldana, the number three commie, the other day. It's just too volatile here. What if they hold free elections and beautiful Cuba"—he gave it the Spanish pronunciation, *Coo-ba*—"decides to become the fifty-first state?"

"Then you're fucked, Foley."

I must have been smiling. He said, "Don't be so happy about it, or you won't get your fee."

And I thought this was a *pro bono* case. "My fee?"

A smile added lines to his creased face. "How's ten million sound?"

"Like a symphony," I said.

As if on cue, a trumpet sounded. Women in multicolored feathery costumes began descending stairs to the main stage. The music blared, and the stage was a procession of bare limbs and exposed breasts. Under the feathers, the costumes were scanty, halter tops and bikini bottoms cut high on the hips. Long-legged women of varying hues began swaying to a Brazilian beat. A tall cinnamon-skinned woman swiveled to the front of the stage, holding a cordless mike, and began singing in Spanish.

Foley watched the stage without noticeable interest. Achieving his goal seemed to leave him empty. All that loot and maybe he felt, so what? For a lot of us, it's that way. Striving for the goal is often better than attaining it.

"Don't care for the show?" I asked.

"They haven't changed the acts since Meyer Lansky used to sit over there, his back to the wall." He gestured toward a corner that had a commanding view of the stage. "Like falling into a time warp, Vegas thirty years ago."

His mind was drifting. But then so was mine. Did he say ten million? "What do I have to do for the money?"

"Be my lawyer, for chrissakes. Negotiate the deal. I'll give everything back in return for full immunity plus a finder's fee or a reward, whatever you want to call it. Keep me from being the most famous thief on two continents."

"You'll need complete transactional and use immunity."

"That's all your department. You figure it out, transmit the offer, do the paperwork, and guarantee me it'll stick. Got it?"

A fat round seed fell off one of the towering trees and plopped onto the table, just missing my beer. "You haven't told me how much you want."

"What do you think it's worth, Lassiter, finding and returning the priceless heritage of a nation?"

"How about a Boy Scout merit badge and a thank-you note from Yeltsin?"

Above us, the dancers had changed costumes. The same amount of legs, breasts, and buttocks were showing, but now the band was playing "The Girl from Ipanema." A table of what looked like Saudi sheiks behind us was humming along.

"I'm not greedy," Foley said, "and this is standard procedure. Insurance companies pay off all the time to get back precious art. I deserve to be compensated. First, get my expenses covered. That includes your fee plus what it cost me to get the stuff here. Bribes, shipping, something for Castro for letting me in. Figure forty million."

I used a pen to make notes on a cocktail napkin. "Forty million for shipping and handling."

"So my services got to be worth two hundred million, don't you think?"

"You're the client," I said. "It's your call."

"Two hundred million," he repeated, weighing the words, one at a time. He seemed to like their heft. "So start playing lawyer, Lassiter. You know how to structure the deal?"

Unlike a lot of Miami lawyers, I don't specialize in money laundering. Still, I know the basics. "I'll set up a Cayman Island trust with ownership controlled by a limited partnership on the Isle of Man. A Bahamian corporation can be the general partner, with you owning all the stock. The money will be wired to the trust, and you can make transfers from there to Switzerland or wherever you want to live."

"Good. Get to it. I've got clerical help, word processors, fax machines, everything you need. The art will be on a ship in international waters. I get the money on execution of the documents, at which time I'll give them the coordinates, so they can take immediate delivery. Nobody tries to screw anybody, all on the up-and-up. Make sure the paperwork is airtight."

"It will be. A confidentiality agreement, because the last thing you want is publicity. A waiver of the government's right to seek injunctions against transfer of the funds. No frozen accounts, no civil liability of any kind, and of course, complete immunity from criminal prosecution."

Foley studied me. "Can it be done?"

"Sure, on paper at least."

His laugh had no pleasure in it. "This isn't make-believe, Lassiter. This isn't some cute trick like getting a judge to sign an attachment order. This is real. This is money and power, life and death. Take it seriously, pal. Take it goddamn seriously. Understood?"

"If you're looking for a guarantee, you need a new lawyer. I can draft the prettiest contract you've ever seen. All the words will be spelled right, and every copy countersigned in triplicate. But if your old buddies in Washington or Moscow want to put a bullet in your head on the ski slopes some day, I can't stop them. Understood?"

"Just get me the money, Lassiter, and I'll take my chances."

On the stage, a comedian was finishing his act, drawing respectful applause. My Spanish was just good enough to understand the setup and miss the punch lines. I finished my beer. The comedian took his bows, and bullfight music began, a matador waving his red cape at a scantily clad woman who must have been the bull. Foley signaled the waiter for the check, and almost immediately the black-haired young woman reappeared, slinking between tables into the seat next to him. "So, Lassiter, you know what I want?"

"Two hundred million," I said, figuring that was the answer to the question: Just how much money does one man need?

"It has been agreed by the bureaucrats," Severo Soto told me, his voice dripping with disgust. "Your government will give Foley his money and the Russians their art."

Funny how he always called it *my* government, always distanced himself. From the beginning, he had planned to return to his homeland, had never become an American citizen.

"Everyone should be happy," I said. "In a roundabout way, the plan succeeded. The thefts have been stopped, the reformers saved from embarrassment."

We stood on a street corner in Old Havana near the ornate Grand Theater. Soto was leery of talking business in the hotel room. Hundreds of men and women on Chinese bicycles streamed past, headed for work. A skinny teenage boy in torn sneakers approached us, offering to exchange pesos for American dollars at triple the exchange rate. I picked up a few one-peso notes as souvenirs and studied one of them. Beneath the inscription, *Entrada a la Habana 8 de Enero de 1959,* Fidel Castro rode triumphantly atop a tank, surrounded by his soldiers. One of Fidel's compatriots, a bearded warrior, held a flag and wore crisscrossing bandoliers. To me, he looked like a young Severo Soto.

I said, "I thought the money might have been a problem."

"They would have paid even more. Money is unlimited to bury mistakes."

"Cheer up. Mission accomplished. Castro won't get his hands on the billion dollars that could save his economy. You can wait for him to fall."

Soto pulled a cigar from his guayabera pocket. A Partagas corona. I had watched him buy a handful in the hotel lobby. Most *exilados* refuse to smoke them until Fidel is toppled.

"I have been waiting more than thirty years. How long can a man wait?"

For a moment, I thought he was reading my mind. But he was talking about Castro, not the cigars.

Soto said, "Returning the art, restoring the status quo, does nothing to aid the just cause of the Cuban people."

I remembered what Foley told me at the ballet. Soto was the one who wanted to drive the nail into the coffin of communism. "Hey, be happy with a wash. It's better than Castro getting all that loot."

We walked past the Floridita Restaurant where, Miami Cubans say, a bartender first mixed rum with lime juice and sugar. The sign above the entrance read, *La Cuña del Daiquiri.* We passed old stucco apartment buildings pockmarked with age and neglect. We crossed a street of wooden bricks that had to be three centuries old. A jacaranda tree blooming with purple flowers gave us an umbrella of shade at a street corner. Best I could tell, no drug dealers lurked under the branches. From a courtyard not fifty yards off a main street, a bare-chested man was pulling a bucket of water from an underground cistern.

An open truck stopped in front of one of the restaurants that cater to hard-currency tourists. Skinned pigs gleamed yellow in the sun; hundreds of flies buzzed over the carcasses.

"The people have no meat, but *La Bodeguita del Medio* can feed the *turistas* all the pork they want." Soto puffed on his cigar and blew aromatic white fumes in my direction. "Do you care for lunch?"

I wasn't feeling hungry just then.

We had walked several more blocks when Soto said, "It is a crime to return the art."

Funny, I thought it was a crime to take it.

"Do you know what we could do with the proceeds from just a fraction of the paintings and gemstones?" Soto asked.

"You could give this city a coat of paint."

"I could equip an army, or I could feed the island for a year. I could build factories and roads and hospitals. Or I could make a revolutionary statement the world would never forget."

Now what did that mean?

The old dreamer. An errand boy, his daughter called him. Burned out, Foley said. But Soto wasn't reminiscing about past glories. He was looking to the future, and again he was carrying a gun. When he closed his eyes, he must have seen sugar cane workers abandoning the fields and streaming into the mountains, lean men in fatigues cleaning their weapons in a tropical downpour. He heard rifle bolts clicking into place, smelled cordite and gun oil, felt the tingle of quickened heartbeats.

"Do you have a sense of irony?" Soto asked. He tossed his cigar into the street. "The art was the product of corruption. The Russian peasants starved so that the Romanovs could have diamond eggs. Is it not ironic that the handiwork of such evil could now be used for the benefit of the people?"

"But it won't be used at all. It's going back to the museums. No more art for wheat. No more sting operations. Socolow got the word, remember. The U.S. doesn't want to interfere in the internal affairs of a sovereign nation."

Soto barked a humorless laugh. "*Sí,* just as your government didn't want to interfere in Guatemala in '54, but that didn't stop the CIA from overthrowing Jacobo Arbenz. Just as you didn't want to interfere in Panama in '64, but U.S. troops still killed a score of protesters, to say nothing of the illegal invasion of that sovereign country in 1989 in order to kidnap General Noriega. How far does American respect for sovereignty extend? Not to Libya, Cuba, or Iraq. I am sure Sukarno of Indonesia and Nkrumah of Ghana would have been surprised to learn that the U.S. doesn't interfere in their internal affairs. What would Allende say if he were alive to say it?"

Nobody ever called me a knee-jerk patriot, but all this America bashing was getting on my nerves. I was also beginning to wonder if coming back to Cuba had jarred a screw loose in the old man's head. "I'm no expert on world affairs, but you're leaving out a lot of the good. *My* government also gave you a job and a home and the freedom to say what you want. Frankly, I'm worried about your priorities down here."

Soto looked away, pretending to admire an old church. "I have said too much. Do not fear. I am a good soldier."

I knew that. I just didn't know in whose army.

25

THE FIDELISTA

We were on Agramonte Street nearing the Maximo Gomez monument when the driver stopped and pointed to his left. Severo Soto nodded, rolled down his window, and spat in the direction of a baroque palace of arches and columns. "The *antiguo palacio Presidencial,* decorated by Tiffany, occupied by the pig Batista. How unfortunate he did not die there rather than in his bed in Spain. Now, it's the *Museo de la Revolución.*"

The driver headed out of Old Havana on the Malecón just as the sun was setting. Behind us, the city was bathed in a pink glow, softening the focus, concealing the decay. We were on Fifth Avenue, the broad tree-lined boulevard of foreign embassies, when Severo Soto spoke to the driver in Spanish, and we took a sharp left turn in front of the Presidente Hotel.

The setting sun was at our back. My sense of direction told me we were headed away from the ocean. "The marina is to the west," I said, "and we're headed east."

"There is something I want to see before we do our business," Soto replied.

I had left Foley sitting at his table at the Tropicana roughly twenty hours earlier. Soto spent the day at the U.S. Interests Section, fiddling with a satellite up-link telephone, speaking in coded English to his superiors at Langley. He conveyed my messages and gave me theirs as we worked on details of the agreement. I already had prepared the first draft of the paperwork. An assistant attorney general made some revisions, then I made some more. Soto sent and received the documents by fax. Later we would meet with Foley, review the papers, dot the *i*'s and cross the *t*'s. Just another day of lawyering, but somehow it didn't feel the same as settling a slip-and-fall at the Porky Pig market.

Had Foley *really* said ten million?

The taxi pulled into a large square dominated by a huge obelisk. "The Plaza de la Revolución," Soto told me. "Formerly, Plaza Cívica."

"Folks do a lot of name changing around here," I said. "Maybe after Castro's gone, they'll change it all back. Like Leningrad to St. Petersburg. How about a Parque Soto in Old Havana?"

"I never had such ambitions. It is enough for me to be a lieutenant in the eternal war for justice."

He stared at the monument, and something nagged at the back of my mind. What was it?

Present tense.

It is enough for me . . .

Soto *was* still a soldier. "What war?" I asked.

"Do you know nothing of history, the struggle against neocolonialism, fascism, and racism?"

"That sounds like Castro's rhetoric."

"Rhetoric? Is that what you call it?"

"What now, are you going to defend the guy who put you in prison and threw away the key?"

"I don't condone his Stalinist repression of dissent, but I have never disagreed with his philosophy or principles. Have you ever listened to even one of his speeches to the Movement of Nonaligned Nations?"

"No, I seldom have six hours to kill."

"His are the words of a giant who has prevailed against the concerted efforts of eight American presidents to overthrow him. Fidel has been shaped by Cuba's tragic past, four hundred years of domination by the Spanish, fifty years by the Yankees."

"And now thirty years of glorious independence."

He looked toward a statue of the Cuban poet José Martí at the base of the spire. "You are being sarcastic, are you not?"

"Yeah, in case you haven't heard, Marxism is dead, but here you are, the number-one fan of the All-Pro commie dictator."

"I told you I can see Fidel's faults, but—"

"But he's the lesser of two evils, right?"

"Sí, compared to the imperialists—both American and Russian—Fidel is a *santo,* a saint. He believes in Cuba for Cubans, an independent country free of control by outsiders."

"I don't believe this. All this time, I thought you wanted to overthrow Castro."

"My philosophy has been consistent for thirty-five years. Am I not entitled to my beliefs, my freedom of expression you Yankees always speak about?"

But where does philosophy end and action begin, I wondered.

Soto motioned for the driver to get moving. "We were the children of the centenary, Fidel Castro Ruz and I. In 1953—the one hundredth birthday of José Martí—we attacked the Moncada fortress in Santiago de Cuba. You should have seen Fidel then. Rugged, clear-eyed, full of purpose. Did you know he was a lawyer?"

Just like Gorby and little old me. I wondered if the clear-eyed bearded one ever defended a condom-in-the-salad case.

"The attack failed," Soto said, "and we were both arrested. At the trial, Fidel gave a brilliant speech. He told the world, 'History will absolve me.' " Soto pulled a Partagas from his guayabera pocket. He rolled the cigar under his nose but made no move to light it. "We were both imprisoned on Isla de Pinos, then exiled to Mexico. But we never gave up. We planned for a Cuba where every child could read and write and have doctors and nurses provided by the state, where we would get fair prices for the sugar and fair wages for the workers. We would burn the casinos and send the whore-mongering Yankees home. Eventually we sailed from Tuxpán on the *Granma* with eighty-two men. Eighty-two men to fight a war! Do you know what Castro said as the lines were cast off and we headed toward what I believed was certain death?"

" 'Who brought the Dramamine'?"

Soto's eyes were thirty-five years and hundreds of miles away. " 'If I set off, I arrive; if I arrive, I enter; if I enter, I win.' "

"And he won."

"*We* won! Not that it was easy. Camping in the Sierra Maestra mountains, recruiting villagers for the rebel army. Fighting and running and fighting again until Batista fled like the coward he was, and eight days later, we rode triumphantly into Havana."

"And one dictatorship was replaced with another."

He shot me a look. "But the children *can* read, and there *are* doctors for all."

"And Mussolini made the trains run on time."

"Perhaps we should not speak of politics," Severo Soto said, striking a match to his cigar, then puffing at it until an orange spark glowed at the tip. He exhaled a wisp of smoke toward the monument, and without turning to me said, "It is beautiful to behold, is it not?"

"What, the statue?"

"The art. You saw it, all gathered together."

I thought of the warehouse, the paintings and sculptures, the coins and jewels, the intricate eggs and ancient artifacts, the treasures of long-dead nobles and czars. I thought of the golden bunny in Crespo's clenched fist. "Yes, I have seen it all."

Soto's eyes glistened. "It is beautiful, is it not?"

"It's the stuff dreams are made of," I said.

Surrounded by Canadian yachts and luxury craft from South America, the rusty Polish freighter creaked against its lines and rested low in the water, its paint faded, an unlikely bearer of a priceless treasure. Maybe that was the idea. The *Polonez* was moored at Hemingway Marina, which sits on the shoreline of the Great Blue River, as Ernest Hemingway called the Gulf of Mexico. According to a sign near an outdoor restaurant, the writer started a marlin fishing tournament here in 1950.

Soto and I followed Foley down a ladder. The freighter smelled of diesel fuel and stale air. Foley turned the wheel on a watertight hatch. We stepped over a metal rise and into the hold. Ten metal containers the size of trailer-trucks lined the bulkhead, five on each side. We sat at a wooden table bolted to the deck. A crewman brought us a pot of *café Cubano,* then left, sealing the door behind him.

"Hey, Soto, you'll be a big hero back at the Farm," Foley said. "You'll get a gold watch."

Severo Soto's dark eyes flared. "You are a man without principles. You are a servant to expediency."

"Wrong, my friend. In the end, I'm loyal to my country, as you are to yours. I just gauge the way the wind is blowing and try to make a buck out of it." Turning to me, Foley said, "Or two hundred million bucks, eh, Lassiter?"

"I'm going to drink my coffee and let you boys play your macho spy games," I said. "When you're done wagging your dicks, let me know, and we'll talk about the logistics for getting this old tug into the Gulf Stream."

Soto looked toward the steel containers. "Perhaps it is not too late for the wind to shift. What makes you think Fidel will let you take the art now that it is here?"

Foley laughed like a man holding four aces. "What's he going to do with the stuff, sell it at Sotheby's? Become an international fence? He can't take the heat. He'd lose the moral high ground. The few friends he has left would scorn him. The Russians would write him off if they haven't already. The Chinese would stop sending bicycles, then where would he be, buying roller skates from the North Koreans for his great revolution?"

"And what if we just took the ship away from you?" Soto asked, his voice even and soft.

We? At first I thought that included me. Then I realized *we* referred to his old *muchacho* Fidel.

"Why would you do that?" Foley asked. "The Company's making a deal for pocket change. The Russians get their art, and everybody goes home happy."

"I will not be happy," Soto said, his voice still betraying no emotion, "and I will not be home."

Foley smiled. The look was familiar. Did it come just before or after he broke Kharchenko's finger? "Hey, Lassiter, you said we had a deal. Now this old geezer's changing the terms, holding me up for a piece of the action."

"I don't think that's what he's doing. Foley, I think you've got a problem here."

"Problem? I been dealing with problems since 'Nam. Look,

Soto, you're screwing around with the wrong guy. I don't care how many people you bayoneted back in '58. You give me any shit, you'll be shark bait in the Florida Straits."

Soto shrugged his shoulders. "It is not so terrible to die for a cause that is just." He sipped at the sweet, syrupy coffee, calmly showing Foley that he had no fear. "The riches you have stolen can be used for the people. If you do not agree to cooperate, I will use all of my power to obtain the principled result."

"What power? Soto, you're two cans short of a six-pack."

"We are at the crossroads in history," Soto said, barely above a whisper. "Eastern Europe has fallen. The Soviet Union no longer exists. It is now or never for the Cuban people."

Foley slapped the table with his hand. The sound echoed off the metal bulkheads. "You senile old bastard! So that's what you're talking about. Giving the merchandise to Alpha 66 or whatever you guys call yourselves these days. A bunch of pot-bellied old farts in fatigues, tromping around the Everglades, shooting tin cans with .22s, pretending they got Fidel in their sights." He looked at me, shaking his head with disgust. "Is that it, Lassiter? He's gonna fund an army of Calle Ocho shop-keepers?"

Below us, I heard the pumps working, and somewhere on the dock, a whistle shrilled. A crane groaned from the top deck, as provisions were loaded. I looked at Severo Soto, his eyes dispassionate, his face placid. Another war to fight, or was it the same one? I thought of his ceaseless condemnation of the Americans and the Russians, the glorious memories of the revolution, his friendship, even adoration of Castro. He was a man of contradictions and conflicts, but in the end, his loyalty never wavered. Soto was a Cuban patriot, and regardless of their differences about the means to achieving a *Cuba Libre,* so was Fidel.

"Foley, you've got it wrong," I said. "Señor Soto's not talking about the counterrevolution. His war is the ongoing struggle of the socialist people of Cuba. He wants arms and food and consumer goods. He wants to protect communism, not destroy it. *Socialismo o muerte."* Foley looked as if he didn't understand, so I spelled it out for him. "Come smell the *café Cubano,* Foley. The art, the money—it's all for Fidel."

For long moments, no one spoke. Above us, the crane continued to groan. A metal cable whined. Something thumped against the upper deck. There were the hydraulic *whooshes* and mechanical *clunks,* and the soft, padded noises that come from deep inside ships. Foley's pale eyes studied Severo's implacable face. Minutes passed. Somewhere above us, I heard water dripping against metal, a *ping-ping* that seemed to pace itself with my breaths.

"So the great anticommunist turns out to be a *fidelista,"* Foley said finally. "A double agent, sucked in by the cult of personality. The last of a dying breed, aren't you, fella?" He sneered in disgust, stood, paced around the wooden table, then sat down again. He looked like a man who didn't know how to express his anger and frustration. "Are you out of your fucking mind? Look what Castro did to you."

"I still have one arm," Soto said.

"Look what he did to your country, aligning it with the Soviets."

"Unfortunately, your government gave him no choice."

"Look what he did to his buddies in the army, General Ochoa and General de la Guardia."

"They betrayed him," Soto said.

"And you? What will you do, give him the ability to stay in power a couple more years, postpone the inevitable. He's a dinosaur, a snake, a bearded grandmother."

Soto never raised his voice. "Fidel will survive with or without the Russians. Hard currency now will give him time to pursue what we planned in the mountains in '56."

"Christ, listen to him!" Foley exploded. "Lassiter, help me out here. Earn your fee."

"Señor Soto," I said, "you are a man of high ideals. Becoming an international criminal will not advance your cause."

Soto shook his head sadly. "The international criminals are the Western nations. For hundreds of years, they have exploited the peoples of Latin America, Africa, and Asia. They stole the gold and silver, plundered the sugar, coffee, cacao, tea, and cotton. They have endless thirst for the raw materials of the third world. Your own government commits heinous acts of international terrorism in pursuit of oil. But no force on earth can shackle human dignity and freedom forever. José Martí said that 'rights are taken, not asked for; they are wrested, not begged for.' "

Foley slammed his fist down, sending the coffeepot skittering across the table and crashing to the floor. "Bullshit! I've been to a hundred countries, and I've had it up to here with that third-world bullshit. In case you been asleep the last few years, let me give you some news: The Iron Curtain has fallen down."

"Cuba hasn't fallen," Soto said. "Fidel will lead us to our destiny."

Robert Foley ran a hand through his short brown hair and seemed to be sizing up his situation. He didn't ask for his lawyer's advice. The U.S. government had approved the deal, but Soto was threatening to blow it. From every indication, he wanted to steal the art, leaving Foley high and dry, and depriving a deserving lawyer of a ten-million-dollar fee.

Unless Soto was bluffing.

Maybe he didn't have any authority from Castro. Maybe he *was* out of his mind. If Fidel wanted the art, why weren't there troops surrounding this old tug right now? That's what I was about to advise my client when I heard a noise above us. A shout in Spanish, the *thump* of boots on steel, three dozen men descending ladders to the hold. The hatch swung open, and they fanned out into a semicircle with military precision. The men wore fatigues and combat boots and carried Kalashnikov rifles.

Foley sat still as a statue while a Cuban officer approached. The officer said something in Spanish. Soto nodded. Two soldiers came forward and positioned themselves on either side of Foley, who finally stirred. "First bastard who lays a hand on me is gonna lose a vital organ."

The officer leaned close and whispered to Soto, allowing him to remain seated, showing him respect.

Foley's voice grew louder. "Soto, I got a deal with the Company. You can't go freelancing, you crazy bastard!" Foley's eyes darted from the soldiers to me. "Lassiter, what the fuck's going on?"

Soto had told me, but I hadn't been listening. Now it was clear. "Señor Soto detests the Russians," I said, "and it doesn't matter who's in charge: Gorbachev, Yanayev, Yeltsin, or a committee of Siberian polar bears. The Matisse that hangs in his study, *Satyr and Nymph,* reminds him of Russia and Cuba in just that order. He hates Cuba's dependence on the Russians. He wants Cuba to be a free, independent socialist state, not under the thumb of the Russians or the Americans, because both are corrupt." I looked at Soto. "How my doing?"

"You are a more thoughtful man than I had believed. What are your politics?"

"Don't have any. I distrust all politicians, but I've always believed in the American dream. I believe anybody with guts and brains who's willing to work hard can make it."

"The sad truth," Soto said, "is that there is little difference between American capitalism and Russian socialism, even when there was such a thing. The essence of capitalism is profit from the sweat of others, and so too was the essence of Russian communism. The elite in Russia were just as fat as the robber barons in the States, and the poor were just as poor. Gorbachev's *perestroika* merely mimicked the West."

Foley barked a laugh. "Wake up, Soto. The Russians need the Americans."

"To go to a market economy, that is true. But it is shameful for an avowed Marxist to do so. And why did the old guard seek to oust Gorbachev? To reform their socialist society to conform to the founding principles, to say with Lenin that 'the state is the proletariat, the advance guard of the working class'? No! They believed the system is theirs for the plundering. In Russia, as in the States, it does not matter who is in charge. Each is equally corrupt."

Foley eyed the two soldiers who hovered over him. "Soto, you know what you hate. The Russians and the Americans like each other. We have the same desires, the same needs."

"*Sí,* you all need to be rich. But to be rich, some must be poor. Who is to speak for them?"

"Who appointed you? Why don't you hold an election here and see how many votes Fidel gets, or did you see what happened in Nicaragua and decide not to risk it?"

Soto showed a sad, tolerant smile. "Lenin also said that 'liberty is so precious that it must be rationed.' There will come a time for free elections, but only after Cuba is already free, not when it is quarantined by your government and indentured to the corrupt Russians. The Americans now say Cuba should follow Russia's example, but should we prostitute ourselves again to be handmaiden to both the Russians and the Americans? Or should we be strong and independent? Should we—"

"Make a revolutionary statement the world will never forget," I said.

Foley threw up his hands. "What the fuck does that mean?"

"I don't know," I said. "You'd better ask Señor Soto. It's his line."

"It is not your concern," Soto said. He snapped orders to the officer in rapid-fire Spanish. The two soldiers grabbed Foley by each arm and lifted him from his chair.

Soto's voice was soothing. "You will not be harmed, Señor Foley. There is a hacienda for you in Cienfuegos. Two hundred acres not far from the bay. You can watch the *pesetero* ferries and the cargo ships unloading at the fertilizer plant."

Foley struggled unsuccessfully to free his arms. "Fertilizer plant! What the fuck are you talking about? I've got a villa waiting for me in Lausanne."

"Not feasible, I'm afraid. Your property here is adjacent to our first nuclear power plant. It is quite scenic, really, right on the water. You will live comfortably there on a pension as if you were a retired colonel in the Cuban army. Life will not be luxurious, but neither will you starve."

"Starve! There's two hundred million dollars being wired today to my account on Grand Cayman."

"No," Soto said, "I countermanded that order. The money will be wired to your account in Aruba."

Foley rubbed his chin. His eyes were moist. "I don't have an account in Aruba."

"Ah, how unfortunate. Perhaps the account number I provided Langley was incorrect. I suppose we will have to impound the funds for safekeeping."

We again.

"You thief, you cocksucking communist crook!" The soldiers tugged at Foley, pulling him toward the hatch. I remembered

Foley subduing Kharchenko so effortlessly, but now, surrounded by troops with automatic weapons, his body went slack, his feet dragging across the deck. The last words I heard him say were to me. "Lassiter, what are you going to do about these bastards?"

I didn't know.

"Sue them?" I suggested.

26

CUATRO DE JULIO

Severo Soto didn't say where we were headed. After the soldiers left with Foley, there was only a skeleton crew left on the freighter. All Cubans in camouflage gear. Maybe the Polish crew got a hacienda next to Foley's. Soto stood on the bridge with the captain, a wiry, leather-skinned man with white hair and grease-stained clothes.

The captain coaxed the *Polonez* from the dock and we chugged eastward. Gulls dipped and cawed and taunted us from their feathery heights. At first, I thought Soto was taking our precious cargo to a more remote site at the eastern end of the island. Las Tunas maybe. Then I watched the position of the sun off the port side. We were headed northeast, riding the Gulf Stream across the Straits of Florida. A strong southeasterly wind whipped up whitecaps in our path. Ninety miles due north was Key West, but our heading would take us east of the curving chain of islands. I stood on the deck in my jeans and Dolphins jersey, watching the whitecaps appear, build, and die. Overhead, four U.S. Air Force jets streaked in formation, heading back to Guantánamo.

Soto had disappeared into the hold, telling me to wait for him. The old freighter pitched gently through the small waves, the motion making me sleepy. A crewman offered me a can of guava juice and a piece of sugary pastry.

Half an hour passed before Soto reappeared and greeted me with a silent nod. We stood on deck, shoulder to shoulder, elbows leaning on the rail, watching the waves break, staring at the sea. Studying the great green depths quiets a man. We look into our species' past, the beginning of life in the salty waters, and it stills us. The endless vista compels contemplation. Beneath the surface, the sea teems with life.

And danger.

And death.

Finally, I said, "If my bearings are right, Andros Island is off to our east."

"Sí."

"If we continue this heading, we'll hit Grand Bahama Island tomorrow morning."

"Sí."

"We're taking the art to the Bahamas?"

"No."

Soto drew a Partagas from one of four pockets in his guayabera. He had trouble lighting it, so I helped out, cupping my hands around his, shielding the wind with my back. We stood that way a moment, huddled together, and he looked up, studying me intently. Did those dark eyes seem to soften for just a moment?

"Jacobo, have you lived a full life?"

"I don't know what you mean."

"Do you have any regrets?"

Still, I looked at the sea.

Regrets.

Who hasn't looked back and considered the road not taken? We're not handed an itinerary when we start out. Most of us get where we're going by accident. A kind word from a math teacher, and the student aims, knowingly or not, toward engineering. A thoughtless rebuke and the young violinist surrenders his dream.

If we're lucky, we take a path where we can do some good along the way. My first career had little social utility, other than providing televised entertainment interrupted by sixty-second accolades to the glory of various beers, cars, and insurance companies. My second career has even less. Now, I'm one of the players in a game where justice is dispensed nearly as often as the Red Sea is parted.

Regrets.

I wish I'd been faster then, smarter now. I wish I could paint a picture or build a bridge. I wish there was a woman—just one—who had lasted. A best friend and only lover, a soulmate, not a cellmate.

After a moment, I said, "We all have our regrets."

"Have you accomplished all you have wanted? Have you left your mark?"

"My name's not in the NFL record book," I told him, "and I doubt it will be in any history books."

"Perhaps you are wrong." But he said it in a whisper I barely heard above the droning of the diesels and the whine of the tropical wind.

Dusk came quickly, and still we stood, side by side, as the sky deepened to a dark purple, and the light softened. The whitecaps were tinged with pink from the fading light. "You think I am misguided, a foolish, deformed old man living in the past," Soto said.

I didn't know if it was a question. "You've confused me. First I thought you were a rabid anticommunist, a right-wing nut like so many of the *exilados* in Miami. Then, I find out you're a charter member of the Fidel Castro fan club. Now, I don't know what's up your sleeve."

"Nothing!" he exclaimed, pointing to his empty right sleeve flapping in the breeze.

It was a silly joke, and so out of character for the dour Cuban that it convulsed me. And then him. Maybe it had been the tension of the day. I didn't know. We stood there together, sharing the moment of a Caribbean sunset, laughing into the wind. He was puffing a cigar now, its smoke whipping away.

I watched the setting sun, which appeared off the bow. "We're angling to the west."

"Sí."

I tried to figure how many miles we had covered. If I kept this up, I was going to qualify for a Sea Scout badge. "We're headed to Miami!"

Soto didn't say a word.

"You pulled a double whammy. You're taking the art to Miami. You've got Foley under house arrest or something. All that Castro-as-demigod was your cover. You're recovering the money *and* the art. You're still a CIA operative."

Still, he was silent.

A strange bundle of emotions. Anger. I'd been double-crossed. The government had never meant to honor its deal with Foley, and I was part of the deception, even if I didn't know it. But just a bit of exhilaration, too. A sense of awe at how slickly they'd done it, turned the tables on the biggest thief in history. To say nothing of his formerly ten-million-dollar lawyer.

"We *are* headed to Miami," Soto said. "But if the rest of your theory is correct, if the U.S. recovers the money, why did Fidel assist us? Why do we have the use of Cuban troops and a Cuban crew, and why were we permitted to leave the island when Foley's deal was to share the riches with the Castro government?"

I didn't know. What was it Foley had said? That I was half right, as usual. "Maybe the State Department made a deal," I guessed. "Castro gives up the money and the art, and the U.S. drops the trade embargo."

"Politically infeasible," Soto said. We stood quietly another moment, listening to the *slappity-slap* of the waves against the hull. "Think. You have come to know me. What is it I would do with the full consent of Fidel?"

"I can't figure it out. If you're returning the art—"

"I never said I was returning it."

He saw I didn't understand, so he motioned me to follow him. We circled the deck and took a ladder into the hold. Below deck, the steel bulkheads rattled with engine vibrations, and the air stank of sweat, grease, and fuel. Soto turned a wheel at a steel hatch, and we stepped into the cargo compartment. One of the crewmen, a skinny, olive-skinned man who hadn't shaved this week, sat at the wooden table. What looked like an oversize car battery was at his feet, a simple electrical panel in front of him. On the deck was a spool of white wire. Or rather, half a spool. The rest was strung across the deck and around the steel containers that held an unfathomable fortune. The other end was connected to the battery, which, in turn, was connected to the electrical panel. The crewman had a shotgun in his lap.

I knew what it was, but I couldn't say it. Soto did me the favor. "Plastiques."

"Why?"

He didn't answer, but he didn't have to. He was right. I had come to know him.

I could make a revolutionary statement the world would never forget.

It hadn't meant anything then, but it did now. The crewman shifted in his chair and cradled the shotgun. I listened to a pump below us and Soto's breathing next to me.

"I was wrong," I admitted. "I figured there were only three choices: Give the art to the Americans, to the Russians, or to Fidel. I never thought you'd destroy it. But for you, it really is a double whammy. Castro gets the two hundred million to buy bicycles and bread, and you get to make the greatest revolutionary statement of all time."

"Lo entiendes? So you understand?"

"Maybe not all of it. But it has something to do with destroying objects of bourgeois fascination. While the peasants were starving, the nobility had jewelers making diamond-studded clocks. Am I on the right track?"

"Yes, but that is not all. With one fiery blast, I will show the world the value of its gilded objects. I will blow asunder the worthless canvas and meaningless gold. I will turn your silver chalices and precious pearls into shrapnel. I will take five hundred years of decadence and vanity and turn it to silt at the bottom of the sea. And the two of us will join it there."

Oh.

Just then, scuttling a couple billion dollars in baubles and adornments didn't seem that important. Losing the semiprecious hide of Jacob Lassiter, ballplayer-turned-barrister, was another matter.

Footsteps above us. Two crewmen clambered down the ladder and stepped into the hold. Swarthy, lean men in their twenties in jungle fatigues wearing sidearms. Soto spoke to them in Spanish, then turned to me. "They will protect you until we reach our destination,"

Protect me. Communists and fascists alike always have such a cute way of twisting words into their antonyms.

The four of us climbed back to the top deck in silence. On the deck, my two protectors maintained a polite distance of five yards. The nighttime breeze had turned cool, so why was I sweating? The air was thick with diesel fumes. Again, Soto and I stood at the rail. From overhead, suddenly, a *whompeta-whompeta* drew our eyes skyward. A helicopter, its searchlight aimed at us, scanned the freighter. From the bridge, a crewman was shouting in Spanish at Soto, who simply nodded. My bodyguards edged closer.

With the wind from the east and the copter approaching from the west, I hadn't heard it until it was nearly above us. Descending now. My first thought: the Coast Guard to the rescue. Or maybe Army Special Forces, rappelling down on undulating ropes, armed with automatic weapons. Hey, I'd settle for a Miami Beach SWAT team. But it wasn't the authorities. A private chopper. Lower now, I saw it clearly. Beige, rounded nose. I'd seen it before. It used to sit on the deck of Yagamata's yacht.

The noise deafening now, the helicopter was just a few feet off the stern. I squinted my eyes against the blast of wind. When it touched down, a door to the passenger cabin opened and out stepped Matsuo Yagamata. He turned back toward the cabin. A hand reached out, and he grabbed it. The hand belonged to Lourdes Soto, who hopped gracefully onto the deck of the freighter. The two of them ducked under the whirling blade and walked toward us. A moment later, the engine revved, and the helicopter took off, veering to the west, and disappearing into the night.

Lourdes looked toward me and then directly at her father. She was wearing an all-white warm-up suit and running shoes. Her dark hair was windblown. Yagamata, short and chunky in a dark suit, looked tense. As he approached, he shot nervous glances at the armed crewmen. When Yagamata and Lourdes reached us, there was a brief moment of silence. Soto looked impassively at them both, then angrily shouted, *"Lourdes, no deberías estar aquí!"*

"Por qué no? How else would I save you?"

Yagamata looked Soto squarely in the eyes. "Señor Soto, you have proved your point. You are a great patriot. But what you intend is a great waste of both human resources and irreplaceable objects of beauty."

Soto turned to his daughter. "You should not have told him."

"I did it to save you, Papi."

It hit me then. Lourdes knew. She knew everything, including the fact I'd be on board.

Yagamata reached inside his suit coat and withdrew a black velvet pouch from a pocket. Loosening a drawstring, he poured something into his open palm. It looked like a thick gold chain. "Have you ever seen such magnificence?" he asked, holding it up in the light from the bridge.

The surprise from inside the Trans-Siberian Railway Egg. Yagamata's favorite toy, the little gold train by Fabergé. It sparkled in the glare of the deck lights, the intricate details of the engine and cars nearly surreal.

"What you have on board is several hundred thousand times what I hold in my hand. You must comprehend that!"

Soto nodded. "It makes my statement all the more significant. The treasure of the pigs destroyed."

"The art belongs to the world!" Yagamata thundered.

Funny, Yagamata had acted as if it belonged to him.

Soto was expressionless. "What I have begun cannot be halted."

"Spare the artwork," Yagamata pleaded, gesturing toward the hold. "Spare yourself and the lives of your men."

Yagamata replaced the train in the velvet pouch and slipped the pouch back into his suit pocket. His little game of show-and-tell didn't seem to have the desired impact. "Individual lives are meaningless," Soto said.

"I can broker the sale of the art," Yagamata said. "You will have hundreds of millions more for your cause. Let me help you."

"The money," Soto said, "is important, but the principle even more so. The socialist revolution cannot be financed by the slavery of the masses. Your so-called works of art will die a death far more glorious than that of the peasants whose blood gave birth to such gluttony, such excess."

Soto turned to Lourdes and said something in Spanish. Lourdes responded angrily. Her father spoke again, softly, apologetically, his eyes moist. He moved toward her to embrace, but she turned her back to him. Severo Soto walked away, pausing only to bark a command to a shotgun-toting crewman who stood straighter, his eyes flashing from Yagamata to me and back again.

I went to Lourdes, who moved toward me and stepped close. "I didn't come back just for Papi. I came back for you, too."

I put my arms around her. Our faces touched, and I caught the sweet scent of her hair, the fresh-scrubbed womanly essence of her skin. "Your father won't do it now, will he? Not with you on board."

"There's a lifeboat. It was intended for any of the crewmen who change their minds. They're all handpicked disciples of Fidel and Che Guevara. They want to die for a glorious cause."

There is a time for a man to be a man, and another time to look for a soft place to land. "Much room in that lifeboat?"

"Plenty, but Papi wants you *en una pira fúnebre.*"

My look told her I didn't understand.

"Cómo se dice en Inglés . . . on the funeral pyre. Papi says the revolutionary act is enhanced by destroying a symbol of the reactionary colonialists."

"Me? I've never even voted Republican."

"Papi wants to make the largest possible statement. That's why we're going to anchor off South Pointe Park, just a few hundred yards from the beach."

"Why?"

"What's tomorrow, Jake?"

"Sunday."

"Cuatro de julio, the Fourth of July. Papi wants to blow up the richest cache of art ever assembled during the celebration of what he calls your counterfeit freedom. It's his poetic side. If he could, he'd like to have people singing 'the rocket's red glare' when he pulls the switch."

Bombs bursting in air, I said to myself.

Usually, at sea, I sleep the sleep of the innocent. Maybe it's the gentle pitching, the faint *whoosh* of water against the hull. On the other hand, I sleep the same way in the woods or in a mountaintop cabin. So maybe it's the sense of detachment, of being removed from the bustle of everyday life. So ordinarily, I am a two-hundred-twenty-six-pound slab of concrete in my bunk. Not tonight. I could have been worried that this was my last night on the planet Earth. And I was. But I also was sharing my bunk with a hundred-eighteen-pound lady who was lithe and warm and giving. We kissed and held each other, and I stroked the slopes and curves of her. We maneuvered into positions that stretched the cruciate ligaments of my bad knee, and she laughed when I fell with a thud to the deck. But she welcomed me back, and later, much later, I held and kissed and nuzzled her as the orange light of morning streaked through the porthole.

What would you eat for breakfast if you thought it was your last? Steak? Caviar and smoked salmon? I had *huevos rancheros* because that's what was served in the small galley. Then Lourdes and I stood on the deck, watching the Florida Keys to our west. I recognized Big Pine, Bahia Honda, Molasses, and Fat Deer Key as we continued northeast in the Straits, keeping the Great Bahama Bank well to our east. It was a hot July day with wispy clouds on the horizon. It didn't seem to matter if I got a touch of sunburn.

Lourdes and I were standing at the rail as we passed close to Sombrero Key where the earliest European to live in Florida made his home. Hernando d'Escalante Fontaneda was shipwrecked in the Keys around 1545 and spent the next two decades mapping the islands he called the *Mártires,* or martyrs. He identified one Tequesta village called Guarugunbe, the place of weeping, and another, Cuchiyaga, the place of suffering. Happy campers, those Tequestas. Soto would probably consider the Spaniards to have been plundering colonialists. And, of course, he would be right.

In the afternoon, Lourdes talked to her father, who stood sullenly on the bridge. When I tried to join them, a crewman waved a military .45 under my nose and gave me the impression I wasn't wanted near the controls. Through the glass, I watched Lourdes argue with her father, gesturing with both hands. He listened grimly, shaking his head, occasionally saying something I could not hear. Then he turned his back to her and spoke to the captain. She flung her arms in the air one last time, then rejoined me on the deck.

"I guess you didn't convince him to give up his ideals and join the Hialeah Rotary," I said.

"This isn't funny. I pleaded for your life and his."

"What did he say?"

"That his life wasn't worth saving." She looked away. "He asked if I loved you."

"To which you responded . . ."

"I told him no . . ."

Until now, I had always appreciated candor in a woman.

". . . But that I liked you, that you were a good man who was not his enemy. He said you are meaningless as an individual but important as a symbol."

I watched a wad of sea grapes and other flotsam ride the midget waves into the hull of the freighter. I watched the water change color from bright turquoise to deep indigo as the depth changed along our route. I watched three dolphins jump in unison off the starboard side where motor yachts and oil tankers crisscrossed the Straits.

I allowed myself some heroic imaginings. If life were a B-movie, I would break a mirror and, holding it to the sun, bounce messages to a Coast Guard cutter just waiting to rescue a few billion dollars in art and a halfway honest lawyer. But I didn't know Morse code. Or I would dive off the side and swim to shore. Maybe two or three miles, nothing to it, except a couple of jellyfish stings. But my protectors would gun me down before I hit the water. Or I could overpower Soto and hold him hostage. But he would order his crew to blow us all up. That's what he was going to do anyway, right? But what about Lourdes? Wouldn't he want to save her? Maybe, but what had Soto said? *Individual lives are meaningless.*

"Jake, I'm sorry. I really am."

Maybe it was the wind, but Lourdes had tears in her eyes. "It's not your fault," I told her.

"Not just about this. About ever getting involved with Yagamata and Foley. I did things . . ."

She let it hang there. So I helped her out. "You did what your father asked you to do."

"Yes, he had this planned all along, I'm sure, that somehow he would help Fidel. So Papi asked me to provide him with information while I worked for Yagamata. And when the operation was threatened, when it appeared we would be stopped inside Russia . . ."

Again she couldn't continue. Just like her father, she puzzled me with her riddles, the words unsaid. Sometimes the best way to get a reluctant witness to talk is to ask a pointed question. But often, it's best to just remain quiet. Let the silence invite an answer to the unspoken question.

"I had to help," she said. "I was there when it unraveled. I knew he would ruin everything unless he was stopped, and when . . ."

Who was *he*? She didn't say.

Unless he was stopped. Okay, let's count the bodies, going backward.

One potato. Kharchenko, of course, but Foley did that.

Two potato. Eva-Lisa, who wasn't a *he.*

Three potato. Crespo, dispatched by Kharchenko.

Four. Vladimir Smorodinsky.

. . . He would ruin everything unless he was stopped, and when . . .

I grabbed her by the shoulders, pulled her close, and looked her hard in the eyes. "The reason you offered to help me in the Crespo case was to make sure I wouldn't get too close to the truth—"

She turned her head away.

"—And to report to Yagamata if I got too smart. Of course, if I did, you could always run me down with a forklift." I took a deep breath. "Just like you did to Vladimir Smorodinsky, who would ruin everything unless he was stopped."

As I spoke, I pictured it. Lourdes and Yagamata watched from the offices overhead as Crespo lay unconscious on the floor of the warehouse and Smorodinsky, battered and woozy, headed for the exit. Lourdes raced down the stairs, hopped onto a forklift, and chased Smorodinsky down, spearing him like a fat olive on a toothpick. Oh, she can handle that forklift, all right. She could have killed me if she had wanted to. But she didn't. It was her father who would have that honor.

"You and Yagamata cooked up those phony affidavits," I said, "not to save Crespo, but to keep him quiet, to protect you. When it didn't work because I wouldn't use fabricated evidence, and when Crespo looked like he would crack, you had him killed."

She began sobbing. "Not me, Jake. Yagamata ordered Kharchenko to do it. You must believe me. Yagamata did it for the money and his obsession with the art. Kharchenko did it for his politics. I only followed orders. To me, it was just a job."

She collapsed in my arms, seeking comfort and forgiveness. Still holding her shoulders, I gave her a shove. She landed on her bottom, looking up at me with disbelief.

"That only makes it worse," I said.

27

THE LITTLE ENGINE THAT COULD

The freighter stayed wide of Fowey Rocks and came up along Key Biscayne. I caught sight of the lighthouse at Cape Florida just as the sun was setting. Music blared from the outdoor band-shell at the marine stadium, and a score of boats skimmed across the bay and into the open water. By the time we crossed Government Cut between Fisher Island and the southern tip of Miami Beach, it was dark, and the water was crowded with boats angling for good views of the fireworks. Offshore, half a dozen freighters and a cruise ship lined up, waiting for tugs to take them into port in the morning.

The two crewmen with sidearms had been my shadows for the past three hours. One stayed on each side of me wherever I went, except to the head, where one went in, and the other stayed outside the door.

"Want to hold it for me?" I asked the one who ventured inside.

"No comprendo."

"You guys flip a coin, and you won, is that it, José?"

"Mi nombre no es José."

I returned to the deck, and the two crewmen followed. I can understand a little Spanish if it's spoken slowly. From the guy who wasn't José and his friend who was Xavier, I learned that tomorrow's edition of *Granma*, the Party newspaper named after

Fidel's boat, would carry the story of our heroic act, including the names of all the martyred crew members. Mine, too, I guess. My footnote in history. So these bozos were trading their lives for a half-inch of newsprint.

"I want to reason with you two," I said to Xavier. "This is pointless. Ridiculous. *Estúpido!*"

They exchanged looks and shrugged. I heard footsteps on metal stairs. In a moment, Lourdes appeared and walked quickly to me. On the deck, crewmen were preparing her lifeboat. The gray haze of dusk was backlit by a fiery pink glow to the west as the sun dipped into the Everglades.

Her voice was barely above a whisper. "I know what you think of me, Jake. Believe me, I'm sorry for what I've done. Now let me help you." When I didn't say a word, she lowered her voice even more. "I'll be the only one in the boat. You could jump over . . ."

"What about Yagamata?"

"He knows all hell will break loose and doesn't want to answer questions on shore. His helicopter will be back for him. He's headed straight to the Bahamas. He has arrangements to return to Japan."

I took a small measure of solace in the fact that Yagamata was leaving empty-handed. Lourdes grabbed my hand and laced her fingers through mine. "I could create a diversion for you, Jake."

Next to the lifeboat, Soto turned and gestured for his daughter. Without a word, she left me and walked toward him. I stayed put and thought about Matsuo Yagamata. He had ordered the killing of Vladimir Smorodinsky and Francisco Crespo.

Francisco Crespo.

How I've let you down. I promised your mother I'd take care of you, and I promised myself, too. I wanted to protect you, to return the favor. Okay, so you were never going to win the Congeniality Award. But who knows what you went through in Severo Soto's workers' paradise? I remember tossing the ball with you one day in the postage-stamp backyard behind your mother's place. The clothesline was heavy with drying laundry. You wore my jersey, and it hung to your knees. You couldn't catch a football with a butterfly net, but you yelped and scampered and we had fun, then ate your mom's *arroz con pollo* with flan for dessert.

On the shore, lights flicked on along the boardwalk that fronted the beach. I could barely make out the rocky groin that jutted into the sea. Below us, a lifeboat was being lowered into the water. Lourdes sat alone, looking straight ahead, holding her seat as the boat stuttered down two sturdy lines toward the sea.

A *boom-boom* from the shoreline startled me. Above us, the fireworks had started. Great flashes of yellows and greens, an occasional burst of crimson. Starbursts of silver floated toward the sea.

I turned to Xavier. "You're going to die, *muerte,* for nothing. *Nada.*"

Overhead, a *whoosh* of a rocket, then a *pop-pop-pop* like cannon fire. A shower of sapphire streaks fell from the sky.

"C'mon, whadaya say we go down into the hold and stop this. *Pare!*" I motioned to I'm-not-José. With my index finger, I pretended I was firing a gun at Xavier.

The two of them chattered something in Spanish. All I recognized was *"Estas loco,"* and after Xavier looked at his watch, *"Cinco minutos."*

Oh, shit. No time to use my impressive powers of persuasion. "You guys are really a couple of assholes," I said, laughing. They laughed, too.

Overhead, between the whistles and *ka-booms* of the fireworks, I heard the *whompeta-whompeta* of the Italian helicopter as it descended toward the stern. Over the side, the lifeboat was nearly in the water. I heard Lourdes's shouts even over the roar of the helicopter. She was screaming in Spanish at her father, shaking her fist. Soto and every crewman on deck, including my two companions, were staring at her. If this was the diversion, I didn't know how it could help me. Everyone's attention was diverted all right. Everyone was looking straight at the lifeboat. No way I could get to it. Meanwhile, the helicopter touched down.

The helicopter!

I could make a run for it. The lifeboat had reached the water, Lourdes still screaming. I'm-not-José was saying something to Xavier, both of them looking toward shore where multicolored laser beams were piercing the sky. I put both hands on the rail and vaulted over, landing twelve feet below on the steel deck. I hit and rolled, trying to take the pressure off the knees. It worked, but I turned an ankle, and my shoulder thudded hard against the deck.

I limped toward the stern and the helicopter. Yagamata was just ducking under the whirling blades when I called his name. He stopped and turned, looking puzzled. He stood, frozen for a moment. Then, realization crossing his face, he rushed toward the door of the passenger cabin. He had it half open when I slammed into him. It was picture perfect, just the way Coach Sandusky used to teach it. My shoulders were squared up, my legs pumping. I didn't have the leverage because of my throbbing ankle, but still it was a good stick. I caught him in the middle of the back and smashed him into the door. I could feel the wind go out of him.

With my arms still around him, I slipped a hand into his suit pocket and pulled out the velvet pouch. A second later, the little gold train was in my hand. I backed off a few feet and held the chain over my head, twirling it like a lariat. The rail was only six feet away.

Yagamata turned and faced me. He was breathing hard, his face red. "Are you crazy? What are you doing?"

"Hitching a ride."

"My pilot is armed. He will shoot you if you enter the aircraft."

"Tell him to throw his gun onto the deck."

"No."

"Then say good-bye to the little engine that could."

By now, my two companions had scrambled down a ladder, and I'm-not-José was pointing a .45 at me.

I positioned myself in front of the rear gas tank on the helicopter. "Tell him to back off."

"Don't shoot!" Yagamata yelled at I'm-not-José.

"Take me with you!" I ordered.

"You're crazy! They'll shoot us down." He was shouting, but his voice barely carried over the roar of the helicopter.

"Your train's going into the drink in ten seconds."

I leaned over the rail and dangled the trinket of an emperor.

"No! Something must survive this madman. Give it to me!"

"Take me. Tell the pilot. Now!"

"Give it to me," he repeated, his mouth tight.

Over my shoulder, I saw Xavier hustle toward the hoist where the lifeboat had descended. Probably to get orders from Soto. I'm-not-José still had the gun trained on me. I wondered how much time I had.

Yagamata yelled something in Japanese, lowered his head, and came at me, flailing away. Like much in life, it caught me by surprise. His fingernails tore at my neck as he reached for the train. I ducked and pivoted away from his claws, intending to smash him in the gut with a left. Which is precisely when my ankle decided to desert me. It gave way and I dropped to the deck. Yagamata grabbed the gold train from my hand.

I started to get up, but he was behind me. He was quicker than he looked. I felt a sudden, sharp pressure on my neck. He was using the train as a garrote. It bit hard into my flesh, choking me and drawing blood at the same time. He had one hand on the engine and one on the caboose. I struggled to my feet, wheezing, and he leapt onto my back, inexorably tightening the chain. I tried to hit him with a backward elbow smash but just grazed his ribs. I tried to work a finger under the chain but couldn't do it. My Adam's apple wanted to explode.

I staggered in the direction of the helicopter, wanting to turn and bang him backward into the fuselage. Still he rode me, his knees digging into my sides. I straightened up and tried to shake him off. I heard the piercing shriek of giant rockets from the shore and the *whompeta-whompeta* of the helicopter. I caught a sidelong glance of I'm-not-José, now with Soto and Xavier standing next to him. Three guns were pointed at us.

I took two more steps, and again I tried to buck Yagamata off, hoping to flip him over my head, praying my ankle would hold. I have strong legs from the days of running up stadium steps in full gear, but still he stayed put.

My energy was nearly gone, my vision blurred. Loss of air was dragging me under. Another step, one last try. I flexed my knees, lowered my head, pushed up on his legs with my hands. Then I jumped, a little hippity-hop, a bucking stallion desperately trying to toss its rider.

I felt the pressure lessen on my neck and heard a *whompeta-clunk-whompeta.*

Everything happened so fast. So many sensations.

My load weighed less.

My shoulders and face were covered with something red and sticky.

Everything seemed so quiet, though it couldn't have been.

Soto, Xavier, and I'm-not-José were looking down at a spot on the deck a yard in front of Soto's feet. Looking up at them was Matsuo Yagamata. Or, more precisely, his severed head. His eyes were open. So was his mouth. He seemed startled.

The rest of him was still on my back, my arms clenched tight against his legs. A gurgling sound came from above me. Blood sputtered from what had been his neck and flowed down his body, drenching me. I hurled the body to the deck where it landed with a thud. The dull, heavy weight of a dead man.

The pilot revved his engine and took off, and I rolled underneath the ascending helicopter. Soto shouted something at his crewmen. I hoped it was "Don't shoot."

The first shot *ping*ed metal. I hit the deck and rolled toward a ladder that descended into the hold. The second shot was wild, probably high.

I hobbled down a ladder into the hold, hearing shouts above me. It couldn't have taken more than thirty seconds. Another minute to get in, maybe take a shotgun blast in the chest, but maybe the gun would jam, and I'd take down the crewman at the control panel.

I was at the steel hatch. Door closed. I tried turning the wheel. It didn't budge. In frustration, I slammed the wheel with my fist, cursing. It still didn't move, but my hand flared with pain, then went numb. I whacked the door with my shoulder. An old rotator cuff with a grudge reminded me of its existence. The compartment was sealed tight from the inside. I couldn't open the door with a blowtorch.

So this was it. Not even a chance to die like a man.

Footsteps on the ladder above. I turned and headed for the stern. My ankle was starting to swell, and I was galumphing along at a half trot, half limp. I heard a tinkling sound that seemed to be coming from me. I touched my neck. The gold train, dripping Yagamata's blood, was still hanging there, the engine and caboose intertwined into a knot.

Two compartments to pass through to get to the stern. Shouts from behind now. I forced myself not to turn. A gunshot, ricocheting off metal, then another, this one banging loud and close.

I crouched low and stumbled along. At the same time, I was zigzagging as much as I could along a narrow corridor. It reminded me of hopping through the tires on the practice field, the coaches studying stopwatches.

Time.

How much time?

Two minutes maybe.

The anchor chain came through a well at the stern. Thick, greasy steel links. I took two giant steps and leapt onto the chain. Then, squeezing my body against it, I lowered myself through the well. In ten seconds I was in open space and could drop into the water. Except that my jeans were stuck. Somehow the fabric was caught in a joint between two links of the chain. I pulled against it, but succeeded only in lodging it deeper. Then a grinding sound from above me, the motor that operated the winch. They were hauling the anchor, trying to pull me back into the well.

A huge explosion above me—God, this is it!—a shower of light, and I winced and closed my eyes. I opened them to discover a sunflower of exploding fireworks, a symphony of cannon bursts. The Grand Finale of the celebration.

I dangled there a moment, then felt the great steel chain rising. As it did, the links creaked. I pulled back once again, harder, and felt the rip as I tore out of my blood-soaked jeans and tumbled into the water. I started swimming, a version of the Australian crawl fueled by overwhelming fear. After ten strokes, I discovered I wasn't moving. I floated for a second, getting my bearings, and was swept backward. I was pointed toward shore but was moving toward Bimini.

Riptide.

Of course. We were about an hour from low tide. Strong southeasterly winds had built up the surf. The churning water carves depressions in the sandbar along the beach. Water falls in from both sides of the depression, and rips back out to sea, carrying out shells, fish, and scared-to-death lawyers.

I turned around, heading away from shore, and started swimming again, this time with the rip current. Mark Spitz couldn't have kept up with me on his best day. I felt strong and smooth as the current lifted and carried me. I fought the urge to look over my shoulder to see how much distance I had put between myself and the freighter. I just kept reaching and pulling and kicking . . .

And then the blast.

It lifted me from the water and tossed me down again.

And then the second one. The first, I figured, was the plastique, tearing apart the hold, smashing every statue and coin and painting and artistic doodad Foley could steal. The second would have been the fuel tanks, blowing the freighter apart.

I don't know how far I was thrown. I remember I could no longer swim. My ears rang and my head throbbed and my limbs were numb. I floated on my back, and then face-down, and then on my back again. Salty waves washed over me, filling my nose and mouth, and I went under. Was I drowning along with the da Vincis and Renoirs and Gauguins? I came up and floated some more, opened my eyes, and couldn't see.

I rode a breaking wave toward shore, but the riptide pulled me out again. I went under, came up, and bumped into something. I flipped onto my back, looked up, and saw a face peering down at me. Pale, with wet dark hair plastered to her forehead. Her mouth was moving, but I couldn't hear a thing.

Above me, the sky was aflame. The water stank of oil and diesel fuel, and fire skittered across the surface of the waves. A piece of hot metal brushed my leg. What looked like burning newspaper floated in the breeze.

Again, I looked at her face, Lourdes leaning out of the lifeboat, reaching for me. I couldn't hear, but in the shimmering light of the blazing ocean I saw her mouth my name. She reached down and tried to hoist me up. She couldn't do it. I struggled to pull myself over the side of the lifeboat, but fell back into the water.

Finally, she wrapped a line around me and let me float there alongside. She put a hand on my cheek, cupping my head. When she withdrew, her hand was covered with blood and she shrank back.

Then I rolled over again onto my back and watched the

flames dance across the water, black smoke billowing into the nighttime sky.

My head stopped throbbing, and I suddenly wanted to sleep.

I felt no pain.

No fear.

No nothing.

28

FALSE DAWN

Dr. Charles W. Riggs makes house calls.

This neither boosts the spirits nor stabilizes the blood pressure of his patients, none of whom has ever survived.

Except me.

I lay in bed sipping papaya juice and reading the newspaper, which was filled with its usual collection of *mondo bizarro* Miami news. A man getting off a flight from Bogotá was stopped by customs agents at M.I.A. when they saw him walking stiffly through the inspection line. A closer look revealed packets of cocaine sewn into his thighs, beneath the skin. Miami's customs inspectors are a jaded lot. They've caught folks who swallow condoms filled with cocaine and have found the drug in every orifice known to man (and woman). But the do-it-yourself plastic surgery was news, even here.

The sportswriters were still ecstatic over Miami getting a major league baseball franchise. More realistic was a columnist who suggested some ingenious promotions, including "Uzi Day," in which all kids got toy submachine guns, "Cartel Day," with box seats for drug kingpins, and "John Doe Day," with free corn dogs for anyone in the Witness Protection Program. Maybe you have to live here to appreciate the humor.

Then there was the usual epidemic of burglaries, as always, with a Miami twist. Stolen lawns were the latest in larcenies. In the middle of the night, thieves roll up newly sodded lawns and cart them away. Mia-muh, you gotta love it or leave it.

A stream of visitors flowed through my coral rock house in Coconut Grove. Granny Lassiter tromped in, carrying bags of groceries. She stocked my shelves with her homemade kumquat preserves and calamondin marmalade, then baked a tart Key lime pie. She whipped up some conch fritters and sautéed fresh shrimp with lychees, ginger, red peppers, and passion fruit. I nibbled at the shrimp, then downed a jelly jar full of her white moonshine and slept for the next twenty hours.

Emilia Crespo brought me a steaming pot of *arroz con pollo.* At least I wasn't going to starve to death. Emilia stayed in the house, cooking, cleaning, mopping my feverish forehead, and whispering prayers into my ringing ears. Pain radiated from lacerations on my leg—infected by the gunk that floats in our waters—and I looked up at her through a haze. She seemed so far away, and I didn't know which one of us was drifting. When my head cleared, I told her how the man who killed her son had died an excruciating death. She listened silently, then said something in Spanish and crossed herself.

Charlie Riggs sat by my bed for a week, occasionally peeking under the bandages at my ruptured eardrums, claiming to see all the way through. I insulted him by asking for a real doctor; he told me he had graduated medical school *summa cum laude;* and I reminded him that was before the discovery of penicillin.

Cindy stopped by, delivering a get-well card signed by four of the eight members of the management committee of the law firm, along with written reminders that my time sheets were incomplete for May and June, thus putting an automatic hold on my draw for July.

I lay in bed and watched news reports of the memorial service for Severo Soto, hailed as a great anticommunist by his old cronies in Alpha 66. The TV camera caught a fleeting glimpse of Lourdes Soto coming out of a Little Havana church, her eyes hidden behind dark glasses. I wrote a condolence note, not knowing what to say, filling the white space with platitudes. Two days later, she phoned, asked how I was, and said she would come by the house for a visit. She never did. When I finally called her apartment, a recording said the phone had been disconnected.

I awoke one day to the sound of a glass swizzle colliding with ice cubes and the scent of burnt lemon. Mickey Cumello, my favorite bartender, sat next to the bed, making me a martini with Plymouth gin.

Marvin the Maven stopped in, carrying a box of chocolate-covered cherries, which he proceeded to devour, sucking the juice off his thumb with slurping sounds. Just wanted to cheer me up, Marvin allowed, saying he was looking forward to the retrial of my chicken case next month.

Then Abe Socolow paid his respects. He brought garlic bagels, cream cheese with chives, and a college football magazine, then stood awkwardly at the foot of my bed.

"What's going on, Abe?"

"Whadaya mean?"

"What was it the paper said, 'an explosion of unknown origin'?"

He took off his suit coat, looked up at the ceiling fan, and probably wondered why there was no air-conditioning.

"Why the cover-up?" I demanded. "Why no mention of the art?"

"What art?"

"C'mon, Abe, don't pee on my leg. Granny was fishing off the rocks at South Pointe day before yesterday. She told me the place was crawling with federal marshals, and a barge was in place, dredging the spot where the freighter blew up."

"All true."

"So what'd you find? Did anything survive?"

"Sure." He allowed himself a snicker. "A couple tons of rocks."

I propped myself onto one elbow and leaned toward him. There'd been a ringing in my ears and I wasn't sure I'd heard him.

Socolow pulled a cigarette out of a pack, watched me scowl, and slipped it, unlit, into his mouth. "What was supposed to be the coins turned out to be rocks. Like in your head, Jake. The statues, slabs of concrete. Paintings, just newspapers stuffed into wooden crates."

"I don't believe it."

Outside my window, old *mimus polyglottos,* the mockingbird, was chirping his song. In my bedroom, Abe Socolow was pacing and berating me. "You're an okay guy, but a half-assed lawyer, Jake. Where was your due diligence? You never inspected the goods. How's your malpractice coverage, anyway? If I was in charge, I'd have the government sue you for the two hundred million that's in Fidel's bank account."

Suddenly, there wasn't anything wrong with my hearing. "You've got it backwards, Abe. I didn't represent the government. I represented Foley. Your guy was Soto. If he hadn't been so wound up in his revolutionary rhetoric, maybe he would have taken inventory. The last time I saw the art, it was in a convoy of trailer-trucks headed east on the Airport Expressway."

"Right. Foley went straight to the port, where he intended to put everything on a ship to Cuba. Unfortunately for him, Nikolai Smorodinsky and some pals from the Russian Agency for Federal Security were waiting. They're all ex-KGB agents still trying to atone for Kryuchkov taking part in the coup. They relieved Foley of the contents of the trailer-trucks, which by now ought to be under lock and key in St. Petersburg."

"Then you knew all along that Foley didn't have the art."

"No way." Socolow pulled out a pack of matches and lit his cigarette. "The Russian government didn't want to admit that things were so far out of control, so they never told Washington that Kharchenko had gotten out with the biggest load of treasure anyone had ever seen. Of course, we knew it from our sources in Finland and from tapping Yagamata's phone here. But in the eyes of Yeltsin's people, the art was never officially stolen, so it was never returned. They simply clammed up and didn't tell us a thing. Hey, regardless of the form of government, the Russians are still a secretive bunch who hate to be embarrassed."

"Foley," I said. "What about Foley?"

Socolow paused long enough to blow smoke in my direction. "Picture him, Lassiter. For an hour or so, he was the richest man in the world. Then he's left holding nothing but his dick. On one hand, he's lucky to be alive. The Russians could have killed him. But he looks at it differently. He's going crazy, figuring how close he came. He has a freighter at the port, but no cargo, at least not until he gets a bright idea."

I shook the cobwebs out of my head. "He pulls a scam. Even

if he doesn't have the art, he can pretend he does. He loads the freighter with rocks and newspapers and heads to Havana."

"Right. Foley tried using his contacts with Cuban intelligence to worm his way onto the island, but they thought he was full of shit, a guy saying he had billions of dollars of art on a Polish freighter that could barely float. So they call their most valuable double agent, one Severo Soto, who confirms Foley's story because the CIA tells him it's true. The CIA, of course, was relying on information provided by one Jake Lassiter, who reported that Foley had the art on trucks leaving the warehouse. When Foley turned up in Havana, everybody just *assumed* he had it, can you fucking believe it?"

The mockingbird was growing louder. Its tune reminded me of a piano concerto. Tchaikovsky maybe. "Of course," Socolow continued, "by this time, Soto had his own plans."

"A revolutionary statement," I said, "a funeral pyre of capitalist treasure."

"Yeah, turns out he blew himself up on a garbage scow."

"So, the Russians get their art back, and except for giving two hundred million in foreign aid to the bearded dictator, the mission was accomplished."

We both thought about it a moment. "What about Foley?" I asked.

Socolow looked for an ashtray and couldn't find one. He tapped his cigarette into the neck of an empty Grolsch bottle. "Yeah. The last we heard, that shithead was swinging a machete in one of Fidel's cane fields. As you can imagine, the boys at Langley didn't shed any tears. Hey, we even recovered a load of stuff from Yagamata's house. All of it in perfect shape except for some fancy egg that was supposed to have a train inside."

"Fabergé's Trans-Siberia Railway Egg."

"Right. You know about it?"

"I've heard of it," I said, with less than complete candor.

"The egg was in Yagamata's gallery, but the insides were missing, and so was Yagamata. I don't suppose you know anything about that."

When given a choice, I prefer not to lie. Sometimes I stall. "About what?"

"About the train . . ."

Sometimes I evade. "What would I know?"

". . . and Yagamata."

And sometimes I just tell the literal truth. "His love for the art was obsessive. I always thought he might lose his head over it."

Socolow scowled, told me he had work to do, and left.

I swung my stiff legs over the side of the bed and tried to sit up straight, fighting off the dizziness. I reached under my mattress and pulled it out, a shiny twenty-four-carat gold choo-choo train. There was an engine, a tender, and five coaches. Each car was connected to the next by a tiny gold hinge, and they folded together like a penknife. A pretty piece, all right. It took a brilliant artist to conceive it, great craftsmen to execute the handiwork. It was one of a kind, and probably could not be duplicated today. But I couldn't imagine killing for it, and I wouldn't want to die for it. Enough people already had.

Two weeks later, Charlie Riggs said I'd been an invalid too long. He wanted to get me out on the water. I said no thanks.

He tried to entice me with an invitation to chase bonefish in the flats off Key Largo. I declined because of the lobster mobsters. For two days each summer, just before the commercial season begins for the spiny lobster, every jerk with an outboard motor gets to trample the coral and shoot spears at all living creatures in our shallow waters. Not that it's legal to spear, hook, or trap the little crustaceans. You're supposed to catch them by hand or hand-held net. You're not supposed to take egg-bearing females and undersized lobsters of either sex. But these bozos don't care, and I wasn't about to get speared, shot, or just plain annoyed while fishing.

So why did I let Charlie talk me into a ride on his old Boston Whaler?

To talk.

We said to heck with the flats and headed into the ocean in fourteen hundred feet of water, seeking a measure of solitude. Charlie had the binoculars out looking for osprey and frigate birds feeding on small fish at the surface. In the food chain hereabouts, the dolphin—the bluish gold fish, not Flipper the marine mammal—chase tiny fish to the surface where the birds eat them.

We follow the birds and find the dolphin, which, with any luck, will be in Granny Lassiter's frying pan by sundown.

I used a light spinning rod baited with a yellow feather and came up with some seaweed. Charlie used mullet and got a strike from a five-pound dolphin. It jumped, fought, ran, fought some more, skipped along the surface, then gave up. Charlie hauled it in, wriggling, and tossed it into the cooler. "*Coryphaena hippurus*, a magnificent animal. Fast and full of fight."

I was still casting when Charlie pulled in his second one, a blunt-headed iridescent blue female. I leaned back and rested awhile, watching Charlie enjoy himself. After a moment, I said, "I still can't figure it out."

"A little more wrist," Charlie advised.

"Not that. What was I doing, trying to help Francisco Crespo or find out something about myself?"

"Either way, you tried to make a difference."

"And either way, I still couldn't tell the good guys from the bad. Every time I thought I knew, they changed the players or the rules."

Charlie chuckled. "Things are seldom what they seem. Skim milk masquerades as cream. The new world order makes it even more confusing, Jake. It's hard to realize, but old enemies are on the same side now. Still, there will always be loners like Foley and Yagamata, who are just in it for themselves, and an occasional throwback like Soto who thinks he can change the world by force. Most everybody else seems willing to let individuals control their own destiny."

"But I didn't do anyone any good. I didn't save Crespo or Eva-Lisa. I didn't save anyone."

"Sure you did, Jake. You saved yourself."

We stayed the night at a rundown motel on the Gulf side, then got up at four A.M. for a second try. Except for the slap of water against the hull, it was quiet as a tomb as we headed out the channel. A velvet black sky was filled with diamonds, and a feathery breeze blew from the southeast. Charlie and I sat looking at the heavens in the silent comfort that two good friends can savor without self-consciousness.

When we reached what Charlie promised would be a hot spot, I baited my hook. Charlie tamped tobacco into his pipe and scratched at his beard. "You see my matches?"

"Too dark," I said.

After a few moments, on the horizon to the east, an orange glow cut through the darkness.

"False dawn," I said.

"No. That's the real thing. Sun's coming up."

"Too early, Charlie. That's the phony one. I remember."

"Twenty bucks," Charlie said, goading me.

"You're on. In the meantime, tell me one of your stories I haven't heard in a while."

Charlie harrumphed. "Ever tell you about the Doomsday Rock?"

"What's that, an engagement ring?"

"An asteroid big enough to cause an explosion a billion times bigger than Hiroshima."

"Where is it?"

"Nobody knows. But theoretically, it has to be out there, hurtling toward us right now. The Earth gets hit by one every five hundred thousand years or so. The blast causes a dust cloud that changes the climate, kills off the plant life. It's probably what did in the dinosaurs. To demonstrate the effect, imagine my bait box is an asteroid." He leaned over and picked up the box. "You see this, Jake?"

"Of course."

"Thought so," he said, laughing.

I reached for my wallet, handed the old buzzard two tens, and told him to finish his story.